ALARM! PAIN! ALARM!

Risa ambrov Keon scrambled up the slope to where Sime fought Sime with deadly intent. Yet even as Risa raced to aid her fellow guard, three Simes carrying a Genhunter's net joined forces to entrap Risa.

Risa evaded her attackers but one of them netted Muryin, heir of the House of Zeor, and dragged her to higher ground. As the rest of the party from the Householdings arrived, the Sime holding Muryin hostage pressed a stiletto against the terrified child's eye.

And as the Householders froze in horror, the enemy leader shouted, "One more step, and the House of Zeor is dead!"

ZELEROD'S DOOM

A Sime/Gen Novel

Jacqueline Lichtenberg and Jean Lorrah

The Sime/Gen Universe is an Original creation
of Jacqueline Lichtenberg

DAW BOOKS, INC.
DONALD A. WOLLHEIM, PUBLISHER

1633 Broadway, New York, NY 10019

DAW Book Collectors No. 682.

First Printing, August 1986

1 2 3 4 5 6 7 8 9

PRINTED IN U.S.A.

My work on this book is dedicated to Katie Filipowicz, the first stranger to write me a fan letter on my first novel, *House of Zeor*, the prequel to this book. For ten years she has been insisting I write the rest of the story of Hugh and Klyd. When I went to Kentucky to stay with Jean and finish this book, Katie took her vacation and came to work with us on it, slaving tirelessly, even over the Fourth of July and her birthday.

And through Katie, this book is dedicated to all the enthusiasts of the Sime/Gen Universe who would have done the same in Katie's place.

If you're willing to look at the universe from other peoples' points of view and provide them what they need to survive, if you're willing to embrace your adversary, if you can't believe *any*body could be so *stupid*, so *careless*, or so *cold hearted*, then *Zelerod's Doom* is for you because you have made this book happen.

Jacqueline Lichtenberg
Murray, Kentucky
July, 1984

My dedication is also to Katie Filipowicz, for yeoman service above and beyond the call of friendship. Katie gave up a real vacation to be caught in the middle between two squabbling authors breaking their necks to beat a deadline and at the same time create the best book possible. She slaved at the word processor, tolerated our fussing, and is single-handedly (or actually double-handedly, as she is a touch-typist) responsible for the first version's getting done by deadline. Every writer should have a Katie!

I would also like to dedicate it to the hundreds of fans who have helped to shape the Sime/Gen universe with their comments and encouragement. We would like to hve your comments on this book, too—please contact us through *Ambrov Zeor*, P. O. Box 290, Monsey, NY 10952. If you require a reply, please enclose a stamped self-addressed envelope.

Jean Lorrah
Murray, Kentucky
July, 1984

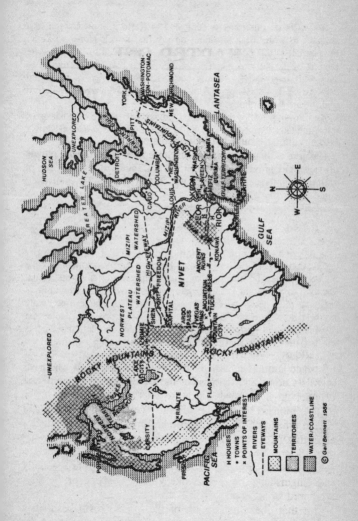

CHAPTER ONE

Unwelcome Visitors

Hugh Valleroy could not believe his eyes.

On the field before him, scarlet, gold, green, and purple tents and pavilions were being raised. Thousands of people in holiday finery trampled the mud. Horses, wagons, carts, and even dogs were decked in red ribbons. Aromas of strange foods spread through the morning air. The noise increased by the minute as more and more people arrived.

After the beige world of the gypsy wagons, the gaudy display of Gulf Territory's famous Spring Fair seemed more like a Choice Auction than a trade fair. Valleroy turned to the man beside him, and asked only half rhetorically, "Klyd, are you *sure* this is where we're supposed to meet her?"

Klyd Farris, Head of the House of Zeor and official emissary of the Nivet Territory Tecton, snapped, "Of course I'm sure! Must you question everything I—"

Valleroy schooled his concentration to give Klyd a bubble of peace amid the riotous emotion. Valleroy was here as Klyd's Companion, to protect the trained sensitivities of the channel.

The moment Valleroy went to work, Klyd sighed and waved a hand in a helpless little gesture, two dorsal tentacles emerging from the orifices near his wrist in graceful emphasis. "Sorry."

"My fault," replied Valleroy. Klyd was a Sime, visually indistinguishable from Gens like Valleroy except for the tiny, whipcord strong tentacles.

But that one modification of the human form bespoke a world of inward differences, such as the Sime senses, one of which allowed a Sime to perceive life energy fields.

Klyd sighed. "Let's not argue. We've got to find her."

A third member of their embassy, Ediva ambrov Dar, emerged from the gypsy wagon behind them. Eight years younger than Valleroy, she was renSime, not a channel like Klyd. Ediva was the foremost mathematician of her generation, successor to the famous Zelerod. In fact, their journey was a result of her crusade to convince the world that Zelerod's Doom was at hand.

Wearing a full-length ceremonial cape of Householding Dar's colors, deep blue-green and gray, she carried a cascade of brilliant blue material: Klyd's cape. She was almost as tall as the two men, not as broad shouldered, but strong in the wiry, Sime way. "Sectuib Farris, Sosectu Rior," she greeted cheerfully, "even though it's so warm here, shouldn't we wear our Householding cloaks?"

Back home, people would still be bundled up in woolen capes against the last sharp winds of winter; here in Gulf Territory the grass was already green, trees budding, some in bloom. On the teeming field, many workers wore the colors of the two Gulf Territory Householdings, Keon and Carre.

Klyd took his cloak from Ediva's shoulder, revealing one beneath it, Rior's flame orange touched with Zeor's distinctive blue. Rior, Valleroy's House, was a daughter house of Zeor.

Valleroy took his cape, and Ediva's eyes met his. They'd had no privacy on the trip, and he was sure she also felt that as a deprivation, soon to be remedied. The thought warmed him in a way he hadn't felt since his wife had died.

Still holding eye contact with Ediva, he kept his professional attention on Klyd. Abruptly, Klyd turned to scan the scene behind Valleroy. "Kitty," he called, "have you found her?"

Valleroy turned to find Kitty ambrov Rior approaching with a businesslike stride, her Rior cloak billowing out behind her. She was a Gen he had trained himself to move confidently among Simes. In the intimacy of those years, just after his wife had died, Kitty had become infatuated with him, and he had mistaken it for love. Two things had come of it—their son, Jesse, now six years old, and Kitty's more mature realization that it was the ideals of Rior, not Valleroy himself, that had captured her love and devotion.

"Sectuib Farris," replied Kitty when she was close enough, "the Sectuib Keon is in the infirmary tent. They said she's expecting you, and you could go right in." She glanced at Ediva, clearly aware of the unspoken attraction Valleroy felt. A hint of a smile danced over her face, and Valleroy knew she was letting Ediva read with her Sime senses that Kitty was no rival for Valleroy's affection.

"Hugh!" said Klyd, sharply calling Valleroy's attention back to business. Then he strode into the maelstrom of color and sound, his cape flapping behind him.

"Kitty," said Valleroy, "see if you can get things organized here. We'll be right back. Come on, Ediva." Valleroy took off after Klyd, catching up as he worked his way through a crowd of Simes. He put an inconspicuous fingertip on Klyd's elbow. "It's not wise for Gens to run among junct Simes." Juncts were those Simes—the majority—who killed Gens for selyn, the life energy Gens produced and Simes had to have to live. Such Simes regarded Gens like Hugh and Kitty as their legitimate prey . . . and this fair would certainly be teeming with them.

Klyd slowed and curiously scanned the people about them. "Hugh, there's something very strange here."

They were passing a gaudy purple and green tent with red and gold triangular pennants flapping merrily. A small band was tuning up, and tables and chairs were being set out. At one side planks were propped on sawhorses to form a bar.

As they paused to watch, Ediva commented, "Shiltpron music mixed with porstan—and Gens?"

More than half the workers were Gens, but not slaves or drug-deadened pen inmates. They were young, bright, laughing, high on enthusiasm, teasing the Simes who worked with them as if unaware of the danger of provoking a Sime to kill. Risa, Sectuib ambrov Keon, had claimed that Gulf Territory was rapidly approaching the lifestyle of a territory-wide Householding. Could it be true?

Studying the ambient of that tent, Klyd said, "No Companions. No channels. Except for the woman directing them, the Simes are junct, but the Gens are low field. Some channel has taken their selyn in donation. No Simes are in need. I doubt if there'll be any incidents—but—''

Yes. But, thought Valleroy. Anything that either startled or caused pain to one of those untrained Gens could provoke a junct Sime to the kill—draining the Gen's system of life energy so brutally that he died in agony, nerves burnt out. Close friendship, even love, could not prevent Sime instinct from turning on a Gen, given sufficient provocation. "Something else to ask this Sectuib Risa ambrov Keon about."

"Charge her with, I'd say," answered Klyd. As he spoke, a wagon backed up to the pavilion to unload porstan kegs. Two Simes leaped onto the heap of kegs and tossed them down to a pair of Simes who stacked them behind the bar. Kegs flew through the air in a steady arc. All four Simes augmented—used extra selyn to strengthen their muscles—as if Gens were so cheap that each Sime could kill two a month.

Ediva shuddered. "Negligent! No, criminal! I'd like to take her apart with my bare hands!" Ediva was disjunct. She had accomplished the agonizing withdrawal from the kill to join Householding Dar. In the Householdings, channels like Klyd took selyn from Gens without hurting them, and gave it to the renSimes, who could thus live without killing.

At Dar, Ediva had learned of Zelerod's Doom. The mathematician Zelerod had discovered through statistical analysis that with Simes living longer and therefore killing more Gens, the point would come within a few generations when the Sime and Gen populations would be equal. The Simes would kill the remaining Gens in order to survive and die of selyn attrition when there were no more Gens. Humanity's only alternative was to live as Householders lived.

Valleroy was not so sure that what he saw about him was "criminal." It was obviously possible for Gens to interact much more freely with Simes than they did in Nivet Territory, perhaps possible for *any* Gen to give Simes selyn directly, given the proper attitude and training. Klyd and other Tecton leaders, though, would not hear of such experimentation, pointing to centuries of statistics on Sime/Gen intimacies with horrifying rates of failure. But much had been learned over the last few decades. The Tecton, the organization of Nivet Territory Householdings which had sent Klyd on this mission, was Sime-dominated and overprotective toward Gens. Perhaps the Gulf Territory Householding organization—if only two Houses could form an organization—was different.

Ediva turned away from the flying beer kegs, repelled, and Klyd called after her, "Ediva, wait! We mustn't jump to conclusions. We're strangers here. We might not know what we're zlinning!"

Good, thought Valleroy, hurrying after them. *Maybe seeing Sime/Gen interaction in operation will open his mind.*

In the center of the fair grounds stood a huge mortared brick hemisphere cupped around a rusting heap of iron. A plaque bore an inscription in oddly curled script. THIS BLAST FURNACE IS PRESERVED IN MEMORY OF THE FIRST PROFITABLE PARTNERSHIP BETWEEN KEON AND LAVEEN. TO FREEDOM THROUGH COOPERATION.

Klyd circled the monument, Valleroy following, to find a white tent, its round green and red flags marking it as a dispensary and hospital. "See there?" prompted Klyd, pointing with two tentacles, "The infirmary is well staffed and large enough. *That's* not negligence."

The white tent swarmed with channels and Companions wearing Keon and Carre colors. A wagon unloaded cots and bedding at the rear of the tent. Gens made up beds while Simes arranged bricks for a hearth.

Klyd circled the tent, gesturing Valleroy to keep his distance as Klyd zlinned with Sime senses for the distinctive nager—selyn field—of a channel such as Risa Tigue must be.

"She's not here," he announced with a shrug.

"There's the Keon Pavilion," pointed Valleroy. It was easily the largest tent at the fair—bright red and white—set across a broad avenue formed by tents and stalls. And it was already in full operation. "Let's try there," he added leading the way.

Before they reached the open awning shading the front of the pavilion, Klyd confirmed, "She's there!" He cut through the line of customers waiting to go in, stomped the mud off his boots on the matting provided, and said to the guards, "Sectuib Keon is expecting us."

The pavilion was made of alternating strips of solid red and translucent white, giving the interior a warm pinkish glow. Glass cases displayed intricately wrought jewelry, decorated household items, and a series of plaques identifying Arensti design awards. Precious and semi-precious gems, gold, silver, and assorted burnished alloys created effects from gaudy to infinitely refined. But the overwhelming impression was "rich." Some display cases did not have protective glass. Many things were out in the open to be handled—or stolen. A few clerks roamed behind the counters or helped customers, but most of them were Gen—incapable of zlinning the intention to steal, or a quick hand movement behind their backs.

The place was not crowded. A new customer was admitted only when someone left. But there were more Simes, Gens, and even children roaming about than the few clerks could watch. Risa Tigue once again seemed a foolish manager.

Valleroy noticed a young man—a boy no more than fifteen, but obviously established as a Gen—standing near a case of gleaming jewelry. He wore a Householding ring displaying Keon's ruby crest. He was tall, with striking blue eyes that lighted on the visitors at once, but Valleroy was not sure why he noticed the boy until he realized Klyd was signaling him. Valleroy turned to the channel, to protect him from the Keon Gen's nager. Anything might irritate Klyd at the moment.

The boy stepped forward with a formal bow. "Keon extends greetings to Zeor, Dar, and . . .? Please forgive me for not recognizing your Householding, Naztehr," he said to Valleroy, who saw him note the white lining of both his cloak and Klyd's, and frown in puzzlement. But he asked no question which might offend.

"Rior," Valleroy supplied. "We have come to meet with Risa, Sectuib in Keon."

"We're expecting you. You are most welcome. I am Morgan Kreg ambrov Keon, Second Companion. Please come this way."

They found the Sectuib in Keon at the back of the pavilion, a tiny woman with dark hair in a neat coil at the back of her neck, and pale, freckled skin. Although Valleroy knew she had to be in her mid-thirties, she looked as if she were hardly out of First Year.

But her attitude was that of a woman grown and fully in control. "This flour is spoiled," she was saying to the abashed Gen before her. She dipped a delicate hand into the sack, and Valleroy smelled a yeasty odor. "Either you were cheated, or you are trying to cheat me."

"Or both," put in a nearby Sime, a middle-aged man with iron-gray hair, dressed in a tailored business suit at odds with the casual dress of the rest of the fair-goers. But it was his eyes, not his attire, that caught Valleroy's attention. A strange air of calm overlay a hidden sadness in their depths—an expression Valleroy had never seen before today, but which had looked out at him time and again from the eyes of older Simes they had passed on the fair grounds.

Sensing Valleroy's surge of curiosity, Klyd murmured, "Semi-junct. The place is full of them, Hugh. Dangerous."

Dangerous? In the days of the first channels, before the founding of Zeor, the Sime/Gen community of Freedom Township must have felt like this, the generation of Simes too old to disjunct—to stop killing forever—limiting their kills to two or three each year and living on channel's transfer as much as possible. How could the Tecton ever hope to fulfill its cherished dream of uniting Simes and Gens, without accepting—and respecting—a generation of junct Simes willing to encourage their children to disjunct?

The Sime man eyed the embarrassed Gen with the flour, saying, "And you want to give the Gens citizenship, Risa?"

"Shall we revoke all Sime citizenship because some Simes are cheats or fools?" she responded, wiping her hands on the much laundered, paint spattered smock she wore, several sizes too large for her diminutive frame. Gingerly, she shoved the sack toward the Gen. "Take this away—and don't you try to sell it anywhere at the Fair, you hear?"

"Yes, ma'am," the Gen replied, and began trying to haul the opened sack away. Embarrassment made him clumsy; the sack toppled and spilled.

A pungent aroma oozed from the breached sack, and Valleroy thought he saw maggots. His gorge rose, and he turned away, clamping down control in order not to nauseate all the Simes in the tent.

Risa swung around, attention attracted despite Valleroy's

efforts. "Ah, there you are at last!" She wiped her hands thoroughly, shrugging out of the smock and tossing it to the huge Gen she'd apparently borrowed it from. Valleroy recognized the blond giant by reputation: Risa's husband and First Companion, Sergi ambrov Keon. The Sectuib extended her tentacles, smiling as she repeated, "Keon extends welcome—"

Valleroy had closed off his awareness of Klyd and Ediva out of politeness, and now was caught off guard by a sudden move from Klyd. Before Risa had taken two strides, Klyd spun, raking the tent with an expression of growing horror. Then, his weathered complexion paling, he charged across the tent, detouring around the Keon Second Companion who had resumed his post by the jewelry case, and plunged out the door.

Stunned, Valleroy glanced at the Sectuib ambrov Keon, who no doubt thought she had just been snubbed by the emissary from Nivet Territory. No time for apologies—Klyd had obviously sustained a systemic jolt of dangerous proportions or he wouldn't have fled like that. He plunged after the channel, squeezing through the tunnel in the crowd already closing behind Klyd, Ediva right on his heels, berating himself for exposing Klyd to whatever it was, hoping he could repair the damage with his own nager.

Sectuib Risa ambrov Keon stared at the retreating backs of the ambassadors she'd meant to honor lavishly. Since she'd pledged Keon, she'd heard endless stories about the skittish and unpredictable Farris channels, but this was the first time she'd—almost—met one.

"Now what the shen caused *that*?" asked Tannen Darley, one of Keon's major investors and probably their best friend in the territory legislature.

"I'm afraid we've upset our visitors, Tan," she replied. "I'll try to straighten it out." With a sidewise glance, she gathered her Companion, and raced after the ambassadors.

Despite her short legs, she outstripped Sergi as easily as Klyd outdistanced his Companion. But Sergi was in superb condition, as well as long-legged and used to chasing after Simes. He caught up with her as she slowed to confront her guests, who had stopped near the Monument.

"Please wait!" called Risa as the group turned toward the gypsy wagons that had brought them. At closer range, she added in a normal voice, "I've no idea what offended you. Please tell me and let me correct it."

The Sectuib Zeor answered in the clipped accent characteristic of Nivet Territory, "You really mean that." His head tilted as he studied her nager, and she held herself open to the scrutiny. Amazed, he said, "You set trained Companions to bludgeon Sime sensibilities, to inhibit freedom of choice, and you've no idea what you're doing?"

Despite her best intentions, the man's attitude infuriated her. She put her hands on her hips and looked up at the channel, who stood a good head taller than most people. "Bludgeon? *Bludgeon!*" She carefully controlled her voice. "Our Gens broadcast a quiet, tasteful *suggestion*, reminding customers how much easier it is to pay our fair prices than to deal with the law. It is unobtrusive, subliminal—"

"Unobtrusive!" roared the man, his eyes widening.

His Companion sought to spread calm through the ambient nager, and Sergi swallowed his own outrage and joined the effort. Klyd glanced at the renSime woman with him, and repeated, "Unobtrusive?" seeking corroboration.

She said, "Well—I did notice it a little when Hugh stopped shielding us."

More calmly, Klyd asked, "It really wasn't—?"

Klyd's Companion stepped toward Sergi and inserted a low voiced comment. "It was my fault. Is there someplace where we can talk?"

Risa said, "I have a shielded office in the dispensary tent. I won't ask you to return to the pavilion."

They filed through the maze of insulating draperies to a triangular section between two treatment cubicles. This small office used the insulated walls of the adjacent cubicles to cut the chaos of the ambient nager. As they walked, the Gen said, "Klyd, it was my fault. I dropped the fields when I—"

"I felt that," interrupted Klyd as Risa felt the Gen's gorge rise at the memory. "When you dropped the fields, that racket her Gens were making hit me full blast—thought I'd faint for a moment, but I'm not injured. We must take our transfer soon."

Why haven't they done that already? Could something have happened on the trail? Zlinning as unobtrusively as she could to evaluate the situation, Risa didn't find their fields far enough out of balance to account for the channel's erratic behavior. *Surely a channel of his reputation can cope with a trivial degree of need.*

As she led them into the office, she motioned to an idle assistant to bring chairs and trin tea. It would take time to untangle this touchy situation.

As they jigsawed themselves into the tiny office, Risa admired the Companion's skill with the Farris. But an intuition flickered at the edge of her awareness. *There's trouble there.* Something jarred their nageric harmony. Personality conflict? Something *must* have happened along the way; no channel would travel with a Companion with whom he had some basic disagreement. Their capes told her they were not of the same Householding; perhaps Klyd's own Companion had been lost along the way. No wonder he was in such a state!

When their tea arrived, Risa motioned the renSime to serve, hoping hot trin would soothe ruffled nerves. She settled behind the desk as they traded introductions. The Gen was introduced as First Companion of Zeor and Sosectu Rior. Risa exchanged a confused glance with Sergi, who had said nothing so far. Her husband would have to become accustomed to the voices and accents of their guests before he could understand them perfectly, for he had suffered a hearing loss in an explosion years ago, when enraged juncts had attempted to destroy Keon's steel mill.

She saw and zlinned, though, that Sergi had assessed the situation between these two men, and he, too, found it impossible to understand how a Gen could perform the duties of a Companion and at the same time run his own Householding. The designation also told her they *were* regular transfer mates. So why the tension between them?

"Let me welcome you with all the hospitality at my command and apologize if anything here has distressed you. Sergi has told me how sensitive Farris channels can be. Perhaps our quiet message seemed like a raucous bellow to you, Sectuib Zeor. If I'd realized, I'd have had them cease the moment you walked in—especially Mor, our son. He shows promise of being as fine a Companion as his father, but he is established only a year. He has strength, but only time will give him judgment.''

Clasping the tea glass holder—one of Sergi's gorgeously wrought metal carvings—between four tentacles, Klyd said graciously, ''I apologize for losing my temper. The reason is obvious.'' He opened both hands, fingers spread as he dropped his show-field, and an incredible amplitude of need washed over her. And something else—yes, entran. She never suffered it herself, but when some channels, accustomed to taking selyn from Gens and transferring it to renSimes, suddenly ceased working, their systems could cramp up painfully. *No wonder he's hypersensitive. How could they let this get out of control?*

She marvelled at Klyd's ability to mask his true state. That was, of course, a channel's stock in trade, and only a channel of superior ability could penetrate the illusion. Risa had never run up against anyone who could fool her senses as he had. So Farrises were as good as rumor said. Obviously they paid for it—this man could not be expected to think clearly in his condition. She gestured to the dispensary. ''In a matter of hours, we'll be in full operation. You're welcome to work off entran here, Sectuib Zeor.''

Risa felt Sergi check astonishment. Klyd held back his acceptance just a hair too long, and Risa wondered if he had perceived her pity. Having such a sensitive channel around would improve her own show-field technique.

Hugh answered, ''We'd be glad to contribute our skills. We have nothing quite like your Spring Fair in Nivet Territory. Juncts and Householders never mix so freely.''

Risa answered politely, ''That's just the reason I invited you here, to see for yourselves what cooperation with juncts can do. We've no reason to increase our Border Patrol as the Nivet government is urging us to do. But we're delighted they've sent a Householder to negotiate. You will see, perhaps, what your junct colleagues could not—that the Wild Gens can become valuable allies. Sectuib Zeor, when you've explained to them what we're doing here—''

''Junct *colleagues*? Sectuib Keon, I fear you've misunderstood. I speak only for the Tecton—the Householdings of Nivet. The juncts of Nivet far outnumber us, and we are obliged to abide by their laws. The Tecton has sent me in hopes that I may convince you where the Nivet emissary failed, for it is urgent and crucial that this border be fortified.''

Risa had studied the maps. The islands of Sime Territory surrounded by Gen Territory had shifted over the centuries, one Sime Territory amalgamating with its neighbor until Nivet stretched nearly across the center of the continent. But there was a small, vulnerable yet strategic corridor between the east end of Nivet and the west border of Gulf across which Freeband Raiders operated occasionally—and which the Gen Territory government wanted to garrison and fortify, effectively cutting off Gulf-Nivet trade as well as Raiders. Nivet claimed that the only way to stop the Gen troop movements was for Nivet and Gulf to cooperate in handling the Freeband Raiders before the Gen troops moved in permanently.

"I speak for Gulf Territory as a whole," explained Risa, setting aside her consternation. She had always envisioned the Tecton as a powerful entity in Nivet. "Here, Householders are very active in territory government, as are semi-juncts and nonjuncts not affiliated with Householdings."

"Not affiliated—!" Hugh gasped in astonishment.

"Reserve judgment," the channel warned his Companion. "Please go on, Sectuib Keon."

"We would like to cooperate with your territory, and both of its governments," Risa continued. "However, we believe that acts which the Gen Territory governments can interpret as aggression—such as increasing Sime armies along our borders—can only delay the alliance with the Wild Gens that is our ultimate aim."

She could not miss their open skepticism, but she continued, "See it, zlin it for yourselves. There's hardly any market here for Wild Gens. There are no unlicensed Raiders willing to deal with Genrunners. The activity of our Licensed Raiders has fallen off sharply in recent years because of the diminishing market for Wild Gens as Choice Kills. Perhaps your junct government couldn't appreciate that achievement, but I assume the Tecton would."

Klyd nodded assent, adding, "But it is very hard to believe that such a thing has in fact been achieved."

"You see the proof about you. This used to be the time of the spring Choice Auction. No Gens are sold for the kill here. Customers come to trade for other merchandise. Sectuib Zeor, we have made life easier for our junct colleagues—they have jobs, physical comforts, and plenty of selyn. A growing percentage of younger Simes are nonjunct or disjunct and remain friends with their friends and relatives who turn Gen. Not only do we have no market for Wild Gens—in a few years we'll have the Wild Gens coming to the fair to trade! Why should we alienate potential allies by setting a Sime Army in their back yards?"

Hugh had settled into the Companion's role, sheltering Klyd from what little nageric noise filtered through the insulating material. The channel sipped his tea and replied cautiously, "Your reasoning would be impeccable if your facts were complete. On the way here, we saw numerous signs of Gen Army troop movements. Not your neighbors, Sectuib. Troops from New Washington. They are deploying against the growing activity of Freeband Raiders in this corridor—"

Freeband Raiders were bands of homeless Simes who swept through the countryside stealing and killing Gens, murdering Simes, high on the kill. Hard times added to their numbers, as good people who had lost everything joined the hopeless hordes. Once they had been a scourge that periodically swept through every territory, Sime or Gen, but now—

"We don't have that problem here anymore," Risa told her visitors. "You really must tour our Territory. We have peace here—Sime and Gen in profitable cooperation. Let us show you—"

Just then Klyd cocked his head to one side, his eyes going unfocused as he zlinned. He stood, moving so that Sergi was not between him and the outer wall of the tent. Frowning, he said, "Something's coming! Zlin that?"

Risa stood, turning toward the lightly insulated outer wall. But she got nothing unusual. "It's just the fair. There must be four or five thousand people here now."

"No," insisted Klyd. "Way beyond the fair. Come outside!" He turned on his heel and strode out, leaving Risa flatfooted for the second time in less than an hour.

Sergi said, "Farrises are noted for their sensitivity. He's likely zlinned something important."

Risa charged after Klyd. Outside, the pace had picked up. Thousands of Simes and Gens were buying, selling, laughing, entertaining. Klyd had walked up a guy-line securing the dispensary tent and was standing well above the heads of the crowd, surveying the territory to the north.

As Risa started to join him, Klyd called, "It's Freeband Raiders—fifty or a hundred—riding this way at a full gallop. Ten—fifteen minutes at the most. They must be attracted by the ambient of this crowd."

Fifteen minutes' gallop. He can zlin that far and even grab the field nuances? I don't believe it.

Risa zlinned Sergi's tremor of warning. The years had taught her to heed her Companion's instincts. She about-faced and began shouting orders to Keon members. In moments, a band of channels and Companions was mounted. Tannen Darley came out of the Keon pavilion, heard what was happening, and began directing the many Simes who owed loyalty to him.

Risa gave Klyd, Hugh, and Ediva horses from the common pool. By the time they reached the northern edge of the fairgrounds, they'd gathered several hundred renSimes, some mounted, some not, but all days short of need.

Mounted on the gorgeous black stallion with white stockings Sergi had presented to her at her last Pledge anniversary, Risa deployed her reception committee in a huge semi-circle, the Gens in the middle to attract the Raiders. Then she rode off to where Hugh, Klyd, and Ediva sat. "I can zlin them now," she told Klyd. "Where could they possibly have come from?"

"Try to capture some of them alive," Klyd said grimly, "and ask them. But we saw signs of such activity all across the corridor between Nivet and Gulf."

"Some? We'll take them all alive," asserted Risa.

She caught a wisp of unvoiced sarcasm in Hugh's nager, but he kept silent. Freeband Raiders wasted selyn as fast as they could in order to kill again and again, seeking the most grotesque and dehumanizing ways to kill. They were rarely taken alive. She would demonstrate just what Gulf Territory had achieved and win these people over quickly.

Klyd seemed dubious as well, but he asked, "Where would you like us stationed?"

"Right here," she replied. "Just watch. You'll see something you won't believe." *Besides, in the state he's in, Klyd doesn't belong down there.*

They could hear the thunder of hooves from the Raiders now, and the ambient nager roared with vulgar anticipation. Hugh focused tightly on his channel. Apparently they could set aside their problems to work together. Good. Risa didn't dare think what would happen if this Sectuib were tempted to a kill while in Gulf Territory on her personal safe-conduct.

Valleroy put out one hand to touch Klyd's wrist, intensifying his effort to protect the channel from the chaos that would erupt below them. His other hand he extended to Ediva, hoping to protect her, too.

Klyd pointed to a rank of Companions deployed to meet the Raider attack, projecting an enticing field. The trained Companions, of course, could not be killed by any renSime's attempt to draw selyn, though the Raiders loved to slaughter such Gens by flaying, burning, or the slowest method available.

The Raiders' spearhead struck, bursting from the lush underbrush at the edge of the fair grounds—their horses lathered and panting, barely able to maintain the gallop their riders beat out of them. And those riders!

Scarecrow thin, dressed in filthy rags or mismatched stolen finery, they showed the effects of their lifestyle in sunken cheeks and starvation sharpened features.

Risa sat her mount beside her Companion, watching with calm satisfaction as her people maneuvered to meet the charge.

How can she be so calm? Valleroy, despite his best professional efforts, was tensed against the images raging across his inner vision—memories of young Companions full of confidence sent into a panic and killed by Freeband Raiders such as those below. Perhaps Risa had never witnessed such a thing. Perhaps if she did, she'd come to realize how important it was to fortify her borders. But something deep inside of him wanted her to be right. *The world ought to be the way she thinks it is. It ought to.*

The Raiders' line smashed into the defenders, and they swung from their exhausted mounts onto the rank of Gens awaiting them, oblivious of the force arrayed against them.

"Half of them are in attrition!" exclaimed Klyd.

Attrition, the state just before death for lack of selyn. Those Simes had to get selyn—and they would take it regardless of the consequences.

"I zlin it," replied Risa. "The Companions will give them transfer. Don't worry. There'll be no kills."

The first Raider fell upon his "victim." The Companion accepted the scant body with upraised arms, letting the Raider get a grip on his forearms with his handling tentacles. They were too far away for Valleroy to see the tiny pink lateral tentacles, one on each side of each arm, weaker than the four handling tentacles. The laterals were composed almost entirely of selyn-conducting nerves. When the attacking Sime made a fifth contact point, usually by pressing his lips to the Gen's, invisible selyn flowed from the Gen body into the Sime through the laterals.

Valleroy edged closer to Klyd, noting that both channels were now in channel's functional mode, their own nervous systems protecting them from the brunt of the nageric assault. He, himself, was anticipating the soaring joy he'd feel when his selyn-saturated tissues were relieved in transfer.

But pleasure wasn't what the Raiders sought from their victims. They sought Gen pain and terror.

They didn't get it from Risa's Companions, though. As each Raider drew selyn, a channel or a renSime plucked him off the Gen and wrestled him to the ground, lest the Raider murder the Companion for cheating him of a kill. Valleroy thought he recognized Mor, Risa's son, in the midst of the fray, and was sure of it when Risa and Sergi stirred as the young man went down under a tangle of Raiders. Valleroy's heart pounded, almost as if his own son Jesse were down there—

Klyd nudged his horse closer to Hugh's. "Don't become involved," he warned in his professional voice, quiet with a penetrating calm that was more than the absence of tension.

Valleroy dismissed the wild images and concentrated on supporting Klyd. "Relax, I can handle it." And moments later, Mor was again mounted and shouting commands.

The action was soon over. The Raiders were corralled by a wall of renSimes and channels—the Gens safely out of the way of the vengeful Raiders. Replete with selyn now, they easily had the strength to rip a Gen into pieces. And they had the psychology to enjoy it.

Klyd told Valleroy, "No kills—not even any murders."

Valleroy breathed a sigh of relief. "You took a terrible risk, but I'm glad you won, Sectuib Keon."

Risa said, "Not so much of a risk. You see, when Gens trust Simes and cooperate, there don't have to be any deaths. We'll put the Raiders in the Pen for the time being—"

"I'm impressed," admitted Klyd.

The Pen would be the stoutest building in town, for it was the stockade which usually housed the greatest wealth of the town, the Gens raised to be killed by taxpaying Simes. How could Risa, a Householder, have the authority to send her prisoners—Simes at that—to the Pen? And how would such Simes react to being treated like Gens ripe for the kill?

But before he could say anything, Klyd nudged his horse about and zlinned the far distance again. "Sectuib Keon, have you given any thought to what those Raiders were fleeing from?"

Risa's eyes unfocused as she zlinned and Klyd read it for them all, "Three—maybe three hundred fifty Gen Regular Army troops. They've seen atrocities, and they won't see any difference between you and those Raiders."

Clearly, the Keon Sectuib had not planned for this. She took a deep breath and called, "Come on, Sergi!" She signaled to her herald, and without waiting for her Companion to turn his horse, she arrowed her stallion full tilt into the disintegrating defense lines.

CHAPTER TWO

The Farris Mystique

Valleroy stared after Risa, dumbfounded.

Klyd muttered, "And I was beginning to think she had the makings of a decent executive!"

The woman, her Companion riding at her side, was shouting orders from her horse. The lesser channels zlinned the approaching Gens. The renSime Hugh had seen in the Keon pavilion with Risa regrouped his band of well-trained juncts.

Shouts rose, whips cracked and snaked high, and the herald's horn blew. Whatever else these people might be, they weren't foolish enough to live so close to a Gen border without adequate civilian drills.

This time, the defense configuration was reversed—Simes out front to meet the charge, Gens behind them. "Has she got *channels* on her point?" asked Valleroy, scandalized.

"I'm afraid so," replied Klyd.

Valleroy sensed the conflict in his friend. It was hard for a man like Klyd to avoid physical danger, allowing others to bear the brunt of attack. But only the Householding that protected its channels and Companions survived. Valleroy knew from personal experience that Klyd was no coward.

The small knot of Raiders was near the back of the lines, surrounded by Sime and Gen sentries. The remainder of those attending the fair—mostly renSimes—formed up into regiments, moving out to support the local populace.

The Gen cavalry burst out of the dense underbrush, their uniforms dulled by river mud, their horses ghostly under a coating of sweat. They came and came, seeming far more than Klyd had estimated.

Still beyond the average renSime's zlinning range, the Gens opened fire. But Risa's ranks didn't waver.

Valleroy felt Klyd go into working mode, and knew people must have been hit—pain reaching need-sensitized Farris nerves despite the shield of his own replete field. He fought his horse to a stand. "Let's go help in the infirmary."

But Klyd wasn't listening. He raised one hand, dorsal tentacles pointing, reins twined through his fingers. "There's Risa! Behind the center of the line!"

"If they get her—"

"I hope not. I have to know if she's worth making an alliance with," Klyd replied grimly.

The two forces, Risa's standing, the Gens' charging at full gallop, met and interpenetrated. Simes—even channels—were dying or being tempted to kill.

"Are most of those Simes disjunct?" Valleroy asked, as much to keep Klyd's attention on him as to learn something.

"A good many. More semi-juncts, though."

The battle swirled and churned closer, Risa's side giving ground. Valleroy edged closer to Klyd, who kept drifting away to zlin the distance more clearly. Ediva was frozen in her saddle, tentacles and fingers gripping the reins. Her eyes slid out of focus, betraying the Sime's hunting mode—in which she could attack and kill by sheer reflex. *She's disjunct*.

"Klyd!" warned Valleroy.

The channel reached a tentacle to Ediva's wrist. As a Gen, Valleroy couldn't zlin the fields shifting to protect the renSime, but for years he'd perceived *something* when Klyd worked. As Ediva relaxed, he edged his horse to enclose her between the two of them, and locked into Klyd's body rhythms.

Ediva looked from one to the other of her protectors, and then back to the battle before them as if it were a mirage. Suddenly, her eyes widened.

Five Gen troopers in tight military formation were driving their horses up the rise toward the three of them. Two of the Gens had rifles aimed, two had sabers out, and the remaining one—apparently the commanding officer—drew a mean looking blade as they encircled the noncombatants.

In all the years Valleroy had been with Klyd, he'd never seen the channel carry a weapon. Nor would he allow his Companion to go armed. He considered himself a deadly weapon, pledged to save lives, not take them.

Ediva had no such philosophy. Her Householding made an art of personal combat. Their pledge included never being the aggressors, but those Gens were attacking.

Before even Klyd could react, Ediva drew her feet onto her saddle, and, augmenting, leaped at the Gen leader.

The two tumbled downhill as the other Gens spun to cover her. Valleroy never saw what she did, but when the two came to rest, she had disarmed the commander and was holding his own knife at his throat. "One move and he dies, messily."

She said it in heavily accented English, Valleroy's native language. He hadn't known she knew a word of it.

Klyd scanned the frozen Gens. "You have nothing to fear from us," he called in English, dismounting. Valleroy was sure Klyd didn't mean to move so smoothly, to float down like some preternatural menace. He was intent only on getting closer to Ediva, to grasp the fields before she was provoked by Gen fear.

Valleroy dismounted and worked closer to Klyd. He told the Gens, "Battle's over for you—and you're lucky. These folks won't kill you or sell you to be killed." *I hope.* Even if Risa ambrov Keon had the power to keep these Gens out of the Choice Kill Auctions—would she?

Klyd had reached the commander and Ediva. Valleroy could only admire Ediva's self control. Klyd said, "Carefully now, Ediva, let him go."

She seemed about to argue—Klyd wasn't *her* Sectuib—but then she sighed and loosened her grip. Valleroy saw the commander's eyes widen as tentacles slid across his throat.

She backed off a few paces, slightly downhill from the rest of the group, her back to the battle line.

Klyd's attention was on the commander, and Ediva's was on Klyd, as the Sectuib in Zeor said conversationally, "Welcome to Gulf Territory. Your stay will be more comfortable if you ask your men to stop fighting."

The man's lips trembled as if about to break into a snarl of defiance. "Only if *you* deliver to us every last one of those rotten, mother-killing—"

Valleroy interrupted, the man's voice triggering a cascade of memories. "Harris Emstead! Of all—how—you were in New Washington—"

The man's eyes narrowed, emphasizing the fine pattern of cracks weathered into his skin. His gray eyes matched his salt-and-pepper hair, but his figure was still as trim as a twenty-year-old's. Valleroy, too, had aged, having passed forty, but Emstead had a memory like a trap. "Valleroy? The translator? A Turnie?"

"No!" Valleroy went closer, still mindful of the fields. "I'll explain! Just stop the—"

"Mister Emstead," Klyd said anxiously, "you must surrender quickly before someone accidentally gets killed."

Valleroy eyed the channel, stunned. *There hasn't been a kill yet?*

The commander eased to his feet to meet Klyd's eyes, but before he could respond, Klyd shouted, "Ediva!"

Another knot of combatants was upon them. Ediva was engulfed by mounted soldiers.

Valleroy was cut off from Klyd, fighting for his life amid a forest of horses' legs and bayonettes. It had been years since his time as an Interrogator and sometime Agent for the Border Patrol, and he'd never been particularly good at unarmed combat.

With his field so high, every blow that landed on him would send magnified agonies through Klyd and any other nearby Sime. He dared only to run, not fight.

He rolled, dodged, spun under a horse, bounded to his feet and doubled over, zigzagging, knowing Klyd would never lose track of him.

As he ran, heart pumping, he recalled being held captive with Klyd, used as a weapon against him. Licensed Raiders had done that—supposedly civilized Simes whose business was Raiding into Gen Territory for the Choice Auctions.

But his own business had been interrogating Simes for the Gen Army and Border Patrol—he almost gagged at the memory of caged Simes dying of attrition as he relentlessly questioned them. He had been another person then.

Suddenly two Gen riders came at Valleroy, leaning down as they split to pass on either side. They caught him under the arms, lifted him, then deposited him before Harris Emstead. A blur, and Risa and Sergi were there, a mounted force of Simes and Gens surrounding Emstead's remaining command.

Simes flicked among the mounted Gens, dragging them off their horses and disarming them with augmented strength and Sime speed.

Risa, so small she could barely get her knees around the stallion she rode, shouted in piercing female tones which could penetrate battle noise, "Surrender and no one else will be hurt! This is a mistake—you don't mean to attack a peaceful township!"

Her English was strongly accented, overlaid with the Gulf Territory cadence as well as using Simelan vowels for English ones, but her grammar was perfect. Emstead got the message, as four Simes imprisoned his horse, one woman extracting the reins from his hands, pointedly caressing his skin with tentacles.

I hope she's a channel! thought Valleroy, though the woman wore nothing to associate her with either Keon or Carre.

Emstead's lips tightened. Then he nodded, and spurred his horse through the press so he could grab the horn from Risa's herald—who was also Sime.

Emstead blew a single, tearing note that floated out over the churning company. His men stood down, suffering themselves to be disarmed.

Risa edged her horse over to Emstead, explaining in a "be reasonable" tone, "A lot of people have been hurt. We've got to get our medics out onto that field before any more die. When everything's cleaned up, then you and I are going to have a long talk over a good dinner."

Valleroy had wormed his way to Emstead's horse, capturing its nose to soothe it. "She means that, Harris," he called up to Emstead as Risa held out her open palm for the horn.

Slowly, examining her eyes, Emstead handed it over. "Now," said the Sectuib ambrov Keon, "we don't have facilities to imprison so many, so I'm asking your word that your men will stay where they're put and do what they're told. Then I want you to organize your medics. We'll find a tent for you to use as a hospital—ours can't handle all your wounded, but I'll send a few channels to help. Susi," she said to the Sime woman who had captured Emstead, "will you help the Gen medics, please?" Without waiting for an answer, she continued, "We'll take your men with *transfer burns*"—she used the Simelan term—"into our infirmary. Sergi!"

She had everyone swarming into a new configuration with a few shouted orders. *She's a Sectuib all right,* thought Valleroy as he was conscripted into her medic corps.

Joining the medics was the quickest way to find Klyd. So he went to work, ignoring the background sound as Emstead's orders were passed down chain of command.

Valleroy knelt beside a channel with a bullet wound near the heart, holding the fields, trying to staunch the selyn loss so the woman could control her own bleeding. Then she was on a stretcher, headed for the critical ward, and somebody told him her Companion was dead.

He helped a renSime, skull grazed by a bullet, one ankle broken, to hobble to the wagon come to collect the less seriously wounded. *But where's Klyd?*

Working toward where he'd last seen Ediva and Klyd, he stumbled over a corpse three-quarters buried in the dirt, trampled by the horses. It had been a Gen soldier.

He dug a renSime out from under a dead horse—crushed ribs, blood oozing from his mouth, concussion, two broken legs, mercifully unconscious. Valleroy was grimly happy he hadn't given transfer this morning after all. His field was so high, he might even save this one's life.

He took the Sime to the infirmary where a channel forced a transfer into him, Valleroy's field a tourniquet, keeping selyn from pluming away through the wounds. *But where's Klyd?*

Surely the channel would have spotted Valleroy by now! Exposure to channels simulating need, and to renSimes who'd fought themselves into real need, had his selyn production soaring and his system aching with surplus selyn.

He asked everyone he met, "Have you seen the channel wearing the blue cloak?" But the answer was always no until he asked for a phenomenally good channel, a stranger here.

Then, people answered, "That way." But always a different way from the last person's pointing finger.

The afternoon sun was already slanting from the west as he returned to the infirmary. Someone had raised the wall of the tent facing the old town of Laveen. It made an extended roof, covering the less seriously wounded who lay on blankets or sat waiting for treatment.

Seeing no sign of Klyd, Valleroy asked a man with a broken leg, "Would you know where they've put the injured Gen soldiers?" *It would be just like Klyd to dive into the very worst sea of Gen pain and fear!*

The man described a tent Valleroy remembered—the shiltpron parlor.

Valleroy worked his way out of the infirmary, lending aid here and there as requested, but intent on finding Klyd. He came out in the west portico area where a channel/Companion team was doing triage while a group of renSimes served blackeyed peas and hot, fresh corn cakes to anyone who could eat. A familiar voice hailed him, "Hugh!"

He turned, and found Ediva lying under a Gen's saddle-blanket, one arm stretched out from her side. Her upper lip was swollen, and one eye was darkening. Her short hair stood up in spikes around her head, and there was a black smudge across her forehead. But relief swept through Valleroy, washing away a tension he hadn't known was there.

"Has Klyd seen you?" he asked kneeling beside her. Her arm, especially the bicep, was swollen and purple, but no bone ends stuck through the skin, no blood. More relief.

"No," she answered. "I thought he was with you."

Valleroy squirmed around to spot the triage team, summoning them with a wave. The channel consulted a clip board. "Oh, yes, the collarbone and dislocation. Get to you in about an hour and a half." He looked down at Valleroy. "You off duty? Sit here then, but be careful, she's a renSime." And he hurried off.

Fully half the cases who had been waiting when Valleroy arrived had been taken inside. A couple of flatbed wagons took stretcher cases away toward the town and Householding. He really couldn't fault Risa's *organization*, but nothing they did was quite like home. There, at least, he'd never have had any trouble locating Klyd.

"*This*," he said indicating her arm, "isn't serious?"

Ediva roused herself to answer, "It hurts when I let it, but the channel said there's no nerve damage." Injury to the selyn transport nerves running up and down a Sime's arms could mean death.

"What channel?" he asked suspiciously. For something

like this, at home, they'd call in a Farris. But Klyd was the only Farris in this whole Territory—and they had no sense of how to use him. They also didn't know how important Ediva ambrov Dar was to the world.

"The Sectuib—Risa. Hugh—don't leave." Tears leaked from the corners of her eyes, and she was shaking, pain and sudden relaxation leaching away the last of her bravery.

Sergi's hands massaged Risa's back as she stood up from treating another mangled Wild Gen. "He's dead," she whispered, leaning into her Companion's soothing fingers and blinking tears away as the nerve-shattering deathshock receded. Her eyes strayed over the rest of the tent full of Gens, their medics plying their crude—and often needlessly painful—trade. She and Klyd had saved some lives and some limbs the Gen butchers would have amputated.

The Gens were grateful once they realized they were being helped and not just being saved for the kill. Yet they didn't understand the price the channels paid. She'd already sent three others away, saturated with Gen pain and fear. Klyd was still working tirelessly. She couldn't fault him as a channel. He threw himself into the work, and his temper had steadied as his entran was relieved. His need, though, had become ever more obvious to her, if not to his Gen patients.

Klyd was nonjunct, unlike herself, having never killed for selyn, and so under less stress from this kind of thing. But so was Susi Darley, and she'd had to send the young woman away from here an hour ago.

But who would dare tell the Sectuib in Zeor that he was overdoing? Only his Companion, but Hugh seemed to have disappeared. Perhaps she could set him an example, then, for she realized that keeping up with the Nivet-Territory channel had become a kind of challenge, and she could not afford to let such personal feelings interfere with her common sense.

"Sergi, work with Klyd for a while. I'm going to take a break and see how Colonel Emstead is doing."

Sergi seemed about to object, but then followed her gaze to where Klyd was struggling with a Gen thrashing in convulsions. He swallowed hard, and made for the visitor, focusing his attention. Risa retreated toward the door of the tent, pausing to admire Sergi's performance. He had such precise control that she hadn't felt a jolt when he shifted his attention from her to Klyd, and though he was barely four paces away now, she could hardly perceive him.

Sergi got a grip on the thrashing man, holding him still so Klyd could work on his caved-in skull. Risa turned to leave as they began murmuring together.

Outside, a team of children were serving the out-Territory Gens a dinner of peas, beans, and onions, cornbread, citrus juice, and fresh fruit. She heard some grumbling from the men, and caught her daughter, Virena, telling one of them, "Well, if you don't like our food, you can catch a rabbit and eat it like a dog!"

"Vi!" exclaimed Risa. "These people are our guests! You must always be polite to guests, no matter how rude they are to you."

"Yes, Mama," the girl replied, only partly chastened. She was very much Risa's child, looking considerably younger than her fifteen years and showing no signs of changeover, though her birth characteristics had foretold she would be a channel. Risa wasn't worried; she had changed over at sixteen with no problems.

"Apologize to the gentleman," Risa prompted, laying her hand on the back of her daughter's head, tentacles—out of sight of the Gen soldier—twining gently into the child's hair, which was coming out of its braids.

Vi smiled disarmingly at the Gen soldier, and said, "I am sorry for calling you a dog. We have two dogs at home, and they're really very nice." Risa tightened her hand slightly, not enough to hurt, and Vi ended her left-handed apology at that ambiguous point.

Harris Emstead came up, flanked by his lieutenants.

"A word of explanation," Risa said to him. "The children are serving you because the adult Gens are with the injured, and I don't want Simes so close to your men just now. We haven't given everyone transfer yet—" *I'll be working through the night on that!*

Someone had explained the Householding lifestyle to the man, for he said, "I suppose they haven't thought of that." He waved to the listening soldier. "Pass it down." Then to

Risa he said, "We can't fault your hospitality—especially after the approach we made—but you did promise a talk. My men are anxious about what's to become of them."

"Oh, you'll all go home as soon as we can spare you an escort to the border. First we must attend the injured."

Before he could answer, Sergi came up behind her, and she turned around. His expression was cold, though his nager was controlled. Vi was staring at her father, not used to seeing him look upset. "What happened?" Risa asked in Simelan, not to be rude but expecting a technical answer.

Sergi replied in English, "Klyd said you require me more, and I was hampering him. I should have told you that would happen, but I was hoping—"

He is hurt! "Was he rude?"

"No—tactful. He asked me to find Hugh for him."

To Emstead she explained, "A channel gets used to working with certain Gens. In a critical case, it can make a difference." But to Sergi, she suggested, "Send Dinny to find Hugh. You and I must have a talk with the Colonel."

Sending Vi back to her task while Sergi dispatched the young Companion, Risa decided to invite their Nivet Territory visitors to the conference so they could see how cooperation with the Wild Gens beat fortification against them.

She sent Emstead and his remaining lieutenant to her office under the care of some Keon Companions who'd just come off duty, then took Sergi's arm around her shoulders and walked close to him, telling herself, *Pull yourself together. There's an opportunity here—somewhere!*

"Risa," said Sergi thoughtfully as the parlor tent came into view again, "Do you suppose, before they leave, you might arrange for me to work more closely with Klyd? Maybe after he's had his transfer? I know I could do it—when he's in condition to have some patience."

Feeling his tremor of eagerness, she wondered why she'd worried about a channel hurting her Companion's feelings. Klyd was the most intriguing challenge Sergi had met in a decade, and what he learned from Klyd, Sergi would teach her. "I'll do my best. But be prepared. I think you'll find he's the semi-hysterical type who overreacts to everything."

He looked down at her. "You think so? I've heard things

like that said of Farrises. They're a different mutation from the ordinary channel, you know. That sensitivity is genetic.''

''So you've—hey, isn't that Dinny coming?''

''If you say so,'' replied Sergi.

The light was failing, and Risa realized she'd identified the boy by his nager. ''News of Hugh? I hope nothing's wrong. Klyd really needs that transfer tonight.''

From the way Sergi clamped down on his field, Risa intuited he'd be delighted to give Klyd transfer. *Shen, I could really get to hate Farrises!* But she couldn't blame a Companion for being attracted, and she didn't dare allow personal feelings to interfere with her judgment of the Nivet representatives.

Dinny, intent on his mission, arrived at the tent a few seconds before Risa. She followed him through the insulating tent flap and stopped in her tracks.

The depressed skull fracture patient was dead, a blanket over his face as if to hide the nakedness of death.

Klyd bent over a stretcher still held by two of Emstead's men, carrying one of the more accomplished Companions in Carre. The ambient nager was ashen with the fading field perturbations of the Companion. As Sergi entered behind her, Risa zlinned the Companion, badly nerve-burned by an attacking Sime and thus deep into transfer shock.

Klyd didn't spare a glance for Risa as he muttered at the stretcher bearers, ''You shouldn't have brought him *here*, but put him down. I'll do what I can.''

One Gen stretcher bearer grumbled, ''Found him in a pile of bodies. Wouldn't turn anyone over to those—''

''Shut up, Norris,'' snapped the other. ''I seen this guy do miracles.'' And he lowered the stretcher.

Risa, edging forward to get a better reading, kept her field level, masking Sergi to give Klyd a working space. She inserted herself into the nageric pattern, facing Klyd over the supine Companion. There was only one way a Companion of this caliber could have been burned like this—gang attack by Raiders. *Maybe they panicked at being put in a Pen? That could have been bad psychology.* But where else in town was strong enough?

Then she concentrated on zlinning the problem before them, welcoming Klyd's field control.

Blood pressure too low, capillary seepage around brain and spinal column, pulmonary edema. As she watched, the man's heart went into weak fibrillations, then stopped.

She let up her grip on the fields, fending off the deathshock. "He's gone. How'd this happen?"

A Gen started to answer, but Klyd snapped, "Stand back!" He stripped the patient's shirt off, wrestled the inert body onto its side, and took a grip, spreading his two left hand laterals over the sternum, and his right hand laterals across the upper back, enclosing the heart area.

Risa gasped as the ambient nager split with a clap of inaudible thunder. Everything went black, and when her senses cleared, she was slumped against Sergi.

Before her, the Carre Companion was on his back. Klyd leaned over him, fisted both hands on his sternum, and bore down hard, as if trying to break his breastbone. She was about to protest, when the Companion's heart gave a flop and a whump and picked up a weak but normal rhythm.

She stared, zlinning, as the purple receded from the Companion's coloring and his nail beds took on a healthy glow. *I don't believe*—. She twisted to glance at Sergi, who was staring at the Companion, equally dumbfounded.

She looked back at the Companion, not healthy but living. Out of her gradual realization that maybe they didn't know *anything* about what channels could accomplish, came a flash of blinding insight on how to turn this whole debacle to a real profit—to get Emstead to grant them a travel corridor to Nivet Territory so they could send First Year channels there to be trained.

But just then she saw Klyd's lips paling as they had earlier that morning. His eyes glazed over. His face went slack. His nageric control loosened. She pushed Sergi toward Klyd. "Sergi, quickly. He's about to faint."

Her husband caught Klyd's shoulders as he tilted over, and she felt Sergi inducing him to breathe by breathing deeply himself. But he made no attempt to lock onto the channel's fields as a Companion should.

"Sergi—what are you doing? *Help* the man!" She started to reach for Klyd's arms, laterals extended.

"No, Risa!" Sergi commanded. "You don't know how to

handle a Farris, and *neither do I*! Where is this man's Companion?!''

Astonished at Sergi's vehemence but trusting him, Risa merely zlinned Klyd cautiously, observing without attempting control of his fields. But as she was probing for his problem, Klyd was forcing his eyes open, struggling to sit up.

He focused on Sergi. "Thank you," he whispered on a shaky breath. But he retreated from both Risa and Sergi, hugging his knees.

"I'm sorry Sergi couldn't help you—" Risa began.

"He did the right thing," Klyd replied, his voice still weak. "He's not trained to cope with Farrises."

Risa squelched her automatic defense of her Companion in favor of diplomacy. "Your patient's doing fine." That was what she'd want to hear, in Klyd's place.

He turned to the Carre Companion, zlinning though his own systems were in painful chaos. "He'll have to be treated very carefully now, or he may never work again. Did anybody ever find Hugh? He's not very far away . . . over there, somewhere." He waved a tentacle, but lowered his forehead to his knees and held his breath. She could feel his plea for Companion's support and Sergi's struggle to resist it.

Risa moved back, motioning Sergi away, and turned to Dinny, who had plastered himself next to the entry as if trying to draw his nager up and become invisible.

The Companion answered from there, "Hugh ambrov Rior is in the main infirmary tent, working, and asking everyone where Klyd Farris is. I told him to stay there and I'd bring him."

"Good," answered Risa, and asked Klyd, "Can you walk?" *He'll have to take that transfer now. There's no other way to restore his systems.*

Klyd raised his head, bewildered. "No—bring Hugh here. I must treat the patient."

"You can't do him any good in this condition," argued Risa. She admired stubborn adherence to duty, but this was too much. She spoke to the two Gens still hovering beside the stretcher, "Would you two carry the Companion to the infirmary? We've got better facilities for him there."

As the dazed Gens picked up the stretcher, casting wide-eyed glances at Klyd, he struggled to his feet and stood swaying, fending off Sergi's arm. Gradually, the nageric turbulence in Klyd's vicinity died away, and there was a semblance of that cleared bubble he carried around with him when working. "I—think I can walk."

Then, as if putting his hands and laterals into an open flame, he placed one hand on Sergi's shoulder and the other on Risa's. "I—could use some help, though."

Klyd became steadier on his feet. Though he was touching them both, his nager barely interpenetrated theirs.

Outside the infirmary, despite the heavy insulation, even Risa flinched at the torrential nageric pain and unfillable need. Klyd, however, walked into the white hot nager as if it wasn't there. *And he complained of my guards emoting too strongly?* But she vividly remembered how his face had gone white. *Maybe his ethics were more offended than his sensitivities?* She'd never met anyone who'd faint over offended ethics before.

But she could not deny what she'd just zlinned him doing, nor the awe as he let go of their shoulders and strode through the maelstrom as if it were of no moment. But her original judgment of him stood. His strength was so brittle, so unpredictable, it might as well be a weakness.

Only a few lesser injuries still waited for treatment. Risa automatically searched the ambient for acute problems, and slammed into a mighty, throbbing, seductive Gen nager.

Gasping, she caught at Sergi. They moved to see Hugh kneeling beside that renSime—Ediva ambrov something—his eyes almost closed, the most serene expression on his face she'd ever seen outside of bed, and his fingertips wandering over the renSime's arm.

The woman was breathing slowly, selyn fields twined deeply into Hugh's—not quite a transfer grip, but the most articulated and facile field work she'd ever zlinned a Gen doing without a channel to shape and focus the effort.

It hardly seemed necessary. The renSime was not badly injured. A slightly cracked collar bone, minor contusions and abrasions. Though it looked as if the arm had been painfully swollen—something tickled her memory. She'd examined this one earlier, not recognizing her as the other Nivet ambassador. She'd lost her Householding cloak, and her face had been swollen and badly bruised, her nager reduced from augmentation and some sort of trained pain blocking. A vision of the arm as it had been swam into her healer's mind. *Shen and shid! A Companion alone couldn't have—*

As Klyd carefully moved around Ediva to face Valleroy, Risa stole a glance at Sergi and reminded herself never—ever—to dictate limits to his abilities.

Seeing Klyd, Hugh sent a smile of unutterable welcome and bone-deep relief washing through the ambient, weakening Risa's weary knees.

Klyd, however, did not respond. His fields were still hardened. Risa could not read a flicker of emotional reaction through that shell-like casing, and so was utterly unprepared when Klyd said, voice shaking with outrage, "Hugh ambrov Rior, how *dare* you!"

CHAPTER THREE

Fair Exchange

Valleroy looked up from Ediva and saw Klyd—no apparition this time. He let his relief show, happy with his work on Ediva and glad they could now have transfer.

"Hugh ambrov Rior—how *dare* you!"

Valleroy controlled his recoil and disengaged from Ediva. Calming Klyd with his nager, he replied, "I was careful—"

Then he saw Klyd's pinched look, his bruised sunken eyes, his trembling fingers—*His hands never shake*. And how ghostly Klyd's presence seemed. He could hardly feel the need he saw. Absently, Valleroy suggested to Ediva, "Sleep now," and reinforced it nagerically so the renSime drifted off. "Risa, could we have privacy?"

A tremor passed through Klyd's body, but he didn't yield

control. As they followed Risa toward the office they'd used that morning, she said, "I've arranged a dinner this evening with Harris Emstead and his officers. We'll show them we're civilized. With you two in good shape, we ought to accomplish a great deal."

Hugh acknowledged the invitation, then asked Klyd professionally, "How did you get into this condition?"

Tightly, the channel answered, "Fibrillation shock on a thrice-burned Companion."

Valleroy winced away from visions of the possible results if Klyd had failed. "Without me there—"

"Risa sent Sergi to me. I'll be all right—"

Hugh stared at Sergi, his sense of violation turning to anger at the Keon Companion. "You touched him?"

"Not nagerically," insisted Klyd. "Sergi knew enough not to make matters worse. He could have learned to work with me once—probably could now—but he *hasn't* worked with Farrises." He added, "It's strangely terrifying walking around among people who don't know what *this* means."

He fingered his distinctive black string tie and braided black belt. Once, Valleroy hadn't known what they meant, either, or even that they had a meaning.

Risa said, "How can you expect people to know that means something? Lots of people wear ties or belts like those. You should wear a tag or badge—something that won't be taken for decoration. But never mind that now. Go have your transfer. Then we'll talk." She and her Companion left them in the shielded office.

"It was my fault," Valleroy told Klyd. "These folks seem almost like home after the gypsies, but I shouldn't have let us get separated."

"That's the least of what you shouldn't have done," Klyd answered coldly.

That was the last straw. Bone-weary and totally out of patience, Valleroy rounded on Klyd and let him *feel* what Ediva had been suffering. In a cold, professional voice, he listed her injuries before he'd worked on her, then added, "And *they* hadn't the decency to call you to examine her!"

"Hugh—they had no reason to think she required *my* skills. But *you* did."

"*You* were not to be found. Ediva was alone among strangers, hurting—what if there'd been damage to her selyn transport nerves? Think what she means to this world!"

Still cold and hard, Klyd said, "I *am* thinking! Hugh, what if Zelerod's successor goes junct!"

"I told you," Valleroy replied adamantly, "I was careful. I wouldn't endanger Ediva's disjunction."

"You have no concept of how your field affects Simes. Your touching a renSime is cruel seduction. When Ediva's next need hits, she'll want a Companion, a Gen she can't possibly *affect* in transfer. No matter which way you turn it, that's cruelty."

Holding his temper, Valleroy fixed his eyes on his shoe tips, and said what he'd said a thousand times and couldn't seem to make Klyd hear. "RenSimes are people, too. Just because you were born a channel, you have no right to deny others what only a Gen can provide. As long as the only trained Gens are trained to serve channel's need, then the only Gens who dare touch renSimes are Companions. If that's cruel, it's your rules that are cruel." He met Klyd's eyes, and added, "Can't you see it would have been immoral of me not to heal Ediva?"

"I see that you think so," Klyd answered heavily. "But you still don't understand junctedness, or how 'delicate' Ediva is. If I can ever make you understand, perhaps you'll have sense enough to keep your field away from helpless renSimes, but right now I can't—can't—cope with it."

No Companion could resist such a plea from a channel in need. Absolutely nothing else mattered when Klyd's field reached out, meshing into a firm grip.

Valleroy focused on the channel, knowing how tenuous Klyd's control had to be to force such a plea from him.

Klyd dropped into the reclining desk chair.

Valleroy sat on the desk, gathering Klyd's hands to examine his lateral tentacles.

He coaxed the small, pink-gray lateral tentacles out of their sheaths and onto his skin, relaxing, remembering good transfers, letting his body respond to need, knowing Klyd's Sime senses would share every nuance of Valleroy's emotions.

Klyd's eyes sagged shut. Valleroy said, "I've a confession

to make," not sure Klyd could hear him, but knowing he zlinned intent behind his words. "When the Gen Army attacked us and we were separated—I remembered when we were captured by the Runzi Raiders—how Andle caged you beside me, in hard need but unable to touch me. I didn't know then what he was doing to you. But I do now. I don't think I'd have the strength to go through that again.

"But if Harris Emstead had taken us captive, things wouldn't have been any better. He would probably have me flayed alive right in front of you, not really understanding what he was doing, just seeking military information.

"Klyd, I wouldn't mind dying, but I couldn't stand hurting you. There was a time when I couldn't have believed such a statement. Now, I can barely understand how any Gen can be near you and not want to relieve that—that scream that's coming out of you right now. I can even admire Sergi—if he really didn't work your fields. But I don't trust him anywhere near you. If we don't do this transfer now, I'll do nothing but worry about you—seeing you keeling over dead, or twisted into paralysis—or worse—"

Klyd squirmed away, complaining, "Do you have to dwell on such horrors?"

"Do you have to take such risks?" countered Valleroy.

Klyd's eyes gradually refocused, the strain of ironclad control gone, for Valleroy's work had damped the oscillations in the channel's systems. He showed only the normal symptoms of need as he got to his feet.

Klyd paced. "Look, you've restored my systems. Sergi couldn't have done that, and I know you won't deny me transfer when I ask. But not yet. Not now."

In disbelief, Valleroy asked, "Why not? Klyd, you've got to be at your best for that dinner meeting!"

Klyd paced a circle, never moving away from Valleroy, aching with the suppressed fear of death which was the worst part of being in need. "I'm too upset over what you did to Ediva. Talk about me taking risks! And the mood you're in—Listen to yourself, raking over bad memories. Our transfers haven't been good lately, and this could be the worst yet. I can't even make myself touch you."

Valleroy went cold all over, nerves screaming as if somebody were pulling them out by the roots. *If it's that Sergi, I'll—*

Klyd closed the distance between them in two strides, and seized Valleroy by the shoulders. "No, no, Hugh. You're the only one here who can stand up to my draw—especially when I'm like this. I don't think I *could*—*ever* take a full transfer from anyone else willingly, any more than you'd offer to anyone. I'd rather wait than ask another Companion to partial me. I hate partials and shunt-splices, Hugh. They give me headaches for months."

"You're telling me denial exercises are better?" Valleroy couldn't keep the sarcasm out of his words.

Klyd conceded grudgingly, "We can't get away from each other, but we can't go on like this, either."

"I keep trying to talk about it—"

"But it never seems important before turnover, and afterwards—"

Turnover, the point mid-way through the month, when a Sime had used up half the selyn in his system and began the descent into need. After Klyd's turnover, Valleroy often visualized himself prone at the edge of a cliff, holding Klyd on a rope that just stretched and stretched, taking him further and further away.

"I think," said Valleroy, "philosophy is *never* important to you. A channel lives from disaster to emergency, hoping for the strength to deal with the next crisis. And a Sectuib—Zeor's bigger now than it was in your grandfather's day. Some day, we've got to take some time—go away maybe—and thrash this whole thing out. We do agree," he grinned, "we can't live like this."

"All right. We'll do it, very first chance. But now," he sighed, "you've got to give me some time."

"You're *out* of time!" retorted Valleroy sharply. "I'm calling a Companion's Demand on you. If I'm really First Companion of Zeor, you'll heed it."

Klyd looked as if he'd never seen him before, and Valleroy was sure he was hypoconscious, seeing with his eyes alone. In Klyd's state of need, that indicated either supreme control or a severe nervous disorder. Valleroy asked, "In the battle, did you take a blow to the head?"

"No," Klyd answered absently. "You *are* an officer of Zeor, Hugh, in spite of heading your own House. I can't disobey you. But I don't think you know what you're doing."

But he did. A bad transfer now would be worse than none. *So it won't be bad!* Valleroy summoned the image he'd had of Klyd when he'd first offered him transfer: valiant, noble, heroic, trustworthy. But perhaps Klyd had always been too foolish to take care of himself, and Valleroy had just not understood. Well, now he did. "I'll control this transfer."

"Yes, Naztehr," Klyd answered reluctantly.

Valleroy took control of the fields, yearning to unload the energy his body produced in such abundance. It seemed, just before transfer, that he was drowning, suffocating in his own selyn. Valleroy had never met another Companion who experienced it this way and long ago had stopped talking about it. He knew his experience was the Gen counterpart to Sime need, but Simelan had no word for it, so he just thought of it as need.

He held out his arms, enticing the channel with his field and waiting for him to raise intil—the condition in which Klyd would not resist taking selyn from the nearest source.

He felt Klyd go hyperconscious, able to sense the world only through Sime senses—a condition called hunting-mode in a junct. But to Valleroy it promised fulfillment, not pain and death. He was serenely confident as Klyd seized his arms, clutched them with his handling tentacles, and extended his laterals into contact position. They were bathed in ronaplin, the conducting fluid for the invisible, intangible energy, selyn.

Valleroy relaxed as Klyd seated the fifth contact point by touching lips. He had no idea what untrained Gens sensed at this moment that scared them and turned the sensation to pain, the pain juncts craved as the peak of the kill. What he felt was a delightful washing of energy from cells and nerves, balm that spread well-being through him, releasing an up-welling optimism and sense of invincibility.

He could feel Klyd sharing that feeling in the increasing speed of the transfer. He craved more, and sought it aggressively, knowing that this "pushed" selyn into Klyd, rather than requiring him to "draw" it. This was the way transfer should always be.

But then, at the halfway point, Klyd grabbed control. Valleroy became a harmonic string, resonating to a perfect note, but not originating it. It was only a fraction of a second, but he tried to regain command, berating himself for slowing beneath Klyd's demand rate. But Klyd wouldn't release control, he attacked as a junct might.

Valleroy's speed and capacity matched Klyd's so closely that nothing Klyd did could hurt. But as they wrestled for control, the anticipated pleasure eluded them both. Klyd's body had acquired enough selyn to survive the month, but his spirit had been cheated of rejuvenation. His handling tentacles left Valleroy's arms, dropping them in mid-air. He shook his head sadly. "I didn't mean to do that. I told you I couldn't—"

But Valleroy couldn't take Klyd's feelings into account. He felt disconnected from reality—as if his nervous system had been packed away in cotton. And he knew from bitter experience that it would stay that way for two weeks, then get progressively worse until their next transfer. It was worse than he could ever remember. "I know why you did that! You're afraid I'd go to Ediva if you made me post! Dammit—I know I can't have transfer with her, but you've got no right to keep me from loving her!"

"Hugh—no! Listen to me!"

"I've done enough listening to you!" He charged for the door, but Klyd caught him half way there. There was no way to counter Sime strength with Gen muscle. He took a deep breath, gathered control of the fields, and turned, forcing Klyd to drop his hands.

"I said," repeated the channel, "I'm sorry. I didn't mean to do that. I couldn't help it."

"Do you hate me that much?" Valleroy asked in wonder.

"No! It's just—Hugh, what you did to Ediva is *monstrous*! You are so powerful—you frighten me."

"You don't trust me."

"Most of the time I do. It's never how you treat me, only what you *believe* in. Your beliefs are so dangerous. I know you're not callous, but it's hard to make myself believe it sometimes. Can't you understand that?''

"You honored my Companion's Demand."

"Of course. My judgment might have been wrong. Householding wisdom insists there are times only the Companion can judge rightly. And only the Companion can discern when those times are." He scrubbed his ronaplin-smeared hands together. "Let's wash up, see to Ediva, and go meet Harris Emstead and the officers in Keon."

The large table in Risa's pavilion office had been set with a table cloth, sparkling candelabra, and Keon's best china. As Sergi checked the wine he had ordered from Keon's cellars, Risa asked him, "Why did you disobey me, Sergi? When I told you to help Klyd?"

"I could have hurt him badly if I'd tried to engage his fields."

Risa said, "You act as if the man were made of spun glass, while his own Companion shoves him around—"

"His *own* Companion," Sergi agreed. "Hugh knows exactly what that brittle Farris strength can and cannot take. Farrises are . . . like copper, Risa. One of the most efficient conductors of energy in existence, astonishingly malleable and resilient—up to a point. But when that point is reached, the slightest stress—and it shatters. I've got the years of training and experience to handle copper. Hugh has it to handle Klyd Farris."

"Well, I hope Hugh handles him into a good transfer, which I suppose you'd characterize as melting down the copper to start over?"

Her husband grinned at her. "Perhaps that's why with you it's like a blast furnace, to produce molten steel?"

They were still chuckling when Harris Emstead and his officers arrived, followed by Risa's and Sergi's son and daughter, Mor and Virena, both freshly scrubbed and dressed in their best clothes. It amused Risa to see Vi playing "grown up," while her "little" brother towered over her and already had the adult grace of a Companion. *That will change once Vi changes over.* She had no desire to hurry her daughter; Risa had been pushed into responsibility early, so she had given her children the chance to enjoy childhood.

The Gens were hungry, but Risa was determined to wait the full hour she'd allotted the Nivet ambassadors. She poured another round of trin tea and urged Emstead to sample another variety of liquor they imported from beyond Gulf Port. Susi Darley came to the tent flap.

Risa called, "Come in, Susi. Where's your father?"

"Asleep . . . finally," the young channel answered.

Risa started. "Susi, what happened? Is Tan ill?" She knew he hadn't been among the injured.

"No more than usual," the other woman replied. "He augmented in the battle and went into crisis. But he couldn't kill. I finally got transfer into him. He'll be all right in the morning."

But between the two women hung the unspoken question, "What about next month?"

Tannen Darley was one of the many semi-junct renSimes who supported Keon's efforts to disjunct the territory. Too old to disjunct, he had taken fewer and fewer kills over the years, accepting channel's transfer most months. But every few months any Sime who had not completed disjunction had to provide his selyn system a real kill, or he would die.

The Pen system was still in full operation; both Keon and Carre knew full well that it had to be left to die of neglect. They never, ever spoke against it despite what their members might feel about raising human beings, drugged out of fulfilling their potential as people, to be killed that Simes might live.

However, Simes who had accepted Householding beliefs with their hearts, but whose bodies were too old to overcome the need to kill, eventually lost the mental survival technique of dismissing pen Gens as animals. One day even the dullest could not be seen as anything but a potential person, and from that day onward, the semi-junct Sime was on the road to an agonizing death.

Risa had watched Verla, her first friend and business partner in Laveen, die that way three years ago. Now Tan Darley, dear friend, staunch supporter—

"Oh, if only we could find him the right Companion!" Susi said wistfully.

"We'll keep trying," Risa assured her, but she had no real hope. There was little chance of finding a Gen capable of providing direct transfer to a renSime and being satisfied in the process, for the Gen's satisfaction appeared to be the crucial substitute for killbliss. There were a few such transfer pairs, but so far no Gen had proved the solution to Darley's need—except those he reluctantly killed.

Susi proffered a sheaf of papers. "You asked for the report on the Raiders."

"Oh, yes." Risa took the documents, but her attention was still on Susi. "Will you be all right?"

"Of course. But since Daddy can't be here, I doubt I could contribute much. There are still people waiting for transfers—"

"Go ahead," Risa told her, not that she had any right to order Susi about. The girl had trained at Keon but had chosen to offer her services as channel and healer to her home town of Laveen. Other channels had followed her example over the years. There was now hardly a community in Gulf Territory without an independent channel or two.

Even the most hardened juncts were discovering that channel's transfer was tolerable when it meant extra selyn for augmentation. And many juncts discovered they were not so hardened after all, as years passed with no more selyn shortages, and Gulf Territory's overall standard of living improved dramatically.

That was what Risa intended to show the ambassadors from Nivet—and her unexpected Gen Territory guests as well.

Risa studied the papers Susi had brought, saying to Emstead, "Please excuse me, Colonel. I believe I have news here of those you were chasing."

She read it through, then summarized in English, "We have twenty-three junct—uh—"

Sergi supplied the English term, "Freeband Raiders."

"Yes, Raider prisoners. Despite everything, none of them has killed. One of Carre's Companions nearly died, but he's recovering. Some fifteen of the Raiders are young enough to change their ways, perhaps live normal lives. The rest we'll turn over to our government for rehabilitation."

"I was hoping we might negotiate that point—" started the Colonel, but was interrupted by the arrival of Hugh and Klyd, followed by Ediva.

Risa couldn't believe her eyes. "Ediva, you shouldn't be out of bed!" she exclaimed.

The renSime had one arm in a sling, and a bandage around her head. Her face was still bruised. "I'm fine now that Klyd's worked on me. I know I wasn't invited, but Klyd thought—"

Risa's gaze went to the Sectuib Zeor. She couldn't believe what she zlinned. He'd had a transfer of sorts, and his systems were back into a normal balance, but she'd never have believed anyone carrying a field like Hugh's could possibly deliver such a rotten transfer. "Dare I say you shouldn't have been working?"

"With Hugh's support, it's no bother," answered Klyd. Sliding into functional mode, he walked over to Emstead and extended his hand, Gen style. "I don't believe we've been properly introduced." He recited his name, explaining briefly why his party was in Gulf Territory. Gingerly, the Colonel touched Klyd's fingertips and withdrew.

Risa motioned for Sergi to call for dinner while she made the rest of the introductions and seized the initiative again. "The rest of this report is casualty statistics. Klyd, that Carre Companion was the worst burn, and there were no kills." She made no effort to disguise her pride. "Take a look."

"Thank you," he said, passing them to Ediva, explaining to Emstead that she was their mathematician.

Risa rearranged the seating to compensate for Klyd's condition, putting Sergi on one side of him and Hugh on the other. That still put Sergi's good ear toward Risa, for he could understand her voice better than any other. Then Mor, Emstead's aide, and Emstead between his aide and Risa. A place was set for Ediva on Risa's left, next to Virena.

Sergi opened a bottle of fine wine from North Eastern Territory, the best in their stock, and Risa set herself to keep the talk light.

Klyd, not the slightest bit hungry despite having had transfer, expounded on the different culinary traditions of Nivet and asked the Colonel about where he grew up. Soon he had Ediva explaining Zelerod's Doom, with Hugh supplying words Ediva didn't know in English.

As the main course was taken away by silent renSimes, Ediva reached across the table to scribble on a notepad Emstead took from a breast pocket. Though their alphabets were different, numbers were the same everywhere, and Emstead was beginning to believe what she was proving. Risa, the best bookkeeper in Gulf Territory, couldn't always follow, but she comprehended the logic and had always taken Zelerod's Doom seriously.

As Emstead realized the powerful motivations behind the Householding lifestyle, he began to thaw, perhaps feeling less a prisoner and more a guest.

The talk flowed easily until after dessert. Then Vi politely excused herself—in relief, Risa noticed. The girl was clearly bored by the adult conversation and glad to run off to play. But she had performed perfectly, disarming the gruff soldiers with her petite charm. Risa made a mental note to explain to Vi later how important it was to show their out-Territory visitors the normal family life here.

Emstead, toying with the unfamiliar trin tea, said offhandedly, "I must confess I'm surprised to find materials and even individuals from such far away places here."

There were barbs of fear in his nager. Risa started to speak, but Klyd beat her to it. "You're wondering how we got here despite your patrols designed to keep Simes out of Gen Territory."

The Colonel smiled ruefully. "I don't expect you to reveal military secrets—"

"There aren't any," said Klyd. "But there's a lot of space out there, and very few of your soldiers. Simes can sense them at a distance. It's as easy to avoid patrols as it is to attack them. Raiders attack, we avoid."

"And you trade," Emstead added.

"Among Territories? Of course," answered Klyd.

Risa had the opening she'd been trying for. "I think you can see it's to your advantage to distinguish between Householders and Raiders, can't you, Colonel?"

"Well, to be perfectly honest—"

Risa interrupted, "We don't kill, we don't trade in Gen lives, and we *do* trade in a large range of goods. This is a trade fair, Colonel! Not everyone's a Householder. Many Simes here do kill. But they don't try to steal our Gens, and they don't attack Householdings or those allied to us because we trade with them to great advantage. Many of them wish they didn't have to kill Gens to live, and children of such people won't ever have to kill because of the Householdings and the channels. This may be the last generation of juncts— killer Simes—in this Territory. But if your army destroys Keon or chokes off our trade, it won't be. Tell me, which way is better for your people?"

"You put a strong case, young lady."

Risa saw her grown-up son smothering a grin, but ignored it. "Colonel, my proposal goes even further. We can also trade with you! There'll be profit all around, and the clearer that becomes to Gulf citizens, the faster the transformation will occur. The Raiding will stop."

"The Raiders we chased in here showed no sign of stop- ping and no mercy for those they slaughtered," answered the Colonel levelly, but his nager surged with outrage and skepti- cism. "I must take some of them home for questioning, or I may as well not go back. That group wiped out a small farming community. I wish I could show you what it was like—infants and children crying among the dead bodies, older children hiding—"

"And where do you suppose," Mor put in, his youth making it impossible for him to keep silent in the face of such ignorance, "those savage Raiders came from?"

"From right here!" Emstead spat.

Risa grabbed the report off the sideboard. "Twenty of them were born in Gen Territory." She tried to read the names of the towns, knowing she was mangling the pronunci- ations, but intent on making her point. "I suspect those are places over by Nivet Territory because that's where they'd flee after going through changeover, and where they met up with the hardened characters who're leading them. They're probably all suffering deep psychological scars from killing family members in First Need. After that, what can a few anonymous faces mean? It's just striking back at those who'd murder them if they could." She softened. "Colonel, they're barely more than children. What do they know of life, except what you've taught them?"

He had no answer. Face white, he just stared at her, nager in turbulence.

"Fifteen of those kids I'm going to keep. There's a good chance they may never kill again. The three leaders and the two older ones I can't help. I'm turning them over to the Territory Government. They'll probably be able to rehabilitate the two. They may kill for the rest of their lives, but they could become honest citizens. The three ring leaders—" She couldn't control a shudder, wishing Sergi's appetite hadn't induced her to eat so much. "—will probably be executed."

"Then let me have them," insisted the Colonel.

"I can't do that," said Risa. "We have laws here."

The Colonel sat forward, thrusting his chin out. "You said you want to trade. What will you take for them?"

Risa gritted her teeth to stop a sharp reply. How could Emstead think that of them? That would make them no better than Genrunners!

Mor said, "Householders don't trade in human flesh."

"They're prisoners of war," argued Emstead. "Also fugitive criminals."

"No," insisted Klyd. "They're victims of tragedy."

Risa said, "I can trade with you."

Klyd reacted, but she held a "bear with me" in her nager, and he subsided warily.

The Colonel leaned back in his chair, seemingly thinking of playing them off against one another. "Let's hear your proposition."

"Pick a few of your men and stay here for the fair—a week at most—and I'll allow you to question the prisoners." She zlinned Klyd, not letting her eyes waver from the Colonel's. Sergi understood and was laughing inside. Her son struggled not to grin openly.

Comprehension dawned in Klyd's nager, followed by a shiver of respect. She was getting Emstead to *buy* what she couldn't give him as a gift, for the prisoners would verify what Risa had said. Gen Territory suffered mostly from their own cruelty to their children, and the price Emstead would pay for this information was just what she wanted him to do—stay and shop the fair for items they could later trade.

Oh, Klyd Farris ambrov Zeor, you are getting your first lesson on how to run a Territory!

"Done!" said Emstead with the air of one who'd just put one over on an adversary.

The dinner ended on a celebratory note. When Emstead and his aide had been escorted back to their men, Risa curled her tentacles around a glass of trin tea and said, "I wish we could sit and gloat over that little victory, but I'm afraid Sergi, Mor, and I must dash off. We've got a heavy dispensary schedule."

Klyd said, "I'll help."

Remembering his speed and tireless capacity, she knew she could really use him, but— "Are you sure?"

Hugh stepped forward. "At home, I'd certify him fit to work dispensary. I'd like to assist, though."

"Hugh, you're about to fall asleep."

Risa considered Klyd incredibly polite to have sat through the meal with a Companion who had made such a mess of their transfer. And he was finding the gentlest way possible to get rid of him.

"I would be honored to work with you, Sectuib Zeor," offered Mor. "I realize I have a great deal to learn."

"And you, too, are tired," Klyd pointed out. "You have the potential to be a great Companion, Mor, and with your Sectuib's permission I will work with you tomorrow or the next day, when you're rested enough to profit from it."

"I do dispensary best when I'm asleep," Hugh put in. "You've often said so. Awake, I'm a distraction."

Sergi laughed, and Risa couldn't help joining, partly in a relief she could not explain that Klyd had not accepted Mor's offer. "I've said the same of Sergi many times. All right, Sectuib Zeor, though I don't usually expect my guests to work all night. We'll tell our controller to rearrange the schedule."

Valleroy woke with a start. Risa was at the door of their cubicle, a happy renSime passing her on his way out while Klyd filled in his report on the transfer.

"Dickart!" Risa greeted. "Good enough?"

"Perfect!" replied the renSime. "Never better, though I honestly couldn't take even him as a steady diet."

"You'd never be asked to," assured Risa. "But I was worried. He's nonjunct."

"Well," temporized the renSime, "I couldn't tell that."

Risa reached up to put a hand on the man's shoulder. "I'm glad. Go see to your wife now."

Risa turned to Klyd. "My report forms slowing you down?"

"Oh, no, once I adjusted to their sketchiness."

She walked over to him as Sergi came in with a tray of glasses in the ubiquitous ornate glass holders, and a huge crockery pot of tea. The aroma brought Valleroy wide awake as Risa looked over Klyd's shoulder asking, "Sketchiness?"

Klyd pointed. "Ours usually require the quantity of selyn here, the speed curve estimate here, and transient thresholds and innates here, if the channel can make it. Then the recipient's quality estimate—" He turned, looking up with a quirked eyebrow as if she'd reacted oddly.

"Let's discuss that later," Risa suggested as Sergi handed out tea glasses. "Sergi and I are going to the Pen in a few minutes, to see to the Raiders the other channels couldn't handle. You can get some rest. Leave the reports for later."

Klyd accepted a glass with two tentacles, holding the quill pen in his fingers. "Oh, I'm not tired."

Clearly, Risa didn't believe that. She looked exhausted. Valleroy strolled toward them, mindful of where Sergi had posted himself so as not to imbalance the fields. "I suppose people who aren't accustomed to Farrises might read the situation wrong. Take my word for it, Sectuib ambrov Keon, Klyd really has been enjoying the work."

"If there's more," Klyd added, "I'd be delighted to help out. And you are to be complimented. I've learned a great respect for you through your people. I'd like to help with the Raiders because they are, in a way, my people. Their presence here is due to the failure of Nivet's Tecton, and Nivet's junct government."

"I understand," replied Risa. "However, I can't help noticing. Your transfer was not as good as it should have been—not surprising considering the circumstances," she added with a glance at Valleroy. It didn't fool him. The woman obviously thought him a clumsy blunderer.

"The best thing to dispel a negative post reaction," Risa continued, "is augmentation. It'll be pretty hot later; if you'd like to go out and run, or otherwise work off some selyn, early morning is the time to do it."

Klyd smiled at her. "I've always found that the best cure is work. I'm in much better condition now than I was last night." Valleroy noticed that he made no defense of his Companion; what was the use, with the evidence of his ineptitude still clear for her to zlin?

Risa's eyes went out of focus as she zlinned Klyd, obviously considering him her patient for that moment. "You do seem somewhat recovered. So, if you're not too tired, I could use any help you'd care to offer. Hugh," she turned to him, "I know *you* must be too tired."

"No—I slept most of the night, as promised."

Risa ignored that, saying to Klyd, "I can't give you Mor for this; he's never seen it done and will observe how Sergi and I handle it. I could assign Korin, though."

"But I've never worked with him," Klyd pointed out. "Forcing transfer on Freeband Raiders requires close teamwork. Hugh and I have been a team for many years." His tone closed the subject. Risa shrugged and invited them to have breakfast before the trip into town.

In Laveen, a group of channels and Companions was waiting for them beside the poles flying the green pennants proclaiming to all juncts, "Here any honest taxpayer can get a Gen to kill." Hugh remembered the first green pennants he'd ever seen—and Klyd's offhand attitude. Now he knew the channel must have been zlinning him for reaction, and he was ashamed of what he'd felt then.

Despite years in Sime Territory, his disgust never abated. If he were Sime, he knew he'd hate himself as much as those Raider kids probably did—and defy the world to punish him for his depravity. Now, though, he had to steel himself to clinical detachment so as not to distract Klyd.

They were greeted by the older man Valleroy had noticed yesterday, the man with the haunted eyes. He was introduced as Tannen Darley, representative to the Territory legislature and owner of the Pen. The pretty young woman who had captured Emstead was Susi Darley, the man's daughter, a nonjunct, fully-functioning channel! What kind of alien world *was* this, where the Gendealer was semi-junct, and his daughter operated as a channel, independent of any Householding, from a dispensary in the Pen?!

"But this is where people come for selyn," Susi explained. "It's only logical to have a channel here—makes it easier for people to choose transfer over a kill. Their neighbors don't have to know which they came in for."

"It used to be," her father added, "that most people wouldn't admit openly that they'd accepted transfer. Nowadays, though, many people would rather not have all their friends know when they've been forced to kill."

Valleroy heard the faint edge of regret in the man's voice, and knew he must be one of the latter. But why, then, remain a Gendealer?

"Oh, I still *own* the Pen, but I don't *run* it anymore," Darley replied when Valleroy had the temerity to ask. "I'm pitching in this morning because the staff can't handle all the extra work. Besides, it's good politics; my constituents see that when they can use my help, I'm not afraid to get my hands dirty."

Or your clothes, Valleroy noted. Gone was the smartly-tailored suit of the political campaigner; this morning Darley wore a plaid work shirt and denim trousers, obviously put on clean but already spattered with blood.

The stain matched in freshness a similar stain on Susi's otherwise immaculate white apron, beneath which she wore an outfit similar to her father's. Work clothes. Her dark hair, yesterday arranged in shining curls for the fair, was this morning slicked back into a braided coil like Risa's. The severity only served to emphasize her magnificent blue eyes, fringed with thick black lashes.

It struck Valleroy as strange that he should only now realize that Susi Darley had the most beautiful face an artist could ever ask for a model. But she was totally unconscious of her beauty, intent wholly on the business before her—and on her father, whom she was carefully protecting from shifts in the ambient, although the man had obviously recently had transfer, if not a kill.

Risa led them away from the Darleys, into the building complex, a sturdily constructed fortress with thick, defensible walls. Inside, smaller buildings, neatly whitewashed, were set among gardens and small tilled plots. Only the thick bars on the windows proclaimed this a Pen.

The roof of the building they entered was thermally insulated, the walls and windows well-caulked against drafts. And, it was clean—not even the usual odor of packed bodies permeated the Pen. Beyond an office they came to a corridor lined with closed cells. A large lavatory facility opened off the far end, and on either side were medical treatment rooms.

"You can take that one," said Risa. "This will do me."

Klyd nodded, and explored the room briefly. There was a bed, cabinets full of jars and medical implements, a sterilizer, a scale, and a white-sheeted examining table. Light came from nicely designed and maintained oil lamps—not much soot, plenty of bright light.

Klyd took off his jacket, saying, "She gave me the room with heavier insulation. Perhaps this alliance *will* work. But I'd like to see Carre and the rest of the Territory. It can't all be like this. One thing's for sure—they don't have drought here!" He shoved some papers around on the desk, adding, "Tell them to send in the first one."

The Raider, a stickfigure thin youngster, darkly tanned, was dragged struggling all the way by two renSimes who had to augment to match the Raider's furious strength.

"Let him loose and leave us," Klyd instructed.

The woman renSime attendant looked at Valleroy as if asking his permission before freeing the killer Sime. Valleroy stationed himself to Klyd's right and braced.

The renSimes let go and slammed the door. The Raider leaped for Valleroy, for even low-field he carried more selyn than the average Gen. Klyd intercepted and twined the Raider's lateral tentacles with his own, letting the boy take his fifth contact point lip to lip.

An inaudible snap, and it was over, the Raider coming out of hunting mode to stare at Klyd in total bewilderment. Then he disengaged, roaring obscenities. He went for the desk chair, lofting it to sweep the glass-fronted cabinets to destruction, but Klyd caught the chair's legs and wrestled it from the young man's grip.

"If you're goin' a execute me, why'n't just leave me in that cell to rot in attrition?" the boy demanded.

"You're Wanted in Nivet, aren't you?" asked Klyd.

"What's it to you?"

"If you've never Raided out of Gulf, you've not yet broken the law here. With a clean slate, you could start a new life."

The sullen glare told Valleroy what nageric comment the Raider made to that. Klyd called the guards to take him away and sank into the desk chair. "He's one of the leaders. If they free him, he'll be at it again within the year, no matter how fervently he promises not to. He won't live much longer in any case. He's a channel."

"Shen!" swore Valleroy. Junct channels rarely lived long lives.

"Maybe the next one won't be so bad."

She wasn't—though the drill was the same: Valleroy as the target, Klyd intercepting to feed in the unwanted channel's transfer so smoothly the Raider hardly knew she hadn't killed. Since Valleroy had learned what was involved in the junct's satisfaction, a peak of Gen terror coupled to nerve-burn pain, he'd often marveled at Klyd's ability to simulate that without ever having experienced it himself.

Four more young Raiders passed through their hands, Klyd always striving to initiate conversation after the transfer, only twice succeeding.

One of the young men was in love with a woman who'd been treated by Risa and come out crying hysterically, begging him to come into the Householding with her. "She said," he reported, "the fake kills were horrible, but for a chance at life it's worth it. She's pregnant. Maybe that's why she thought transfer was so bad."

"You can do it," encouraged Klyd, "if you support each other." He walked the youth to the door. "Just because you're Sime, you don't have to forsake the love of your children. You can make their lives better, if you work as hard as your parents did—and don't make their mistake."

After the young man had gone, Klyd swore, "Pregnant! Shen and damn!"

Hugh also shuddered. The woman did not yet know she would have to choose between the life of her unborn child and her own disjunction.

After the last of the Raiders had fought through the ordeal, Risa and Klyd, Sergi and Valleroy gathered in the small staff lounge off the building's front office, where they were served muffins with nut butter and honey, tea, and fruit. Sergi ate hungrily, Risa nibbled at a muffin, and Hugh enjoyed fresh fruit such as was rarely available at home. Klyd refused all but the tea.

Sometime during the chaos of the night, one of Keon's members had explained to Valleroy that the First Companion in Keon was partly deaf, the result of a long-ago explosion. Now he reassessed his opinion of the man, understanding why he had said so little at the dinner last night in a room full of strangers. He also noticed the way Risa's comments to Sergi were accompanied by gestures, and how frequently she communicated with him by gesture alone.

Valleroy had intended to get to know this man who was also both artist and Companion, and from the evidence all around them clearly found much more time than Valleroy to pursue his art. *But I can't trust him. A day or two of training and he'll think he's a Farris expert. If he tried to handle Klyd—* No! Sergi was a professional.

It was easier after transfer to thrust aside foolish jealousy, especially when, his vision no longer clouded by Gen need, Valleroy could see that Sergi was totally devoted to Risa.

Valleroy's fingers itched for a brush or a bit of charcoal as he watched their host and hostess interact. Risa tiny, dark, dynamic; Sergi huge, fair, Gen-graceful. They could not have been further mismatched physically, yet they worked together as smoothly—

As Klyd and I once did, the thought came unbidden.

Valleroy forced it away, letting his artist's eyes arrange a portrait in chiaroscuro. Risa would be easy to draw, with those piercing dark eyes, that stubborn pointed chin. Sergi's features were more regular although his eyes were so dark a blue that Valleroy had not at first been sure of their color.

The man's nose had been broken at some time, probably part of the same injury that had impaired his hearing. The slight irregularity was not disfiguring; in fact, it added a certain ruggedness to a face that otherwise might be too soft for his well-muscled body.

The man runs a steel mill, too, Valleroy recalled. Companions might be tough and lean from keeping up with Simes, but only heavy daily work put that kind of muscle on a Gen. He certainly didn't *have* to do it—there were plenty of Simes and plenty of selyn to let them augment—which meant he worked because he wanted to. What kind of conditions allowed a First Companion so much time for other pursuits?

Plenty of channels, he realized, and plenty of Companions, too. These people were not confined to only those channels born in the Householdings. Susi Darley was not unique, and someone had told him that eight years ago the law had been changed here in Gulf Territory to allow a freeborn Gen to go to a Householding at establishment, provided he had the permission of his nearest Sime relative.

There was even talk of giving Gens full citizenship although the Householders feared that such discussion was premature. Until the Pens were no longer necessary, too many Simes had to delude themselves into perceiving Gens as less than people. It was a bitter pragmatic decision to do the *possible*, disjuncting the Sime population gradually and letting the number of kills dwindle year by year, instead of yearning after the *impossible*, attempting an abrupt end to the kill and having the juncts rebel to save their lives.

The Householders here hated the Pens as much as the Householders of Nivet Territory did, Valleroy realized. *The difference is, here they are willing to settle for an unpleasant compromise to achieve progress, while in Nivet we accomplish nothing because compromise with the juncts is considered too dangerous.*

The Sime-dominated Tecton was as guilty as any junct of seeing Gens as less than people. As far as Valleroy knew, the Nivet Householdings had never attempted anything like the program Keon was implementing with such success. Wasn't that another example of their blindness to Gens as people? While they proclaimed that Householding Gens had to be protected at all costs, their obstinate separatism from the Nivet populace and government meant that every year millions more Pen Gens were "protected" to death.

But now was not the time to bring that up. Klyd and Risa were already disagreeing. Best not to add fuel to the fire.

They had begun by exchanging notes on their cases, estimating prognoses in a professional rapport that wakened Valleroy's hopes for the future alliance. Risa ended with the comment, "Now you can see why we don't require any increase in our Border Patrol."

"Don't? Why, everything that's happened since yesterday only underscores the urgency!" Klyd stopped.

Risa just stared at him.

He elaborated. "What about the war you've caused by letting Emstead question your prisoners? What about the Nivet citizens who'll give their lives in defense of their homes and children because of what those Raiders say?"

Valleroy explained, "Those Raiders speak English. Emstead can play on their Gen upbringing. Risa, you've got them post. If they decide to 'tell Emstead off,' they'll give him information we can't let the Gen Army have."

"I don't believe—you can't have missed what went on here!" exclaimed Risa.

"And you can't see beyond your Territory border!" retorted Klyd.

"Of course I can!" Risa said, leaning over the small table, eyes bright with a distant vision. "I've got Emstead in my pocket! He'll go home with stories of what he's seen here, and they'll send offers of trade. One of the things we'll offer in trade is to take in their Sime children."

"You're dreaming!"

"If you don't have a dream, how can you make it come true? We've done it before, on a smaller scale. There's no reason it can't work all over! Think of the goods and lives lost to the Gen Border Patrol every year. Once the Gens are dependent on what we can provide, we'll ask for caravan escorts to Nivet Territory. And that's only the beginning. Within two years I'll be sending you my First Year channels for training. You know more about channeling than we do. You'll train some of our brightest youngsters—and we'll train yours in whatever you find here that you'd like to take home. We can accomplish so much more if we cooperate.''

Klyd looked at Valleroy, who took a deep breath and tried to burst her bubble gently. ''The kinds of functions Klyd has impressed you with can't be learned by any but the Farris channels. We know; we've tried.''

She brushed that aside. ''Well, there's still plenty of knowledge to exchange. Take a few days after the fair and go down to Norlea. Visit Carre and Gulf Port. I'm sure you'll find much here of value. The few times I've been to Nivet to trade, we've made a good profit.''

Klyd leaned away from her fiery presence and said, ''If we do that, I want two things in return. First, I want to be present at all of Emstead's interviews with the Raiders. I'll do the field work so his nager won't get to them, and perhaps they won't blurt out too much. And second, I insist you return to Nivet with us—bring Sergi and whoever you'd like—make a similar tour.''

''You drive a hard bargain, Sectuib Zeor,'' replied Risa.

''As do you, Sectuib ambrov Keon,'' admitted Klyd.

She thought it over. ''I'll require a month after the fair to prepare for such an absence. Will you stay that long?''

Klyd consulted Valleroy with a glance and Valleroy assented. He couldn't have hoped for better.

Valleroy held his peace until they were outside the Pen stockade. ''You really fooled her. You made her pay you for doing what you really wanted to do!''

''Don't chortle too loudly. We were maneuvered.''

Risa watched the door close behind her guests, leaning back in her desk chair. Sergi said, ''Risa, I think you did it again.''

''Did what?''

''What you did to Emstead—one of your bargains.''

''Don't be too sure. Whatever else he may be, Klyd's no fool. He wouldn't have concluded a tricky deal while in such condition. Therefore he didn't feel he was giving anything up to get what he wanted.'' She zlinned his nager, too tired to shift her gaze.

Sergi hitched one knee over the arm of her chair and put an arm around her protectively.

She answered his unspoken question. "No, I won't have to try to manipulate him much longer—as soon as he sees our interests are in accord."

CHAPTER FOUR

East Nivet

The journey to Nivet Territory was more of a strain emotionally than physically. Spring rains bogged down the wagons, but the weather was warm and the gypsy caravan they joined long experienced at moving wagons over any terrain. Sometimes it seemed to Risa, as she and Klyd tried to zlin the best way to get through somewhere, that the gypsies knew the way by magic. But who could ever understand gypsies? They operated by the wisdom of experience passed down through many generations of travelers on these same trails.

When they reached the ford across the Mizipi, where they would leave Gen Territory and come into the open as House-holders on the west bank, they found the first flood waters already rushing dangerously. In a month it would be impassable. Once across, unless they returned immediately, they would have to remain on the other side until the Mizipi calmed to its summer flow.

And that was where Tannen Darley had to turn back.

Tan had insisted on accompanying them as a representative of the Gulf Territory government who was not a House-holder. Susi, of course, traveled with her father, for she knew as well as Risa that although he seemed fine after she forced yet another transfer into him, kill-crisis was rapidly approaching.

The water was running too swiftly at the ford to let them

swim the horses across, so everyone pitched in to build rafts. In the middle of the work, Tan collapsed.

As the channels eased his system back into normal function, he was forced to admit that he had become more liability than asset. "Every time I augment," he confessed to Risa, "I feel selyn draining away—and I know I'm speeding the day I'll have to choose—" He shook his head wearily. "If I'd been able to kill before we started, I'd be good for six months or more on transfer."

But he had not been able to kill and possibly never would again. One of the gypsy wagons, with Gens to serve as camouflage to the Gulf border, took Tan and Susi Darley home. Risa watched the wagon dwindle into the distance, her throat tight with tears. She would probably never see Tannen Darley alive again.

Sergi stood at her shoulder, his sorrow as strong as hers. He understood and shared the terrible price they were paying to better the world for their children: the painful deaths of some of their closest friends.

But though their party dwindled by two at the river crossing, it was soon increased by one. At the end of the second day of raft building, as they rested before negotiating the crossing at first light, the Sime sentries zlinned a Gen rider approaching, heading directly toward their camp. Risa quickly recognized his nager: Harris Emstead.

"I knew this was the only place you could cross the river," he explained. "If I hadn't found you here, I'd have gone on to Keon figuring to meet you along the way."

They had sent Emstead and his men home from Gulf Territory loaded down with presents and with a written invitation to the Gen government to consider a trade agreement. According to Emstead, the word of all his soldiers was not enough to prove that they had actually been in Sime Territory, had been well treated—even touched by Simes without being hurt. Fantasy, mass hallucination, or trick, they were told. The treaty offer was confiscated by Emstead's commander, his men separated and sent off to the most distant and dangerous posts.

Emstead himself had been given a choice of dishonorable discharge without pension, or of finding proof of his story. "I don't trust General Dermott," he told Risa. "He suggests you and Mr. Farris come to him to prove your intentions. But you ask Hugh Valleroy about Dermott. He hasn't changed at all. He's bucking for commander-in-chief of the Territory army. Torturing information out of Simes high in the governments of two Sime Territories would give him the favor he wants."

The man's bitter sadness, and the truth of his opinions, rang in his field. "Then are you seeking sanctuary here?" Risa asked.

"No. That is, yes, in a way. I want to take home irrefutable proof that your peace offer's in good faith; proof I can take over Dermott's head to the government!"

Other than hostages, which Risa would not consider, she could not think of a way to prove their intentions. Nor could Klyd or Hugh, although Hugh confirmed Emstead's assessment of General Dermott. So they decided to take Emstead on their journey and see if they could find the proof he sought.

As they proceeded through Nivet Territory toward Zeor, Emstead did nothing to shake their trust in him. Still, there was that suggestion in his nager of something left unspoken. . . .

The two Rior Companions, Hugh and Kitty, rode with Emstead at first. As they slogged their way through the marshes, the three conversed in their native language, English. At the first night's camp, Virena offered the Colonel a plate of food.

"Thank you," he told the child, one of the few phrases he knew in Simelan.

"You're welcomed," the girl attempted in English.

"No, it's just 'welcome,' " Emstead explained. "Tell you what—I'll help you with your English, and you can teach me Simelan."

Risa doubted that the man could learn at his age, but soon a lively contest went on around the fire, several Gens joining in as they carried their savory vegetable stew, seasoned with herbs Gens relished, to eat in a group downwind from Sime noses.

Sergi abstained from the dish, as he would neither leave Risa's side this close to turnover, nor offend her with the aromas of foods both poisonous and objectionable to Simes. Besides, his appetite tended to wane in sync with hers each month—not that a stranger might notice, considering how much food it took simply to keep his large body functioning.

Risa nibbled at the bowl of plain vegetables Sergi placed before her, but her attention was on their daughter and the circle of Gens at the other fire.

Korin and Dinny, both ambrov Keon, spoke English with a Simelan accent. Korin was a skilled Companion; Risa had brought him just in case Virena should change over before they returned home. That, though, was a very long chance; her real reason was to expose the Keon Companions to new experiences. Especially Zeor techniques.

Gens grew from new experiences; sometimes they seemed more flexible than Simes. She watched Emstead relax with the other Gens. Finally he gave up on Simelan for the moment, and asked Korin and Dinny, "Were you born in a Householding?"

"I was," said Korin.

But Dinny replied, "No, I was born in Norlea, but my mother brought my sister and me to Laveen when we were just little kids. She was junct, but she wanted us not to be, so she put us in school at Keon. When I established—" At Emstead's questioning look, he explained, "—turned Gen, started producing selyn—I pledged the Householding. Sis changed over, and by that time Mama was pretty sick, so Sis took over running the business."

"So because you turned Gen," said Emstead slowly, "you lost your inheritance and your family just as a Sime does in Gen Territory."

"Oh, no!" Dinny protested. "I'm a stockholder in Keon, and Keon is a partner in Verla's Shiltpron Parlor and lots of other businesses. As for family, that's the reason I'm a little late in my development as a Companion. I spent a lot of time my First Year with Mama. There couldn't be a channel with her *all* the time, and a Gen could ease her through crises when a Sime couldn't. Only after she died, could I really put my mind to Companion's training."

Risa noticed Hugh and Kitty listening intently. In Nivet a child of juncts who entered a Householding was separated forever from his family. How could they expect to attract people to their lifestyle in any large numbers until they healed that fatal rift?

By the time they reched Zeor, Emstead was determinedly trying to communicate in Simelan, resorting to English only when no one could decipher the gibberish he made of it.

Zeor was a surprise; adjoining a small city nestled in beautiful rolling hills, its exterior looked much as Keon's had years ago, when Risa first arrived. *This* was the most famous and successful of all Householdings?

Alone in their comfortable guest quarters, Risa watched Sergi examine the curtains and hangings in deservedly-famous Zeor patterns.

"Does it meet with your approval?" she asked her husband.

"Oh, yes," he replied. "The design is incredibly textured. I might try working that pattern in silver. It would make a beautiful necklace for you; no, don't shake your head. Do you know how you frustrate me, refusing to wear jewelry?"

"I always wear the starred-cross you gave me," she replied, "and my Keon ring and our marriage band. That's enough. If you had your way, you'd decorate me with baubles like ribbons on a maypole!"

He laughed. "Well, when I tried sculpture, you wouldn't let me exhibit my best work!"

"I hardly think displaying a nude bronze of the Sectuib in Keon would add much to the dignity of the Householding! That was the one time in my life I wished I had some artistic talent, Sergi. Oh, how I'd love to turn the tables on you! You're the one who should be painted or sculpted."

He captured her and pulled her down onto the bed with him—no passion, just the warm contentment of being together. "You have plenty of talents to suit me," he told her.

That evening they had the chance to display one talent they shared as Zeor's dining hall was cleared for a party in honor of the visitors. As they waited for the festivities to begin, Harris Emstead joined them. Risa was saying to Sergi, "You can see that Zeor is prosperous—the fabric mill and dye works have to be worth seven fortunes—but their buildings are merely adequate, their heating system is antiquated, they still huddle behind walls, and they don't spend anything on comfort. Did you notice the dishes here in the dining room? Good quality, solid, serviceable pottery, beautifully cared for—but not a single gracious, sensuous piece in use. The duty chef told me why." She stopped to glance sidewise at Sergi.

He sighed. "All right. Why?"

"Because if they display their real wealth, the juncts may attack the 'perverts who can live that way because they don't have to buy Gens.' And you saw the scars of battles on their walls. The Nivet juncts regard Householdings as an economic threat!"

"You sound as if that pleases you," said Emstead, his puzzlement reflected in his nager.

"This Territory is a vast market for our products," she explained. "If we help them solve their problems, in a few years the Householdings will open their gates and trade with the juncts—who won't want to be junct any more. Then they'll be willing to make treaties with your people, Harris."

"I hope so," the man said flatly. Risa zlinned something in his nager, but could not tell what it was he hid from her. She—and every other Sime in their entourage—knew the man had not told them the whole truth about why he had joined them. Yet what he *had* told them zlinned true, and so she trusted him—with reservations.

Dinny ambrov Keon arrived with his shiltpron. Zeor members stared at the Sime musical instrument in Gen hands, but Risa smiled inwardly, waiting for the surprise to come.

The shiltpron was designed to be played with both fingers and tentacles. Dinny had learned to finger the audial strings when he was a little boy, taught by Ambru, the Sime musician whose talent had made Verla's Shiltpron Parlor famous all over Gulf Territory.

Ambru had died before Dinny established, and left the boy his shiltpron, with the admonition to play it to make people happy, as Ambru had always done.

When Dinny's mother lay dying, one of her greatest comforts had been to have her son play for her, and out of his sorrow had come his discovery that although he had no tentacles with which to set the instrument resonating nagerically, he could do so with his selyn field.

Now, as he began to play, conversations hushed one by one, attention captured by the soft music. Other Companions picked up the swelling nageric resonance, and the dining hall soon rang on two levels with the poignant melody.

Risa saw Hugh slip away, returning almost immediately with a sketch pad. Dinny was anything but handsome—thin, pinched features, straw-colored hair that fell limply over his forehead—but when he concentrated on his music, he was beautiful. *If Hugh can capture that on paper,* Risa thought, *he's as great an artist as Sergi.*

The haunting melody came to an end. The enraptured audience did not even breathe, and to the zlinning Simes there was for one moment nothing but the pulse-pulse-pulse of selyn production and consumption, as if in that one shining instant every heart, Sime and Gen, beat as one.

Then held breaths had to be released, and a murmur of astonished appreciation broke the spell. Dinny looked up, grinned, and broke into a lively dance tune. Couples whirled into the cleared center of the floor, everyone there so accustomed to compensating for need cycles that the nageric flow underscored the music in sweet harmonic rhythm.

Risa and Sergi started together, but moved through changing partners around the floor. Risa loved to watch her husband dance, marveling anew at his command of his huge body. Half-way around, he met his daughter. Risa saw Vi giggle as her father bowed to her, but she curtsied properly, and let Sergi swing her. Even tinier than her mother, Vi was lifted right off her feet, but she landed laughing, and went on with the dance without losing a beat.

Hugh was still sketching, Ediva now looking over his shoulder.

Kitty ambrov Rior joined Harris Emstead at one of the side tables. The music ended when each dancer was back with his original partner. A new tune began, Zeor members with fiddle and guitar joining Dinny.

This dance was an old one, done in groups of four couples. People sorted themselves out as the introduction played. Kitty pulled Emstead to his feet, insistently drawing him into a group consisting of Risa and Sergi, Bethany and Uzziah ambrov Keon, and Klyd's daughter Muryin and a Zeor Companion named Dsif. Like Vi, Muryin had not yet changed over, but was expected to become a powerful channel. The two girls were quickly becoming friends.

It was a thoroughly safe group for Emstead to relax in: everyone except Risa and Uzziah was Gen or child, Risa was a channel, and Uzziah was high-field and so thoroughly fixed on his wife that Risa doubted he could touch another Gen. They were one of the first such couples, but certainly not the last. Nonjunct, Uzziah had been increasingly volatile and unpredictable on channel's transfer and four years after change-over had begun having bad transfers despite the best efforts of every channel in Keon.

Eventually Bethany, his wife, could stand it no longer. Not a Companion, she had never given transfer, although of course she donated through the channels. One month she did not show up for her donation appointment, and by the time Keon's controller tracked her down, she had seduced her husband into transfer . . . and both were alive, well, and happy.

All Uzziah's crankiness and health problems disappeared as if by magic. Risa saw no reason to forbid what had turned out to be a healthy relationship, and her judgment was confirmed as Uzziah became one of the most reliable, even-tempered Simes at Keon. He and Bethany had been transfer mates for eleven years now; their oldest child had changed over last year, and was caring for two young siblings while their parents went on this journey.

So Risa had no qualms as Kitty, blond curls bouncing, pulled Emstead into their configuration on the dance floor.

The Gen soldier did not dance well, but he surrendered gracefully. Once committed, he went doggedly through the motions, memorizing the steps and performing them, even though without art.

Hugh Valleroy watched the man who had once been his commanding officer as he went through the motions of the dance. He had to admire him; it had been hard enough for Valleroy, as a much younger man, to adjust to what he had found in Sime Territory.

Valleroy's fingers flew, and he tore one page after another

off his pad as he tried to capture the dance scene in quick, lively sketches. But as he drew Muryin's coltish grace, Virena's pixy charm, Risa's and Sergi's polished cooperation, he missed something—someone.

The Sectuib in Zeor was not at his own party.

Slowly, Valleroy's interest in his art drained away as dance followed dance and still Klyd did not put in an appearance. Eventually he knew, not knowing how he knew, that what had detained Klyd was bad news. Abandoning his sketchpad, he slipped as unobtrusively as possible from the dining hall and went to the Sectuib's office.

Klyd looked up. "Hugh. I was about to send for you. Trahan was just in with a report: there are massive troop movements in Gen Territory."

"That's what Harris Emstead couldn't tell us," said Valleroy. "Klyd—he really *couldn't* trust us with—"

"I know," Klyd replied with a placating gesture of two dorsals. "Even if he had known, which I doubt. This is new, within the past week."

"But Emstead's a good enough soldier to predict it," said Valleroy. "We've got to send someone out there."

The channel's expressive lips curved in a grim smile. "You anticipate me. Unfortunately, Rior has the largest number of suitable Gens."

"Fortunately," Valleroy countered. "Don't worry, Klyd. Within the week I'll have three or four loyal, well-trained Gens who grew up out there on their way home, to act as eyes and ears for us. There's one problem, though," he added, gut wrenching. Klyd had just reached turnover. "I'll have to go to Rior to arrange it."

"No, you won't."

Hugh whirled. In his concentration on Klyd he hadn't heard Kitty ambrov Rior come in behind him. "I knew there was something wrong when you suddenly left," she explained. "Hugh, you must accompany Klyd on this journey. He has to be at his best before the Tecton, and you must speak for Rior."

"Kitty's right," said Klyd, an admission that made Valleroy's blood stir, but he was torn. The people to be asked to risk their lives were loyal to *him*.

"Hugh, I'll go myself," said Kitty, planting herself with all Gen strength before him. He knew her determination, saw for one moment in the set of her jaw, her shining hair, the image of the son she had borne him. To protect Rior—to protect Jesse—he had to let Kitty go, for of all the Gens in Rior, she was probably best qualified for this assignment.

And she was a born organizer, never forgetting a detail. He had seen her time and again cut through chaos to create order. Rior respected her; with Hugh's writ empowering her to act for him, she would command the loyalty she had to have if people were to risk their lives—as she would risk hers.

His throat ached, but he nodded and sat down at Klyd's desk to write the order sending the mother of his son to play her part in preventing the ceaseless battle between Sime and Gen from becoming the war that would end everything.

Leaving Zeor and the foothills of the Oza Mountains behind, the caravan journeyed into farm country, but the crops were sparse here compared to the lush growth Risa was accustomed to in Gulf. At first she thought it was because spring came later here, but then she noted how much drier the air and earth became with every passing day. This should be the time of spring rains; instead they encountered only one rainy morning all the way from Zeor to Konawa.

The deeper into Nivet Territory they traveled, the more glad Risa was that she'd insisted Klyd tour Gulf. As she surveyed the city of Konawa, nestled in the crook of a stream they called a river, her confidence grew. She smiled at Harris Emstead, who had ridden up beside her without hesitation, no longer giving a thought to whether she was Sime or Gen— and thereby keeping a steady field almost as comfortable as that of a Companion.

"So that's the capital," the Gen soldier said. "I had no idea Nivet Territory was so huge!"

"Only the regional capital," said Sergi, riding up on Risa's other side. The rest of their caravan lumbered off the sorry excuse for an eyeway onto the road into the city. "Nivet is more than twice the size of Gulf."

Sergi looked at the puny river where Virena and Muryin were wading, collecting rocks. "Look at the children," he said. "By the time they're grown, they'll have a much better world to live in. And if they remain friends, perhaps they can improve it even more."

Now Risa was glad she had brought Virena because Klyd had brought his daughter on this last leg to Konawa. He planned to send Muryin with another Householding caravan to the channel's training school, far out west somewhere.

Risa thought the child a bit young for training, surely two years shy of changeover into a Sime, but Klyd insisted Muryin would change over before winter was past.

"I can't deny," Risa had told Klyd, "you know more channels' science than we do. Perhaps we can trade for that knowledge."

"The knowledge is free," Klyd had countered, "to any House that supports the Channels' School at Rialite. If Keon pays the tithe, you can send Virena there."

"I'd like to look the place over myself first."

"I'll see what can be arranged," he had told her.

Now she sat her horse, watching the two girls gathering bright riverstones. Today she'd have to render a final decision on Virena's future, a decision over which she and Sergi disagreed.

At least Mor had shown a sense of identity. Risa smothered a smile as she recalled Klyd's astonishment at Mor's "provincialism." The Zeor channel had worked with the boy at Keon, praising his skills. Then he had said, "I once invited your father to come and train with me, perhaps eventually to pledge unto Zeor. At the time, Sectuib Nedd required him, and had he not given priority to his own House, he could not have been the Companion Zeor wanted.

"But you, Mor, have the same potential as Sergi. You're young. Keon has plenty of Companions and no channel up to your potential. I invite you to train at Zeor and consider devoting your life to excellence."

Risa had held her breath, wondering just how impressed Mor might be with Klyd. True, Mor's potential was frustrated at Keon. Twice she had taken transfer from her son in order to satisfy his need to give and to develop his system. But her torluen with Sergi meant they could not function at their best after transfer with anyone else. It also meant Mor had never yet had transfer with a channel who fulfilled him.

But her son had replied proudly, "I'm honored at the invitation, Sectuib ambrov Zeor, but when my sister changes over, she'll need a Companion of my capacity. With my Sectuib's permission, I'd come to train at Zeor but only to bring new skills to Keon. When Mother returns and frees me from my duties as temporary Head of Householding, I will ask permission to do so, if your offer still holds."

Later, though, Mor confided to his parents, "I'll go to Zeor because their transfer skills are so important to Keon. But what I'd *really* like to do is learn Dar's unarmed combat! Did you see their Gens in the battle, Dad? They were taking on Simes—and those Raiders didn't know which end was up!"

Risa had decided then that, yes, she could let Mor go. Keon's virtue was freedom; if the boy wanted Zeor training, or even Dar training, he'd have it. But Ediva had explained that unless he pledged Dar he could learn only the basic exercises, since the higher skills were a matter of daily discipline and practice with one's peers, for life.

So, promising to tell him all about Zeor on her return, Risa had left her son in charge of Keon. The responsibility would mature him further, she knew. He would be ready to decide what to do with his life when she returned.

And once she saw it, she knew Mor wouldn't pledge Zeor. The skills would intrigue him, the disciplines challenge him, but he was too much like Risa to spend his life chasing a tenth decimal place in dynopters of selyn!

Klyd turned the Zeor grain wagons over to the consignee, and sidled his horse over to Risa and Sergi. He was a completely different man than he'd been when he'd first appeared in Keon's pavilion. Apparently, he and his Companion had ironed out their differences. "I'm sorry, Sectuib Risa, but it looks like you aren't going to see Rialite just yet. This dispatch just came."

Sergi nudged his horse closer so he could peer over her shoulder. After the usual formal salutations, it read:

The Agenda for this Special Session of the Tecton has been amended. Session Opening has been moved up to the morning after the New Moon, and deliberations will begin over Nivet Territory Bill #66, providing for the confiscation of 8% of all Householding Gens establishing during the next calendar year.

All other business is tabled for the duration of this emergency.

Risa looked up at the Zeor Sectuib. "Confiscation?"

Sergi explained to Emstead in English. The man fumbled for the loose white enameled chain about his neck, a symbol of Keon's protection, although he was not a member. Risa felt him fight down fear, conquer it. She zlinned the nager of the experienced soldier prepared for battle.

"It's not unexpected," said Klyd glumly, "but we'd no idea they could move this fast. People believe the Gen shortage is due to the food shortage, and that that is due to Householdings keeping too many Gens alive."

As he spoke, Hugh moved up beside him. The Companion added, "The Genfarmers blame the kill-shortage on their being denied the best breeding stock—Householding Gens. Public sentiment will sweep that bill through the junct legislature."

Risa schooled herself not to look at Sergi as he fought down disgust at being considered prime stud. "Klyd, you've got to fight this—" she started.

"We will," he interrupted calmly, "but the session will be longer and more involved than I'd anticipated. Your plan to sell us food is the key, but I'll have to lobby to get the agenda changed which will take time, so you can't go on to Rialite tomorrow."

"That's all right," said Sergi. "Virena can go on to Rialite with Muryin."

She hasn't changed over yet, thought Risa. *She probably won't for a year or more; there's no reason she can't go see the place.* To Klyd, she said, "Of course, we'll stay as long as necessary. As for Virena," she frowned at Sergi, "we'll decide later if she goes on tomorrow or stays until we all can make the trip."

"Good enough," agreed Klyd. "For now, we'll all do well with a hot bath and a good meal. The Tecton hospice boasts the best insulated guest quarters in the city—and you are, of course, Zeor's guests." He turned his horse and moved away.

"Come on, Sergi," said Risa, "let's collect Vi."

"Good idea," he agreed. "We'll leave it up to her."

"That's *not* what I meant!" She nudged her horse into a trot, refusing to think about what Vi would choose. Father and daughter were Householding bred. Risa, brought up as a successful merchant in a junct city, had developed the shrewd skepticism which had made Keon a real power in Gulf. She couldn't let her daughter, her heir, grow up without that trait.

"I know how you feel," Emstead said unexpectedly. "They seem so young to make such big decisions. I remember when my daughter told me she wanted to marry; I thought she was still a baby! But she was only a year or so older than your little girl. Now I have a granddaughter, very much like those two." Risa knew their Gen Territory guest was wondering if he'd ever see his daughter and granddaughter again.

Signs of impending crisis were everywhere in Konawa. Gaudy posters proclaimed this or that faction would provide a monthly kill for each Sime. Some pointed out that the current Pen Gen Distribution System had been devised by a Householder, Ediva ambrov Dar, and was thus suspect.

Government posters announced regulations against claiming a Pen Gen before hard need. Risa noticed boarded up, failed businesses. Dirty, unkempt children threw dung at the line of Householders, shouting obscenities.

In the center of town, their caravan came to a dead halt in the midst of a crowded street. Up ahead, the ambient rang with anger, fear, pain—

Risa stopped zlinning, but Sergi reached over and plucked her from her horse onto his, laying his arms along hers to shield her laterals. "How did you know?"

"I don't know what it is, but it's something horrible."

Uzziah ambrov Keon slid down off his horse and wormed his way forward. Cheers rang out from the crowds blocking their way. He returned pale and shaking. "Executions," he managed to get out. "I didn't zlin, but I couldn't help seeing—" He fought nausea. "They were excising a woman's laterals!"

Despite Sergi's warmth against her, chills ran through Risa. Her husband's hands closed convulsively over hers as he whispered, "What kind of barbarians—?"

Gulf still had a few capital offenses, but even when life had been less sacred, there had never been such a hideous method of execution even for hardened criminals!

Risa squirmed in Sergi's arms, to look around him at Klyd. Guessing what she was thinking, he edged his horse up close enough to say, "It's a new law. They're executing black-market Gen dealers, Choice Auction and Gen Parlor operators whose businesses were made illegal last year. Death by attrition is too slow to satisfy the crowds these days."

Risa had heard the Sectuib in Zeor speak in many tones in the weeks she had known him, but never before had she heard such bitterness in his words.

Their caravan stood trapped, the Simes trying not to zlin, everyone trying not to hear, see, or smell the madness in the plaza ahead. When the crowd dispersed, they turned into a side street and wended single-file through the narrow lanes rather than pass through the place of execution.

Finally they reached a square surrounded by the capitol of the junct government. It was grander than anything in Gulf and was capital only of the Eastern half of the Territory. Yet the Gulf citizens' tax burden was a feather compared to what these tortured people paid.

They rode straight through the square, passing a fountain surrounded by trees. In the center of the fountain was a sculpted stone tableau of a caged Sime clinging to the bars with fingers and tentacles, an unmistakable look of agony on his features. Attrition, supposedly the worst death known, death by the gradual depletion of selyn. *But now they've invented an even worse form of death!*

Emstead did not understand enough to be affected, and Risa decided it was not the time to enlighten him.

Sergi rode with his nager closed up to a polished shell, in such concentration that even when they were out of Virena's earshot, he said nothing about the problem she now posed. *If only she were safely home at Keon!*

Klyd stopped the column of riders outside a neatly painted white clapboard house, three stories tall. The porch stairs fanned out from double doors, over which was painted in discreet lettering, TECTON FIRST YEAR WAYSTATION.

Klyd came back to where Sergi and Risa had stopped,

flanking Vi. "Here's where you'll be staying, Virena. I've arranged for you to have a room next to Muryin's."

Vi nodded, leaning forward to catch her friend's attention, but Risa said, "I thought we were staying in the Tecton hospice."

"There's nothing for children to do over there." He gestured to the building shadowing the waystation from behind. "I thought, at least tonight, Virena would stay with Muryin."

"At the waystation, of course," agreed Sergi. Risa had to fight not to be overwhelmed by the firmness in his nager. She'd chosen a dominant man but didn't intend to be dominated by him. "Sectuib Zeor," he continued, "is very considerate to house the heir to Keon in the most well-armored, well-defended building available."

What? She zlinned the waystation, noticing now how opaque it was to her Sime senses. The windows were placed carefully for defense. On the roof was a fire fighting system. The back was flush against the huge Tecton building, and to either side stood buildings angled to defend the front.

It was an armed fort, designed to look innocent.

Klyd provided the last word. "There's direct access from within the hospice, so you may visit back and forth."

"Virena—" said Risa.

"I'll be fine, Mama," her daughter called, guiding her horse up the line to where Muryin had dismounted.

The Zeor group was escorted to rooms on the upper floor of the Tecton hospice. Risa went through the courtesies, restraining her desire to get Sergi alone. When she thought they had privacy, there was yet another Gen at their door with a thick file of briefs, compliments of Sectuib Farris.

She thanked the messenger, then shut the door with a firm snap. Turning, she threw the file onto a marble table and stalked her husband, who was inspecting the view. "All right, let's have it. Why did you override me—and in public, too?"

Astonished, he asked, "Are you worried about your image? I assure you, it's no tarnish on a Sectuib's reputation to take the advice of her First Companion."

"I am not worried about my shendi-fleckin' image! I'm worried about my—our—daughter! Our heir, the future of

Keon and all of Gulf Territory! These—these Tectonists—can't handle their junct relations and I don't want them corrupting—"

"I know my daughter," insisted Sergi calmly, "and I know which side would get corrupted!" He put his hands on her shoulders. "Risa, you aren't *afraid* are you?"

"Yes!" she shouted, infuriated by his calm. But then she controlled herself. "You know I am. Vi can take care of herself in most situations, but—"

"—but this town reminds you of how you lived before you disjuncted. You'll never be comfortable with what you once were. You were so old when you disjuncted."

"But I did disjunct, I never even think about killing!"

"And neither will Vi. The Tecton hates the kill as much as we do. Maybe more, because they live amid so much of it."

"And *that's* what I'm afraid of! Don't you see? Hate causes warfare between Householding and junct. I don't want Virena to *hate* juncts. I don't want her to see their violence, like that execution today, or associate with children who saw the juncts murder or kill their families. She's too *young*!"

"And you were too young? Didn't you bring her here to learn, just as you learned from your father?"

"Why are you always tying me in knots?"

"I don't intend to. We both love Virena. She's going to be a channel with your strength, so we've got to give her a chance to develop your character to go with it. She's old enough—"

"She's *not*! Changeover is late in our family. She's still just a child!"

He drew her to him, cradling her tiny body against his massive chest. "I know, Risa. I know." She felt the tears he wouldn't shed, that she couldn't shed this far into need. "It's so hard to know what's best for your own child. But Vi's a tough kid. Responsible. Level-headed. Trust her."

She thought back to her first trip to Nivet with her father. Yes, she'd seen things he'd tried to shelter her from. "All right, Sergi. All right."

Still, she couldn't trust anyone or any place just *because* it was Householder run.

*   *   *

The conference with Risa and Sergi lasted until dawn. Valleroy closed the door after them and leaned against it. Klyd still bent over the littered table with Ediva. Leaders of maybe twenty Householdings had been here during the night, listening to Risa's offer, pledging their support.

"You two can work some more," Valleroy said, knowing he wasn't heard, "but I'm going to sleep."

Even though Klyd wasn't far enough into need to require Valleroy's presence, he stretched out on the divan rather than going to bed.

Klyd glanced up before the door signal sounded. "Hugh, would you get that?"

He hauled himself up, opened the door, and leaped back as two Tecton-uniformed figures charged into the room. Daggers gleamed at their belts; only juncts carried daggers.

Ediva jumped away from the table and crouched, ready to take on both the Sime and the Gen.

The two strangers held their arms wide, the man showing tentacles spread in a gesture of peace, the woman's Gen arms bare, hands open. "We came to talk."

Klyd came forward, squinting in the uncertain light from the oil lamp. "You're—aren't you Enid ambrov Noam?"

Valleroy knew the name, but she denied it. "No! We're Enid and Amos Kaneko of Kaneko Herbs and Simples."

Klyd came closer, not wary now, and Ediva relaxed her stance, remaining on guard. Klyd said, "You *were* ambrov Noam. I chartered your House—daughter of Zeor and Imil—"

"Not *our* House!" corrected Amos. "We owe neither Noam nor Zeor any loyalty."

Klyd recoiled as if slapped. "Then why have you come?"

"To issue fair warning," said Amos. "Without our help, the Tecton is doomed, and our help comes at a price."

"We don't want the Nivet government to confiscate your Gens," said Enid. "We have relatives—"

"It would lead to war," argued Amos. "We're offering the Tecton our support against the confiscation bill. We have junct friends in high places. They'll help if you guarantee them transfer from Householding Gens."

"But—" protested Valleroy.

Klyd's hand closed over his shoulder. "He doesn't mean

our donors, but our Companions. This man left Noam twenty years ago with his wife in protest of the Householding policy that wouldn't allow him transfer from her.''

"Not just for ourselves, Sectuib," said Amos. "We left to make the world a place where every Sime can have Gen transfer. It works for us.''

"For you," said Klyd, "but it won't work for everyone."

"You'll make it work," said Enid. "Channels must arrange safe pairings instead of keeping us apart.''

"Offer the juncts Gen transfer," urged Amos, "and they won't take your Gens for the kill.''

"Nor would they be satisfied," answered Klyd. He was right. Juncts hated Householders because Companion's training spoiled the best Gens for the kill.

"They'll learn. And so will you. You want our help, that's our price. Don't let that meeting open tomorrow unless you're willing to pay that price.''

The two were gone before Valleroy could figure out what the threat meant.

"Klyd?" asked Valleroy.

"He's zlinning," supplied Ediva.

Valleroy waited until Klyd came back of his own accord. "What was all that?"

"I don't know," answered the Sectuib absently. "They surely have survived, despite the odds. I wonder how they get the juncts to accept them? She could never handle a killmode attack—even by a renSime. I don't. . . .''

That wasn't what Valleroy had meant. He had just realized that those two people were already living his ideal—not in far-off Gulf Territory, but right in the heart of Nivet!

CHAPTER FIVE

The Tecton

Risa agreed to send Virena with Muryin to Rialite, assured by Klyd that they'd be free to follow in a month or two. Sergi was right; Virena had a deeper maturity than Risa had suspected. When Risa asked her, "What do you expect will be the hardest part of training at Rialite?" she answered, "Remembering their philosophy is so deadly serious to them. I really like Muryin, but she believes everything the Tecton says. I don't know if she can learn to think for herself."

Too soon, Risa arranged herself behind her formal escort, facing the tall, gleaming wood doors of the Tecton meeting hall. It had seemed ridiculous to carry their Keon banner all this way, but amid the colorful panoply of this ruling body of Householdings, she'd have felt shabby without it and their full-dress capes.

A line of Householding delegations stretched along the corridor, restless, keyed up, whispering. At a triumphal burst of sound, they started forward at a brisk march. As the Zeor delegation passed, Klyd gave Risa a confident wink, then grinned at Sergi.

He followed his searing blue banner into the meeting room. A rousing crescendo was followed by the creak and groan of leather chairs, the clatter of banner shafts being planted in holders, and a rising whisper cut off by a musical refrain. That was their cue.

The doors swung open, and they faced a very elderly Sime dressed in a hooded white cloak: the Tecton Marshal.

He bowed low, executed a crisp about face, and bowed again toward the room. As she'd been coached, Risa bowed to the room with him while the rest of her delegation remained upright. Then the Marshal paraded them about the room, giving her time to take it all in. Suddenly the ceremoniousness didn't seem such a waste of time, for she was also aware of being sized up.

There were over a thousand people in the room, most of them channels and Companions of high rank. The powerful but harmonious ambient nager couldn't be zlinned through, but it didn't sap her strength.

When the music stopped, the Marshal declared the session open. The opening ceremonies were followed by a rapid procedure to set aside the agenda and proceed to the matter of the food and Gen shortage.

A murmur went around the room, one word coming clearly to Risa over and over: "Zeor." Did Zeor hold the prestige, or was it Klyd himself who'd won them?

Just as Klyd took the podium to introduce Keon, Risa felt a mild disturbance in the ambient behind her. She turned full around as her daughter hissed, "Mama!"

"Vi! What are you—?"

Sergi turned as Virena darted out and knelt behind their chairs. Her whisper shook. "It's Muryin. She thinks she's going to change over and kill somebody!"

"What? Muryin's in changeover?"

"I don't think so. Dsif is with her, and Mr. Emstead, but she's screaming and crying. Mama, she scares me!"

"No wonder," said Sergi. "Vi, sometimes Farrises have a real hard time at changeover, and it takes a top-notch Companion to give them First Transfer so they won't kill. But Dsif *is* that kind of Companion, so there's nothing to worry about. Now what set Muryin off?"

"The drovers say they aren't going to Rialite. They have to go somewhere else instead because of a riot. And Muryin says now we can't go at all!"

Sergi said, "Of course you can, with another caravan later, or with us. Tell Muryin that, and don't come back here unless she really is in changeover. Dsif will know; if he hasn't sent Mr. Emstead away, she's definitely not."

Virena said, "I'm sorry, Daddy, Mama—but Muryin's acting so *wild*. She thinks she's going to kill someone!"

"Well, she's not," said Risa. "Vi, we are surrounded by

the best channels and Companions in the world. If that doesn't reassure Muryin, remind her she is the heir to a Householding and must learn to think a situation through, not indulge in hysterics.''

"And I'm the heir to Keon," their daughter said. "I should have thought of that myself instead of bothering you in an important meeting." She stood, set her chin determinedly, and left.

"Farrises!" Risa whispered to Sergi in exasperation.

Up on the platform, Klyd was finishing, ". . . and so I give you, Sectuib ambrov Keon."

Shuven! I've got to make a speech! She hadn't given it a thought—had made no notes—never required any at home. But here—her accent, her ignorance of their formalities, suddenly made her feel helpless. Sergi urged her to her feet.

She hadn't heard a word Klyd had said to them, had no idea where to start. Gulf Territory meetings rarely amassed more than a hundred officials, and she knew each one, their biases, their opinions, and their personal objectives. These were all strangers, and she dared not fail!

Oh, Dad, you never trained me for this!

Valleroy watched the tiny woman who wielded the power of an entire Territory approach the podium, walking in a slow, dignified manner. She'd blatantly defied protocol to comfort her daughter.

Wish I had her stage presence. He stood at Klyd's left, facing the Tecton as Klyd's Companion even though he was not ambrov Zeor. It was the first time they'd ever done it, an audacious move. But if in the crush of greater events they could get away with it, when things settled down it would be accepted beyond challenge.

"Risa's got stagefright!" whispered Klyd in utter disbelief. "Or—what could her daughter have said?"

Valleroy followed as the Sectuib strode forward to meet Risa. "What is it?" he asked anxiously. "The children—?"

She whispered back, "They're fine, just disappointed because the train couldn't take them to Rialite today. I told Virena we'd take the next one with them, and—" She broke off, astonished at the effect her words had. But she didn't know the danger to Muryin.

"Muryin's changeover!" protested Valleroy.

Klyd cut him off. "We'll deal with it later. Risa, come!" Extending a dorsal tentacle to touch her fingertips, he handed her up the steps to the speaker's podium.

Valleroy followed, schooling his heart rate back to normal. Muryin, only daughter of the first woman he'd really loved, meant more to him than he dared let himself know. That Klyd was her father made her more precious. And Rialite was the only safe place for her now. *She'll make it in time.*

With expert stagecraft, Risa waited just the right moment beyond total silence, then spoke in a musical voice.

Both pairs of doors at the rear of the hall burst open. A cadre of rough-clad Simes, whips held at the ready, pushed the Honor Guards into the room at knife point.

A woman shrieked, and the crowd shrank from the intruders. Most Simes here were channels, noncombatants by definition, taught to respond to a threat by moving behind other Householders. Otherwise this ragtag group of fifty or so could never have interrupted an assembly of thousands.

Klyd squeezed up to the podium and struck the "Come to Order" chime. It tolled out over the racket, startling the invaders to a halt. If Klyd had used nageric modulation, the junct Simes, such as these appeared to be, must have felt it like a searing shock.

"Send your leader forward," said Klyd into the sudden silence. Then he glanced at the Chairman, offering him the mallet of his office. The Chairman, an older man, declined with a weak gesture of two tentacles.

The ranks of intruders split. Two figures emerged: Amos and Enid Kaneko. Enid strode to the foot of the podium and whirled to confront the assembly. "We're here to see that you consider the only alternative to losing your children to the Pens—offering Gen transfer to any Sime in need."

Amos joined her, adding, "We'll stand quiet while you discuss it, but we'll know which Houses support us."

Klyd whispered to Risa, "May I?"

She stepped back. "Go ahead."

To the room, Klyd said, "The House of Zeor is flatly opposed to countering the government threat of confiscation with an offer of Gen Transfer. This is not the time for such a measure. Zeor proposes we offer *channel's transfer* to those in need, and we support Imil's proposal to fund a public education project on Zelerod's Doom."

Out on the floor, several people shot to their feet, shouting variously, "Point of Order!" "We already have both those programs!" "There's no budget!" "How can we—"

"These proposals and many others will be introduced," shouted Klyd over the attendant uproar, "and discussed and voted on in this assembly. No Householding will yield to coercion. We respect the authority of the government of Nivet Territory—not the spokesmen of a rabble."

Then why did you recognize these people instead of having them thrown out? Valleroy wondered, frustrated. For one bright moment he had thought Klyd was going to admit that direct Gen transfer for renSimes was possible, even if not the solution to the current dangerous shortage. Instead, he had called the people who practiced Valleroy's philosophy "rabble," undermining their case before they could even speak.

While Valleroy balanced on the balls of his feet, expecting the intruders to erupt into violence at that provocation, Klyd briefed Risa on the Kanekos. The intruders scanned the ambient warily, zlinning that they had garnered no sympathy.

Klyd placed the mallet on its hanger beside the chime. "The Sectuib Keon has the floor, and her proposal would seem germane to the junct complaint of kill-shortages. Sectuib Keon, will you speak before this entire assembly, or shall we eject the non-credentialed?"

She replied, "No, let them hear." She raised her voice. "I'm pleased to address any and all of our Nivet neighbors." She gestured gracefully to where the Keon delegation sat. "Gulf Territory recognizes your lifestyle as legal. You may wish to speak to Uzziah and Bethany over there."

Valleroy felt Klyd bracing as he compared the two couples. *He's afraid someone's going to get killed,* thought Valleroy. He'd seen it himself, much too often. His own House of Rior was composed of many Simes from out-Territory and young Gens stricken with Householding idealism. He had to be constantly on guard against compassionate Gens offering transfer to Simes in need. With people like Amos and Enid or Bethany and Uzziah as examples, idealistic youngsters could die luring Simes into junctedness. The tragedy of the junct condition, leaving not even the most beloved Gen safe—continuing in life only by taking lives—was worse than the death of the Gen who was killed.

He'd worked more than a decade to curb that Gen idealism although he was certain it grew from the Gen's natural physical need for transfer.

But Klyd, raised in-Territory, knowing juncts intimately, didn't believe Gens had such a need. Too many generations of tragedy showed that the kill couldn't be stopped except by Sime self-control and denial. That's how his ancestors had done it; that's how all Householdings had done it.

Only he's wrong. As long as there are humans, we can't stop transfer mates from finding each other. We've got to create a world where that's the expected and natural way to live. Simes have failed. Now it's up to us.

Valleroy forced his attention back to Risa's speech.

". . . Gulf Territory can—and will be delighted to—feed your Gens. You've been tottering on the brink of famine for three years, with worse ahead. But your Territory's rich in raw materials and technology retrieved from the Ancients. On the road, I saw a bundle of pelts no larger than *this* that would supply the average Pen with rice for a week.

"We can trade—to both our profits. Both the Houses and the Towns of Gulf are eager to do so. I'm empowered to sign a trade agreement on behalf of Gulf Territory. We don't intend to see you destroyed by need. We're ready to act—now."

For a protracted moment there was silence. Then they were all on their feet, shouting their enthusiasm.

People jammed the aisles, conferring with their allies. Valleroy heard Klyd congratulating Risa, but he was watching the juncts pushing toward the Keon delegation. Granted there probably wasn't a Gen on the lower floor they could harm, but—

"Klyd?" He looked behind him to where Risa, Sergi and Klyd huddled with an assortment of Tecton officers. "Klyd?" He focused his attention on the sensitive channel.

Klyd turned, eyebrows raised in query, and Valleroy gestured to the stream of outsiders amid the Householding capes. "Is that safe?"

Klyd climbed onto the podium to zlin. Valleroy could see one of the intruders shouting at Amos Kaneko, gesticulating.

"That junct with Amos, in the brown and green vest, is in need, high intil, too."

The man was now shouting at Enid, who pointed at the rear doors, clearly ordering him to leave. As the junct became ever more furious, Klyd leaned over the podium and called to the Marshal's assistants, "Evict the angry one—gently. Give him transfer if necessary."

Two young Sime women moved to obey, but their way was blocked by excited delegates.

There was a scuffle; somebody went down. Valleroy couldn't see it all, but inferred from Klyd's clenched fist and helplessly lashing tentacles that the junct had attacked someone—Gen, undoubtedly. Klyd charged down the stairs toward the action, Valleroy on his heels, vaguely aware of Risa and Sergi shoving along behind them.

Amos leaped over the pack of struggling bodies. There was a scream. Valleroy almost ran into Klyd as the channel stopped.

Dinny ambrov Keon lay on the floor, jerking feebly. The junct stiffened as Amos' limp body slid from his tentacles. Enid screamed in agony. Klyd's hand clamped onto Valleroy's wrist and his eyes bulged. *What's the matter? He's zlinned kills before.*

But this junct had taken a Gen, then killed a Sime.

Risa slipped through a narrow gap in the crowd, leaving Sergi trapped behind. Klyd lunged forward and seized the junct killer, as if to give him transfer. Risa knelt beside the Keon Gen shiltpron player, and a moment later Sergi was at her side. Valleroy narrowed focus to attend Klyd, not at all sure what the channel was doing.

The junct Klyd held gave a rattling groan and melted to the floor—dead. Enid stared from the corpse to Klyd. "You killed him!" Klyd raised his hands to his face, but continued to stare at the corpses while Valleroy hoped he could provide enough shielding for Farris nerves.

Some nearby channel said into a bubble of silence, "No, he was a channel. No wonder he wanted a Householding Gen. But he died of nageric shock."

Klyd knelt beside Risa, who had Dinny in a transfer grip, but had not made lip contact. He held his hand over the man's chest, frowning deeply. Then he shook his head. "It's no use, Risa."

She shot him a venomous look and bent over her patient. But she must know Klyd was right. As Klyd turned to Amos' body, Sergi took Risa's shoulders, his big hands almost wrapping around the tiny woman. He whispered in her ear, no doubt reinforcing it nagerically.

At last she sat back on her heels and leaned into her Companion's chest, heaving a sigh. "Dinny could have handled it, but he was too low field. He was stripped, not burned."

"I'll put that in the next dispatch," said Sergi, it being the First Companion's duty to keep records of marriages, births, deaths, and changeovers.

Klyd closed Amos' eyes with two tentacles, then used his tentacles and fingers on the arms to force the dead Sime's tentacles to retract. He worked with a peculiar concentration, as if there were some significance to his movements other than courtesy.

Then Risa's eyes found Klyd's. Her lips tightened. "We all knew the risks."

"You're Zeor's guests. It's as if it happened under our roof. There's no restitution great enough for a life."

"My husband's life!" Enid suddenly found her voice. "It's your fault—all of you with your fine Householding ways! If that man had had a transfer mate to turn to—Ohhh, oh, Amos!" She knelt beside her husband's body.

Risa gathered herself, once more Sectuib not merely woman, and went to look down at Amos, the dead junct, and Enid. "A Householder gave his life, trying to protect your husband."

Enid stared at Risa. "How can you side with *them*? You said you were different, that you believed. You're not to be trusted. None of you!" She turned and fled the assembly.

Silence spread through the hall. The elderly Marshal worked through the press to survey the bodies, then removed his white cloak to cover Dinny ambrov Keon. Two of his assistants removed their cloaks and draped the other two bodies as he raised his quavering voice. "This session has not yet been adjourned!"

Stillness gripped them, a sense of consternation. Then Klyd bowed formally to the Marshal, led the way back to the podium, struck the chime, and proclaimed, "I call this session to order!"

While they cleared the aisles, Valleroy heard Sergi say to Klyd, "In Gulf, we no longer have unidentified channels like that."

"We have many," admitted Klyd. "Either we identify them when they're too old to disjunct, or the young ones want nothing to do with the Householdings." He added, "There are huge sections of Nivet where there are no Householdings, no working channels at all for a day's ride in any direction."

Valleroy saw Risa eye the room, estimating the size of the Territory from the number of banners displayed, and how sparsely distributed Householdings were. She seemed awed.

Eventually, the Chairman took the podium and restored order, the Marshals took their places, and stillness descended.

The Houses voted to trade with Gulf. The next step would be to propose it to the Territory government, sending a representative who could convince the West-Nivet Tecton and then speak to the juncts on behalf of the whole Tecton. Who could that be other than Klyd—backed by Risa?

And if she really had no idea how big this Territory was, a trip across its length would teach her. Then they'd see if she could provide enough food to make a difference.

Also, there was Muryin. If the Tecton sent representatives, they'd be on the road in a couple of days.

He glanced at Klyd, who was staring off into the distance as if zlinning. *He looks like a channel just after changeover, marveling at selyn fields.*

He watched Risa as it was moved, seconded, and passed unanimously to enter Dinny ambrov Keon's name into the Memorial to the One Billion who had given their lives in the cause of Sime/Gen unity. The Tecton could confer no higher honor.

Risa could not offer a motion to the Tecton, so Valleroy, knowing Klyd wouldn't do it, stood to claim the floor, his

Rior cape flashing flame amid the brilliant blue of Zeor. The Chair recognized, "The First Companion of Zeor, Sosectu Rior."

Valleroy noted the preposition, "of," not "in." He said, using a Sectuib's syntax, "Rior moves that we send Sectuib Klyd Farris to solicit the support of Tecton Nivet-West, then approach the Territory government at Capital with Keon's plan of trade. Rior further recommends that we invite the Sectuib Keon to accompany our Representative on this vital mission."

"So moved. Seconded?"

There was a deafening shout of acclamation.

"So ordered. If there be no objections, the Marshal will proclaim this session adjourned." History had been made.

CHAPTER SIX

The Ruined Lands

For the next three days, Risa was busy in meetings with Householding and Territory officials. Even if, as Hugh said, Klyd had not traveled out of Zeor much these last years, he had not lost touch with the controlling forces in the Tecton.

He taught her much about the way Nivet functioned. To convince them Gulf's offer of trade was sincere and feasible, she offered generous credit on the initial year's purchase. It was to Gulf's advantage to have their neighboring Territory strong and able to control the Freeband Raiders.

But Risa didn't reveal all of her vision. Nivet's juncts had to learn that the Householding lifestyle would be to their economic and emotional advantage before a full partnership could begin. The Householders had to see how juncts who depended on them would defend the Houses. She recalled the long struggle, the violence, the deaths that had plagued her first efforts to befriend Laveen Township. Her brother had died on the threshold of a promising life because of her haste. She wouldn't make that mistake again.

She sometimes glimpsed Klyd and Hugh, sitting over tea with Muryin in the dining hall, or interviewing trail guides. Once, she walked into a shouting match over Klyd's obsession with the details of Amos' death, Klyd insisting only tragedy could come of the lifestyle Amos and Enid had attempted. Hugh retorted, "Let's stop dwelling on all the ways people can die, and concentrate on Simes and Gens *living* together. Klyd, if something is *right*, there has to be a way to accomplish it. Isn't that a Zeor axiom?"

Wearily, Klyd answered, "Yes, it is." It sounded like capitulation.

Later that night, she found Sergi sprawled in the big chair in their room. She sat down on a pillow on the floor, and delivered the good news, "It's going to work, Sergi. Hugh's on our side. And he'll win. Companions always do."

Sergi agreed. "Ten Houses are pledged to follow Rior's lead. Most are young Houses who've chosen Gen Heads, Sosectu like Hugh. And the number's growing. They call their philosophy 'distect,' whatever that means." He flashed her a smile, "They're impressed by you."

"Are they?" she countered innocently.

The grin broadened. "Not as much as I am."

Her response to him as pure *Gen* redoubled. Her need had become acute sometime that day. She let intil rise, knowing he'd sense it as a blatant invitation.

Tomorrow both of them would share a more cheerful outlook—which would be good for Virena, too. Together, without need anxiety, they could handle any dangers on the mysterious inner plains of this continent.

Hugh Valleroy was glad he wasn't in charge of moving this group. In addition to the Keon members going west with them, there were Muryin and Virena, two Zeor Companions, Ediva and the ten Guards hired from Householding Dar, plus Lenis, their trail guide, and her four scouts: thirty people, and forty-five horses.

As they left town, a dry wind scoured them with grit.

Valleroy rode with his eyes slit and a bandanna over his face. When the wind slackened at sunrise, Risa rode up beside him and Klyd. "Is the road this good all the way west?"

"This isn't the eyeway," answered Valleroy. "That runs a day's ride north, through an Ancient Ruin we'll avoid."

"It's been years since I've been on this road," said Klyd. "Lenis says the main eyeway has deteriorated since the drought, so it'll be hard going."

"That must be slowing trade down."

Risa never considered anything but commerce, reflected Valleroy. It must be boring being her Companion, though Sergi seemed anything but bored this morning.

"The drought's brought trade almost to a standstill anyway," said Klyd.

Valleroy remembered how much time they'd spent in Gulf Territory pinned down by torrential rains and spring floods. *What's wrong with the world? Could the Church of the Purity be right in saying God withholds the blessings of the land from the wicked?* He couldn't believe that being Sime, or even junct, made one hopelessly immoral.

Harris Emstead spoke up. "We've heard of the drought west of the Mizipi, but we had no idea it was like this! My daughter and her husband took in his brother after he lost his farm. It dried up one year, and the next year's winds blew his topsoil away."

Risa and Sergi were riding side by side now, seemingly lost to everything but one another. Valleroy envied them—until he caught Klyd's sharp-eyed stare. He ignored it, and kicked his horse to keep up with Emstead. "Better not get out ahead, Sir. Let Risa ride scout."

"No use 'Sirring' me anymore, Hugh," replied Emstead. "No one will *ever* believe what I've seen here. Just look at those two, Sime and Gen—hell, back home, who'd believe that *any* two people married long enough to have teenage kids could still be so deep in love, let alone—"

He cut off as Risa turned to glance at them. "It's all right," she said. "We know we're unusual, though Sime/Gen marriages aren't, in Householdings. What Sergi and I have is called torluen."

"What's that?" asked Emstead, while Valleroy frowned.

Such relationships were pure myth, as far as he knew. And they thought *Klyd* was a mystic?

"It's a special relationship between a channel and a Companion who are matchmates," Sergi explained. Then he had to explain that Simes and Gens had frequencies of selyn resonance as distinctive as facial characteristics. Matchmates were people whose frequencies *and* capacities were so similar that they were irresistibly drawn to one another.

"In a channel and a Companion," Risa took up the explanation, "those forces are very powerful, and when two people work together and have transfer together, they . . . adjust until their resonances . . . harmonize. But it's not only physical; caring deeply for one another also affects their fields. And the result can be lortuen or torluen."

"What's the difference?" Emstead asked.

"No real difference," said Sergi. "It's just Simelan syntax. Lortuen means the channel is male and the Companion female; our situation is called torluen because the channel is female and the Companion male."

"But it only happens between a man and a woman?" their Gen visitor pursued.

Risa smiled. "No, but in lortuen or torluen there is a . . . sexual component. Love, in the romantic as well as the compassionate sense. I suppose that makes orhuen rarer— that's between channel and Companion of the same sex. There's no sexual component. I guess that's why the poets aren't much interested in writing songs about it!"

They had slowed their horses to talk, and now Klyd caught up to them, hearing Risa's last comment. "Surely you can do better than to fill our guest's head with myths, Risa. Next you'll be telling him to beware of wer-Gens!"

"It's Simes who have to beware of them," Risa replied. "Actually they're rather nice once you get to know them," she added. Sergi returned her grin, sharing some private joke. "Besides," Risa continued, "if you're as sensitive as you claim, you certainly know by now that torluen is no myth."

"What do you mean?" Klyd asked blankly.

"You've zlinned Sergi and me deeply enough to notice—"

"Risa, don't be absurd! You two have a dependency strong enough to be debilitating if you let it, but you aren't anywhere near perfect matchmates. As to torluen, there's certainly never been a case in *my* lifetime, nor my grandfather's either! I doubt there can be such a thing. It's a romantic notion made up in the early days of Householdings to explain dependencies people just didn't want to break. Any deep dependency can *feel* as if death were preferable to breaking it, but I can't credit the idea of a dependency so deep it *causes* death when broken!''

Sergi spoke up. ''Klyd, I *know* what happens between Risa and me. You don't, and you never can.''

''Didn't you say,'' replied the Sectuib in Zeor, ''you've given transfer elsewhere, Sergi? And Risa, your son told me you took his transfer to provide him the best first experience possible in Keon.''

''Of course,'' said Risa. ''We're not as out of touch as you think over in Gulf. It's hard, but Sergi and I do break step occasionally—in case there should be an emergency in which we *can't* have one another for transfer. That's one of your own rules, Sectuib—and it's a good one.''

''But one you would be *incapable* of following if you were in torluen. Thus, by definition, you are not in torluen—for which you should be grateful. Even a strong dependency can threaten the ability of a channel or a Companion to do his work . . . and that can lead to tragedy.''

Risa and Sergi looked at one another, shaking their heads. Obviously they saw Klyd's assessment as just another Farris technicality. Valleroy agreed. If they wanted to think of their relationship as the romantic torluen, what harm did it do?

Harris broke the uncomfortable silence. ''Well, if it's that rare, I guess that's a bit of Simelan I don't have to learn. We've been talking so much, I haven't been paying attention to the road. How far have we come today?''

Klyd knew as well as Valleroy that the Colonel hadn't lost track of their position, but he took the cue to change the subject. ''We're moving along the southern edge of Nivet. When my grandfather was a boy, there were lots of little Sime Territories all around Nivet—which was only what we now call 'West Nivet.' When the Gens pushed into the region, Simes in outlying Territories moved closer to Nivet for protection. The smaller Territories disappeared, and Nivet amalgamated the larger ones.

"This—" he swept his hand at the desolation dotted with tumble-down gray buildings and dead vegetation,"—was once prime Genfarm terrain. This time of year it should be green with new crops. These Genfarms fed themselves and sold huge surpluses, so many farmers moved here for the easy profits. Then the land started to go bad. The amateur farmers didn't know crop rotation and worked their best Gens to death trying to force crops. The best workers were also their prime breeders. They lost everything when this drought hit, and that's nearly destroyed Nivet's economy."

Risa stared at the desolation, the blankness of her expression conveying more eloquently than words how hard it hit her. "This can't be repaired in a year—or even five."

"Having second thoughts?" asked Klyd neutrally.

"No, just getting a better idea of the problem. I don't think it'd help if we sold you irrigation supplies! Even if this land was once fertile, it's desert now!"

"It's been deforested," Harris Emstead spoke up. "They made that mistake in some of our own farm areas. My son-in-law's brother planted trees, but the drought killed them. The only way to reclaim land like this is by reforesting to stop the erosion. It will take a generation of careful management to create a new layer of topsoil."

The road narrowed where loose dirt had covered half of it, and they strung out in single file, ending the discussion.

That night they camped by a river ford. Lenis ambrov Frihill, their trail guide, cautioned them not to mix with the other travellers gathered there.

"I heard whispers in town," she told them quietly. "We may have been followed. I'm sending two of my scouts back along our trail. I'll speak to those prospectors; it would be expected of Frihill. Meanwhile, observe security precautions, especially you children!" As they set to pitching camp, she disappeared into the trees.

"What does she mean, expected of Frihill?" asked Risa.

Valleroy explained as he pulled down his saddlebags. "Frihill specializes in Archaeology. With our Dar contingent, Lenis would be willing to go right into the heart of an Ancient Ruin."

"She seems nervous, though," observed Risa, preparing to lead Valleroy's horse off to their picket line.

"Then she's got good reason," replied Valleroy.

Muryin and Virena came to deliver a load of firewood. "A Patroller told us not to waste the wood," said Muryin. "As if we were despoilers!"

"He's just doing his job," replied Valleroy.

Emstead had been listening to their conversation without comment. Now, with only Valleroy and the two girls within hearing, he suddenly asked, "What's a wer-Gen?"

Virena giggled. "Hugh is. My Daddy is."

The man frowned. "Someone from Gen Territory, who's turned traitor?"

Vi replied confusedly, "No, my Daddy was born at Keon. Juncts used to think Householders practiced witchcraft, and turned some of their Simes into Gens to produce selyn!"

"They couldn't understand Gens who associated with Simes without fear," Valleroy explained. "What you've been doing since you joined us, Harris. No, you're no Companion . . . but you're not the same man who chased those Raiders into Gulf, are you? You've learned that on this side of the border are people with homes and families like yours. That make you a turnie?"

"I guess so," Emstead said sadly. "But I've got to go back. Hugh, there *must* be tangible proof that Simes who don't kill aren't a myth like wer-Gens! Help me find that proof!" He knelt to lay the campfire base. "Even if I have to go back without it, my granddaughter must be told Rior exists."

He looked up at the two girls handing him kindling. "You girls both think you're going to be Sime—"

"We *are*," Muryin and Virena chorused.

"But you know you won't kill anyone. I want Bonnie to know that, too . . . just in case."

"Mama says that's what everybody really wants," said Virena. "That's how we're disjuncting Gulf Territory. Maybe we can disjunct Gen Territory, too!"

"Vi," Valleroy began, "the word 'junct' can't be applied to Gens."

"Why not?" asked Virena. "There are junct Gens in the Ancient Ruins."

"What?" asked Emstead. "More wer-Gens?"

"Oh, no," said Valleroy, "the Wild Killer Gens are only too real. Out-Territory, children who survive turning Sime hide out in the Ancient Ruins. The same thing happens here sometimes, especially far in-Territory, where it's hopeless for new Gens to run for the border. Some of them develop into gangs almost like Freeband Raiders. They entice Sime prospectors and explorers with their fields—then murder them. Sometimes they even kill them."

"And then they eat them!" Muryin said with a child's relish for gruesome details.

"Now that I'll *never* believe!" said Emstead. "It's not fair of you to gang up on me that way!"

"They're telling you the truth." Ediva joined them, to set water on the fire to boil. "The ambrov Dar occasionally clean out such gangs, when Simes wish to reclaim something from the ruins. They're as vicious as the Freeband Raiders—and no wonder, since they grew up in junct society and know the Simes will kill them if they don't strike first."

"But how could an unarmed Gen kill a Sime?" Emstead insisted. "That's not possible."

"Yes, it is," Ediva contended.

"Oh, maybe with the kind of combat training *you* people have, but you're talking about runaway kids."

"No, the murder of a Sime can be accomplished by any Gen who can keep his presence of mind under Sime attack— not easy, I'll admit, but when you have nothing to lose but your life if you don't learn fast—" She glanced toward their distant neighbors, screened by tree trunks and twilight. "Let's show him, Hugh. He's donated selyn, and pulled his weight all this journey. He ought to know how to defend himself if it should ever become necessary."

Valleroy shuddered. It was knowledge he had seen used only once; it had made him sick at the time, and even sicker after Klyd explained the full implications. But Ediva was right. Emstead had earned the knowledge. *And she's Sime.*

Ediva extended her arms to Valleroy. He lectured, "You know a Sime's handling tentacles are harmless. Only the little laterals on either side of the arm draw selyn and can kill

Gens. The laterals are practically raw nerves—selyn conducting nerves. A Sime lives on selyn.''

''I know all that,'' said Emstead.

''But you're not putting it together,'' Valleroy explained.
''When a Sime takes a Gen in transfer grip, the same grip
used for the kill—'' Ediva put her hands on his forearms,
wrapping her handling tentacles about his arms in total trust.
''—he's completely vulnerable. You see where my hands
fall?'' Very, very gently, he wrapped his fingers around
Ediva's slender forearms, right over her lateral sheaths.
''When those lateral tentacles are extended, the nerves are
even more vulnerable. One good, hard squeeze, and the Sime
will be dead.''

He saw amazement, then horror spread over Emstead's
face. ''I—I never knew such a thing was possible!''

''Even after all the Simes your army doctors dissected?''
Valleroy asked, remembering that he hadn't known the secret
until Klyd revealed it.

''Let go of her, please,'' the man said. ''You're making my
skin crawl!''

Ediva smiled as Valleroy backed off. ''He's speaking the
truth, Hugh—which means this is not the information he will
take home to get his commission back. We must finish the
lesson. Harris, if ever you must use this technique, do not use
half measures.''

''Never point a gun unless you intend to use it,'' he
replied. ''I understand.''

''No,'' said Valleroy. ''A gun can make a wound which
will eventually heal. This technique makes only *fatal* wounds,
or instantaneous death. I hope you will grant even the most
jaded Raider the latter.''

''What do you mean?''

''Make sure the Sime's *dead* before you drop him. If you
merely injure those selyn transport nerves, he'll take hours or
days to die—in the worst agony imaginable. I—I did that
once,'' Valleroy confessed. ''That is, I taught someone what
to do. She left the Sime merely unconscious, and I didn't
know any better than to leave him that way! What's worse,
he was a junct channel.''

Clearly, the difference between renSimes and channels was

unimportant to Emstead; his face showed he had come to see all Simes as people and would never willingly torture one again. Valleroy knew what memories of Sime interrogation he had stirred up; they had haunted his own nightmares when he had gone through the same realizations Emstead now faced.

"Very well," Emstead said firmly, "if I ever have to do that, I'll make sure I kill my attacker."

"Not kill," said Muryin. "Murder."

"No, not murder," Emstead corrected. "It would be self-defense."

"The terms don't translate perfectly into English," Valleroy explained. "By convention, the word 'kill' is used strictly for death by selyn movement; everything else is described as 'murder,' although that word may have other connotations in English. If we ever achieve unity, the lawyers will have a field day making the languages match."

"No—wait," Emstead protested. "You called the Gens in the Ancient Ruins *Killer* Gens."

"Some," said Ediva, "learn a thing even more terrifying to a Sime than what we've just taught you: the Companions' trick of giving a Sime a fatal shock with their selyn fields. Obviously, not all of them learn to do it; but those few strike fear into Simes, for they don't have to get close enough to touch . . . to kill."

"Do me a favor," said Emstead. "*Don't* teach me to do that!" He got up and left, the girls following discreetly, taking the responsibility for a guest of their Houses.

Ediva looked after them. "He may need that lesson. Maybe we *should* let him take it back to Gen Territory. Gens able to defend themselves could at least postpone Zelerod's Doom."

Valleroy began to string a laundry line, knowing they wouldn't see water again for days. "That's your need talking. We have years before the real crash."

"I did my figuring before this drought. In Konawa I heard there's drought in Norwest Territory, too, and a Gen shortage and a Raider problem. We might not have even another two years. Hugh, we're not going to make it."

Got to cheer her up before Klyd gets here. "I'm going for a swim before the light's gone. Join me?" Valleroy focused on feeling good and clean after the day's ride. "Come on, you'll feel better!"

"All right!" She rose and peeled off her clothes as Valleroy fished soap out of his saddlebag and led the way across a long stretch of mud to the water.

Ediva stood up on a rock, arched and dove cleanly into the water, her Sime senses telling her the depth. Valleroy, soap bar on a rope around his neck, followed. He wouldn't have dared dive if he'd been alone.

He surfaced and found Ediva waiting. "Here, soap my hair for me and I'll scrub your back."

He scrubbed the bar across her hair, one arm around her shoulders to hold position while he treaded water.

Her body was comfortable against his—sparse, angular, Sime— Maybe tonight—

Ediva groaned and shivered against him with rising intil. Recovery from her wounds had rephased her need cycle into sync with Klyd's. Valleroy had had her in transfer grip not half an hour ago; abruptly he realized she was fixing on him.

He let go and backpedaled. "Hey, I'm sorry. I forget you're not a channel." He brought his fields under strict control, easing gently out of the nascent linkage.

She faced him, her voice husky with anguish. "I—take that as a compliment. Klyd must be—the luckiest Sime alive."

He worked now as if she were a shenned channel. "Go to Klyd. He'll serve you." But the real message was the way he managed the fields: withholding, but not rejecting.

Half-hypnotized, she nodded, splashed out of the water, absently grabbed her clothes, and trotted barefoot across the mud.

"Shen!" swore Valleroy softly. *That was the dumbest—the stupidest—what would I have done if I'd goaded her into attacking me?* The idea of transfer with someone other than Klyd sent crawling horror through him.

He swam to the rock and found Klyd staring down at him. From the look on the channel's face, he'd gathered the essence of the scene. And he was in need.

He said, "You've upset her. She wouldn't stop."

"She thought—Klyd, I wouldn't—let me go explain—"

The channel forestalled Valleroy's charge across the mud.

"*I* will take care of Ediva. She needs a transfer, not a philosophy lecture." He started down the shore side of the boulder. Then he hesitated. "Maybe you *wouldn't* give anyone else transfer—but *could* you?"

Valleroy watched him go. There was only one channel Klyd might consider giving him up to: Muryin. But Klyd had brought Dsif for her. *Is Klyd worried Dsif can't handle Muryin?*

Back at camp, the children were pushing and shoving, squealing and chasing each other. Klyd had gone with Ediva and another Sime who was up for transfer, to find a place where they could disrupt the ambient nager without disturbing nearby juncts. Lenis returned with bad news about the roads; the drought was destroying everything. "Where's Klyd?" Valleroy told her. "He should have taken guards. Well, when he comes back, tell him I want to see him."

"Sure," agreed Valleroy.

Lenis went off, shouting orders for camp security.

After dinner, Valleroy and Dsif collected the dishes. "I'll finish this," volunteered Dsif, glancing over his shoulder. "You'd better tend to Sectuib."

Klyd was coming out of the dark. Valleroy ached in sympathy with the channel's need, but Klyd shouldn't have been feeling that bad. "Did Ediva give you such a hard time?"

"Only one abort. She's fine now, a miracle after what you did to her at Keon—and again tonight."

"I wasn't thinking about transfer, either time. It's the *woman* who attracts me, Klyd," he protested. "I don't want her transfer!"

"I know. That just makes things harder. When you're high field and she's in need, she can't see you as anything but Gen. You're a shedoni-doomed fool, Hugh Valleroy."

"Yes—and you're the one who has doomed me to it," Valleroy replied, wondering if the channel realized what he had said. "Shidoni" meant death by attrition; "shedoni" meant *execution* by attrition, for breaking the law. *I've broken some precious Farris law—and you're punishing me for my compassion, for being Gen.* But this time he didn't say it, remembering the last time he had shared his "morbid" thoughts with Klyd. "I'm sorry. I can't make myself stop falling in love with her."

"At least you've admitted it to yourself. It's good, Hugh—after Aisha—it's been so many years. . . ."

"I never thought it would happen with a Sime. I can't even tell if she feels the same."

"She'll let you know in her own time. But what are you going to do if—"

"I won't let her attempt to take transfer from me."

"I don't doubt your ability," answered Klyd. "You handled her beautifully *after* you realized what was happening. For that, I can trust you tonight. But she told me her need nightmares have been focusing on you. The worst ones are where you are Sime and she's Gen, and you attack to kill her. Awake, all she can think of is being near you. Do you know what that means for a disjunct renSime?"

"Her disjunction resolve is being challenged. She fears Gen attack, and that's just one short step from attacking first." He spoke analytically, but inwardly he was shaken. He'd been sure when he'd healed her that he had not engaged her systems. *I'd have felt it!* "If she's having such nightmares about me, I have to admit I made a grave error at Keon. What can I do to help her?"

"I don't know. I can't surrender her to the juncts—Zelerod's successor rejuncts! How could anyone think she believes her own figures? And she couldn't live junct, you know."

It was Valleroy's turn to gaze off and struggle to regulate his breathing. "I healed her because I thought she might die. I couldn't stand losing her."

Klyd sighed tremulously. "I can't think now."

Valleroy took a step toward him, one hand out in invitation. "Why do these things always come up just before our transfer?"

A tentacle twined firmly about his fingers, pulling him closer. "Ediva's condition is vaguely reminiscent of Amos' just before he abandoned House and ran off with Enid. And there was something in the way Amos died—I've zlinned it before, but never attached any importance to it." Klyd shook his head. "There's so much we don't understand yet, but if we can identify these peculiarly sensitive renSimes, we'll develop support for them."

That Klyd would summon the effort to think of others,

feeling as bleak as he did in need, melted Valleroy's heart. If anyone could make Valleroy's cherished vision a reality, it was Klyd. All he asked in return was a touch, a steady support, and the selyn Valleroy's body ached to get rid of.

"Don't do that," whispered Klyd, "unless you're ready to follow through."

They moved along the beaten trail toward the hulking Ancient ruin they were using as a selyn shield.

"There shouldn't be a price tag of suffering on every human relationship," Valleroy insisted. "I still say we must build a world where Sime and Gen are free to create whatever relationships they individually choose. Freedom to choose includes the risk of wrong choices, but to be denied choice is to be denied humanity."

"If we could find an objective way of evaluating those risks before running them . . ." Klyd pondered; then, "Help me with Ediva, and maybe together we'll discover the key."

Klyd's vision kindled Valleroy, as it always did. There was such kinship between them, he marveled they could ever lose that sense of oneness. *This will be a great transfer.*

CHAPTER SEVEN

Loss of a Companion

"Whew!" breathed Risa as the sharp intil spike blurred away behind the Ancient ruins. "Sergi, leave the rest of the trin tea there."

Sergi set the pot on a stone near the edge of the banked cooking fire. "You said you had the second watch."

She couldn't miss his disappointment. "I do. Klyd has first watch, and he'll be on soon, wanting tea and food."

Sergi's nager was a dim flame, dancing with excitement. "They seem irresponsible, postponing transfer so long."

Risa shook out her bedroll. "Klyd was so busy in Konawa, he had seven secretaries working 'round the clock! I just hope need depression didn't affect his decisions! Why can't I *trust* him?"

"He's a terrific channel—even as Farrises go."

"You would notice that."

"Jealous?" he teased as he stripped off his shirt.

She asked herself if her reaction to Klyd were just Sime jealousy. Klyd was the first channel they'd met who could attract a Companion like Sergi. *No. Sergi and I share more than that.* "No," she denied, watching him strip. "But if you worked hard at it, you might inspire me to jealousy."

"I was just kidding."

"I know," she laughed, and stripped. "I've got to stay alert for half an hour. Want to go for a swim—in the dark?"

"You'll give poor Lenis fits."

"She'll get used to us. Besides, there's nothing out there as far as I can zlin except a few thirsty animals minding their own business."

Klyd poured hot trin tea for himself and Valleroy. "Risa is always thoughtful." There were also some bread and beans left near the fire.

Valleroy sipped the warm brew gratefully. He felt as if it ought to be dawn, with birds singing and laughter everywhere. Instead, it was the dead of night, lit by a slice of moon. "I thought Risa was covering your watch."

He gazed toward the river. "She was until I returned."

"Oh." From Sergi's look that morning, those two were as post as Valleroy now felt. "Oh, Lenis wanted to talk to you!" Klyd started to get up. Valleroy knew that if Klyd moved now, he'd never eat. "I'll get her. Keep my tea warm."

Valleroy found the guide's fire near the horses' picket line. Lenis and Dsif were talking. Dsif looked up at Valleroy and grinned, sensing his post condition.

Lenis, a renSime who couldn't have missed Valleroy's field drop either, said, "Is Klyd ready to talk to me?"

"Ready to leave his first meal in days to talk to you."

She stood up. "I'll go over there."

Dsif stood to walk back with Valleroy, but Lenis turned to stop the two men. "After we get the business out of the way—well, maybe I'll just see how post a channel can get."

"There are times," said Dsif, "when a Companion is not welcome. I think I'll get some sleep."

Valleroy shrugged, then wandered to the Dar campfire.

Ediva stood with her arm around the waist of a Gen called Dazul ambrov Dar. They were with the other Dar in a circle around a pair of Simes. Two long staves lay on the ground between them. They clapped the staves together and beat them on the ground arhythmically, while another Sime danced barefoot between the flashing staves.

Meanwhile, two other Simes juggled five spinning knives in an arc over the dancer's head. The dancer's tentacles flashed into the arc of gleaming steel to snatch a knife. Everyone cheered as the dancer leaped out of the circle.

As part of Valleroy's mind was telling him to retreat and leave Ediva to her post-transfer partner, she turned and shot him a grin that weakened his knees. Then she leaped between the clattering staves under the arc of knives.

He strangled a cry of dismay, fearing to disrupt her concentration. If she missed a beat, those staves could smash her ankle. But Dar was a House specializing in the martial arts, and this must be child's play for them.

But Ediva was raised by a whip maker in a junct town.

He tried not to project his fright into the ambient nager. He couldn't have succeeded if he'd been carrying more selyn. His mouth was dry, his palms sweaty by the time Ediva had missed two snatches at the arc of knives.

He had to close his eyes against the vision of her lateral tentacles sliced through, and he missed her third and successful snatch. He peeked as the cheer went up, and saw her toss the knife to the ground, where it stood quivering while she strolled toward him.

The clapping tempo slowed, the rhythm became steady, and the knives in the arc were reduced to four when the Gen Ediva had been standing with jumped into the center.

"Dazul's very good," she said, wiping her face. "It's just a game, helps to work off frustrations. Don't watch if it upsets you."

"I didn't mean to be a distraction."

She bowed. "Rior's manners are irreproachable."

He grabbed her shoulders, pulling her away from the circle. "Good manners? Listen, I owe you an apology."

"No. I owe you one. Dar conditions renSimes to channel's transfer. I didn't mean what happened in the river."

"Neither did I. I shouldn't have touched you earlier, either. I'm supposed to be the professional at this, and I—Klyd told me you had trouble taking transfer."

She turned, the distant fire gleaming on her sweating face. "He shouldn't have said anything—"

"He had to. I had to give him transfer. But it's a professional confidence." In a rush of honesty, he added, "He told me your nightmare."

She buried her face in her hands. "I'm sorry!"

"I'm Gen, but I understand need nightmares. Klyd has to share his with me because I have to treat the condition. Truthfully, sometimes I think they're contagious."

Astonished, she said, "You're not joking."

"I don't condemn you for your dreams. Next time you're in need, I'll be very, very careful."

"But you would shen me, wouldn't you?"

"I doubt I could stop myself," he said candidly. As a disjunction specialist, he'd said the like many times. "But I'd never hurt you—not even if it cost me my life."

She zlinned him. "I believe you. But let's not worry about it now. Lenis and Klyd have decided not to frustrate one another. Do we have to stay frustrated? I've taken precautions, but if I got pregnant, Dar would welcome the offspring of such a Companion."

Raised without a father, Valleroy often had to remind himself that any child born in a House never lacked family. He gathered her into his arms, luxuriating in the feel of woman. "The problem is, Ediva, that with you—I think I'll come to need something permanent."

Valleroy woke to the vague gray of pre-dawn light. He was twisted in Ediva's bedroll with her scant body draped over him, her snores in his ear. For a moment, he thought that had wakened him. Then he heard the strangled scream.

He was running before the scream ended. Ediva followed, hopping tender-footed to where the children slept.

Klyd and Risa were already there, bending over Muryin. Risa turned to Virena, who was sitting up groggily. "Go back to sleep. It was just a nightmare."

Harris Emstead came up, saying, "Let me."

Valleroy watched him tuck the sleepy child in and knew he missed his grandchild. Virena surrendered to sleep, dead to the world, limp as a sleeping baby.

Lenis and one of her scouts paused a few feet away, and Klyd motioned them back to patrol, saying, "No problem."

Muryin was wide awake, blankets twisted, underwear rolled up as if she'd fought through the night. Klyd put a hand on her shoulder and searched her face, zlinning. "Come, let's have tea and talk about it," he suggested.

Muryin agreed, flipping her hair back. Younger than Virena, she was nearer the threshold of maturity.

By the time Valleroy returned from dressing, Klyd, Muryin, and Dsif were toasting bread on long sticks while waiting for the teapot to boil.

Klyd moved over to make a place for Valleroy on the log. Muryin pulled her stick out of the fire, the bread smoking deliciously, and held it toward Valleroy. "Careful, it's hot," she said in unconscious imitation of her father warning a Gen.

Valleroy pulled it off the stick. "Thank you."

"What's wrong with me, Dad?" asked Muryin suddenly, hopelessly. "Why do I have such terrible thoughts?"

. Klyd explained to Valleroy, "For the last few days, she tells me, her dreams have centered on killing in First Transfer—nothing atypical of pre-changeover in a Farris, but I didn't expect this for another six months." Klyd took the pot off the fire, added tea leaves, and set it aside to steep. "But I think we still have two or three months. You'll be at Rialite in plenty of time, and I expect to be there before you change over. But I'll talk to Lenis about picking up our pace. Tomorrow I'll send a messenger ahead with one of her scouts to make sure there's a train at Mountain City to take you on to Rialite."

Muryin forced her hands not to mangle her bread and cheese. "Is that necessary?"

"Probably not," Klyd grinned at Dsif, "but your Companion will be happier."

She pulled herself into her best grownup pose and answered gravely, "In that case, we should." She cracked a tentative smile and let herself be sent back to bed.

Klyd sighed, and slid his heels away as he leaned back on the log. "She's frightened, but shen she's brave!" He glanced at Valleroy. "You missed the part about her having lost the sense of when her changeover would be."

Shidoni! "That's unusual, isn't it?"

Dsif answered, "In a Farris, yes. Something's disrupted her internal clock. She may be a premature changeover."

Klyd asked, "Dsif, are you sure you can handle it?"

Dsif considered before answering. "The transfer, yes. But there are Farris pathologies I've never dealt with."

Klyd nodded. "I'll monitor, of course, but I doubt there'll be complications. I just hope she doesn't change over on the trail." He scooped preserved fruit onto his bread. "Eat, then I'll take your field down. There're renSimes at turnover today."

Dsif met Valleroy's eyes and made a face. But all he said aloud was, "Yes, Sectuib."

Valleroy commiserated. No Companion liked not working, and Dsif had been held for Muryin for over a month. Klyd wouldn't risk his not being ready when Muryin was.

As the days dragged on, Risa's dismay grew. She'd been *told* how big Nivet was, and she'd seen the map, but it just hadn't sunk in until she crawled across it on horseback.

As far as a rider could see, as far as she could zlin, there was *nothing*. Maybe once a day they passed the remains of a shack, with some scrawny Simes and underfed children. More often the ramshackle dwellings were deserted—the people dead, scattered, or turned Raider.

After days of riding under the relentless blue sky, the lack of trees, the flatness, the resounding *silence* of the stark landscape, and the nageric featurelessness of the horizons began to tell on Risa's spirits. Sergi felt it too, as did the whole Keon contingent—a sense of being outside the firm confines of reality.

Despite ingrained Keon courtesy, the strain finally spilled onto an outsider—Klyd.

One night, camped at a waystation recently sacked and burned and the water cistern emptied, they huddled about their campfires. Klyd paused by the Keon group, Risa not noticing him as she listened to Ediva explaining to Emstead how the discouraging news from Norwest Territory moved up the date of Zelerod's Doom. She watched Harris Emstead, finding no fear in his nager as he concentrated.

Behind her, she heard Bethany's voice raised in fretful complaint, "Why can't you mind your own business!"

Risa assumed Virena had been asking impertinent questions again. She started to say, "Virena, ask me about it later—" Then she noticed Klyd zlinning Uzziah and Bethany from a distance in his abstracted way that annoyed everyone so.

She stood and turned. "What seems to be the problem?"

Klyd apologized with a formal bow. "I was most impolite. I beg your indulgence."

"You must be tired. Come, sit with us. Bethany, why don't you and Uzziah check the bed sites for snakes?"

When the couple had gone, she said quietly to the other Sectuib, "I've noticed you probing those two. Maybe *I* can help you?"

"No, I don't think so. It's just—I can't quite put my finger on it. Perhaps they'd allow me to deep-probe them?"

Risa hid her shock. Well, here in Nivet maybe it wasn't an offensive request. "We're all uncomfortable here—as you must have felt in the rainforests and bayous. I'll talk to them about it in Capital."

Emstead said, "I'm sorry, but I've no idea what just happened. Would it be rude to ask for an explanation?"

"Not at all," Risa replied. "Bethany and Uzziah are transfer mates as well as husband and wife, which isn't done in Zeor. Being curious, Klyd zlinned a bit too deeply."

"I still don't understand," said Emstead. "They're Sime and Gen, like you and your husband. Given Sime/Gen marriage, what difference does transfer make?"

"Uzziah ambrov Keon is a renSime," said Klyd.

Emstead threw Risa a helpless glance. She elaborated.

"Channels can do their work only with Companions to serve their need. Our work, as Klyd defines it, is to prevent Simes who aren't channels from taking selyn from Gens."

Bewildered, the Gen soldier said, "I know channels have to take selyn from *frightened* Gens because the other Simes would kill them. But if a Gen *isn't* frightened—I've *seen* what happens, from that very first day we rode into Gulf Territory! If Bethany isn't afraid, why shouldn't she give her husband transfer? I've gathered from you two it's—"

"Delightful," put in Sergi. "An emotional high, a peak experience, especially with someone you love."

"Then why—?"

"Because," Klyd interjected, "the renSime on Gen transfer has no conditioning against taking the first Gen who comes along, willing or unwilling, if his transfer partner is unavailable. A Sime who kills will never again be satisfied by transfer."

"He can disjunct," Emstead said firmly. "I've *been* asking questions, Sectuib Farris; I know the basic facts."

"No, Harris," Risa reminded him, "a Sime cannot disjunct after First Year."

"Oh—yes, I remember. But I don't understand why you don't simply educate all your Gens not to be afraid. People aren't afraid of what they understand."

"Are you saying you're not afraid?" challenged Klyd.

"Of you? I understand only a trained Companion who's spent years developing his selyn capacity can provide for a channel, but channels don't want people like me. No, I'm not afraid of you, nor am I afraid of someone like Uzziah. I'm sure I could give transfer without getting killed."

"Harris, that's courage talking, not fearlessness," said Hugh, glancing to Klyd for corroboration. He was right. If a Sime attacked Emstead, he'd attempt transfer in *spite* of fear, an act which would leave him very dead.

"You're not ready," Risa told him gently. "You may be one day; you're right, facts drive out fear. In Gulf, we teach our children all the facts we know, so new Gens won't fear. Along with our program of identifying channels among the juncts, education has reduced kills to the minimum. In another generation, juncts will be a vanishing minority."

Emstead mulled that over. "That's a problem. As a troop commander, I want courage in my men, not fearlessness! Men who truly lack fear also lack caution. They charge headlong into danger and get killed—murdered. They die."

Ediva spoke up. "You are a wise man, Harris Emstead. The uses of caution are taught in Dar. You aren't ready to judge Sime attacks, so if a junct attacks you, use the technique Hugh and I taught you; don't attempt transfer."

"But go on learning facts," added Sergi. "And forgive Klyd if he seems impertinent in his search for information," he added, to Risa.

Risa acknowledged her Companion with a nod. Klyd was more than half scientist, she realized, and part of his boorishness stemmed from his absorption in his puzzles, his ability, honed by channel's work, to go into total concentration at the flick of a nager.

They left the waystation when one of Lenis' returning scouts reported movement on their backtrail that zlinned unfriendly.

The next waystation was intact, well supplied with food, but low on water. The next one had been destroyed.

Two days later they were on short water rations, enduring the dry heat that made Risa shiver at dusk and waken with cracked lips. Lenis' advance scout returned with a stranger who took off his wide-brimmed hat and waved them off the trail, shouting, "Wagon-train coming!"

From the heat haze and dust emerged wagons drawn by as many as twenty mules, two Sime drivers per wagon, and, in the distance, Gens. Cargo *and* a Pen shipment in the same train? And no Dar guards? Risa rode forward with Sergi, Klyd, Hugh, and Lenis, to listen to the exchange of news.

The wagon master, a junct renSime, met them at the side of the road. "Can't stop t'chat, folks. Stock's too tired to get started again. How's water up ahead?"

"Bad," replied Lenis and outlined the situation.

The wagonmaster was old, skin leathery, teeth missing. He absorbed the news phlegmatically. Risa concentrated to cut the old man's dialect. "We hada shovel our way through some of them passes. You got two, mibbe three days to the Tuck River—it's near dry. Where you headin'?"

"Mountain City," replied Klyd. They would lay over there and split their train, so he and Risa could go north to Capital while the children went on to Rialite.

"Don't recommend it, I don't. I tried t' make a delivery there, but Raiders had it surrounded. Barely got 'way with our cargo—picked up the gov'ment Gens later. Their Guards died in a 'ttack by a small band o' Raiders."

He surveyed them. "Say, ain't that a Zeor claok?" They were covered with ocher dust, but bright blue showed at the creases. Klyd introduced himself.

"Shen! Here I am starin' death down the gullet, an' I meet a living legend! Well, you take a little advice from an old wagoneer. The sooner you get offin' this 'ere eyeway, the safer. Go into Tuck, and take the Gypsy Trail north to Ancient's Valley.

"Keep on Gypsy Trail north a day, you come on a big lake. Circle the lake, but watch out—ain't called Bandit Lake fer nothin'. A couple small towns can sell you supplies—if'n they'll deal with Householders. Pack melt be givin' plenty o' water, but high up it could snow yet.

"Ancient's Valley's mined out, so go 'round it t' the big eyeway t' Capital. Tell 'em to close this here eyeway and send troops t' Mountain City 'afore it's too late. There be bandits takin' tolls on the d'rect road to Mountain, an' a mudslide closed Mission Road. Alla tribes usta live here are movin' south, an' the Gens live there don' like it. You tell 'em Biskor said so, an' nobody knows these parts like Biskor. Biskor ain' gonna travel this road no more. They gotta fin' 'nother way t' get Gens to Konawa nes winter."

Klyd said, "We thank you, Biskor, for the good advice. We have little to offer in return, except a warning that our rear guard has spotted a large angry group behind us. Pass them with all care and give our regards to Konawa."

Risa watched Biskor join the end of his train, the Gen cage wagons lumbering over the hillocks of blown dirt. She coughed and fixed her attention on Sergi. "Closing this road," she said to Klyd as the wagons crept past, "will mean much higher prices in East Nivet next winter. The citizens won't stand for it. Some will spot-raid on their own, and the Gens will retaliate. What's the population of Nivet?"

Ediva edged her horse nearer Hugh's as the cages went by. "Before winter—about a million and a half Simes, not counting Freebanders. But more have died than have changed over, and thousands moved to other Territories. The biggest drop is in Genfarm stock."

"Never mind," said Risa, knowing she'd paled under her sunburn because Sergi nudged his horse closer and focused on her, fighting down his own shock. If even a percentage of Nivet went renegade, Gulf's militia could not handle it. She had come to give her economic solution to Sime/Gen enmity. Now she was fighting for the survival of her homeland. If she failed, Virena and Mor would inherit a House in ruins.

Hugh had translated for Emstead, who now said, "If *more* Simes start raiding us, our government will declare war. We haven't had an all-out border war in over twenty years. Hell and damn! I don't want to fight you people! And I can't fight against my own!"

Risa was still short of turnover, easily able to banish the spectre of failure. "We *will* find a solution. Right now, I think we'd better move on."

As they rode into the wagons' dust, Risa said to Klyd, "We're not prepared to fight our way into a city under siege. And if we did, could the train to Rialite get out?"

Klyd answered, "I'm more concerned about what has become of our scout and messenger. If they've made it into the city, will they still be expecting us to follow?"

"We can't send anyone else after them," protested Lenis.

Klyd asked, "Have you ever used Gypsy Trail?"

"Years ago, when Frihill was mining Ancient Valley. It isn't much of a road, but if Biskor's wagons got down, we can ride horses up if we trade for mountain ponies at Tuck."

"Is it that steep a road?" asked Risa. "I thought the real mountains were far north of us."

"Most people trade horses at Tuck. Of course, we could wait until we get to Ardo Pass for better horses. But at Ardo they'll have the advantage of us—because we *must* trade before going on up to Capital."

Now this, Risa could understand. "Maybe we'd best go on into Tuck, ask some questions as we trade, and plan from there. We're not outfitted for mountain snow travel."

"If it did snow, it would melt quickly. Snow isn't our problem," said Lenis, glancing at Muryin, "time is."

Risa felt Klyd zlinning Muryin, worried. But they had two Companions to handle the children if necessary, with Sergi and Hugh in reserve. Furthermore, either she or Klyd could give a channel an emergency First Transfer. And the child showed no sign of impending changeover. Muryin's childish nightmares indicated nothing but how her father's overprotectiveness had scared her.

"Lenis is right," offered Hugh. "If the situation along this eyeway is so bad, we must get to Capital as quickly as we can. Lenis, wouldn't Gypsy Trail be faster?"

"Not ordinarily" replied Lenis. "It *should* have water and forage—but no Patrollers, and no waystations until Ancient Valley."

"Waystations haven't helped us much," said Sergi.

They were still discussing it the next evening when they arrived at the Tuck River. The road dipped to a mud flat surrounding a damp streak, all that was left of the river.

Ediva eyed the area. "Nasty trap that camp would make. Attackers would have the high ground."

"I want to keep the Gens and children out of the wind," said Klyd. "But you're right, we'll post a guard up there." He pointed to some tilted falsestone rising over the lip of the arroyo. "We'll have plenty of warning."

Lenis agreed, ordered camp set, and called them to discuss their options over her maps. It was always chancy to leave the eyeway. Maps of sidetrails were never up to date. "Too bad you don't have military maps," said Emstead. "I'll bet the Nivet army knows what's passable."

It was nearly dark when Risa noticed the ambrov Dar were not going through their evening gyrations. She scanned the rising ground behind them. Neither she nor Klyd had made a sweep in more than an hour.

"I'm going out to scan our perimeter," she announced.

The Dar had pitched camp at the top of the arroyo, but now they were scattered out among the cactuses and sagebrush in what seemed like a skirmish line, invisible to the eye but clear to Sime senses. Risa climbed a chunk of Ancient falsestone to zlin the distance.

At the edge of her range was the group that had been trailing them. That vague nageric haze was mostly Gen.

There was nothing out there for the ambrov Dar to be skirmishing against, so it must be another of their interminable exercises. The children, with Dsif and Korin, were scouring the dry brush for firewood.

She zlinned upriver, then turned back toward the camp, focusing on the group still huddled over the maps, wishing she could decree they go north.

A sharp, searing snap went through the diffuse ambient. And again—alarm, pain. Risa scrambled back up the slope, zlinning through the gathering dusk. At the right end of the Dar line, Sime fought Sime with deadly intent.

She gave the alarm, then forgot Sectuib's restrictions and sprinted toward the fight. But she hadn't reached the action when another and yet another eruption occurred. The Dar nager rang with a peculiar mixture of precision and ferocity.

Suddenly, three Simes carrying a Genhunter's net and whips joined forces to entrap Risa. She relaxed, and asked conversationally, "What do you want?"

"Children," spat one.

They're hunting preGens for a Genfarm! Virena! But then she recognized them. From the Tecton chambers—they belonged to Amos and Enid Kaneko's group.

"She's that visitor," said one of the men. "She'd do just as well as his daughter. Grab her!"

Risa, unarmed and no match for three large men, leaped back. Augmenting fully, she ran toward where she zlinned Sergi, the girls, and the two Companions.

One of the Sime attackers netted Muryin and dragged her up the side of a lump of falsestone twice Sergi's height, while his comrades ranged below, defending their position from the ambrov Dar. A woman was climbing the falsestone now—a Gen. *Enid Kaneko!*

Klyd and Hugh arrived just as Risa did. The Sime on the rock held a stiletto to Muryin's eye. Enid threatened, "One more step, and I'll let him murder her!"

Klyd froze, one arm flung out to stop Hugh's headlong plunge. Sergi, Dsif, and Korin, who'd been circling warily to find a nageric advantage, also stiffened. The ambrov Dar ceased fighting.

"We're going to take her," Enid informed them, "and we'll kill her unless you make the Tecton open the Houses to give Gen transfer to anyone who asks. You do that, and we'll send her home. Now back off—we're leaving!"

"Wait!" Klyd surged forward calling, "Wait! She's close to changeover—you're not a Companion—"

Enid snarled, "I was a good enough Companion for my husband—who died because of *your* prejudices! If your daughter changes over, I'll give her First Transfer and not care if she kills me. Who can live in a world that separates Simes and Gens! So hurry back to your precious Tecton, Sectuib Zeor, or your Heir will be dead—or junct!"

Dsif took two strides and stopped as the kidnappers leveled throwing knives at him. "I'm a Companion. I'll go with you."

Risa felt Klyd's objection die on his lips. Nobody breathed as Dsif moved cautiously forward, talking swiftly. "She's a Farris and going to be a channel. You could never satisfy her, Enid. She'd kill you and turn on your Simes. Or she'd die, and you'd have no hold left on Klyd. He'd turn Zeor on you, and I doubt any of you would survive."

More renegades gathered as he spoke, and Risa feared some of the Dar must have died out there. Klyd was doing something with the fields that blurred out the approaching Dar. She watched and zlinned as Enid assessed her followers. The Simes were edgy, Dsif's words penetrating: they had followed a woman who had no care for her own life—and while she might throw it away in juncting Muryin, that would leave them still alive to suffer Klyd's revenge.

Still talking, Dsif mounted the falsestone to where Muryin had ceased struggling, the stiletto against her closed eyelid. Enid had control of that Sime. Muryin's fate rested on the nager of a distraught, suicidal Gen.

"Enid," Dsif pleaded, "you have suffered a terrible loss, but Amos died for a dream. Harming Muryin won't help that dream come true. Let me come with you so Muryin will be safe while you bargain with the Tecton." As he climbed, his field vied with Enid's for control of the Sime with the Stiletto. While all attention was riveted on Dsif, the surviving Dar were gathering at a distance further than a renSime might notice.

Risa got set to augment fully, climb the falsestone, and snatch the captor's dagger the instant the Dar moved. There just might be a chance—

Suddenly the ambient went searing white—pure nerve overload. It had three centers—Dsif, Hugh, and Sergi.

When it was over, Risa was on top of the falsestone, her hand and tentacles gripping the renSime's hand, still wrapped around the stiletto. But the man was slumped in death. The stiletto was buried shaft deep in the eye of Dsif—whose deathshock slammed through Risa's nerves like nothing she'd ever felt before. Behind her, Muryin strangled back a scream.

Risa's eyes fixed dazedly on the selyn-rich blood of one of the bravest, most skilled Gens she'd ever known. *But he had saved his charge's life!*

CHAPTER EIGHT

Ardo Pass

Valleroy saw Dsif's plan, and prepared to help him slam the renSimes while protecting Klyd. Dsif was high field, Valleroy only quarter-high. "Klyd, can we do it?"

Klyd would never yield to blackmail. Muryin—and Zeor— could be destroyed even if her captors didn't murder her outright. They had one chance.

"Yes," Klyd answered without moving. "I'll take care of the Dar. Do it, Hugh, and don't protect me. I'll signal when Dsif's ready."

Dsif, talking persuasively, mounted the falsestone one tiny step at a time. Then Klyd flicked a tentacle, saying silently, "Now!"

Valleroy contracted his field by concentrating on his center, then flung it wide with all his power.

Dsif lunged for Muryin and knocked her aside.

Simultaneously, Risa streaked across open ground and leaped to the falsestone prominence under full augmentation—almost faster than Valleroy's eye could perceive. She landed on target, seizing the Sime's stiletto hand, but the dagger was already buried in Dsif—blood fountaining.

Nearby renSimes collapsed, some dead before they hit, others screaming in agony.

Enid leaped toward Muryin, but Risa, staggered from the Genslam, nonetheless seized the Gen woman and flung her off the prominence.

Battle erupted. Sergi and Emstead defended Muryin's refuge, Emstead using what they had taught him that first night out from Konawa. He *was* merciful; the attacking Sime died instantly.

Klyd crumpled bonelessly to the ground.

Companion's experience overrode Valleroy's combat training. Forgetting the battle, he focused wholly on Klyd.

With his artist's talent, he visualized moments they had shared: their first transfer under the cathedral arc of evergreen trees, when he'd learned the meaning of need and fulfillment; the day Klyd had dug the first shovel of dirt for Rior's foundation, pledging Zeor's support to Rior as a daughter House; the moment their eyes met over Aisha's dead body, and they'd heard Muryin's first cry, knowing they were both father to that baby; the day Klyd had confessed he could not survive without Valleroy's transfer.

Don't die now. Not yet.

He fought despair until, deep inside himself, he felt the distinctive sensation of selyn field engagement.

The Genslam, followed by Dsif's deathshock, had shocked Klyd's systems, just as it had nearby renSimes', and *stopped* the pulse of selyn consumption.

Klyd responded to Valleroy's imposed rhythm. He felt the channel's heartbeat thumping erratically until it synchronized with his own. He felt his breath, warm on his face. Klyd struggled to focus his eyes. "Muryin—"

Valleroy looked toward the falsestone.

The fighting had ceased. In the distance, retreating figures ran at augmented speeds. Nearby, the fallen were being tended by Risa and the less badly wounded. On top of the falsestone, Muryin knelt over Dsif's body, sobbing while Virena and Korin comforted her. Around Klyd and Valleroy there was a ring of dead bodies where the Dar had defended them as Valleroy labored to save Klyd's life.

Valleroy called for a stretcher team.

"No, I can get up," Klyd protested. "I've got to see to the wounded."

"Idiot," replied Valleroy. "*You* are wounded!"

Risa worked her way across the battlefield, Sergi at her side. A pair of Lenis' scouts brought a litter made from a blanket and two Dar staves.

Klyd struggled up, then bowed his head into his hands as he almost blacked out. Valleroy pushed him down. "We carry you back to camp. Companion's orders."

Klyd had no choice but to lie quietly while the scouts shifted him onto the litter and Risa made a lateral contact examination. Risa had been closer to Dsif's slam than Klyd, and showed no effects at all. If it weren't for her sturdy toughness, they wouldn't have *either* top channel.

She stood back. "I can't zlin any permanent damage. We've plenty of fosebine. You'll be all right by morning."

She signalled Sergi. "We'll tend the wounded. Enid Kaneko is dead, along with two of the Dar—"

Klyd started up. "Ediva!"

Valleroy had last seen Ediva with the crew digging for water in the riverbed. "Go find her!" urged Klyd.

Valleroy's feet took a step of their own accord, but duty brought him up short. "No, I've got to stay with you."

"She's fine," Risa told him. "I saw her with the Dar burial detail."

As they lifted him, Klyd called, "Risa—take Dsif's final donation—please. I—can't do it."

She eyed him with a peculiar expression, then nodded and went on about a channel's business.

Klyd slumped back onto the litter, saying, "Her handicap can be an advantage. I couldn't stand up now if my life depended on it. She augmented into the heart of that slam—

even ignoring *Sergi's* contribution—and came out of it on her feet! Got to admire that woman.''

Sergi helped? A person could do worse than to make such friends.

It was past midnight by the time the bodies were buried, the wounded tended, and the horses—which had been driven off by the attackers—gathered and staked out again.

Klyd had slept under Valleroy's constant attention, a discipline which left Valleroy exhausted yet unable to sleep. Korin and Sergi had worked for Risa, healing.

Korin was curled up under a blanket near the fire, and Sergi was reclining beside Risa, his hat tipped over his face. Klyd, able to sit up now, was drinking tea with Risa, discussing their losses.

"Muryin finally fell asleep about two hours ago," reported Risa. "I gave her a double dose of fosebine. If she sleeps the night through, she'll adjust."

Klyd nodded, but Valleroy thought he accepted the information without agreeing with Risa's prognosis. "You said we lost some horses," prompted Valleroy. "How many?"

"Three. But now we're twenty-four riders, and forty horses. We can trade for enough mountain ponies."

"That wasn't my concern," said Klyd. "Zeor's credit would be good in any case. What do you mean, twenty-four? We only lost two of the ambrov Dar—"

"Sahyiden died while you slept. He'll be remembered."

Sahyiden ambrov Keon had been among those defending Klyd while Valleroy worked to save his life.

"I'm sorry," said Klyd. "I gave Keon safe-passage."

"How could we stay out of a fight to save Muryin? Any child—but especially the child of a friend." She leaned forward so the light fell on her sunscorched face, etching painful shadow lines that for once made her look her age. "Klyd, this alliance can't be just Gulf Territory and Nivet Territory. It's got to be *personal*, too, or it won't work."

He looked at her a long time before he said, "Yes. It must be so. Now—how did they get through our defenses?"

"They bought Gens from Biskor and stayed far enough behind us so we'd think the Gen nager was theirs. Then they dispersed to re-converge on us tonight. I can't imagine why they'd try such a stupid thing.''

"Wasn't so stupid," said Sergi from under the wide brim of his hat. He poked it back and sat up. "They'd stashed Gens to kill when they returned from the battle, and they didn't come at us in need because they knew there weren't any killables with us." Valleroy glanced at Emstead and realized that the man was no longer vulnerable. "They weren't stupid, just desperate. But *why* are they so desperate?''

Klyd nodded in agreement. "That's bothered me ever since Amos died in the Tecton chamber. These people—the leaders anyway—have a sense of desperation that zlins like need frustration. They all belong to a type my grandfather called 'delicate juncts.' If they don't die of winter plague, they develop some debility or disorder, then deteriorate as if the body can't hold itself together any longer.

"The worst tragedy of the 'delicate juncts' is that they die just when their children require parenting the most. Their children often go Raider for lack of guidance. Their grandchildren come to take pride in Raiding and create the huge Freeband Raider combines—such as devastated Maple Territory ten years ago.''

"Grandchildren?" asked Sergi, helping himself to tea and a handful of sunflower seeds.

"My grandfather observed long-range patterns and identified many types. He taught me to identify the 'delicate type' because he felt it was very important.

"Ediva belongs to that 'delicate type.' So did Amos, and a remarkable percentage of his followers.''

Valleroy had heard it all before, but he listened until Klyd ran down, and then offered his usual comment. "It's all academic until you discover how to keep them from dying young. As things stand, Householding 'delicates' don't live appreciably longer than juncts.''

"It's not their lives that provide the clues, Hugh, it's their deaths. There's something—ghostly—about the way they die. Amos was stripped of selyn by a junct channel; Muryin's captor died from a field stunning." He glanced sheepishly at Valleroy. "I didn't mean to zlin that, believe me, but it's important!" He appealed to Risa, frustrated, "It's as if they die *twice* in rapid succession! You were closer—surely you zlinned it?''

Risa looked from Valleroy to Klyd. ''You were zlinning field gradients when your daughter was about to be murdered?''

Sergi, too, stared at Klyd, father to father, making no attempt to hide his shock.

''He couldn't reach her in time,'' said Valleroy, ''but of course he was zlinning.'' Valleroy saw a crumbling of their new accord, and added, ''He had to cue me to the slam.''

Mollified, Risa asked, ''What if the solution to the longevity of the 'delicates' is direct Gen transfer?''

''I have considered that,'' answered Klyd. ''I don't know. They'd be vulnerable to going junct. I wouldn't do that to any ambrov Zeor, so how could I sanction it for anyone else?''

She said, ''There's no point arguing that now. We must decide what to do tomorrow morning.''

''We'll stay here until everyone can ride,'' said Klyd, ''so as not to split our party. I must examine Muryin. A shock such as she's just had could precipitate changeover.''

Risa climbed to her feet. ''I'll check Virena in the morning, too. If we can't all ride, we can send someone into Tuck to bring back wagons.''

''I'm feeling much better,'' said Klyd. ''I'll stand watch while you sleep, and in the morning, if Muryin is all right, I'll ride into Tuck.''

As Risa and Sergi went off to their bedrolls, Valleroy stared at Klyd, aghast. ''Ride—! Listen—!''

''I'll be fine by morning, and you'll come with me. I'm not going to send a renSime into Tuck until I've scouted it. So get some sleep. I'm going to see which of the Dar can go with us without leaving this party defenseless.''

The drought had made Tuck nearly a ghost town, but they were able to rent wagons and buy water. The next night they all stayed in a deserted hotel, replete with dust, packrats, and spiders. But they managed hot baths and laundry.

The following day they traded horses, bought mountain supplies, and prepared to move out at dawn, still considering routes. Klyd stood at the window of the hotel's dining room, gazing into the weed-choked street. He stiffened. ''Risa?''

Behind him, Risa turned from braiding Virena's hair. "What do you zlin?" she asked, coming to the window.

Klyd said, "Come on! Someone get Lenis!"

Sergi snapped over his shoulder, "Virena, run get Lenis! She's out back by the barn." And he followed the channels shoulder to shoulder with Valleroy.

They ran west along the main avenue of the town. Coming around the town hall at the far end were two men on horses, slumped with weariness. As Klyd ran toward them, Risa exclaimed, "Those are the men we sent to Mountain City!"

Others of their party had come out of the hotel behind them, and all began to converge on the two weary Simes. "Come on inside—" Risa began, obviously using her field to ease the scout's need until he could have transfer.

The man sighed in relief, then said, "Wait—there are two Gen soldiers behind us. They helped us escape."

Sure enough, Valleroy could see two riders stopped at the edge of town. Harris Emstead moved past the small group and called, "Come on in, boys—it's safe now!"

They *were* boys, Valleroy saw. Neither of them could have been more than twenty. They looked vaguely familiar—

"Colonel Emstead!" one of them cried, sliding down off his horse. "You *are* here! And safe—thank God!"

"Joe—Joey Madison—what are *you* doing here? And Jesson—God, it's good to see you! But why?"

Joe Madison swallowed hard and nodded toward the two Simes. "The Major—he was gonna torture them. After what we saw over in Keon, I . . . I sneaked in to talk to them—found out they knew you were alive."

"We couldn't persuade Major Travers, Sir," put in the one called Jesson. "We were sent to his border outfit for talkin' about what we saw in Keon; he threatened to put us in the stockade if we didn't shut up. Dammit, I wouldn't have my right arm if that lady right there hadn't of healed it!" he said vehemently, looking toward Risa.

"So," Madison continued, "we decided the army was wrong. And that's the end of my career. My Dad—"

"He'll understand," said Emstead, "eventually. Now come on in and eat and rest. There's so much to tell you!"

While the channels gave the two weary Simes transfer,

everyone pitched in to care for the starved horses, and find the four refugees clean clothes, bath water, and a hot meal. It was only after Emstead had tended his men and Klyd had taken their fields down that the Gens rejoined the group.

"What happened to you?" Klyd asked.

The scout answered, "We tried to get through to Mountain City. Can't be done. Gen Border Patrol has claimed the eyeway from two days' ride west of here all the way to Mountain. They're massing to defend that border from the Raiders who've got Mountain City. They'll move south once they've used up everything in Mountain, and the Gens know it."

He looked to Lenis. "We were captured by a Gen Patrol, but these two men helped us escape." He turned his eyes bleakly to Klyd. "Gens hang traitors, you know. We had to bring them along. By yesterday we had to warn them to stay away from us."

"You did well," Risa spoke up. "And both you young men are welcome at Keon; never fear you'll lack a home or friends after what you've done for us."

"Thank you, ma'am," said Jesson shyly, "but I was just payin' you back. I don't know if you remember me, but I'll remember you all my life. I been prayin' for you every day since you healed my arm—though I ain't been inside a church since. After Keon, I can't believe Simes are devils."

Recognizing that the boy had lost something that had great meaning in his life, Valleroy said, "You'll find a church here you'll be more comfortable with—not Church of the Purity, but Church of Unity." Although formal religion had never meant anything to him, he felt a warm glow at seeing the sadness in Jesson's eyes replaced by hope.

Klyd declared, "That's it, then. We go north on Gypsy Trail, and then try to find our way to Capital."

They rode through rising countryside, bleak and sere at first, then gradually greener.

Along the way, Valleroy learned that the two young soldiers had been assigned to Emstead's command just as Valleroy had so many years ago. Emstead had been a captain then, but as he moved up through the ranks he had kept his reputation for turning the "difficult" recruits into loyal soldiers. Difficult recruits were older, or better educated, or more intelligent, and had to be handled with more delicacy than everyday Church of the Purity farm boys to keep them from becoming sullen time servers or candidates for court martial.

Valleroy, whose mother had established as a Gen and escaped Sime Territory, had been ''difficult'' because he had not imbibed the values of a multi-generational family of Gens. His artistic temperament hadn't suited him to army life either. But Emstead had bullied and cajoled him through, displaying the same sound common sense with which he now coped with the drastic change in his life, and then recommended Valleroy for the intelligence service where he had made a short career.

Madison and Jesson had not been friends until they returned from Gulf, bound together by experiences that separated them from the other men.

Joe Madison, Valleroy discovered, was the well-educated son of General Joseph Madison. The General had seen to it that his only son, whom he expected to follow in his footsteps, was assigned to his old buddy Emstead. Jesson, on the other hand, seemed an unusual soldier to be sent to Emstead. Farm boy; uneducated beyond reading, writing, and the simplest arithmetic; raised in the Church of the Purity—the kind of recruit any officer could handle.

''But the boy's brilliant,'' Emstead confided to Valleroy. ''He never had a chance for education, but I planned to get him into officer's training.''

The next day they wound south, then north again, to a wide river roaring with snow melt. At the ford, a large party of Householders gathered, studying the rapids.

Klyd squinted at the mauve and yellow House colors and identified, ''Householding Mountain Bells!''

Lenis said, ''They raise horses in a valley east of here. The Bell mares are the best breeders sold in Ardo each spring. Come on, let's find out what they're doing.''

The Mountain Bells leader introduced herself as Morningstar, second channel in her House. ''We're going to Ardo—haven't you heard?''

''We've been on the trail for the last two weeks.''

''Ardo's been snowed in twice in the last month. Word just

reached us that their spring shipment of Gens was wiped out by an avalanche. We're going up to offer them channel's transfer until the emergency shipment gets there. If they're in bad enough shape, we'll look good!''

Lenis said, ''We expected the storms would be over.''

''Probably are now,'' agreed the native of the region. ''But that won't help Ardo much. With the Gen shortage, it's bound to be weeks before another shipment. If we can get in, it will be miracle enough. Zor, our eldest weatherwatcher, predicts another few weeks of hard freeze up there. He's seldom wrong; it's death to be wrong in these mountains.''

Lenis nodded. ''Then you can guide us around Ancient Valley? It's been years since I've been there.''

She gestured to one who had been studying the river. ''Tirlis was there last fall.''

Tirlis tipped his broad-brimmed hat back. ''First we've got to cross this. Current's vicious. Might lose some horses.''

Valleroy dismounted with Klyd to inspect the river. Risa gnawed her lip, probably zlinning the current and the bottom. Then she asked for his sketch pad.

She scratched a few numbers, then parked the stylus in her mouth and paced off a distance upstream before zlinning the situation again.

Sergi went after her, snatching the notebook before she could say anything. ''Oh, no you don't. *I'll*—''

''Don't be ridiculous,'' she answered, then raised her voice to call to the others over the rush of the water, ''I can get a line across for you. Then we can rig a trolley.''

Tirlis interrupted, ''We don't have enough rope.''

''We have plenty,'' replied Lenis.

In the end Tirlis, using Risa's calculations, made the swim across with a line. They catapulted him dry clothes and firestarters. In two hours they had built a bosun's chair to transport the children, the Gens, and the cargo. Then several of the more river-wise Simes, Risa included over Sergi's protests, got the horses across.

Exhausted but triumphant, they camped on the far bank that night. The harrowing crossing made instant friends between the two groups. When Keon was introduced as a Gulf Householding, Morningstar was amazed.

Risa explained her trade proposal.

"Might work. We can trade horses, wool, and goat's cheese. We could use grain and beans for next winter. There won't be any from the flatland Genfarms this year."

The next morning, they sent a messenger back to their House requesting a voting proxy for Morningstar, who had decided she must go to Capital with them. "We pledge to our Mountain Bells which are heard echoing far and wide, as we expect our deeds to be felt everywhere. We live in the most secluded valley, but we are still part of the world."

Klyd nodded. "So you sent your best to help Ardo."

"Yes, you do understand," replied Morningstar, much enchanted by the Farris presence.

They left two of the lines for the messenger to use to catch up with them and set out into a real climb.

Later, where the trail widened, Morningstar rode between Valleroy and Klyd. "I've been assuming you'll stop at Ardo and help us with the juncts. You will, won't you?"

"Of course. But if the road's open, none of us will be needed there."

"*If* the government Pens deliver! That's become less and less certain lately, you know."

Three days after fording the river, they skirted Ancient Valley on a road rutted by wagons like Biskor's twenty-mule monsters. The cold deepened as they climbed yet again, on the eyeway which stretched south behind them to Mountain City, and north to Capital. Spring thaw had washed out some sections, and giant trees lay across the road.

Morningstar explained, "By now government crews should have cleaned all this up, but they've been conscripted. There's going to be a war."

"There already is a war," replied Valleroy bleakly.

"No," said Emstead. "Not yet, but there soon will be."

The horses, as well as their riders, had to accustom themselves to the altitude. With each succeeding stop to clear the road or detour around an obstruction, they worked more slowly.

"There's only one cure for it," said Morningstar, frustrated. "Time. We won't be able to give decent transfers unless we give our blood time to adjust."

They shared their trail rations with the lowlanders, claiming diet speeded adjustment, but they pushed the pace.

And then came the storm.

It was a freak howler, sweeping from the north, then swirling east on icy winds. Caught without shelter, they were pinned down a whole day under evergreen lean-tos.

Daylight hours were lengthening, however, and the next day they moved camp to a Shrine of the Starred Cross five hours' ride up the road through knee-deep snow.

They found the stone cabin already occupied by a band of gypsies. Valleroy had never seen this tribe before. They had no wagons with them, only donkeys loaded with their goods.

They recognized the mauve and yellow of Mountain Bells, readily acknowledged Zeor, and made room for the sopping wet travelers. Valleroy ended up sharing the Shrine building with all the gypsy Gens as well as the Companions, while all the Simes made camp outside.

When it was quiet, Emstead asked, "What is this place?"

"A Shrine of the Starred Cross," translated Valleroy as he fished his own starred cross out of his shirt and matched it to the one inscribed on the tags of Emstead's white enameled Keon chain. "Nobody knows where the symbol came from. But every child in-Territory knows if they go Gen, they can find safety in a Shrine like this, and a way to the border. They're stocked with provisions and copies of this symbol." He pointed to one hanging on the wall.

Sergi, whittling another of the emblems, added, "Have faith in the starred cross, and do not fear the Sime in need, the sign says. It's true. Surely you know of refugees who've made good lives out-Territory?"

Valleroy answered for Emstead, "My mother was one."

Sergi threaded the new cross on a thong. "Junct law forbids aiding escaping Gens. We don't respect that law."

At the smell of gypsy cooking, Valleroy wanted to join Klyd in the cold. But his field was rising. If he went out to shiver through the night, it would keep the Simes awake. After a while he fell asleep, and when he woke, the gypsies— and every trace they'd ever been there—were gone.

"They left before dawn," reported Klyd, who'd had watch

duty. "They hardly made a sound—the babies didn't even cry." He shrugged. "Gypsies."

The going was rough that day against the new snow. But soon the road melted clear, and they climbed onward.

The trip to Ardo normally took about a week. It took them almost twelve days, the last two fighting over a mountain of snow that choked the narrow entry to Ardo.

"There's nageric texture up there," insisted Klyd when Risa said the place felt dead. "Gens—Simes, too. But it's very weak and far off. Maybe beyond the village itself."

It was noon, the sun brilliant in a Zeor blue sky, when they broke through the last wall of snow and stumbled around a turn in the eyeway where the Ancients had carved the living rock to their convenience.

The corrals and barns, race track and fancy hotels of Ardo Pass, one of the most vital trading hubs in Nivet, lay before them, blanketed with pristine white. There wasn't a human track to be seen—rodent, wolf, horse, even bird, but no human tracks. At the far end of the long, skinny township that lined the walls of the pass, another party could be seen standing dazed after breaking through the ice and snow clogging the northern entry to the town.

Lenis, who was in the lead, moved out into the open, looking about and zlinning. Harris Emstead was right behind her, followed by the two young Gen soldiers and Ediva, with Valleroy and Klyd close behind. The rest of their party were closing in behind, causing a bottleneck at the entryway.

"I don't like the feel of this," said Emstead. He and the two soldiers drew their guns for the first time, as their only ammunition was what they'd carried with them.

"No, that's the government Pen shipment," said Lenis, waving Emstead back. "Put those things away!"

Klyd, from behind the clog of people between them, shouted, "Lenis! Emstead! Look out!"

From one of the pueblos lining the walls, a lone Sime appeared, looking down at them like one of the vultures they had seen in the desert. Lenis looked up, but the Sime's target was Emstead, the closest Gen to him.

Valleroy slid down and darted through on foot, Klyd on his heels.

The Sime leaped!

Ediva crouched to spring. Valleroy changed intention in mid-stride, aiming now to pull her out of Klyd's way.

The Sime was in mid-air, Emstead staring up at him, stock still, certain he could defend himself—

But not in front of those government Gendealers!

Augmenting, Lenis knocked Emstead against Madison and Jesson, caught the Sime as he shrieked in rage and grasped her arms, pulled her into position, and—

Valleroy screamed as Lenis went white with pain when the attacker pressed the nerve centers to force out her laterals. He tried to entice with his own field, knew Klyd was doing the same, but the mindless Sime was crushing his mouth to Lenis'—

Klyd flung himself onto the attacker, augmenting to pull the Simes apart. The junct dangled limply in his grasp.

Lenis fell, equally boneless. Klyd flung the junct aside and bent over Lenis. People were circling them now, channels on the outside of the ring, facing any other selyn-starved Simes who might show themselves.

Klyd drew Lenis into transfer position . . . but never touched lips. He must have known it was hopeless from the moment he zlinned the kill. Emstead bent over them, demanding, "Help her! She was trying to protect me!"

The channel looked up. "It's no use. She's dead."

"No," Emstead choked. "Why did she do that! Why—?"

Ediva, meanwhile, was staring at what seemed to be unevenly packed snow. But it was only a thin layer, over . . . cloth . . . hair—

Risa returned to the center of the circle from zlinning the buildings around them. "He must have been the last," she said as she bent over the Sime. "Now he's dead, too. I can't zlin any more Simes, except the ones at the other end of the pass. So where is everybody?"

Ediva knelt beside a shape in the snow and gently broke away the encrusting ice.

Two figures emerged—two Simes locked together, tentacles twined in Sime/Sime transfer position, mute reminder of what they had just witnessed.

Ediva said, in a tight, frail voice, "They ran out of Gens

during the storm. And of course, they couldn't get out to hunt—so they turned on each other.''

She rose with the kind of calm that indicates deepest shock. Now they recognized the meaning of the shapes under the snow. Hundreds of such shapes.

She locked eyes with Emstead, who was as pale as the dead Sime at his feet. ''Here—,'' she said with the cruelty of unshielded fact, ''—Zelerod's Doom has already struck.''

CHAPTER NINE

Changeover

Valleroy followed Ediva to another lump in the snow. Ediva shoved the snow aside to reveal another ice-shrouded Sime couple locked in a hideous death struggle.

She rose and staggered out into the pass. In the shocked silence, he could hear the strangled wail of her breathing, not quite a sob.

He started after her, and as if that were a signal, everyone else moved to begin the search for survivors. Klyd caught Valleroy back. ''No, Hugh. You're high field again.''

Harris Emstead came out of his shock, and turned to follow Ediva. ''Dear God,'' he said, ''It's not just arithmetic—it's real!''

Madison and Jesson flanked him, staring mutely at their commander as he tried vainly to comfort the woman.

Ediva was *seeing*—and zlinning—the reality behind her sterile figures. She'd been junct—four kills, Valleroy recalled, before she went to Dar to disjunct. She knew, as neither he nor Klyd ever could, what these people had faced. Without a word to Emstead, she turned into Klyd's arms.

Risa and Sergi searched the snow-covered lumps for survivors while the Mountain Bells people forged ahead to the pueblos and the government drovers. Risa joined Klyd, putting an arm around Ediva from the other side. Good. Risa, too, knew what it was to live junct. Perhaps she could help Ediva even more than Klyd could.

A cry went up. "Survivors! This way!"

A Mountain Bells channel clung to a precarious ladder leading to the top floor of the pueblo. Risa and Sergi stayed to protect Ediva from nageric shock. Valleroy followed Klyd.

He climbed three ladders before noticing how insecure they seemed and how high he'd gone. He had to stop and cling panting, vision blurring. *Shen the altitude!*

At the top, Sime hands boosted him into a dim chamber carved from the living rock, icicles dripping from crevices because the fires had gone out.

Others were crowding up the ladder behind him, so he staggered on into the dimness of the next chamber. Klyd's fingers closed over his shoulder, and a torch flared.

They had found about two dozen children. The babies were crying, diapers unchanged for much too long. The older children stared blankly at the walls, unaware of their rescuers. Several were curled in fetal position, not even covered with the nearby blankets.

One of the Mountain Bells channels knelt beside a still form and peeled a blanket back. "Shidoni!" she swore.

As everyone crowded around, Valleroy saw the corpse's face, the same grotesque horror he'd seen outside—death by the kill. *Some poor renSime was driven to attack a child*!

They found the killer's corpse under a tangled heap of babies clinging to it for insulation from the cold floor. The adult who had stayed to care for the children—probably the one most beloved by them—had killed one of them.

Valleroy had to rush outside to vomit. Klyd came and shook him hard. "We've got to tend the living. Get a fire going—melt some snow and find some food for these children. I'll get our supplies brought in. Move!"

Klyd slid down the ladder, sending the rest of their party back for supplies, then approached the Pen drovers. Valleroy rinsed his mouth with snow, watching Klyd give the juncts orders.

They worked fiendishly all day, caring for the children,

gathering the corpses outside, walling them into one of the pueblo rooms that became the town's mass tomb.

Then the Pen shipment's wagonmaster demanded the children. They were orphans—without relatives to claim them. By law, they belonged to the government Pens.

Mountain Bells offered to take them, but of course that was illegal. "Don't worry," assured the junct, "any of them as goes Sime will be turned loose with a stipend, as usual."

They argued, they threatened, Risa offered money, Klyd offered a Tecton job paying much more than the wagonmaster's job. But he was the one incorruptible Pen employee in all of Nivet. Ardo Pass had taught him how desperately Gens were needed. In the end, they had to watch the children go.

Klyd was withdrawn, hardened to living by junct law. Valleroy demanded, "How can you just stand there!"

"We can't steal their Gens. We'd only get the Householdings destroyed."

"They feel we have more than our share of Gens already," said Risa. "That's the attitude we must change—and not by declaring war. In Nivet, the Householdings are outnumbered."

"If you start a civil war," agreed Emstead, "the Gen Army will simply wipe out those who are left."

"We must get to Capital," said Klyd, "and bargain with the juncts—for all our lives."

It seemed much too small a hope to matter against the horror they left behind in Ardo Pass. Knowing he felt only a pale echo of Klyd's pre-transfer depression, Valleroy focused on how much better the world would look after transfer.

Ediva was riding easily among the Dar, scanning the sides of the trail, the picture of need-sharpened martial alertness. But Valleroy promised himself that tonight he'd be with her while she cried out her frustration in post-syndrome.

They camped at a waystation at the crossroads of two eyeways, theirs going north, and one leading west into the high mountains. The station was huge, with sheds and lean-tos for stock, and chambers with separate entries, enough room for all of them to sleep under a roof.

Uphill, a wild berry patch thrived, with newly ripened fruit despite the snow. Korin, Morningstar, and her Companion took the children to pick some.

Klyd and Valleroy ended up in a tiny room, one wall made from the cliff, the others of solid fieldstone. Risa had taken first watch, leaving them free for transfer. Neither channel had been able to think of it the previous night in the pueblo saturated with death and horror.

Valleroy brought in their bedrolls and saddlebags as Klyd built a fire. He dropped the massive burden and collapsed to catch his breath. "Klyd, do you think we could take transfer before you do Ediva's? She's going to be wild in post-reaction, and I want to be with her."

Klyd shoved a log onto the grate, then inspected Valleroy. The deadening weight of need prevented the experience of emotion, but after transfer, the full brunt of any shock, loss, joy, or sorrow hit the Sime as if it had happened that very moment.

"Hugh, it will be better for Ediva if I serve her before our transfer. Channel's judgment. I'm ready for you right now, but I'm going to wait, for her sake."

Stubborn channel. Valleroy obeyed the channel's call as Klyd had obeyed him, distrusting but compliant, and left the room. He stalked off behind the horse shed where he climbed a rock face to the last patch of sunlight. Peaks rose to the west, lit from behind by the setting sun, wreathed in fair weather clouds, a froth of dark green trees clothing their flanks. The pure air sparkled, the sky's blueness penetrated the soul—Zeor blue.

At another time of Klyd's cycle, Valleroy would have been struck to his core by such beauty. Now, all he felt was clinical appreciation. Mechanically, he sketched the scene, hoping to capture its essence, to paint it later.

After transfer—Their last transfer, after Valleroy had admitted he'd been wrong to heal Ediva, had been great. That had rekindled his *need* to paint. Everything—the bleak, the horrible, the transcendent, inspired his hands. He had sketches of Ardo he never wanted to look at again. But this, he wanted to capture forever.

"What's wrong?"

Ediva's voice startled him.

She gasped and retreated, but he flattened his nager. "Nothing. I was trying not to think about Ardo."

It was the wrong thing to say. She blanched. He was on his feet instantly, his arms around her before he knew it.

"Thank you," she whispered, trembling. "Those children had it worse than I ever have, and they managed to walk proudly into those cage wagons. I've no right—"

"You've every right!" he contradicted. *I must disengage, but without hurting her.* He pushed her back to look into her eyes. "Stay duoconscious," he instructed. "I'm going to let go, even though I don't want to." Very deliberately, he told himself, *I am the biggest menace to her peace of mind. I must let go.*

"Wait," she pleaded as his grip shifted. Her arms went around his neck, tentacles sliding onto his skin under the collar of his jacket. It felt delectible.

From the edge of the boulder they stood on, Klyd's voice boomed, "Hugh! What are you—! *Don't move!*"

Valleroy froze, knowing she had fixed on him in a tremulous, unhealthy way.

Klyd circled them. Valleroy kept his attention on Ediva, gradually leashing back his field.

"Good," whispered Klyd. "Now, very slowly, turn your attention to me. *Don't* deny her—bring her with you."

Valleroy knew the drill, but this was *Ediva*. He couldn't bear what it must do to her to have her Gen *prefer* another Sime, right in her own arms.

He felt her tentacles stir, the laterals leaving moist trails on his neck. *She's got a transfer contact.*

If it was torture to taunt her by turning from her to Klyd, what would it do to Klyd if he let her take transfer?

His field gradually lost its grip on her. Almost of its own accord, his attention drifted to lock onto Klyd.

"Good," murmured Klyd, holding out his arms to Ediva.

Valleroy felt a gut-wrenching shift as the field gradients responded to Klyd's machinations. He never spoke of such physical sensations to Klyd. Simes didn't believe Gens could read fields, so it was no use arguing. But he knew when Ediva shifted focus, went hyperconscious, and locked to Klyd's fields.

Klyd said, "Back me up. Ardo Pass has delivered another blow to her conditioning. She may abort."

What have I done? He should never have let her within arm's reach.

In a dreamlike motion, the two Simes drew together. Tentatively, their lips touched. Ediva seized the contact. Valleroy used all his discipline to keep focus on Klyd, to hold him steady as he fed Ediva the selyn she had to have.

Suddenly Ediva convulsed out of the contact, emitting a strangled scream. Klyd flung both hands wide, as if he'd touched open flame.

Valleroy hung between two equally balanced impulses—to help Klyd—to help Ediva. Companion's training won again, for to support Klyd would soothe Ediva's battered nerves. He circled behind Klyd, shutting out the blazing sunset, the bustling camp below, the slice of moon.

In seconds Klyd regained full command of the fields. He knelt beside the renSime, enticing her back into transfer grip. But a moment of flow and she aborted again with a cry of despair which might have been "Hugh!"

It took everything he had not to respond. *This is wrong. She has a right to take from me, if that's what she needs. I wouldn't even short Klyd.*

Risa's voice pierced the rushing silence like a birdcry, "Klyd? I felt—Ediva!"

The channel turned, focusing duoconscious. In a few terse sentences, he filled Risa in. She glanced at Valleroy then asked Ediva, "Would you let me try? I'm disjunct, too."

"She's under my protection. I can't condone—"

"I wouldn't undermine her disjunction! Surely you know that much about me after all this time."

Ediva drew herself up, cradling her aching arms across her chest. "Dar pledges to die rather than rejunct!"

"Don't worry," said Risa, approaching her slowly. "Come on, there's no problem here. Zlin me; I'll show you."

As Ediva went hyperconscious again, zlinning only, Risa glanced over her shoulder at Klyd for his final agreement. "I've got a solid contact. Shall I?"

"Go ahead," said Klyd guardedly.

Valleroy rested two fingers lightly on Klyd's forearm, avoiding the painfully bulging ronaplin glands and prepared to deal with entran cramps when this was over. Klyd went hyperconscious, abstractedly following the transfer.

Valleroy saw Ediva tense with an abort spasm, but Risa held steady and the spasm relaxed. It happened again, and yet again, and then Risa dismantled the contact with a sigh, waiting for intelligence to come back into Ediva's face.

Slowly, the fierce savagery of need melted away from the renSime's features. But there was no eruption of bliss, no wracking tears, no other response. Ediva finally said, "I guess I'm all right. I'm sorry. Thank you." She was still numb with suspended emotions—not post.

Risa shook her head. "No, I'm sorry. That was rough, but at least you've got selyn to survive the month. It will be better next time."

Ediva's features remained blank as she said, "The Dar are expecting me. I'd better go."

Valleroy kept his grip on Klyd's arm so his hand wouldn't stray after her. "I'll—uh—see you later?"

"I'll—be busy." She turned away with that dull, not quite here, manner. "I guess." At the edge of the boulder, she paused to mold her mouth into a smile. "Thank you, Risa. Klyd. I didn't mean to hurt you."

"You didn't."

"I know I did." Her eyes flicked to Valleroy. "He's yours, and I had no right."

She was gone before Valleroy could object, "Klyd, you can't blame her! I—she never touched me. I took her."

Risa looked from one to the other, puzzled. Klyd said, to her more than to Valleroy, "A channel can't be jealous of a renSime's touch on his Companion."

Risa shrugged, and gave them a crooked grin. "I guess not. Good night."

They followed her back to the building.

The fire had warmed their room nicely, and Klyd had left a pot of gruel which filled the room with the aroma of spiced raisins. Chestnuts were roasting, the teapot steeping. Valleroy wasn't the least bit hungry.

Klyd went straight to his saddlebags, digging out a small notebook, reading by the light of the fire. He found what he wanted and settled down to write up the encounter.

"Klyd, don't you think you could record it later?"

"Hugh, this could be important. You couldn't zlin what happened. Risa didn't hold Ediva by responding to her aborts *faster* than Ediva's reflexes; she overrode the abort reflex with sheer inertia. I've never zlinned anything like it. In the midst of it all, there was that odd *stutter* which is so characteristic of the 'delicate type.' I'd never zlinned it quite like that before."

"Klyd," interrupted Valleroy, "Risa almost destroyed Ediva. Didn't you *see*? I've got to go to her. Please!"

But the channel was writing. "We'll have transfer in just a few moments. It's too late to improve Ediva's transfer; let's make sure we learn something from it." He finished his notations, and set the book aside. "Hugh, I shouldn't have surrendered Ediva to Risa. She's *slow* and—I hate to say it, but what she offered was too close to junct transfer. I didn't know what Risa was going to do. I should have asked before giving her permission, but Ediva couldn't wait. She's in a lot worse shape than you'd think to look at her. *Why* did you go up there with her?"

He explained what had happened. Klyd nodded. "So she gravitated to you. If you two are ever going to have a sex life, we've got to sever that tropism." He kneaded his face with a tentacle, admitting, "I've no idea *how*, without killing her. She's old for a 'delicate'."

A commotion outside brought Valleroy to his feet. Klyd strode to the door just as Morningstar dashed into the outer room. "Klyd, Muryin's in changeover!"

Klyd's shock—and his advanced state of need—wiped out the Mountain Bells channel's joyful excitement in making the historic announcement to a dedicated father.

"Come on, Hugh," called Klyd, and slipped past the other channel. "I don't understand it. I checked her just this past noon, and there was no sign."

Morningstar stretched her legs to pace Klyd. "She's just entering stage one, but it's going very—"

"—fast," chorused Valleroy and Klyd. Valleroy finished, "Of course. She's a Farris channel."

"I zlin it," said Klyd and strode out into the night. If it

weren't for the slip of a moon, Valleroy would have lost him as he circled the building to another entrance.

Valleroy hung back to say to Morningstar, "Please forgive him. We haven't had a chance for transfer."

"His temper's nothing compared to my Sectuib's," she assured him. "And this way, he can assign you to Muryin."

That struck such panic into Valleroy's heart that she cocked her head at him, frowning. "Klyd can manage with Korin ambrov Keon, and if Virena changes over, we can reshuffle assignments to accommodate. Don't worry."

"Hugh!" called Klyd from within, and Valleroy gulped.

"Calm down. I'll go find Risa and Sergi," said Morningstar, thrusting Valleroy around the insulating baffle.

He blundered into a warm, firelit chamber like their own. Muryin was being walked around the room by Korin. "I'm so tired. I want to sit down, Korin. I haven't slept—"

"Nobody slept in Ardo. But you're tired because your body is taxed by early changeover."

"All right, Muryin," called Klyd, beckoning Valleroy over to a pallet of blankets he'd arranged near the fire. "Come sit down. I've got to examine you."

"Dad, I'm not an invalid. Tell Korin to go away."

"Later, maybe. Come on, now, be a big girl." As Klyd made full lateral contact, Valleroy knelt behind him, cutting off Korin's hefty nager.

Klyd finally sat back on his heels and said, "Morningstar's right. Stage one of changeover."

Risa's voice came from the doorway. "You doubted her?"

Muryin sighed resignedly. She'd always known, as heir to the House, that she'd have no privacy in changeover.

"Not really," replied Klyd. "But it always pays to check where Farrises are involved. Right, Muryin?"

The girl was staring at her father's arms. She raised her eyes to his face, then to Valleroy's. "Oh, shen! You haven't even had transfer yet. I'm sorry—"

"Don't swear," reminded Valleroy.

"I wasn't swearing," she countered peevishly. "I meant exactly that—transfer interruption."

"Well," said Valleroy on second thought, "you're almost right. But channels get used to that."

"She's too young for such cynicism," said Sergi, advancing cautiously, testing the field variances as he moved.

Morningstar arrived with her Companion, Saiter, an older woman who looked like tanned leather and moved like greased lightning.

Klyd nodded absently, studying Muryin, undoubtedly pondering who'd serve Muryin's First Transfer.

Sergi placed himself gingerly amid the fields, glancing from Valleroy to Korin, "It seems to be among us three. Shall we flip a coin or cut cards?" He grinned at Muryin. "I wish I had an excuse to claim you all to myself."

The girl blushed, then giggled.

Klyd stroked her face. "You've made a conquest!" She got redder. "Teasing aside, we must discuss it. We'll settle it quickly, and your Donor will come to you immediately. Meanwhile, who would you like to stay with you?"

"Virena?"

"Maybe later—choose an adult."

"Morningstar? And Saiter?"

"Of course we'll stay!" Morningstar moved forward.

Klyd backed off, Valleroy with him, and Risa and Sergi moved too, making the exchange an intricate ballet to hold the field gradient steady over Muryin. Klyd said, "Farrises are tricky in changeover, but Muryin is well trained, and I zlin no pathology. Call me if there's any change—and even though she can't zlin yet, hold the fields steady."

Outside, beyond Muryin's hearing, Klyd rounded on Sergi, *"Why* did you do that?"

Risa, her own need clear to Valleroy's trained senses, bristled at the attack on her Companion, but Sergi forestalled her with a gesture, and answered calmly, "I did it to give her confidence." He raised one eyebrow. "It worked, didn't it?"

"Flattery—" started Klyd.

Risa interrupted, "—is adolescent nonsense. You may not have noticed, Sectuib ambrov Zeor, but your daughter is an adolescent. Sergi was speaking her own language—and you can't deny it. It worked."

Klyd paced. "Yes, it did, but she has to know our choice is made by judgment, not preference or chance."

"That makes it my job," said Korin. He was a top Companion and had not been working for months.

Klyd shook his head. "I've studied your parameters when I've taken your field down. You don't have the response time she's going to—"

"You've never taken transfer from me," argued Korin, a measure of how very much he wanted to do it. One never—ever—argued technical matters with a Sectuib. "How do you know—?"

"He's a Farris," stated Valleroy. "If he says you don't have the response—even if he's never touched you and is judging from across the room—then you don't. Period."

Exasperated, Korin shut his mouth.

Klyd continued, "I know Hugh much better, and he's my primary choice for Muryin."

The betrayal hit Valleroy in the pit of the stomach.

Klyd gasped as if he'd sustained a blow.

Into the stunned silence, Risa said, "Obviously, Hugh doesn't want to do it. I'm perfectly willing to release Sergi for Muryin. I'm sure I won't give Korin any problems."

"Then it's settled," stated Sergi, and Risa took his hand and held it out toward Klyd, the gemstones in their Keon Householding rings gleaming in the flickering torchlight.

CHAPTER TEN

Transfer Shock

With Muryin's transfer settled, Risa turned her will to taking her transfer from Korin.

She'd broken with Sergi before, so it should pose no problem—except that she wouldn't be at her best when meeting all those Householding Representatives in Capital.

But for Sergi it wouldn't be that bad. He had worked with many channels before they'd found torluen. Twice the professional Hugh was, he'd handle Muryin easily.

When Dsif died, she and Sergi had discussed this possiblity. Sergi had pointed out, "If she gets a solid First Transfer, Muryin may grow up to be saner and easier for Gulf to deal with than Klyd is."

Risa had zlinned nothing in Muryin's condition to change that. So both Risa and Sergi were startled to hear Klyd say, "I'm afraid that's out of the question."

Risa stared at Klyd, her astonishment plain in her nager, as was Sergi's and Hugh's. Hugh regained control, hardening his nager into a tense shell as he muttered, "Sorry."

Klyd acknowledged with a tentacle but didn't soften his words. "Hugh's the only Companion here conditioned to Farris draw-speed. Sergi, with all respect, you haven't the response times Muryin will require—nor quite the capacity."

Sergi argued, "That's not what you told Nedd twenty years ago. You wanted me for your own Companion then."

Risa submerged her shock. She'd thought Sergi's interest in serving Muryin was merely professional.

Little things he'd said over the last few months—his knowledge of Farrises when there were none in Gulf—all fell into a pattern. Well, it would be good for him to have his illusions shattered. Lifelong yearnings shouldn't be denied when fulfilling them was so harmlessly appropriate.

Klyd answered, "Sergi, twenty years ago you were young, pliable, and immensely talented. But you've spent too many years working to—different—specifications."

Risa controlled her need-temper. She wasn't accustomed to being called a spoiler of talented Companions. Nor would she allow the insult to her husband, who was smarting at the loss of his treasured opportunity. "Sergi is remarkably adaptable, and our differences aren't so great."

She felt a stir of need-dampened amusement from Klyd. "What seem small differences to you have crippled Farrises."

Risa curbed her exasperation with his hot-house-flower attitude. "Muryin's your daughter, your House heir. We cannot argue your choice; we can only offer our help."

Klyd bowed, "Zeor thanks Keon for its most gracious offer. Seldom has a House had such a generous ally."

Nivet formalities! Then she realized Klyd's unspoken question and replied, "Korin, you have my permission to serve

Klyd." *He'll get that Farris experience he wants, even if Sergi doesn't.*

When they'd rounded the building and were out of earshot of the Zeor group, Risa added, "Good luck to him convincing Hugh. Did you catch his reaction?"

"Yes. Hugh's going to abort. Why doesn't Klyd see it?"

Because he doesn't want to. "What makes you think so?" Risa agreed, but was curious about Sergi's thinking.

"Hugh's face at Dsif's burial—the way he looked at Klyd and Muryin. How he blew the fields when Klyd chose him for Muryin. Klyd denies it, but they must have an orhuen. If so, Hugh can't breakstep, even for Muryin's sake, without Klyd's help."

"But if it's orhuen, why does Klyd pretend it wouldn't even *inconvenience* him to take Korin?"

"You don't know Farrises. He doesn't let half of what he suffers show. And he'll be so busy hiding his distress, he won't notice what's happening to Hugh until it's too late." He gazed off into the darkness. "No telling what he'll do to himself tying not to hurt Korin, but he can't accept me because I might overcontrol him. It's a mess, Risa—a typical Farris-made mess."

For Risa's Companion to so harshly criticize a channel was unheard of. "Sergi," she said, "would you mind if we put off transfer until Muryin's settled?"

"Of course I'll do it!" snapped Valleroy.

"But your heart's not in it," prompted Klyd.

"It will be," promised Valleroy. Muryin deserved the best, and he'd just have to find it in himself somehow.

"I know you mean it," agreed Klyd, pacing between Valleroy and Korin with a kind of hopelessness. "Shen!" Klyd swore, "I wish I could let Sergi do it. Maybe if I'd worked with him as Risa wanted—" At Valleroy's hurt, he added, "Not that I don't trust you, Hugh! Or you, Korin—"

"I trust your judgment," replied Korin. "I'm not Farris trained; I'd just hoped to be one day. I could hardly start by serving First Transfer, could I?"

Valleroy saw Klyd's teeth flash white in the moonlight as he grinned mirthlessly, "But you wanted to?"

Korin grinned back, "Could I hide that? Look, I haven't worked in months. I *feel* I could do it, but I'm no judge at this point. I feel I could do anything."

"Then I won't spare you," promised Klyd, grimly.

Valleroy tried to suppress a pang, but Klyd, ultra-sensitive now, whirled and came to him. "We'll be in Capital before Muryin's second transfer, and we'll find a Farris-trained Companion to escort her to Rialite."

Logic doesn't make one whit of a difference, thought Valleroy. For years, Klyd had refused to accept him as Companion because, though pledged to Zeor, he'd founded Rior—on a philosophy which Klyd couldn't endorse.

It had taken Aisha's death bearing Muryin to waken both of them. Now Valleroy was determined Muryin wouldn't suffer another loss of something she'd never had. *I love Muryin as if she were my own blood. Her need will command my responses. She'll have a transfer to remember all her life!*

His determination was rewarded by Klyd's grin, forced up through need though it was. "I'll be there with you," he promised. "You won't require my help, but I'll be there."

"I'd appreciate that." Valleroy was an expert in change-over pathology, for his House was dedicated to rescuing out-Territory changeover victims. But, though he was expert with changeovers with broken bones, gunshot wounds, concussion, or emotional trauma, he knew little of tending the trained Householding children or the channels.

Valleroy returned to Muryin's room. The fire had been built up and more blankets brought in. Muryin had changed into the stark white yawal—a simple smock made from joining two rectangles of material, leaving arm and head holes. It was the garment in which the Pens delivered Gens to their killers, and in the far past, it had become the traditional garment worn at changeover by those who wished to pledge themselves to the House and a nonjunct lifestyle. The custom had stuck simply because the cheap, disposable garment was so handy for a messy process.

Valleroy asked, "Aren't you cold?"

Muryin looked up. "No. Where's Dad?"

"He'll be along. *I'm* going to give you First Transfer."

"You—but what about Dad?"

"Korin will serve him this time." *Is serving him.* Muryin had never known anyone but Valleroy to serve her father, but she took it with equanimity. He added, "Meanwhile, you and I have some work to do, don't we?"

Valleroy replaced Morningstar and examined his charge closely. The familiar routine let him set aside the cold dread that possessed him when he thought of the near future.

"Don't touch me!" warned Ediva, flinching from Risa.

Risa recoiled from the hysterical edge in the renSime's nager. She'd found Virena, Ediva, Emstead, the two Gen soldiers, and two of the Dar in one of the inn's chambers, sorting berries for cooking.

"I just wanted to see your starred cross," said Risa placatingly. She maintained channel's functional mode, aware her need would otherwise irritate Ediva, who was neither post nor in need. The headache from the aborts Ediva had taken off Klyd was controlled by fosebine, but the frustration from the transfer Risa had forced on her would not dissipate until her next transfer—which ought to be normal enough.

"I'm sorry." Ediva put the cross she'd been showing Virena down. "Its only value is sentimental."

"Only?" asked Risa, pulling out the one she always wore. "Sergi gave me this one when we met . . . when he gave me my first transfer, as opposed to kill."

Ediva's eyes suddenly met hers steadily. Then she looked past Risa to Sergi, and her nager went cold.

Risa understood. "Yes. It's easier for disjunct channels than for renSimes because we have Companions. Ediva, although we monitor the pairings very cautiously, we do *not* oppose direct Sime/Gen transfer at Keon. You've seen Bethany and Uzziah. If you were a member of my House, I'd be seeking high and low for the right Gen match for you. But you do have to understand—whoever the Gen is whose need you can satisfy, it *won't* be Hugh ambrov Rior."

Her words brought a shift in the ambient. Ediva hardened against the long-denied dream, but from Harris Emstead came plaintive Gen yearning. When Risa looked toward him, he smiled sadly. "Poor kid. I sure hope you're right that *someone* can make her feel better."

The two young soldiers looked toward their commander, flat incomprehension in their fields—but when Ediva gave Emstead a grateful smile, Joe Madison studied her, confusion clouding his nager. Risa recognized what Madison was going through: that first identification with an individual Sime's purely Sime problem. Soon he'd be perceiving Simes as people with his heart, not just his mind.

Meanwhile, Sergi was avidly examining Ediva's starred cross. "*This* is a work of art." He turned it over, tilting it toward the firelight. "It's not signed, but I'd swear—Ediva, this is a product of genius! Who made it?"

She shook her head. "I was made to promise not to tell who gave it to me, and not to sell it but to pass it on to someone who'd benefit." Her lips narrowed. "Maybe that's silly, but the Dar say good psychology doesn't always have to look true to the objective mind to be effective. I want to give it to Muryin as a changeover gift."

Reluctantly, Sergi surrendered it. "The starred cross definitely works. Give it to her."

"But what if Zeor doesn't acknowledge—"

Virena said, "Muryin told me Zeor pays to have the shrines of the Starred Cross stocked with food all around their area. I'm sure they respect what it stands for."

Ediva asked, "Can I get in to see her now?"

"I think there's still time," said Risa. "Come on."

Virena got up. "May I come, too?"

Risa pondered. Her daughter had been trained for changeover. Sergi said, "Muryin was asking for you. She'd be pleased by a *brief* visit."

Risa, last out the door, heard snatches of conversation erupting in their wake, every third word *Muryin*. Something about Farrises made them the subject of more gossip than anyone. Even the Gen soldiers were asking questions. She could never divine what was so fascinating about them, but on this trip, she'd learned intimate details of six unrelated Farris families. And they all sounded just like Klyd.

Risa preceded them into Muryin's room to command the fields and cushion the effect of their entry. Muryin lay under a pile of blankets, eyes closed, panting. Risa could barely zlin her through Hugh's field, but he whispered, "Transition to stage four. She'll be fine in a minute."

Risa said, "Permission to bring in a renSime, a child, and my Companion."

Without turning, Hugh muttered, "Just hold the fields steady." He paid them no further heed until Muryin gave a huge shuddering sigh, opened her eyes, and sat up.

"Virena!" Muryin exclaimed, then added with adult stoicism, "It's not so bad, really." Her gaze lit on Risa, a wild surmise increasing her selyn consumption. "Is something wrong with Dad?"

"No!" assured Risa. "I came to bring Virena and Ediva. We can't hold much of a changeover party out here."

Ediva held out the starred cross. "For you."

"Ediva, it's gorgeous! But so valuable—I can't—"

"There's a price—two conditions. Never say where it came from, and when the time comes, you must give it to one who'll be helped by it and exact the same promises."

Muryin cupped it in both palms, inspecting the roseate gleam and the intricate carving. Her forearms showed the swollen welts of tentacle sheaths, still sealed at the wrists, the immature organs confined in their fluids. Risa was astonished at how quickly she'd developed. This had to be abnormal. *Where is Klyd, anyway?*

"Put it on," prompted Ediva.

Muryin slipped the chain over her head. "Thank you, Ediva. It's beautiful!"

"I wish I had something for you," put in Virena.

"Your company is enough," said Muryin, reminding Hugh, "Dad said she could come later, and it's later."

"Is it all right, Mama?" asked Virena.

Risa nodded, "*If* you leave quietly when Hugh tells you. Sergi, wait for me here. Ediva, you'd better not stay."

Ediva backed away. "Congratulations, Muryin."

Muryin caressed the exquisite carving. "Thank you."

Outside, Risa heaved a sigh as she let go of the fields. "Have you any idea where Klyd went?"

"Might be patrolling the perimeter," suggested Ediva.

Risa nodded. That was just the sort of warped sense of

duty she'd expect from Klyd. "If you run across him, tell him he should check on Muryin soon."

Circling the waystation in search of Klyd, Risa was delayed by the usual channel's duties—a sprained ankle to start healing, a transfer appointment to schedule, a few reassuring words about Ediva's condition, news of Muryin's progress, and a consultation about a worn shoe on her horse.

Morningstar met her on high ground half way around the perimeter. "Everything's clear as far as I can zlin," she reported. "You haven't had transfer; you can't be on watch yet?"

"I'm looking for Klyd," answered Risa.

"Last I saw, he went that way with Korin."

"Oh." *He can't—oh, yes he could!* She couldn't zlin Klyd because he was in one of the thick-walled inner rooms, with Korin. "Thank you. I'll be back to stand watch."

"Don't worry. I can handle it until Muryin's through."

Risa hurried back down the hillside.

"You can't go in there—private—" One of the ambrov Dar was guarding the entry to Klyd's room, set behind an insulating antechamber. It made an excellent transfer room. Risa couldn't zlin any nageric leakage. "I've got to speak to Klyd."

"The Sectuib gave instructions not to be disturbed."

"His daughter—"

"I heard. He's got it timed. Why don't you wait?"

It was almost midnight. Anything could be happening to Muryin. She weighed alternatives, then said, "I'm going back to check on Muryin. Tell Klyd—"

A surge in the nager announced Klyd. "Tell me what?"

"An hour and a half ago, Muryin entered stage four."

He nodded calmly. "On schedule."

He had taken transfer, but it had only blunted his need. His state was not materially different from Ediva's, though Korin was so low field he could hardly be zlinned.

"Korin," said Klyd, "consider yourself off duty, and—" he turned to the shadowy Gen, "—well done."

Risa sensed his protest, but the Companion only said, "Thank you, Sectuib Farris." He nodded to Risa as he passed, "Sectuib."

As Risa and Klyd walked around the building, he asked, with a semblance of briskness, "You've zlinned her?"

"Only from a distance. Hugh was in control, and I left Sergi—"

He scowled. "Bad move. Hugh can do anything, provided he has no alternative. That's why I took Korin now—to make it easier for Hugh." He paused outside Muryin's room. "She must be near stage five transition, and field sensitive."

Going smoothly into functional mode, Klyd slid through the entry. Risa summoned a neutral field, then followed.

Muryin was indeed at stage five transition, sitting up, braced against the wall, panting.

"You're doing fine," assured Klyd as he came up behind Hugh. "Want me to stay?"

Hugh turned, in charge of the changeover room. "Of course." He noted Klyd's state. "Klyd?"

"I'm fine," he lied. "So's Korin."

Briskly, Hugh said, "We'll discuss it later. Muryin—ready to lie down?"

"If I do, I'll throw up."

"Probably not. Try it. Come on—" Hugh coaxed her onto the heap of blankets. She retched once but held onto Hugh's arms until the heaving subsided. In a few moments, he had her asleep. "Now we wait," he whispered.

Turning to settle himself, he caught sight of Risa. Her need was plain for any Companion to read, despite her masked showfield. "There's no reason for you to stay."

"May we?" asked Risa. "It can't be much longer."

"No, it won't," agreed Klyd as he examined Muryin's arms, without touching. "But Hugh's right—"

"If you insist, we'll leave, of course. But you've often noted how little I know of the Farris mutation . . . this is a good opportunity."

Sergi asked, "Is breakout private to the House?"

"Ordinarily, yes," replied Klyd. "But there are no other Zeor members to witness her, so of course you'd be welcome." Klyd compared the two Companions thoughtfully. Then his attention focused on Risa. "In Nivet, it would be considered an inter-House insult for one Sectuib to ask another if she accepted the responsibility for the results of her decisions. So I won't ask. I just hope you understand.''

"Rest assured, Sectuib Farris," Risa answered, having learned it was more proper to address him by the designation of his mutation than his House. "In Gulf, it would be an insult for any channel to assume another channel, especially one who'd achieved disjunction, had not learned that lesson in First Year.''

Klyd conceded. "Have some tea then?''

Risa didn't want any, but it would be good for Klyd. So she accepted a glass and pretended not to be worried.

They talked. Risa learned more about Farris sensitivity than she'd ever wanted to hear while Klyd strove to enhance Hugh's self-confidence.

By the time Muryin stirred again, coming up on the onset of breakout contractions, Hugh seemed to have overcome his reluctance, maybe because Klyd was no longer a strong focus for Gen attention. But Risa kept Sergi between herself and Hugh, still perceiving a terrible strain in the Companion.

Finally, Hugh knelt and coached Muryin into a sitting position, her hands on his arms. Klyd flanked Hugh on the left, his showfield zlinning renSime. Muryin would not be attracted to him. Sergi took a position to Hugh's right and behind, so the splashby of his field blended with Hugh's, reinforcing Muryin's attraction to Hugh. Risa knelt behind Sergi and just enough to his right to zlin around him.

Hugh coached, "Soon the contractions will be strong, and the membranes fully stretched—feel how the fluids are filling your sheaths?''

Even as they watched, the membranes over the wrist orifices stretched to transparency, six tiny bubbles on each wrist. Risa held her showfield as renSime as Klyd's. Her own changeover had been uncomplicated but exhaustingly long, the breakout and First Kill an anticlimax. She had no reason to relive those moments with Muryin, so it was easy to keep her fields disengaged.

"Now?" asked Muryin.

"Not yet," warned Hugh.

Oddly enough, the high-strung girl took a disciplined breath and overrode the nascent contractions with a strong relaxation. They did it again, relaxing into the trembling verge of the contractions far beyond where Risa would have called for the effort to break out the tentacles. Muryin seemed to be in trance, her selyn consumption remarkably low.

"Can you resist it one more time?" asked Hugh. "You'll be a better channel for it."

"Maybe just once more," she gasped.

"Good. Not yet—not yet, just relax. Let it come, feel the fluids pouring into the sheaths, feel every nerve alive with selyn flow. Just relax into it, go with it."

He continued, and Muryin easily overrode a contraction urge that might have broken the tightly stretched membranes. She glowed with triumph, but Risa couldn't understand how carrying a necessary discipline to abnormal lengths could make one a better channel.

"This time?" Muryin asked. "Please?"

"This time," agreed Hugh. "Ready? Wait . . . now!"

Muryin tightened her grip on the Gen's muscled forearms. Her selyn consumption soared and peaked as the membranes tore, releasing the tentacles, which lashed spasmodically around the Gen arms. Ordinarily, at such a moment the Companion would initiate lip contact and give the transfer. But Hugh held back, field unyielding.

I knew it! But before Risa could say anything, Klyd moved, his showfield rippling into his normal functional condition. He slid his tentacles over Muryin's arms and engaged her new, wet tentacles. Hugh relinquished his place to the channel as if it had been rehearsed a hundred times.

Klyd took off his Zeor crest ring, and held it, with a second ring, out to his daughter. She put her hands over them and Hugh covered their hands with a fold of Klyd's Zeor blue cloak.

"Unto the House of Zeor," said Muryin, "I pledge my heart, my hand, my substance. And unto Klyd Farris, Sectuib in Zeor, I pledge my life, my trust, my undying loyalty—as from death I am born, Unto Zeor, Forever."

"Unto Muryin Alur Farris ambrov Zeor, I pledge my substance, my trust, my undying loyalty, in my own name, born from death, Unto Zeor, Forever."

Klyd put his ring on, slipping Muryin's new ring onto her

finger. Despite the cruel timing, Risa was moved to share a sweet ache with Sergi, such as they knew at weddings and birthings. But Muryin broke the sentimental moment by whispering, eyes wide, "I'm zlinning."

Hugh slid into place. "You're in need—"

Klyd said, "She can't hear you—she's hyperconscious."

Hugh made the final lip contact. Risa could *see* that, but their fields didn't engage. Hugh was holding back.

She waited, unsure if this might be another Zeor discipline, but then Muryin gasped, forced duoconscious.

Klyd was hyperconscious, zlinning abstractedly, and Risa thought, *In that state, he could watch his own daughter die!* She pushed Sergi forward, breaking Klyd's concentration.

Risa, duoconscious, saw Hugh cave in. The fields collapsed around them, shattering into two spheres—Hugh robust, throbbing pain, and Muryin anemic, stilled by shock.

Klyd moved between them, smoothly taking Muryin's tentacles in contact position, but not making the fifth contact, not showing her a Gen field. As she came duoconscious, he said, "Steady. Hugh can't do it."

"No!" protested Hugh. "I can—"

"You froze, and I know why. Don't argue now! Risa?"

"Sergi! Go!"

Sergi moved into position, and with a ghastly sinking feeling Risa felt his attention shift from her to Muryin.

Muryin, still not in extreme attrition, pled with her father. "I can't do this to Vi's parents!"

"Trust me," insisted her father. "I won't let Sergi be overtaxed—I promise."

Sergi wasn't offended. He let Klyd relinquish Muryin to him at his own cautious pace, and then, when their fields were engaged, granted Muryin a quiet, "When you're ready."

She couldn't wait any longer. Sergi's ripe field enticed her hyperconscious and she seized him and drew.

Risa gasped. It was like being caught in an undertow in mid-river. Momentarily, through that nageric current, she felt Klyd go into the distracted state that claimed him so often, but she had no time to be offended. She had to fight the strongest surge of intil she'd ever experienced. Doubled over, gasping, she lost track of everything.

And then, disorientingly, Sergi's selyn gushed into Muryin's virgin system, seeming also to sweep into Risa's own nerves, wiping away the emptiness of need, restoring the balance between her primary and secondary selyn transport systems. It was tainted with Farris, repulsively Farris—yet also ripe with Sergi's signature—beloved, gentle, silly, genius, Sergi.

The swift current swept her along and she went with it, afraid to wake and find need still gnawing at her vitals. In a moment of weak hysteria, she was sure that if she came to in hard need, she'd be willing to hunt a kill again.

Once, long ago, she'd stalked Sergi for the kill, and he'd let her kill him—and then offered to let her do it again the next month because it felt so good. She attacked the incoming selyn with all the savagery of those early transfers with Sergi, and then, tantalizingly, suspended before the peak of satisfaction, it was over.

The world flipped into full sensory reality around her, sight, sound, touch, smell, and even the taste of Klyd's blood where her teeth had cut his lip. As he drew back, disengaging his laterals from around her own, his field still resonated with echoes of Sergi's.

She even felt, ever so slightly, the heady post-transfer sensation, ready for everything Sergi enjoyed doing to her— and having done to him. She had to blink hard to dispel the overlay of Sergi's features and see Klyd, but the moment she found her focus, she spat, "You shidoni-be-flayed lorsh! How *dare* you!"

Klyd was as obviously baffled by her dialect as she was by his, but he got the gist and waved tentacles placatingly, backing toward Hugh as she advanced, like the coward she'd always known him to be. "Sectuib Risa—I didn't— Think! Where would you have taken transfer? I couldn't have done that without Sergi's being the living-pattern." He gave her a crooked smile. "It worked, didn't it?"

Shen! She didn't bother to repress a shudder.

Muryin gasped, and Risa turned to see Sergi struggling to his feet. He went stark white and crumpled to the floor.

CHAPTER ELEVEN

Which Invasion?

Drawing himself in to keep from disturbing Sergi and Muryin with his nageric turbulence, Valleroy was surprised to see Klyd take Risa into transfer position.

A moment later, he forgot his own throbbing guilt when Risa lit into Klyd, screaming abuse. Klyd, heavily into recovery, backed toward the protection of Valleroy's field.

All the thwarted instincts of a Companion wakened, he focused on protecting Klyd's sensitized systems, missing Sergi's attempt to gain his feet until the other Companion went down and Muryin screamed.

Valleroy shifted his attention to Muryin, shielding her from the turbulence Sergi had introduced, leaving Klyd and Risa to handle Sergi's problem. He took Muryin's hands, her new tentacles waving unsteadily as she forgot to control them. "What did I do to Sergi? Dad!"

"Shh," cautioned Valleroy, challenged to hold his own calm. If Muryin had seriously injured the First Companion in Keon— "Let them work on him."

"He's fine," said Klyd. "Just mild transfer shock."

Muryin snatched a hand back and jammed it into her mouth. Valleroy felt her groping toward duoconsciousness and, knowing she had to learn that skill, supported her.

Klyd relinquished Sergi to Risa and came to Muryin, stroking her face with a tentacle. "Don't zlin him now. A Companion's entitled to his privacy."

Muryin asked, "Did—am I conditioned to want Gen pain?"

Valleroy chorused with Klyd, "No!" Klyd let Valleroy speak for the Gen point of view. "A Companion considers such things all in a day's work."

Klyd added, "You didn't feel any pain, did you?"

"I—I don't think so."

"I know you didn't," asserted Klyd. To the Keon pair, he added, "I had every confidence Sergi would be that good."

Sergi tossed and muttered to consciousness, remembered, and struggled to sit up just in time to hear Klyd add to Muryin, "You've nothing to worry about. I'll select your next transfer to make up the slack in your development."

Sergi fell back, but managed to say to Muryin, giving her the title of a channel, "I'm sorry, Hajene. Your Sectuib was right. I had no business trying that."

"It was close," agreed Klyd. "But it worked, Muryin, because you conserved enough selyn so Sergi just matched your capacity. The only problem was the speed match, and Sergi—" He turned to him, "—you amazed me. You started too slowly, but then—" Klyd stared into space.

Sergi didn't notice. "I couldn't believe her draw, but I remembered my first transfer, when Nedd Qualified me a Companion on my first donation. So, I just went with it. Shuven! I haven't felt anything so marvelous since—" He saw the storm in Risa's eyes, and finished, "—since our first transfer. It only hurt when it stopped!"

Klyd said, "From such a Companion, I'd have expected the good sense not to stand up after a scorching like that!"

Risa drew breath, offended, but Klyd ordered, "Hugh, get the fosebine. They both require hefty doses. And you, Hajene Muryin Farris, are going to get some sleep—Sectuib's orders!"

Valleroy helped Risa get Sergi to their room, leaving Klyd to persuade Muryin to sleep, when she wanted to play with her tentacles and learn to interpret fields.

At the door to their room, Risa said with cold courtesy, "Thank you, Hugh. I can handle Sergi now."

Sergi was bigger than Valleroy. Risa's head barely came up to his chest. She was strong enough to lift him, but she wasn't *big* enough. But Valleroy bowed, compelled to mitigate the spiky nager. "Sergi, thank you for doing my job for me. I owe you one—a big one. Risa, try to give Klyd a chance to explain what happened. He *always* has reasons." And he left.

"We'll do better for you next month," Klyd was telling Muryin when Valleroy joined them.

"You can't, Dad," Muryin replied. "That was . . . the greatest thing that ever happened to me in my life! I only got scared *afterwards*, when I thought I'd hurt Sergi."

"You'll understand when you've had a proper transfer."

Muryin's mouth, a perfect copy of her father's, set in a determined line. "You may find someone who can offer more capacity or speed. But nothing will ever be *better*."

Valleroy smiled, understanding what Klyd had forgotten: the first time was the best. For all the incredible transfers he had had with Klyd over the years, as his skill and capacity had grown, that first time under the evergreens would forever remain Valleroy's best transfer ever.

And one day the Sectuib in Zeor would have to accept that there would now always be a close and abiding affection between his Heir and the House of Keon.

Risa eased Sergi onto the bedroll they had arranged for their transfer. He chuckled weakly. "This is embarrassing."

"Sergi, you've nothing to be embarrassed about! You didn't have to play up to that lout by saying Muryin was more than you could handle."

"But she is! Shen, that was her First Transfer. She'll be a third faster and twice as demanding next time, so imagine what Klyd's like! And Hugh serves him easily. Klyd was right; I'm too old, though maybe Mor isn't."

"I'm fed up with this shenned Farris Mystique! He's wrong as often as he's right. He was wrong about Hugh!"

"He was gambling," retorted Sergi. "He had to make a Sectuib's call. He thought Hugh had a better chance than I did."

Offended, she pulled away from him. "You're defending him! Next you'll want to trade into Zeor!"

He put both hands to his head and winced, but she hardly felt his pain through her own outrage. "I suppose you're going to defend his forcing transfer on me!"

He sat up, ignoring the searing ache down his backbone. "Risa! How can I judge? Hugh's right; we have to talk to Klyd, analyze it step by step until we understand."

"Hugh's right! Klyd's right! What's the matter with you? I thought *I* was your Sectuib!" Risa rarely lost her temper, but right now, semi-post and feeling defiled, she couldn't stand Sergi's Householding attitudes. She'd sat in too many conferences, analyzing transfers. "You want me to go and sleep with him, too?"

He reached for her, but she eluded him, appalled at her words but unable to retract the angry nonsense.

"Risa, listen. I'm not half the Companion Klyd gives me credit for! I don't *know* what happened with Muryin. All I felt, until the very end, was *you*—I think Klyd did that by functioning to you. I've never heard of such a thing, but I *know* he was in command of the fields—not me!"

Mentally, she reran the events. She'd lost control after the first nageric surge. "Well, it wasn't me, and it wasn't Hugh. If it wasn't you or Muryin, it had to be Klyd." *I don't believe it.*

"*That's* what Farrises do," said Sergi, "that makes it worthwhile to put up with their 'neurotic quirks.' It's the stuff of legends, and they grab all the glory." He smiled conspiratorially. "But in the end, Keon reaps the profit."

She couldn't help smiling in return. "That's true. You've certainly forged a link between Keon and Zeor's next generation. I wonder what'll happen when Mor meets Muryin?"

On that note, she let him draw her down onto the blankets. But his kiss was dispassionate. "Oh, I hurt too much. Forgive me? I'll make it up next month if you'll wait for me."

He'd never want me to go to Klyd—but he has the good sense not to say he'd stop me if I tried. How can I have been so bloody-shen lucky the night Dad died in the hurricane and I hunted and "killed" Sergi? "I'll wait. If I were post as hell, I'd wait. There's nowhere else to get what I want."

He snuggled her into the crook of his arm. "Then let me sleep. Maybe this headache will be gone in the morning."

The drowsiness from the fosebine he'd taken tugged her down into a light doze with him. Maybe by morning she wouldn't be so disgracefully irrational. *I guess this is what it would feel like to be raped.*

After Muryin fell asleep, Klyd and Valleroy crept away to their own room. It was nearing dawn, the camp wrapped in a profound hush. When they entered their room, Klyd turned to him and took him into transfer position with a deep sigh.

It was only then that Valleroy realized the channel was shaking. "What's the problem?"

"Never mind. It wasn't so bad. We all survived it."

One problem with Farrises; even their Companions can't always tell the damage a strain has done them. He saw that their dinner had been set aside, somewhat scorched, and much of the firewood had been used. Saddle bags and a spare blanket had been arranged to simulate a contour lounge for transfer, so he disengaged and pushed Klyd down on it.

"You had Korin in here?"

"Envious?"

"How could I not be? I feel lousy."

"I know. I'll take your field down in a few minutes."

"Take my field down? As if I were just a donor?"

"The renSimes can use the selyn."

"Yeah." He worked to Klyd, aiding him. "Oh, I don't begrudge Korin. It'd been months since he'd worked." He rested his forehead on his bent knees. "Shen, it *hurts*, Klyd. *Why* did you give Muryin to Sergi knowing she'd burn him?"

"Because you'd have shenned her. You're stronger than she is." Klyd kneaded Valleroy's neck with handling tentacles. "You couldn't help it. I don't know why I'd never accepted it before; you're frozen in sync with me. You couldn't give anyone else a transfer if your life depended on it. Luckily, it never will. There isn't a channel in the Territory, Muryin included, who could force you and live to tell of it."

"But I *wanted* Muryin. Her need—"

"Your fields didn't mesh. I doubt she'd have survived that shenning. She didn't have *that* much selyn in reserve!"

"You mean," he turned, "I might have killed her?"

Silently, Klyd nodded.

Valleroy trusted Klyd's readings of fields and transfer situations. *But—* "It didn't feel—am I so insensitive?"

"No. It's just time I admitted I was wrong about us. Risa was right. We're too close to the legendary orhuen. If I'd known, we might have made it work. But only zlinning you with Muryin made me realize it." He added, "At any rate, I understand now you couldn't have intended to seduce Ediva into a transfer—because you know you *can't*, and nothing in you *wants* to."

That was true—and yet— "Klyd, I respond to her need. It's not a strong response, like to yours, but it's there. When I'm high field, it feels good to hold her. She feels *Sime*, and that feels *right*. That wouldn't be, in orhuen."

"Orhuen is a romantic legend," said Klyd, "built out of wishes and adolescent passions. But the core idea may have *some* truth; given individual selyn production/consumption rhythms, transfer speeds and capacities, then there *could* be a Gen with characteristics exactly mirroring those of a particular Sime. The chances of meeting such a Gen are ridiculously small. But if two such people did meet, it's possible they could never part again and survive."

At Valleroy's alarm, Klyd added, "No, no, we're not that close. Neither are Risa and Sergi. But we're close enough so it does *hurt* and we *resist* interaction with other partners. That's what debilitates me so, when I'm forced to do without you. I'd never realized what caused it—or how much you feel it, too. We'll research it when this crisis is over."

"Is that why I feel so rotten?" asked Valleroy. His field seemed to choke him and there was no relief in sight. He put his head down on his knees again. "Shen and shid, I *need* a transfer! And don't tell me Gens have no such *need!*"

"That feeling isn't due to orhuen, at least not the legendary variety. No other Companion I know reacts this way, and I *will* find out what's causing it. Meanwhile, here's something to take your mind off your miseries. Ediva *is* fixed on you, and it may be partly my fault. Having zlinned Sergi serving Muryin, having served Risa, I can now see my mistake in allowing Risa to force transfer on Ediva.

"At the time, I figured since Risa was disjunct, she could do what I couldn't. She provided the very satisfaction Ediva had forsaken. Usually, that's good for disjuncts, but Ediva's a 'delicate.'

"Hugh, she's fixed on you now. If she attacks you and you shen her, she'll die of the shock."

Through the vision that conjured, Valleroy barely heard Klyd summing up, "And there go all our hopes for surviving Zelerod's Doom. Without Ediva to explain, who's going to believe her figures?"

* * *

For the next three days, the party climbed the steep eyeway north to Capital. Peaks closed in on all sides, and they often had to stop and clear rocks from the road. Late spring brought wonderful days and bitter nights. Risa and Klyd avoided each other. Valleroy brooded over Ediva's problem, but she was so touchy, he hardly dared try to explain.

Virena became ever more lonely as Muryin forged ahead into the adult world. The channels had to take turns instructing her, since any First Year Sime, but especially a channel, could run any mature adult ragged. Virena listened avidly at first, but soon became bored. Not even being Gen, she couldn't get Muryin's attention when the new channel was zlinning.

One night, still four days out of Capital, they camped in a nice waystation. The sky clouded, and wind howled among the peaks. As night fell, it was too dark to see, and the Gens drew lots to pick two of them to sleep outside, giving the Simes on watch selyn fields to zlin by.

Neither Sergi nor Valleroy pulled the duty, at which the channels who had to walk perimeter guard complained good naturedly. Muryin wasn't yet allowed to stand watch because she'd become bemused by the perplexing fields of Raiders or bandits. She called, "I'll take a turn if anyone thinks there isn't enough field to zlin by."

Risa replied, "You'll stand many watches in your life. Don't be so eager to start."

Klyd said, "Risa's right, Muryin."

The look Risa gave him was thoughtful rather than hostile, and that was the beginning of the thaw.

Later that night, Valleroy found Sergi whittling at a piece of wood, a row of figurines before him, each in the wood of a different region. Valleroy knelt to examine them. "What are you making?"

"Chess set. Ever play?"

"Once or twice," allowed Valleroy.

"Virena plays, and I thought I could sharpen up her game."

"May I?" He asked permission to pick up a piece.

"Sure."

"These are gorgeous. I thought you only made jewelry."

"Oh, I make all kinds of things. I made a chess set from

onyx once. One year, when times were hard, Risa sold it. I could never get more high-grade onyx. I hear the best comes from the deep southwest Gen Territory.''

"I don't know much about gemstones," admitted Valleroy.

At the far end of the large common room, the Dar were exercising rhythmically. The two young Gens, Madison and Jesson, were watching Ediva and Dazul teaching Harris Emstead Gen self-defense against Simes. Despite his age, he was determined that, next time he met an attacking junct, he'd have other options than to murder or let himself be killed. Valleroy admired the man's tenacity as he repeatedly ended up pinned, Ediva grasping his arms in transfer grip.

Once more Dazul and Ediva demonstrated, and once more Ediva and the panting Emstead faced off. She leaped—and went spinning over his shoulder! Bouncing to her feet, she attacked again, but Emstead's combat experience was many years longer than hers. He spun and was waiting for her. With a grin of triumph, he tossed her again, and again turned in time to catch her if she came at him a third time.

Instead she stood, hands on hips, laughing freely for the first time since her transfer. "That's wonderful! You've got it, Harris!''

Emstead wiped the sweat out of his eyes and laughed in return. "And you thought I was too old to learn!''

"I never said any such thing!" Ediva protested.

"No, but you thought it," he told her. "Too old, too Gen. But I don't accept 'I can't' from my soldiers—or myself. Come on—let's practice! I've got to keep at it until it's a reflex, which does take longer at my age.''

Madison and Jesson had both risen—in astonishment, Valleroy realized, when they saw their colonel accomplish the maneuver. "Beg pardon, Colonel, Ma'am," said Madison. "Would you be willing to teach that to Jesson and me?''

"Sergi?" Muryin's voice distracted Valleroy.

Sergi set his knife aside. "Yes, Hajene Farris?''

Her face was serious, her black eyes flashing. "I've done a terrible thing, and I have to apologize.''

"What could you have done?''

"You gave me transfer, and I treated you very badly.''

Sergi focused on her. "Oh, now don't think that. It was

your first time; I wouldn't have wanted you to try to control. If either of us owes an apology, it's I.''

"Nonsense," she said, sounding very adult. "You gave me a wonderful First Transfer. *I* felt fine.''

"And my headache's all gone now, zlin?''

Valleroy saw Risa pause on the edge of the firelight, while on the other side of the room, Klyd looked up.

"It was an expensive headache," said Muryin. "It seems to have cost the world a crucial alliance.''

Klyd approached as Risa moved closer. Muryin looked around the circle. "The ambient around here is thick enough to carve chess men out of. And I'm the cause.''

"No, Muryin," put in Klyd, "it was my decision to serve Risa that has offended her.''

Risa looked at Klyd, who returned her gaze openly. Finally, Risa said, "Hugh said you'd have an explanation. I'm ready to listen.''

"Will you have tea with us? Accept our hospitality?''

She settled herself beside her Companion. "Would you accept my hospitality?''

"Instantly. My life is in your hands, Sectuib Keon.''

At Risa's invitation, Klyd took a place by the fire. Muryin retired. The rustic chairs creaked as Valleroy moved to work fields. Klyd had taken down his field a bit each day, but he felt fretful and out of touch with the Simes about him.

Sergi made the tea, which was excellent. Klyd waited for Risa to ask, "All right. Why? Why did you do it?''

"Do you remember what you did—when Muryin initiated the flow from Sergi, and Sergi started too slowly, somehow causing that same, odd—stutter—I keep finding in the 'delicates'?''

"Stutter?''

"Didn't you zlin it? It was quite pronounced in Muryin. Probably not the same sort of thing at all." Klyd shrugged that aside and prompted, "Do you remember what you did?''

"The field surge staggered me, but I was recovering—''

"You were advancing on Sergi," Klyd corrected quietly.

"I—don't— Are you sure?''

"I saw you. Your laterals were out. You were reaching for Sergi.''

"I couldn't have!"

"Risa, zlin me. Am I lying?"

She did zlin him, pondering for a long time before she said, "Probably not. But if I did, I would have pulled up."

"She would have," agreed Sergi. "You don't know yet what strength Risa has."

Klyd said, "I wouldn't allow myself to observe my Companion giving transfer until I'd had transfer myself. I shouldn't have allowed Risa to remain when she was so far into need."

"Why do you take all the blame?" asked Risa. "Doesn't anyone else's decision count? You couldn't have *forced* me to leave!"

Klyd nodded. "Perhaps that's why I didn't try."

"If you really thought I was going to interfere, you could have jolted me hypoconscious without—what you did."

"And what would that have done to Muryin?" Klyd added, "Sergi was having a difficult time, you had to get transfer, and I knew if I bridged, I could help Sergi and get you over the worst of it, too. It worked. It just never occurred to me that you hadn't understood our discussion earlier."

Risa squinted at Klyd. "What discussion?"

"When you addressed me as Sectuib Farris, not ambrov Zeor, I thought you'd finally grasped what 'Farris' means."

"That again!" exclaimed Risa. "You assume the whole world has made an in-depth study of Farrises. It's the same thing as expecting someone to deduce your pathology from your necktie! Don't you realize what consummate ego it takes to blame others for not knowing what you *haven't told them*?"

She rose. "The only way I'll ever trust you again is if I see you learn from this experience. I assume you're capable of that!" She gathered Sergi and left.

Four days later, they crested the highest pass yet and rode down into Capital's wide, tree-lined streets. Double file, they moved along a busy thoroughfare through the main gate in the old fortified walls, now deep inside the town. A crew was reconstructing the gates, augmenting hard, as if time were shorter than the Gen supply.

Off along sidestreets where private dwellings abounded, Risa noted wagons and strings of pack horses and mules being loaded with personal goods. Citizens were deserting this city en masse. One reason was soon clear.

They passed a huge round pillar covered with posters. The section near eye level was reserved for official government proclamations: EMERGENCY PEN PRIVILEGE LIMITATIONS; TERRITORY RESERVE GUARD CALL-UP; CIVILIAN WEAPONS CONFISCATION FOR MILITARY USE; MOBILIZATION MEASURES; FACTORY QUOTAS; GRAIN RATION RESTRICTIONS.

She shuddered as they passed, as did Sergi, but when they saw a line of Simes waiting at the gates of a Pen flying a white flag beneath the green, indicating limited Gen supply, he shrouded Risa protectively in his nager.

The Simes glared sullenly at Householders flaunting their overly ripe Gens. One of them heaved a clot of mud at Risa's horse. Others followed, throwing stones and horse dung.

They picked up the pace, riding without looking to either side.

They turned into a street that ended in a wooden stockade. The well-kept gates opened at their approach and closed quickly behind them.

When the last of the juncts' cries had faded, Risa dared to breathe. Klyd dismounted, striding into the welcoming crowd. They were hustled at once into a briefing, as Virena was taken away to the guarded children's compound.

Klyd embraced a woman Companion wearing Zeor's blue, a light yellow, and the Farris black trim. After a few words, he sent Muryin off with her and turned to the business meeting, saying Ediva must attend this executive session.

Hot trin and good food was served right at the conference table. In the confusion and disproportionate relief and joy in the ambient as people saw Klyd, Risa grasped that a full Tecton session was being postponed while they were brought up to date.

"We thought your party lost," admitted the renSime in charge, who'd been introduced as the Tecton Corresponding Secretary. "We had word you'd left Konawa with a trade proposal for the Nivet government. In fact, the first shipments of Gulf rice arrived in Konawa, on a deal engineered by Householding Theor. They sold the rice to a junct banker underwriting a private Pen. Word is spreading, and there are several more deals in the making.''

Risa grinned. Theor sounded like her kind of people. Klyd asked, ''But why this Tecton emergency session?''

''You haven't heard! The Nivet Council had the Army break into four Householdings. They confiscated all the Gens— even Companions, looted, and torched the buildings. The local militia joined the Army regulars and vented their frustrations—legally.''

Risa's elation vanished. She could not imagine such a thing. From their nagers, the Nivet natives could, though.

The Secretary added to Risa, ''If it weren't for that, and the news from the north, *you* just might sell your idea to Nivet. But now—everyone's preparing to pull out, head south, maybe scatter into the mountains.'' He nodded to Morningstar. ''Mountain Bells should be warned.''

Morningstar asked, ''Warned about what? Has word of Ardo Pass come ahead of us?''

''Ardo Pass? What have the spring horse auctions to do with an invasion of Freeband Raiders?''

CHAPTER TWELVE

Junct Council

Morningstar expressed the bewilderment everyone felt. ''But the Raiders don't threaten Capital. They're holed up in Mountain City, fighting the south Gen army.''

The Secretary blanched. ''Mountain City? That's where *we* were going.''

''It's been devoured by Raiders,'' announced Klyd. ''Tell me about the invasion.''

''Which one? The Gen Army is massing on the northeast,

to push the Raiders down into Nivet by blocking the High Eyeway into the Gen's own capital.''

''Get Harris Emstead,'' said Risa. ''We have with us an officer from the Gen Army—a friend. He can tell us what the Gens are most likely to do.''

''Trust an obvious spy?'' the Secretary asked in horror.

''I'll vouch for him,'' said Klyd. ''Colonel Emstead wants to avoid war between our Territories. When you zlin him, you'll know that's true.''

While one of the Keon party went for Emstead, Ediva, who'd been doodling abstractedly, said in quiet despair, ''Norwest Territory is gone, isn't it?''

''If you've been on the road for the last two months, how could you know that?''

With a wildness in her eyes, Ediva answered levelly, ''The magic of the Ancients, how else?'' Risa knew that was what Ediva's branch of mathematics had been called by the superstitious, since it forecast the future.

''Tell us what's happened,'' prompted Risa. Another year—two maybe—and she could have trade routes into the northern Gen Territory, supplying Nivet with Gen grain, opening the way to peace among all Territories, Sime or Gen. *But I don't have two years.*

The Secretary explained. The collapsing Norwest Territory, desperate for Gens, had licensed its Raiders to go farther than ever into the sparsely-populated Gen Territory which separated it from Nivet—so far that they raided near the Nivet border, competing with Nivet's own Licensed Raiders.

The doubling of Sime raids in that area had brought the Gen Army onto the northern plains. Fighting both the Norwest Raiders and the Gen Border Patrol, Nivet's Raiders brought back too few Gens. The Nivet Government, watching prices soar, outlawed private sales.

Emstead arrived in time to hear that last and waved away Hugh's translation. ''I understand that much Simelan. You've got worse shortages than we thought.''

The Secretary nodded, zlinning him thoroughly before continuing—in English. ''Capital's Choice Auction closed last week. Now rich juncts are competing with the rest for what's left in the Pens.''

Risa said, "Can't the legislators see that forcing licensed Raiders to sell at government prices lowers the incentive to hunt Wild Gens, an incentive already reduced by growing dangers?"

"They're blaming the Householdings," replied the Secretary, "and putting a new tax on us so they can buy Gens in Mountain City's big Gen Market, but now you say there are no Gens left in Mountain. Why haven't we been overrun with refugees from the south?"

"Late snow closed the roads. They're probably dead by now." Klyd prompted, "Go on. Invasion."

"Freeband Raiders, mostly desperate Norwest refugees, are waiting beyond the Divide for the snows to melt so they can take Nivet. Nivet spies report the Gen Army mobilizing on our north border to force the Freebanders south into Nivet."

"I've been out of touch," said Emstead, "but from the point of view of the Army, that's the only solution."

The Secretary nodded. "Raiders and Gens will be fighting in our streets before high summer. If there's no refuge south, I'm sending my family east."

Risa stifled a gasp at the vision of millions of juncts, throngs of Householders with enticing Gens to drive the juncts mad, all pursued by Raiders who had been intelligent, healthy citizens—not the usual pathetic misfits—sweeping across Nivet and into Gulf, followed by enraged Gen soldiers. There was no time for her trade plan to work. "Are there statistics available?" she asked.

Rummaging through a thick briefcase, the Secretary brought out a file. "Our agents lifted these from Nivet's Top Secret files. We can't vouch for their accuracy."

Hugh riffled through the file until he came to a brief note in a neat round hand. "Kitty wrote this." he said. "It's as accurate as anything you'll ever get."

Klyd said, "Ediva can figure how much time we've got. I'll address the full assembly now. Our messengers must be out of here by nightfall."

Despite Klyd's request to dispense with ceremony, Risa felt the woman who chaired the meeting convened it with elaborate formality. Klyd moved with a ponderous efficiency that bespoke total command. *He's a good actor. But I still don't trust him.*

Klyd outlined Risa's plan, already bearing fruit in East Nivet. "But it's too late to avert a disaster that may in fact *be* Zelerod's Doom. Ediva ambrov Dar, who rescued the Pen system three years ago, has been with me to Gulf and back across the south eyeway, gathering data. She's working on new statistics from Norwest which should convince even the juncts who run this Territory that their political solutions to the Gen shortage won't work."

He described the condition of the Genfarm district, the blowing dust, dry waterholes, and deserted waystations, finishing, "Now I hear the Nivet Council has taken four Householdings." He intoned their names, offered a moment of silence, and went on urgently, "We must do more than send out rescue parties. We must stop this! And there is a way." He introduced their forward scout, who'd reported to them at Tuck.

Under Klyd's deft questioning, the scout shyly told his story. The stark facts, however, had a stronger impact than impassioned rhetoric. Hope stirred amid the gloom when he told how two Gen soldiers had helped them escape.

That introduced Emstead, who had been zlinned suspiciously ever since he'd arrived wearing his Gen army uniform. He spoke for himself, in plain but effective Simelan. "One thing is obvious," he concluded. "If the Gen Army, the Sime Army, the Householdings, and the Freeband Raiders fight one another, no one will win, least of all our children and grandchildren. I have *seen* the Doom Ediva ambrov Dar has warned us of."

Klyd took the cue to tell the grim story. When he had finished, they had *been* to Ardo Pass.

Into the silence, he summarized, "So Nivet is under attack from the northwest, the northeast, and the whole of the southwest. There's no refuge—"

"There's Rialite," whispered the Chair.

Klyd heard her. "The Chair reminds me of Rialite. The Rialite community wouldn't hold all of us in this hall, let alone all members of all Householdings. However, my daughter, Hajene Muryin Farris, will leave for Rialite in the morning. Rialite cannot be our refuge, but it may save our children and our Houses. Zeor suggests that each House send one channel of rank to Rialite.

"But we haven't much time. Nivet is surrounded. Sectuib Keon has provided the only workable solution, and she has experience in implementing it. So we must buy time to make it work.

"Juncts are not stupid—nor retarded like Freeband Raiders. I'm prepared to present our solution to the Nivet Council tonight and tell them the Householdings are ready to offer transfer to any junct who asks."

As the last echoes of Klyd's baritone stilled, nobody breathed. *He's doing a complete about face, and right in public, too. He* can *learn from his mistakes!*

"Yes, Risa," Klyd acknowledged. "My august colleague has just realized she's won an argument with Zeor. In Konawa, Zeor declared against this plan. Now, the dangers of the plan are less than those we face if we don't do it. Zeor therefore concedes to Keon and Rior that the time has come for all Householdings to open their gates and offer channel's transfer— and even Gen transfer, at Sectuib's discretion—to juncts in need. We have the Gens, we have the selyn. If we let our Territory perish around us, we will be destroyed along with it."

From around the hall, eyes focused on Emstead, then unfocused as Simes zlinned him. Klyd had spoken in English, yet there was no fear in the Gen soldier's nager. He zlinned as steady as any Householding Gen, only the dimness and lack of engagement in his field showing he was no Companion.

He felt their curiosity, started to rise—but Klyd stayed him with one tentacle: his field spoke for him. His attitude was no longer courage, but confidence. Clearly this Gen could handle a renSime—and if an out-Territory Gen could learn that in a few short weeks, surely most of their own Gens, grown up in day-to-day harmony with Simes, could do the same. Hugh leaned behind Klyd to murmur to Emstead, "They've forgotten that I came from the same place you did."

Hugh's move, along with a ripple of his field, drew attention. Everyone here must know his story, Risa realized. She smiled at the two Gens. What better examples could this assembly have of Gen adaptability? Around the hall, other Householding Gens, many also not Companions, added their assurance to the ambient.

Klyd waited until the unspoken message had reached everyone, then said, "I volunteer to take this plan to the Nivet Council tonight, but I must have a unanimous vote of this body."

After the meeting, Risa wrote a letter to go to Gulf in the dispatch pouch, and a duplicate for her own messenger; gave transfer to one of her renSimes, and was binding up her hair when Sergi came in, dressed in his formal Keon red cloak. Emstead was with him, in dress uniform.

So it was settled that Emstead was to go along. In that case, the more Companions the better.

The junct Council assembled in a room paneled in gleaming wood, with a rich, deep carpet bearing patterns Risa had never seen before. The draperies were insulated, the walls stone behind the panels. An open skylight provided ventilation.

The table, a semi-circle, was also hardwood. The chairs were padded in the design of the carpet. Silent servants showed them to seats at the focus of the semi-circle. They were left alone in silence to wait for the Council.

It was a long, nerve-racking wait—deliberately contrived to stress them. Finally, six men and four women entered and took places at the table. A Sime with a black mustache and a receding hairline swept into the room, zlinned the Householders with contempt, and took the center chair. "Which of you is the Farris?"

As if he couldn't see that! Risa had learned to spot a Farris without even zlinning. They all had that weak mouth, sharply beaked nose, high cheekbones, glittering black eyes, and untamable black hair.

Klyd stood and introduced himself.

"You will remain seated," decreed the central figure without reaching for Klyd's credentials or introducing himself in turn. "This city is in crisis. We've no time for Householder nonsense. State your case before we inform you of our new measures for utilizing Householder resources."

Klyd resumed his seat, ignoring the threat. "I offer the solution to the crisis."

There was no response from the Council beyond silent skepticism. Klyd forged ahead, introducing Risa, explaining her offer of trade. Then he told of the juncts breaking into the Tecton assembly, their demands, the attack on Dinny ambrov Keon, and the deaths that resulted.

"Tedious. What have Tecton politics to do with us?"

"Please bear with me," answered Klyd. "I must relate another incident to show how large and passionate this group is." He described luridly the attack on Muryin at the Tuck River. Then he introduced Ediva. "The architect of the current, *successful*, Pen distribution system has worked out the Gen shortfall expected this winter. Ediva?"

Risa could feel the girl shaking, but then this group of hardboiled juncts could intimidate anyone—except Emstead, who listened calmly. How much of the Simelan *did* he understand? Risa leaned on Sergi to envelope Ediva in a supportive nageric bubble. Klyd backed her. She saw a frown pass over the Councilors' faces, but Ediva soon snatched their attention away from the ambient.

"Here are the shortfall statistics from two months ago, and my projections into this month. I've taken worst-case assumptions throughout." She held up a large sketchpad. "Here is the number of Simes who would, according to the spokesman from Konawa, be willing to take transfer from Companions. This would reduce the shortfall forty percent. Here is the number of Pen Gens that would have to be secured, given the forty percent reduction."

Risa zlinned them. *They can't deny hard facts!*

"This isn't all the Householdings can do," added Klyd.

Ediva turned a page to display another set of figures.

"In truly desperate times, *some* renSimes will take a transfer or two from channels until Gens become available. Projecting from past experience, about sixty percent of all taxpayers will accept channel's transfer for up to three consecutive months. If we add the Gen-transfer option, the Householdings of Nivet can make up the shortfall."

Klyd added, "You'd gain time to stabilize the Territory and mobilize to fight the Raiders. Time for Gulf imports to reduce the death rate of Pen Gens. The coming winter won't be so hard on them if they're not starved this summer. Wouldn't such an increase in selyn supply make it feasible to defend the northern border against the Raiders? We have Householdings along that border. Your troops could move from House to House for selyn replenishment while keeping the Gen troops from chasing the Raiders into Nivet. Between the Gens and your own troops, the Raiders will be wiped out—and those who were solid citizens of Norwest Territory may be lured into Nivet to make new homes.

"Two or three hundred Norwest master craftsmen would help this whole Territory. And—you may be the ones to resettle and command all Norwest, too."

Risa was shocked: first that Klyd knew how to reason like that; second that he'd point it out to greedy juncts like these; and third, that it was working.

The Councilors glanced at each other, sampling each other's nagers, deliberating in whispers—but only briefly.

"This Gen Army officer—is he a captive to be tortured into telling us the position of his troops?"

Emstead understood, it seemed, for before Klyd could answer he replied, in halting Simelan, "No. You already know that. I come to warn you. If the Raiders cut your Territory in two, the Gen Army will follow. Take the Householding offer, and defend your borders."

The leader zlinned in open astonishment. "This is a Wild Gen caught within our borders. We confiscate—"

"He joined us in Gulf Territory and is under the protection of Keon," Risa spoke up at once. "Touch him, and all shipments from Gulf stop. Touch *me*," she added as he focused his threat on her, "and a third force will attack Nivet: a Gulf Territory Army, healthy, determined, and replete with selyn. Years ago, *our* Territory adopted a plan similar to what Sectuib Farris proposes. We have no shortage of selyn. Ever."

Again the Councilors conferred. Risa caught the whispered "threat" countered with "trade," "another army," but "plenty of selyn."

Finally their leader turned back to the Tecton party, and Risa watched what she had seen often in Gulf over the years, juncts saving face when they'd been outmaneuvered.

As if neither Emstead nor Risa had spoken, he said, "Your suggestion has a certain merit, Householder Farris. We will study your calculations tonight and render a decision in the morning. If the figures prove out, we may adopt a version of your plan—instead of simply confiscating all Householdings."

The Councilors rose as one and left the chamber. Ediva turned her eyes to Klyd. "I'm afraid there's been a mistake somewhere—only I can't quite put a tentacle on it."

Klyd put an arm around her shoulders and met Risa's eyes. "Just convince them the figures are correct and let me worry about making up for any errors."

CHAPTER THIRTEEN

Rumors of War

Klyd sent Muryin off to Rialite the next morning. Seeing her off, Valleroy put his arm around her, as much a gesture of love as to warm her with the fold of his cloak. She'd lost the sparse fat she'd had before changeover and had grown a finger's width taller in less than a month. "I'm going to miss you, Muryin."

"Don't make me cry. I want you to remember me as more grown up than that."

"You don't want to go?"

"I wish the world would just stay the same! What if I never see you again?"

"It can happen. We face that every morning on waking, and every night going to sleep." He put his hands on her shoulders. "Let's not part with things left unsaid. Muryin, I *wanted* to give you First Transfer. You *know* how important you are to me."

She blinked at him. "I know. I love you, too." She hugged him. "And Dad—Sectuib—"

"He'd have come down to see you off if he could possibly have gotten loose from the meetings."

She shook a damp curl of black hair out of her face and said, "He came to talk last night. We said our good-byes."

He hugged her, feeling Sime not child, and said, "Take care of Virena for us. She's more important than you know."

Then the trail guide called them to mount up, and Valleroy pushed Muryin away. She resolutely turned her back and mounted, sitting straight and proud in the saddle, holding the reins with the negligence of total command. *There's very little child left in that woman now.*

As the gates opened, Risa and Sergi came clattering down the stairs behind Valleroy and into the yard, where Virena sat astride her mount, huddled beneath her rain cape. Sergi reached up to kiss his daughter good-bye, then both he and Risa stood back as the horses moved out.

Valleroy knew they trusted their offspring to take care of herself, while at the same time they clung together, sharing with Valleroy the same parental shock—*My child is going off without me for the first time.*

By the end of that day, the Nivet Council had decided, grudgingly, to go along with the Householding plan.

The Tecton machinery leapt into motion. Valleroy, with several channels and two First Companions, devised a training manual for volunteer Gen donors.

The communication system that had served the Houses was quickly overloaded, so extra carriers were put on all routes. Certain messages were to be duplicated by the recipient and copies sent to every other House they could reach, so the entire Tecton could function as a unit.

Posters went out informing Nivet citizens that their government had ordered the Houses to offer transfer—not kills—to anyone qualifying for a Pen Gen that day. They were also welcome to bring their children in changeover, to be started off nonjunct. Within a week, feedback from nearer Houses brought objections, problems, and procedure flaws.

Risa had some answers from her experience in Gulf. When the juncts argued that taking selyn from the local Pen Gens created a shortage of kills, she countered, "But it makes sense to reuse Gens."

"Regular selyn draw increases a Gen's resistance to infectious disease," argued Klyd, "not the reverse!" And proved it with public health statistics.

"That's because you feed Gens up fat, while we starve them for lack of money to buy food!" argued one Councilor.

"No amount of money can buy grain that doesn't exist," Risa pointed out. "Cooperate, and Gulf Territory will trade you rice and citrus to keep the Pen Gens healthy."

So the Council authorized Pen Keepers to let channels draw selyn from twenty-five percent of the stock. Each House had to negotiate with their local Pens and citizens. Risa wrote the guidelines on how best to approach the Pens.

Reviewing what she produced, Klyd was pleased. "There are some things here I wouldn't have thought of. Print it!"

When they weren't in committee meetings or arguing for concessions from the government, they were wrangling with the Tecton. Affairs bogged down in the increasing debate until a movement started to give an Emergency Tecton Controller power to act without consulting the quorum.

There was resistance, even outrage. Houses had always been sovereign, the Tecton only a forum for debate. Yet as news came of the worsening emergency, as message riders were lost to marauders, as each House became impatient with the objections other Houses raised, the idea took root.

To Valleroy's surprise, Risa broke the logjam. She took the floor at an assembly that had lasted until nearly midnight, and said, "Why don't you consider *who* might be chosen Tecton Controller? Sectuib Klyd Farris is already performing— to little or no objection—most of the functions of that office. He could do a more effective job with official status."

Klyd had suffered a ghastly turnover and was now slogging through his duties on habit and determination. Now he surveyed the excited assembly, and leaned close to Risa to say, "I wish you hadn't done that!"

The vote was unanimous save for Klyd's dissenting vote. Klyd glared at Valleroy, then rose to make another speech.

Later, pacing the Zeor suite's sitting room, Klyd fumed, "The least I could expect is loyalty from my Companion! I want to get back to Zeor before the battle breaks loose."

Valleroy knew that most of Klyd's temper was need generated. He felt the same. With the heat of summer setting in, his rising field made him feel as if he were suffocating in warm molasses.

Refraining from saying how much he longed to be back at Rior, where his son Jesse had been for months now without either mother or father, Valleroy replied wistfully, "You'll feel better after a good transfer."

Klyd dropped into a divan. "True, but we're not scheduled for two days. I have an appointment with Ediva in five minutes. She's very worried—"

Valleroy hadn't seen her since she passed turnover. "She buries herself in her calculations to deal with need. You increase your dispensary schedule, and she does math. *You*, however, are an especially effective channel when in need; *she's* a lousy mathematician. After she's had a good transfer, she'll suddenly find all the right answers."

Klyd threw his head against the backrest and stared at the ceiling. "Sometimes I wish I were Gen. Such unquenchable optimism." He picked his head up. "You know something? Right now, I can't *stand* your shenned optimism!"

"Maybe because I can't stand your doom-and-gloom."

Klyd heaved himself to his feet. "I've got to go," he said as he swung his cape over his shoulders. He paused by the door, adding, "Let's try not to fight before this transfer."

After Klyd left, Valleroy dragged himself to bed and fell into a nightmarish slumber. He woke with sun streaming in the window. It took superhuman effort to stagger to the shower.

Even after he'd forced down breakfast, he couldn't think straight and his knees felt rubbery. *Could be flu—and after we bragged to the juncts about how healthy transfer makes Gens!*

Bending over to put his boots on, he suddenly realized he was going to vomit. He made it to the hand basin just in time, and stood panting, staring at his bloodshot eyes in the mirror. *Face it. You're sick.*

He went out to locate Klyd, realizing he didn't know where the channel would be now. Nobody else knew, either, and he wondered why this place wasn't run like any decent House, with a duty-board locating the channels.

He happened across Morningstar, coming out of a tunnel that connected the main meeting halls to other buildings. She paused, zlinning him. "You don't look well."

"Don't feel it, either. Have you seen Klyd?"

"No, but stop by the infirmary and get something to settle your stomach, or stay away from the dining hall!"

She hurried away as Valleroy set off for the infirmary. There were no Simes waiting in the foyer. He reeled through the heavy doors and down the varnished hallway. Sunshine from the skylights sparkled dizzyingly off walls and floors. The world spun, and Valleroy fell against a door that swung open, sending him sprawling into a transfer cubicle.

For a moment, he was tempted to stay where he'd landed. Somehow, he didn't feel so bad any more.

Then Klyd exclaimed, "Hugh! What—"

He twisted to face Klyd—and Ediva, who was standing in the doorway behind the channel, wearing shapeless white pajamas. He didn't have to see her arms. Her pinched face and vacant eyes told him just how much in need she was.

Klyd commanded, "Ediva, go back to the room."

The renSime wavered, zlinning Valleroy. The channel shoved her out the door, poking his head out to call to someone, "Take her back to Number Six." Then he closed the door and turned to Valleroy.

The sharp focus of Klyd's attention lifted a good half of Valleroy's discomfort, but the relief weakened him still further. He struggled to get up, feeling foolish. He should have realized Ediva would be here. Apparently Klyd was here to help her assigned channel drive a transfer into her.

Klyd helped him up onto the transfer lounge. "I thought you were in the print shop approving the new edition of *First Companion's Protocols*."

"I should be, but I—" He had no business reporting sick. "Klyd, how is she? She's not going to die?"

"Not this month. But you're not helping her. Why did you come? There's fosebine in the suite to take care of your headache."

He recited his symptoms, and shrugged, "I'm fine now."

Klyd rubbed his eyes with two ventral tentacles and asked all the usual questions: has this ever happened before, when did it come on, how long did it last, have you eaten anything odd? Valleroy answered, feeling silly.

"I can't imagine what it could be," said Klyd. "I zlin nothing unusual, except you're very high field, even for you. I wouldn't want to take you down before our transfer, though."

"No, don't do that. If it's something I ate, I'll be better tomorrow."

Klyd picked up the overturned cart, rummaging for medication envelopes. "Take a dose with water every hour as required. You've no infection, no fever. You're in perfect health."

"You should have told me that before I got out of bed," quipped Valleroy. "Could have saved me some trouble."

Klyd smiled. "See you later." He slipped out, carefully closing the door behind him.

The way he took that exit made Valleroy start to wonder. If Ediva's life were really in danger—right now—would Klyd have told him? Valleroy stirred up his medication, pondering. *What if she dies?*

He pocketed the rest of the envelopes, downed the solution, and left the cubicle. The nausea and weakness were back.

Unable to face the journey to the print shop, he fell into a hall chair to wait out the vertigo. With his field, he had no business staggering around like this.

A door opened across the hall, and a tangible wave washed across Valleroy. Klyd appeared in the doorway, and beckoned as he stepped out and closed the door behind him.

Feeling stronger, Valleroy went to the channel. Klyd zlinned him critically. "Would you be up to an experiment?"

"Experiment?" Alarm thrilled through him. "Ediva—"

"She's aborted twice. The second time, I thought we'd lost her, but Payel stabilized her." Payel Farris ambrov Im'cholee was the channel assigned to Ediva's transfer. Klyd put his hands on Valleroy's shoulders as if to support him as he delivered the next blow. "Her liver isn't functioning properly, and I think she's sustained cardiac damage. Hugh, it's the typical deterioration of the 'delicate type.' "

"She has to live," whispered Valleroy, irrationally. And then, "Is it because she saw me just now?"

"No. This is a special case; I warned you when we first met her. I explained her situation to her—and to her Sectuib. Everyone agrees. There's no point to living if you don't live what life you have to its fullest."

Klyd's hands tightened. "She's agreed to try an experiment. Payel doesn't like it, but he's willing to go along. If anybody can do this with me, he can."

"Do what?"

"A simultaneous induction of a controlled cascade."

"A *what?*"

"An idea I got from Muryin's changeover, another application of the technique I used on Risa."

"Tell me!" demanded Valleroy, afraid to hope.

"Payel takes your field down—just enough selyn to provide for Ediva, to pick up your characteristics." He went on in his clinical tone, tensed against Valleroy's revulsion. "Then, while he gives her transfer, you and I take our transfer right there, providing Payel a pattern. I'm almost certain she won't abort. I believe it'll heal her . . . but I don't really *know* what will happen. I'd consult her Sectuib if she were here. But you're the one closest to her. If you say no, I won't bring it up again."

Valleroy swallowed over a dryness in the back of his throat. "It's still me she wants. That's why she's aborting."

"Yes. But it wouldn't help, even if you could do it. She doesn't have the speed or capacity to evoke the response she craves from you. I want to let her experience your response."

There was never any question in Valleroy's mind that he'd do anything for Ediva. But this— It meant virtually doing transfer in public. Valleroy asked Klyd, "Do you think you can make yourself do it?"

"I don't know. I'll give it my best try. And—Payel won't be touching your core—"

Valleroy nodded. "We've got to try it for Ediva."

Klyd searched his eyes, took a deep breath, and pulled his hands away with an effort. "Let me tell them, then I'll call you."

When Valleroy entered the room, Ediva was lying on the contour lounge, pale under her ruddy tan. The room smelled of aromatic stimulants. Payel and Klyd were dragging a second contour lounge out from one corner. As they fussed over the arrangements, Valleroy met Ediva's gaze.

"Hugh," called Klyd. "Step over this way."

"Right," he replied and forgot to move, forgot he'd heard Klyd at all, he was so caught in Ediva's need.

Using the fields, Klyd pulled Valleroy's focus from Ediva's relatively minor need into Klyd's raging depths.

"Hugh, step over here." Without touching him, Klyd pulled Valleroy over to the second lounge. "Lie down. Drop into level six and relinquish control."

As Valleroy molded the fields to Klyd's specifications, the two Farrises met in the space between lounges. On the periphery of Valleroy's awareness, the channels twined handling tentacles, then made lateral contact with each other, completing the circuit with lip contact. They circled until Payel was on Valleroy's side, and Klyd next to Ediva. Then they dismantled the contact.

Valleroy understood why Klyd required this state from him. His field was so high that, even though Payel was only just past turnover, Valleroy could entice him into a transfer. He'd shen Payel, and that could destroy Ediva. Also, Payel's going for Klyd's Gen would trigger the most primal instincts of a Sime—and though Klyd might not succumb to the urge to attack Payel, he could lose command of the fields, leaving Ediva vulnerable to the struggle between two Farris channels and a Farris-trained Companion. So Valleroy had to remain detached from Payel's touch, simply allowing the channel to draw selyn slowly, superficially.

Distantly, he felt Payel's tentacles searching his arms. There was the momentary flicker of laterals. Valleroy was so deep into his suspended state he hardly noticed Payel's brief lip contact.

Then it was Klyd's tentacles, Klyd's quivering laterals seating themselves on his arms, Klyd whispering, "Relax. I'll control."

He hadn't been warned of that. But before he could argue, or decide not to argue for Ediva's sake, Klyd had made contact and was demanding selyn at transfer speed.

The selyn flooded out of Valleroy with the peculiar sensation he'd craved so desperately for the last month. Yet even the vast relief wasn't enough to stem the realization. *He doesn't give a shenshi-stung deproda for me or Ediva. All he knows is his experiments!*

Some unconquerable reflex rejected the soaring heights of satisfaction, withheld it from Klyd, from himself—from Ediva— while his own need held him in the transfer, surrendering selyn as fast as Klyd took. And when it was over, Klyd held on, shuddering, unsatisfied—lacking the soaring joy and bottomless optimism necessary to conquer the vicissitudes of life.

Finally, with a tremulous sigh, Klyd relinquished the contact, head drooping as he turned away from both Valleroy and Ediva, struggling to recover equilibrium when the transfer should have left him in full vigor.

Payel relinquished Ediva. Her eyes strayed toward Valleroy. The horrid, pinched look had smoothed from her face. Her color was better. But there was no animation in her expression, no trace of post-reaction. *I suppose that was too much to hope for—when I couldn't do my part.*

Payel glanced at Klyd, then asked, "What went wrong?"

Klyd turned bleak eyes on Valleroy. "I thought we'd put all that behind us."

"So did I," said Valleroy.

Payel moved, accommodating Ediva's struggle to sit up. Her mouth worked in disgust. Then, dispassionately, she announced, "Hugh ambrov Rior, I hate you."

When Risa heard of Klyd's experiment with Ediva, she was, luckily, too busy to hunt for the Sectuib in Zeor and give him a piece of her mind. Would he *ever* realize people's feelings were as important as his experiments?

She faced such feelings daily in the Tecton changeover ward, the first one opened to the juncts. Klyd had been wrong again, predicting juncts wouldn't bring their children to be "perverted" by channel's transfer in First Need. The first week, they averaged three cases a day. And word spread.

But Risa had to admit she'd been wrong, too—about the motives of the parents who brought their children to the Tecton. Very few came as the first tentative ones had to Keon years ago, giving their precious children over to a healthier lifestyle than they could ever have. Instead—

The first day she was on duty, two parents dragged a kicking, screaming boy into the changeover ward, demanding, "Here—take 'im an' see he don't kill! That's six kills apiece fer us this year, guaranteed by the Council!"

And that was the first the Tecton heard of the bargain the Council had struck with their citizens.

"I won't be no pervert!" the boy shouted, his struggles using up the last selyn in his system. Sergi calmed the fields, but the boy was not yet able to zlin, and it did little to ease his hysteria.

If the boy died, it could bring junct wrath down upon them. Risa tried reason. "We can't help him if he's too frightened to cooperate!"

"Law says you gotta take him," said the mother. "If he dies, he dies; we get our kills just the same."

Risa tried appealing to the father. "He's your heir. Why didn't you try to persuade him instead of forcing him?"

"She *says* he's my son," the man replied callously, "but I got four more kids at home—two taxin' me outa house an' home fer kills, an' two pre-Gens I hope t'shen establish soon so I kin sell 'em an' git some good outa 'em! This here's the first one I gotta chance t'git somethin' outa."

By this time, the boy had passed out in Sergi's arms—a thin child who had never had enough to eat in his life, and had been sold to monsters so his parents could get kills.

Before Risa could even get their names, the parents took the receipt for the child and fled, leaving the Tecton to cope with the helpless child.

Amazingly, they brought him through. When he was conscious, he screamed and fought, trying to escape—until finally he responded to fields, and Risa and Sergi could control him. Risa's chronic discomfort from the transfer Klyd had forced on her was forgotten in the ever-new joy of bringing a Sime into the world.

Wavering on the edge of attrition, the boy had lost all his fight by the time Risa twined his newly-emerged laterals with hers and gave him First Transfer, pouring love and reassurance into that flow.

When it was over, the boy looked up into her face, then down at her handling tentacles still twined with his. Tears welled up. Suddenly he threw his arms about her neck and cried himself to sleep.

They didn't even ask his name until the next morning when the renSime who had sat with the boy through the night called for Risa. She left Sergi still sleeping and went alone into the new Sime's room.

"Well, you're looking good this morning," she told him. "Congratulations. You're all grown up now!"

Warily, he demanded, "Am I a pervert?"

"Do you know what that word means?" She'd asked her younger brother, Kreg, the same thing when he had resisted going to Keon with her. And this boy gave the same reply.

"Bad. Dirty. Nasty."

"Well, then, you know the answer, don't you?"

"I feel . . . good," he said tentatively.

"You *are* good," Risa reassured him, comprehending that he was groping for a moral definition more than a physical one. "Will you tell me your name now?"

"Do I have one?" he asked. "They sold me—like I'd turned Gen!" He forced away tears. "Don' want the ol' man's name no more. Ain't his son no more."

"You have a home here," said Risa, "but you don't have to stay. Any time you want to go back into town—"

"I can't!" the boy protested. "Not for a year—can't have a kill for a year—save twelve Gens fer other people."

Risa sighed. "The Nivet Council approved our program, but they didn't tell us that stipulation."

"Stip-u—?"

"Rule," she explained. "Well, then, you are a guest of the Tecton for the next year. Do you want to pick a name?"

"What's your name?" he retaliated.

"Risa ambrov Keon."

"Ambrov?" he asked. "Could I have that?"

"It's not exactly a name," she explained. "It means 'belonging to the House of,' and Keon is my Householding. But I knew a man named Ambru, an expert shiltpron player. He'd be proud if a fine young man like you chose his name."

So it was settled, but Ambru still had many adjustments to

make. Especially about Gens. At first he ignored them. But a Gen taught his reading class, and half the students were Gen— including Harris Emstead, Joe Madison, and Bill Jesson, all working on their Simelan.

Risa followed the boy's progress in literacy via Emstead as the changeover ward filled her time. The Gen soldier had little to do besides learn Simelan and teach English. All three out-Territory Gens still practiced martial arts with the ambrov Dar each day, but Emstead was frustrated.

"I feel useless," he told Risa one day, as she was catching her breath in the hallway, preparing to fight down another changeover victim. It had become a routine. Two or three times daily, an adult would drag or carry in a protesting child—or worse, an unconscious victim, suffering psycho-spatial disorientation from being moved while unconscious. The terrifying nightmarish feeling a Sime suffered when his innate sense of position in the universe was disrupted taxed the already panicky youngsters to the breaking point. Nearly half of them died.

Risa was a week past turnover, and the viciousness of the juncts, committing their children to perversions to get kills, grated on her nerves. "I'm sorry, Harris," she said. "I have to go back into that room in a moment, and I'm finding it hard to concentrate. What did you say?"

Emstead's field offered sympathy, although it did not mesh with hers. He had become increasingly comfortable to be around, but she wanted Sergi, who was representing Keon at another Tecton meeting.

"Can you teach me to help you with these kids? Other Gens do. Risa, let's be totally honest."

"I have never known you not to be," she replied.

"I can't stay here forever. Every time a little girl is dragged in here in changeover, I think of my granddaughter. For all I know, she's Gen by now, or she's changed over and been shot down like a mad dog. I keep hoping it won't happen. She's just barely old enough—but I know it *can*."

"I understand," said Risa. "I'm afraid Vi will change over at Rialite, without me. But it's worse for you; at least I know my daughter's in capable hands. You know your grand-daughter definitely is *not*. But Harris, what if you did coach her through changeover—and she killed you?"

His field showed faint alarm. "You think she could?"

"No," she replied. "Unless she were a channel." She sighed, "All right, we'll teach you." She met his eyes. "You've given up on finding proof for the Gen Army of what you've seen here?"

"I'm afraid so. And with war so close, I can't stay here. Risa, you do understand I can't fight my own people?"

"Of course I understand."

"But if we survive . . . after it's all over, I'm going to offer Hugh my help guiding changeover victims to Rior." He set his lips grimly. "I feel so stupid. Those kids in the reading class are passing me by. A few days and they're finished, and I keep forgetting or misspelling words—"

"First, Simelan is their native language," Risa pointed out. "Second, they are in First Year—Gens, too. They can learn faster in that period of their lives than ever before or after. So don't feel bad; you're doing remarkably well."

He shook his head. "Too bad Ediva's so ill."

"What?" Risa was lost at his sudden change of subject.

"Her numbers. Cold, hard, facts. *That* I could take back with me—but without Ediva—if I *understood* her mathematics, I could answer Dermott's questions, make him see we can't ever win by killing off Simes. But now she's so sick, poor kid—"

Klyd's crazy transfer experiment hadn't helped. The next day Ediva was walking around, exercising, figuring the ever-changing selyn situation . . . but a puppet would have had more spirit. And Hugh was worse.

Sergi's soaring field kept Risa on an even keel as long as he was with her, and when he wasn't, she told herself, "He is *always* there when I need him—" and went about her work.

She came out of a room where another child of juncts had just died before his tentacles could break out. Hugh ambrov Rior, so-called specialist in changeover trauma, had been sent for an hour before dawn, but hadn't shown up. Lorina ambrov Carre, a Companion with years' more experience than even Risa had, fought down her own tears as she tried to support Risa. But the gloom of death and the pall of need were too much.

As Risa started for her office to write up the hated report, Ambru came running down the hall, augmenting hard. "Risa! Risa, come quick! Sergi says hurry—big trouble!"

"What kind of trouble?" she demanded, following the boy back to the main Tecton offices.

"He didn't say, but I zlinned somethin' really wrong. Sergi don't usually let things show in his nager!"

She pounded up to Klyd's office, burst in—and found him with Sergi, Hugh, Ediva, Emstead, Madison, and Jesson. The last four wore the loose garments in which they practiced with the Dar.

Although Hugh's field was low, for him, it reeked of depression. He wasn't even trying to control, sitting on the couch crumpling a piece of paper. Sergi moved to shield Risa as she asked, "What's happened?"

"Kitty," said Hugh in a choked whisper. "Kitty ambrov Rior."

Risa remembered the young woman, the mother of Hugh's son. She had gone back into Gen Territory to direct the spy network that brought them most of their out-Territory news. "She was shot by a Gen Army patrol and left for dead," Klyd explained, joining Hugh on the couch, his nager as uncontrolled and dark as Hugh's. "She got back to Rior and sent Hugh a message with her dying breath."

Gently, he pried the paper from Hugh's clutch, and handed it to Risa, his attention on Hugh, sharing his Companion's grief, the first real rapport she'd seen between them.

As she read, she found the source of the nageric gloom. A Genrunner named Simpsin and his Sime contact, Valry Adlay, had been caught in a buy. Simpsin had brought Adlay a string of young Gens, some still children, and Adlay paid in bales of Gulf Territory cotton.

Risa loathed Genrunners. She huddled close to Sergi as she read. The news grew worse, the neat round handwriting becoming uneven and hard to read, another hand taking over when Kitty must have become too weak to hold a pen.

Gens could be as junct as Simes. Adlay was captured and tortured by the Gen Army. Risa had to steel herself to continue. She herself had once been captured, along with Sergi, on a trip across Gen Territory to the Arensti Competition.

They had escaped—but not before she had spent almost two days with her arms cased in the hideous traps Gens used to immobilize Sime tentacles, exerting painful, dangerous pressure on her laterals. Her husband had been able to get Risa away alive—but only when they were safely across the border had he dared stop and pick the locks on the retainers.

It was one of the few times in her life Risa had been debilitatingly ill . . . and as a result, she had miscarried what would have been their third child.

Forcing the memory aside, she read on, only Sergi's steady field allowing her to hold the paper still. Valry Adlay, a junct, had not had a Companion to fool the Gens and free her. They had tortured her to death. And to buy relief from that torture . . . she had lied.

She had told the Gen Army that Nivet Territory controlled the Freeband Raiders! That they had sent the Raiders north, intending to catch the Gen Army in a trap between the Raiders and the Nivet Army, crush it utterly—then invade Gen Territory and harvest Gens to make up their shortages!

Risa's eyes went to Emstead's. His face was grimmer than she had ever seen it as he said, "It's too plausible. Dermott is certain to believe it. We are at war."

CHAPTER FOURTEEN

Wild Gens

"There has to be a way to stop it!" Risa exclaimed, and saw Klyd stare at her in disbelief. As close to need as she was, she should not have been the one to break the gloom—but someone had to. Emstead immediately followed her lead.

"I'll have to convince the Army it's a lie," he said. "Some good news came in with the bad; General Madison, Joe's father, has been put in charge of the western front. *He* might listen before throwing me into the stockade."

"I'll go too," said Joe. "At least Father will know I didn't desert from cowardice . . . and he'll believe *me*."

Emstead looked at Ediva. Even to Gen eyes, she looked unhealthy—a grimness of effort on her face, lackluster eyes, listless movements. "I wish I could take you with me," he told her. "If you'll write up your figures in the simplest way possible, maybe I can show Madison how Simes *know* they have to stop killing, and stop this war."

"I will go with you," said Ediva.

"No!" chorused Klyd and Hugh . . . and Joe Madison! To Risa's surprise, she felt the young man's field attempting to engage with Ediva's. If Ediva were in need, she might actually respond to it—if she weren't fixed on Hugh.

Klyd continued, "You've got to face it; until we solve your problem, you can't go far from a fully-equipped channeling staff."

"Klyd's right," said Sergi. "We may have to fight Gens. We all have to start in perfect health."

"But do try to simplify your figures," Risa added. "I don't understand them either, but between us, Harris and I must make Joe's father accept them."

"I kin explain 'em." It was Bill Jesson, the quiet boy who seemed a mere shadow of Joe Madison. When all eyes turned to him, he blurted, "I never knew there *was* that kind of arithmetic till Ediva showed Joe an' me. But it's all plain common sense oncet somebody shows you."

Emstead was astonished. "Son—to *you* it may be plain common sense, but to me it's worse than Simelan poetry!"

"But he can do it!" exclaimed Ediva. To Madison, she said, "I'll loan you my notes on the explanations I've worked out. But first you'll explain it all to me, so I'll be *certain* you understand. Come on!" Ediva and Jesson left.

Risa said, "We'll want a large enough party to seem strong but not belligerent. Sergi, go see what Gens will volunteer from as many Houses as possible. Tell them to pack their regalia; we'll ride in caped, banners flying."

"I'll find you a white flag," put in Hugh.

"I must get a quorum vote on it, first," said Klyd.

"I leave that up to you," Risa replied. "Send the Tecton credentials after us by fast messenger."

"And if you can't get them," Sergi added, "we'll just make the peace and come back and present it to them."

"But the junct Council—"

Risa said, "The time to inform *them* is when *our* messenger brings you the news that we've got our truce."

She returned to the changeover ward, hardening her heart against being drawn into treating a new case coming in. When she told Lorina she was leaving, the woman could not fight back tears. "Risa, so many children will die here! None of the other channels can do for them what you can!"

"Get some of those shenned Farris channels down here," she replied testily. "They're always bragging how good they are. What makes them think they're too good to help these poor kids? Make them work with real people for a change—do them all a world of good!" *Especially Klyd*. But she could not imagine him deigning to help some poor child of juncts through the worst experience of his life. Recalling his callousness to Hugh's needs at Muryin's changeover, almost traumatizing his own daughter, maybe it was better if he *didn't* come down here to zlin how many new ways these poor kids were finding to die in changeover.

When she returned to their room, Sergi was packing for both of them. "We can't take all the volunteers!" he told her. "I arbitrarily limited our party to fifty, and Harris agreed. "We've got four channels, including you, from four Householdings, their Companions, five more Companions, and the rest donors with a few disjunct renSimes from out-Territory. Oh—be sure to zlin for Ambru. I wouldn't be surprised to find him hiding under someone's cloak!"

"What about cycles?" Risa asked. "We don't want anyone to arrive at the Gen Army camp in hard need or wildly post."

"Some are taking transfer now. Harris says it'll take six days to reach Madison's latest camp. What about you?"

He turned the magnitude of his field on her without enticement. He was ripe and ready for her—had been for three days. But the transfer Klyd had given Risa had been unsatisfactory in quality, not quantity of selyn. She was not coming up short, and transfer would be much better if they waited the two days until she came into true need.

Risa stared at the double bed in the heavily insulated room. How she had anticipated the kind of transfer they hadn't had since leaving Keon: total privacy, no clinical atmosphere, and no public retreat from the transfer area to the place where they could express their post reaction.

She shook her head. "It's got to be out under the stars again. Why do poets seem to think that's so romantic when it really means rain or mosquitoes and rocky ground?"

"We'll make it wonderful anyway. We always do."

By mid-afternoon, they were ready, dressed for the trail, all their finery packed in saddlebags. There were pack horses, too, loaded with peace gifts for the Gen Army. Every Householding had contributed, even though the Tecton session to approve the trip was only getting started.

Risa zlinned Ambru hiding in a straw basket labeled Zeor-designed material. She plucked him out and shooed him off to bring back the cloth, pointing out acerbically that he must know by now he couldn't hide from a channel that way.

He knew. When they made camp at midnight, she found the boy in the midst of a group of Companions, having used their nager as a shield. "What am I going to do with you?"

"Feed him to the Wild Gens," suggested Sergi.

It was not a totally idle threat; the direct route to the border went past a huge Ancient Ruin where such Gens had accumulated the past few months, the Nivet Army too busy and licensed Raiders too superstitious to clean them out.

But the next day they gave the Ancient Ruin a wide berth, knowing whole caravans had been swallowed up.

It was a late summer day, the first chill breezes of autumn wafting out of the mountains almost on the heels of the last chill breezes of spring. Raised in Gulf, Risa was amazed at such a short summer. She rode close to Sergi, and saw him finger his beard as he shivered. He had intended to shave before their transfer, but had learned it was hopeless to try to stay clean-shaven on the trail.

Risa rode close to him, masking his nageric prominence.

Twining the reins loosely around two tentacles, she reached into her saddlebag for her cape. At that moment there was a resounding nageric clap, and Sergi shouted. Risa's horse shied, sunfished, then bolted. The party was surrounded by scraggly Gens in patchwork clothes, rushing at them with weapons raised, howling discordantly.

All of the renSimes and most of the channels had been unhorsed, stunned by the Wild Gens' version of a Genslam. The Companions, still confused, were sitting targets for flights of arrows.

Risa leaped off her galloping horse, landed on her feet, and sped back to the fight, dodging panicked horses. She had to snatch several arrows out of the air before they hit her, but she made it to Sergi, who had ridden after her. She grabbed his bridle and beckoned him to dismount.

"Come on!" she yelled over the rising din of battle and led the way back into the center of their party, gathering the able-bodied as she went.

Emstead was shouting, "Dismount!" for the horses provided shelter from flying arrows. More Wild Gens poured out of concealment. Over their battlecries, Risa explained, "Genslam! Take their fields down as they come at us! Disarm them—don't *harm* them! Gens are too valuable to waste."

They formed a defensive circle, some Simes posted out front to snatch arrows, the channels just behind them, capturing the attackers and taking their fields down to harmlessness. Combat trained Gens then sent the bewildered attackers spinning back the way they'd come.

No one questioned Risa's leadership, but after what seemed like an impossible time more Wild Gens still came at them, while others returned. The rain of arrows hardly slackened. Risa began to doubt they could outlast the undernourished, undisciplined pack of feral creatures.

Emstead, Madison, and Jesson were with the ambrov Dar, disarming their attackers of a growing pile of weapons— daggers, whips, bows, rusty guns they used as bludgeons— even a gypsy telescope. Ambru, barely recovered from the first Genslam he had ever experienced, forced his way to Risa's side, helping Sergi funnel Gens to her.

"Ambru, don't let them—!" she tried to warn the boy of the way the Gens could murder Simes, but though less than a week from hard need, he resisted their enticement, grasping not their arms but their reaching hands, pinning their arms behind their backs until Risa could take them.

Risa began to feel the strain of taking selyn from one Gen after another, with barely a breath between. Sergi took a scratch from a rusty knife wielded by a snippet of a child who squirmed and screamed in his grip until Risa yanked the weapon loose from a clenched fist. She threw it to the ground, and, zlinning the girl, ached at the tragedy. But she could only try to be gentle as she propelled the creature back toward the rocks.

A fresh wave of attackers hit them. Risa knew she had too much selyn stretching her secondary system. They were outnumbered, and none of them could go on much longer. "Augment!" she shouted. "Void selyn!"

Soon the defenders were shrouded in a nageric haze of static that prevented them from zlinning very far.

A gunshot rang out, shattering the ambient. Emstead, seeing a Wild Gen leap on one of the channels from behind, had shot with deadly accuracy. The creature screamed in pain, its ripe nager sending a paralyzing death shock through the haze, blood and brains splattering.

Sergi's attention was divided. Risa took the shock to her primary system, a personal, physical pain.

In need, with too much unassimilated selyn still surging through her secondary system, her depleted primary system lost control of her secondary. She clutched at Sergi, trying for a quick internal shunt of selyn from secondary to primary, not worrying how it would spoil their transfer.

But she couldn't balance it. She felt her body stiffen in a convulsive fit as she began to black out. She had never felt such a thing before. Sergi lowered her to the ground as her awareness of the battle faded.

Then Sergi had her in transfer grip, his lips to hers, his full attention piercing through the chaos to control every minute current in her body.

It wasn't their style. He hadn't done such a thing since before she'd disjuncted, so she was unprepared when he implacably forced the transfer into her.

Her intil rose under his control, her primary system opened to receive selyn. She couldn't control the rate—but it was more than high enough. And it felt good. Shuven! Did it ever feel good. Nothing had ever felt so good. . . .

Each miraculous sensation Sergi's selyn evoked begged for another even better one. She zlinned his senses reeling with the complement of every sensation he caused her. He was so lost in the mutual process his controlling grip had gone lax.

As the flow peaked, she couldn't resist the exquisite mutual satisfaction he offered. Only—at the very last instant, bliss eluded him.

Her primary system replete, Risa's debilitating inner chaos subsided. She finally had the presence to signal Sergi to relinquish control. Hanging at the agony of unfulfillment, he surrendered. She couldn't leave him that way. With one supreme effort, the very kind she'd made with the last few Wild Gens, she stretched herself around a final increment of selyn, drawing it from him with all her speed.

In that peculiar shared effort, something happened akin to the relief of having her ears pop after a steep climb. Abruptly, the ambient nager blasted in on her senses, but in the wake of repletion, as always with Sergi, she toppled to hypoconsciousness, losing perception of the fields, feeling only the stones digging into her backbone. Sergi's weight cut off her circulation, his beard tickled her sunburnt face, screeching Wild Gens beat against their defense lines, and she realized Sergi was obvious. Eyes closed, face transformed to an expression he would never share with another woman, he was kissing her, too post to stop. "Sergi!" she snapped. "Not here! Not now!"

His eyes flew open as she pressed his face away from hers. "Risa?" he begged, as frantic as she felt.

She could hardly stand the hurt in his voice, and was glad she wasn't zlinning. "Yes, dear—it was the most marvelous we've ever had, but we'll finish *later*, understand?" But he didn't understand until four screaming Wild Gens attacked Ambru. The boy was straddling the body of a Dar renSime, shouting for help as their defensive circle crumbled.

Sergi, wild-eyed, grabbed the rusty knife that had wounded him, and rolled to his feet as feral as the Wild ones, defending his mate. Risa forced herself duoconscious as she bounded up, looking for an opening.

But the four Wild Gens focused on Ambru, and their fields built ominously. Before she could react, they snapped their fields in unison, producing a downrushing suction that almost knocked her hypoconscious. She held on, zlinning the peculiar spectrum of responses in the channels, renSimes and disjuncts, as bemused by the plethora of tiny distinctions as Klyd might be. Infuriated with herself, she shook loose and zlinned Ambru, who lay on the ground, paralyzed, terrified as he strained to zlin and could not. He was in hard need. To him it was a sensory deprivation that prevented all possibility of taking selyn.

Leaving Ambru for dead, the four Wild Gens turned on Sergi and Risa, knives raised. Sergi charged, kicked, disarming the biggest one and grabbing him, holding the knife at his throat. Risa had never seen Sergi in a post-rage before. She leaped forward and yelled, "Surrender, or we'll murder him!"

The other three stopped. Sergi's captive squirmed harder, and screamed, "No! Get them!" The other Wild Gens came toward Risa's group, howling.

The other three charged Risa. Ambru picked himself up and—need ruling after the selyn-draining battle—attacked one of them in killmode. The Gen's eyes widened, but he met Ambru's tentacles with his arms out, nager steady, and Risa thought Ambru was as good as dead. Meanwhile, the other two Wild Gens, blanching as if Ambru were an animated corpse, emitted blood-curdling screams that stopped the battle.

Sergi's captive surged against steel-mill toughened muscles. Blood spurted around the knife.

Silence fell, and Risa finally understood that the Gen who hung dying in Sergi's grip had been their leader.

As the leader expired, Ambru and his Wild Gen stared into one another's eyes, frozen in post-transfer adjustment.

One of the Wild Gens screamed, "They're turning us into Walking Dead! Run for your lives!"

They scattered to the farflung cover of the rocks.

Sergi collapsed in a heap over the boy dead in his arms, and wept uncontrollably, "I didn't mean to!"

Risa had never seen Sergi's post-reaction go so sour.

Ambru's assailant tried hopelessly to wrench his arms away from Ambru's hands and tentacles, and Ambru tightened his grip. "No you don't!" he said, shifting his grip down to the Gen's wrists too fast for Gen reflexes to respond.

"You're not dead!" the Gen boy exclaimed. "It didn't even knock you out!" He looked around, his eyes sliding over Risa to appraise Sergi, then the other Gens in the party. "You're—you're Householders!"

"How come *you're* not dead?" Ambru finally asked his prisoner. "You can't be no Companion."

"No, not yet. Sectuib told me—" The boy's words were suddenly choked by tears, then lost in sobs.

"Take care of him, Ambru," Risa instructed. "Don't hurt him, but don't let him go!"

She bent over Sergi, jarring him out of his grief by pointing out the other injured, and he joined her, dazed but recovering. Two Gens and a renSime had succumbed to Wild Gen daggers. Everyone else would be able to travel at dawn.

While she was treating Emstead for a cracked rib, he asked Risa, "How did they sneak up on us?"

"These kids grew up with Simes; they knew how to use these boulders for insulation." She gestured about them. "They probably spotted us from that hill back there, then set the ambush before we got here."

"Yes . . . they got our scout, too," he said. "We found him beyond those rocks. I told them to bury him with the others. What're you going to do with your prisoner?"

"I don't know. Let's question him."

The boy was seated by a campfire, Ambru keeping a wary eye on him as both drank trin tea. They were about the same age, even the same size, for the starved Gen had not filled out to adult musculature, while Ambru was still in the process of leaning out into Sime wiriness.

"What's your name?" Risa asked.

"Bai ambrov Kiereth," the boy replied and fought back tears as he added, "Just Bai. Kiereth's gone." He stared at her, at Sergi, at Emstead. "They said—they'd destroyed *all* the Householdings!" Another tear escaped his control, and he swatted it away angrily. "Shen those juncts! I believed them, and I wanted to kill them all!"

Kiereth was one of the Householdings reported destroyed by the Nivet government weeks ago. Bai, only four months established, had escaped, sure he had no refuge. Risa and Sergi's treacherous post state left their hearts wide open as the boy's story unfolded. Kiereth had been one of three Householdings a day's ride apart, in northwest Nivet. One day they heard of the confiscation and destruction of Orzel, the next day of Trinan—and junct troops were headed their way on the heels of the few refugees from the other Houses.

Cut off from the rest of the Territory by the Nivet Army, preparing to flee northwest, they received word that Norwest was gone. So, with the refugees from Norwest, from Orzel, and Trinan, they had dug in to defend themselves.

"There were hundreds of junct soldiers!" Bai reported. "They burned our stockade gates—murdered all the Simes and Companions, and took the rest of us Gens for market. They said *all* the Houses had been taken, and I believed them!"

He buried his face in his hands, sobbing. Ambru put his arm around him. "Never believe no juncts," he advised. "They were tryin' t'scare you—make you a good kill!"

Anger brought Bai's face up as he shook Ambru's arm off. "What about you? You tried to kill me today!"

"Did *not*!" Ambru replied. Risa zlinned he believed it. "I give you the best shendi-fleckin' transfer ever, *that's* what I done! I'm nonjunct. Never killed, never will!"

Risa let it pass; it was not the time to explain to Ambru that Bai had saved his own life.

"That . . . that was the *first* transfer I ever gave," Bai admitted. "The channels never had much time to work with me because of all the trouble. I donated twice. Sectuib said I had potential, and then the juncts came."

Bai, two other Gens, and six children from Kiereth had been sold to a dealer. Four of the Kiereth children had died on the way. The other Kiereth Gens had been sold, leaving only Bai and two children, who died in the Wild Gens' attack. They murdered the Simes, freed the Gens, and looted the train. The mindless Pen Gens were worthless to them, but they found that Bai was awake and aware.

"I had to prove myself," he explained. "They were a lot tougher than me." He glanced at Ambru, who had the same dragged-up-in-the-streets quality as the Wild Gens. "I wanted to murder juncts, the way they did, so . . . I joined them." He closed his eyes, suppressing tears.

"Juncts burned my home. I saw them murder my mother! Two of them took our Sectuib, and they—they—"

"They murdered him," Risa said gently. "Enough."

"They whipped him—whipped his arms until his laterals were shredded—left him hanging to die by the roadside, with a sign saying, 'Genhoarder.' " His eyes pleaded. "You've got to understand! I had good reason to murder juncts!"

"*I* understand," Ambru told him. "My . . . parents." He spoke the word as if it disgusted him. "They abandoned me in changeover. That's what a lorsh *is*, Bai, someone who'd abandon a changeover victim. Juncts are lorshes."

Bai nodded and continued. Unable to prove himself through physical prowess, he had offered to teach them what he knew of nageric manipulation. He had meant to teach them Genslam—and thought he had, for they had knocked out every Sime in two previous caravans. When their technique had failed twice today, he'd convinced the leader to take four of them in close to a single Sime and blast him. Some of their previous victims had dropped as Ambru had, and he'd always thought they'd died, but the Gens had never waited to see if any would revive. They slashed the Simes' throats, then took their goods and provisions.

"And then, today . . . it just didn't work!"

Risa tried to recall what she had felt from those two nageric impacts. Not Genslam, but something close. Then she remembered the keener perception after transfer. Would Klyd have been able to make anything of it? She'd never studied such details—never believed there was anything *to* study.

While she was thinking, the conversation boiled onward, led by the two youths. Bai was asking, "What Householding are you from?"

"Keon." "Zeor." "Mountain Bells." "Im'cholee." "Imil."

"You're all that's left?" Bai asked, wide-eyed.

"No," said Sergi, "we *represent* all these Houses. There are still many Houses functioning, and you will find a home in one of them. But for tonight you must rest. In the morning we'll figure out what to do with you."

"Just one more question," said Harris Emstead. "Why

didn't you run for the border after you were free of the Gendealers? Was it just that you wanted revenge?''

''Without Householdings,'' the boy replied, ''all Simes would be junct. What would be the use of trying to make a life in Gen Territory when the Simes would just kill off all their Gens and come after us? I didn't think I'd live very long here, but I thought it was no use anyway. How long could it be to Zelerod's Doom?''

CHAPTER FIFTEEN

''Who're You Calling a Farris?''

It took four more days to reach Gen Territory, four days of flat, dull landscape and increasing heat. Finally, when Risa looked back, not even a hint of mountains could be discerned in the haze.

As a Sime, she knew where she was and could return to Capital without a map, but she was fascinated with the way Emstead used the map and a compass, seeming to know their progress as well as she did.

That first day Sergi had ridden in hunched-up silence, still in shock from murdering the Wild Gen. They had not consummated their post-reaction; even if they had been in the mood, the whole night after the battle was spent getting the injured ready to ride at dawn.

The next night they had stayed in a waystation, where a Tecton messenger caught up with them—with their official credentials. Risa wrote a report of the Wild Gen attack to send back with the messenger, Ambru, Bai, and two Gens whose injuries hadn't healed well enough to let them go on.

As she composed her letter to Klyd, Sergi said, ''What can

the Tecton do? If they go out to capture those kids, the government will accuse them of Gen hoarding.''

"I don't *know* what they can do—but soon the Nivet Army will clean the Wild Gens out.'' She hated the harsh anger in her voice. She put down her pen. Sergi slumped on the bed, holding a letter from their son Mor, written two months ago. It was filled with news of goods shipped to Nivet, money and trade items coming in, crops doing well, their metal products selling rapidly. She was annoyed that it hadn't cheered Sergi up as she expected.

Depression and annoyance were definitely not their normal feelings the day after transfer—and *such* a transfer!

Yet ever since, she had fought bursts of inexplicable anger. She rested her chin in her hand and chewed the end of a dorsal tentacle as she analyzed her reactions. She kept losing track of conversations, having to drag herself back from analyzing fields like some shenned Farris—

Or like a brand-new channel! Getting lost in the ambient was perfectly normal for a new Sime, especially a channel. It had happened to her after her First Kill . . . when she had frightened her father with massive mood swings, from delight at each nageric discovery to a deep, mysterious depression when strange dreams assaulted her.

It had lasted only a few days and never happened again. Risa had returned to the strong, stable personality Morgan Tigue had raised his daughter to have. But now . . . the syndrome was related in her mind to being junct—to killing. *Well, I'm not junct anymore. There's nothing to be angry about. I just seem to be zlinning more than I ever could before!*

She moved to the bed and snuggled up to Sergi. He stared vacantly at the letter, not reading. "It sounds as if Mor is running Keon as well as we could," she tried tentatively. There was no answer. "Sergi!"

He seemed to drag himself back from another place. He looked down at his wife as if wondering what she was doing there, then said, "Risa, I . . . I just can't. I'm sorry. I'm no good to you at all.''

"What are you talking about? Oh, for goodness' sake—I'm not interested in making love, either. But I would like to have my husband back. Please, Sergi, what's wrong?''

"I murdered that Wild Gen. I *wanted* to murder them all because they were attacking you."

"To defend me."

"To kill them," he insisted. "And yet . . . I could as easily be one *of* them! So could our son!"

"No, you couldn't," she said, stroking his tense hand.

"Only because we were born in a Householding! It's not ten years since the Gulf Militia cleaned the last Wild Gens out of the Ancient Ruin near Lanta! If I'd run there, I could have been just like that poor kid I murdered."

"And if you'd been born Sime outside a Householding, you'd have been junct . . . just like me."

He drew in a sharp breath, and took her in his arms. "That's not what I meant! Please, Risa, forgive me."

"For what? Reminding me that because of you I have a better life than I ever dreamed of? But I'll never forgive you if you rob me of my beloved Companion."

"I can't help that," he said bitterly. "When I forced transfer on you yesterday, I lost all my self-control. I'll never trust myself again, so how can you?"

"If I can't trust you—if you and I can't rebuild our normal cooperation—it could be the end of the world."

"Did you think I hadn't thought of that? You have to be at your best for the most crucial meeting between Sime and Gen since Rimon Farris met his First Companion. And I wrecked our transfer, and—"

"Sergi!" She pushed away and knelt to look at him. "What do you mean, wrecked? It was miraculous! It took me back to our first transfer together—and then outdid it!"

"I was totally out of control," he reiterated.

"Do you mean at the end? You were unsatisfied because I couldn't take all your selyn. That was *my* fault, not yours. I didn't resent you. I wanted to satisfy you, perfectly."

"Oh, that you did," he said, and added with disgust, "and if you hadn't shenned me out of post-reaction, I'd have taken you right there on the ground, like a dog! And when *that* animal instinct was thwarted, I turned vicious. That poor Wild Gen just got in my way."

She searched her memory. "*You* didn't murder that Gen."

"Oh? Who else drove that knife into him?"

"*He* did." Before he could protest, she insisted, "I zlinned it, Sergi. You were holding him still. You forget how strong you are because you always compare yourself to Simes. But that Wild Gen knew he was being held by a Gen, so he expected you to tire. When he squirmed, he thought your arm would give out and he'd escape. Instead, he drove himself into the unmoving knife."

Sergi shook his head. "You can't read thoughts."

"No, but I can tell you this: *you did not move.*"

His dark blue eyes studied her, and his field engaged hers, a deep personal caress. "You believe that."

"It's true. Ask any of the other channels."

"We don't have a Farris channel with us," her husband replied clinically, "and no one else can zlin nerve impulses and reflexes that closely."

"Shen and shid!" Risa exploded. "You and your shedoni-doomed Farrises! I zlinned *exactly*! Whatever you did to me yesterday, I've been zlinning like a bloody-shen Farris ever since! After Muryin, did you really want one all to yourself?!"

For a moment, his field sparked with denial, indignation, anger. Then, slowly a new emotion welled up, driving the others out until he laughed. With an explosive sputter, he doubled over and roared.

She retreated from him, offended. "It's not funny!" The sensation of having Sergi, of all people, laughing at her grated on her sensitized nerves, but he wouldn't stop. As he laughed even harder, her dismay turned to outrage. "Sergi, what's the matter with you!" She shook him.

He gasped, "You think *Farris* is contagious!"

Suddenly she saw herself through his eyes, spitting fury at being tarred with the same brush she'd laved over the Farrises. Her mouth quirked and her diaphragm knotted, forcing laughter from her reluctant throat.

Finally she was laughing *with* Sergi, and it felt wonderful. Their fields interlocked, they were a team again.

At last, eyes streaming, sides aching, she gasped, "Sergi, you've got to stop!" When he showed no signs of running down, she signalled with their finger touch code. "I can't break it," she gasped. "Help me hypo!"

She was slammed hypoconscious so hard she came up

dizzy and slightly nauseated. *Clumsy—!* But her temper had lost the irrational force behind it. "Sergi, stop laughing."

It was a command, and he responded, collecting himself as if for an emergency. That broke the cycle.

She shoved off the bed, intending to face him at eye level, but her feet and her inner ear wouldn't cooperate, and she had to hang onto his shoulder to keep from falling. "You didn't have to slam me hypo so hard, did you?"

"Slam? Risa, I leveled you just as I always do. I'll never mistreat you again."

She took that in, and patterns began to form. She'd been most irritable when Sergi had been working with her.

She licked dry lips and confessed, "There's another reason I've been so edgy, other than sexual frustration—which is bad enough." She recounted the things that had annoyed her and how she'd been exhausting emotional stamina fighting his touch.

"No," she ended, "I don't *really* think you tried to make me into a Farris. But something's happened to us, Sergi, and I can't take this forever. We've got to help each other."

His professional demeanor composed his features. Suddenly, she was duoconscious again. The room spun hard, and she staggered into his lap with an inarticulate grunt. His arms closed about her, and suddenly she was hyperconscious, but before she could react, she was duo again. She squirmed. "Do that one more time and I'll throw up!"

"Shen! It's true!"

"Do you think I'd lie to you!"

"No," he placated hastily. "You could have been mistaken, but you weren't. Risa, you're just much more sensitive than you used to be! You weren't kidding; I've got to treat you like a Farris!"

She lay cradled across his lap, basking in his healing power. "Maybe it's *you* that's stronger? Your field went sky high this month."

"But this didn't happen then. And right now my field must be zero. Probably it's both of us. We'll ask Klyd—" He stopped, as if waiting for the explosion, but Risa didn't feel even a surge of temper. "Meanwhile, I'll do my best for you, but *you've* got to train *me*, Risa."

When they'd met, he had already been First Companion in
Keon and had seemed wise and knowledgeable as the Ancients as he trained her in channel's skills. "I'm not sure I
can. . . ."

"Just let me see your reactions, let me practice on you,
and leave the rest to me. But let's not have another day like
this one. Don't *hide* anything from me, Risa, even if you
think I can't handle it."

"All right. This world we've built together, Keon and
Gulf, all of it will *end* unless at least you and I can
communicate."

On the fourth day of travel through the monotonous flatlands,
they crossed a line of cairns that marched off to the horizons,
east and west, announcing the Territory border. Other than
that, nothing distinguished Sime from Gen Territory. They
rode on, Sergi and Risa letting most of the train stay ahead of
them, using the endless hours of riding side by side to
practice functionals. As Sergi's field rose, he learned to use a
lighter and lighter touch until he finally laughed, "I honestly
do think you're reading my mind now! I make no effort at
all—just think it, and you react!"

It seemed to work both ways. Since the explosion when the
juncts had blown up Keon's steel mill, leaving Sergi partially
deaf from the blast, Risa had become accustomed to staying
to his good side, facing him when she spoke, and still having
to repeat things sometimes. Now he seemed to understand her
without effort, and it was not an improvement in his hearing,
for he still had problems with other voices.

They passed abandoned farmhouses here and there—not
drought-stricken, but fear-stricken because of raids deep into
this area. Fields of wheat had dropped their seeds with no one
to harvest them, but others were burned-over. Natural fires,
Risa wondered, or deliberate burn-off to destroy cover and
horse fodder?

She rode to the front now, zlinning ahead—miles ahead,
further than ever in her life before, until she zlinned the
chaotic Gen nager that had to be the Army. Emstead rode up
beside her. "If the army hasn't moved—" he began.

"It hasn't. They're about two hours' ride ahead."

The Tecton party dismounted, and transformed their drab

train into a holiday parade. They curried the horses till they gleamed, showing their high breeding. Each one wore the colors of his House, the rider's cloak dramatically draped. All weapons were hidden out of sight—and access.

Emstead put on his full-dress uniform once more. He led, with the white truce banner, followed by Risa leading the pack pony laden with gifts, Sergi with the Keon banner, then the rest of the Houses, each carrying a banner. The net effect was stunning—and not at all warlike.

They rode at a sedate pace, one hour, another. Risa zlinned they were being observed, but they were allowed to come within sight of the camp—still several miles distant on the flat plain—before two patrols closed on them, riding at full gallop, rifles leveled. They were surrounded.

Risa called a halt, and they all sat with empty hands high, as Emstead had explained was the Gen peace sign. Risa speculated it was to show the absence of tentacles—and sat tensed against the memory of the time she and Sergi had been taken just this way.

The officer in charge approached Emstead, his nager in utter confusion at finding a Gen officer leading a coalition of Simes and Gens. Doubtfully, he saluted Emstead. "Sir?"

Emstead returned the salute. "Colonel Harris Emstead, Southeast Division, to see General Madison."

"We . . . were not expecting you, Sir," the young lieutenant said. It sounded more like a question.

"General Madison will know why I'm here," Emstead replied. "Send a man to tell him I've returned from Sime Territory, mission accomplished. These people are friends—and have come, under truce flag, offering alliance."

"Begging the colonel's pardon," said the lieutenant, "but perhaps you'd better deliver that message yourself?"

Emstead didn't look to Risa. He had to appear to be in charge, not under Sime direction. So she offered, "We'll wait here," glad the Gens could not read her consternation.

Emstead rode off with the lieutenant. The rest of the soldiers stayed, guarding the visitors. The Tecton party remained silent as time passed . . . and Risa's imagination worked. She trusted Emstead's judgment in going to meet his old friend first, but suppose things had changed? Suppose

Emstead was now an outlaw, and they threw him in the stockade without listening to him? Or suppose General Madison told him something that called on his loyalty to Gens, against all Simes.

Finally, the lieutenant came back for them, and as the sun threw long shadows they were led toward the camp, a vast tent city. By the nager, there were thousands of men here, but only a few, going about their tasks, stopped to stare. So the camp was not on alert for an enemy in their midst. That spoke well for Emstead's persuasion.

They were led to a large tent, living quarters and office under one roof with a canvas partition between. Emstead stood outside with a taller man of about his own age, with thinning brown hair, but with that same common-sense dignity to his field that had led Risa to trust Emstead.

But he hadn't had Emstead's experience, and his field wavered with mistrust and wariness as Risa dismounted, careful to make no sudden moves. Emstead introduced them and let Risa present the gifts, telling her he had already explained Householdings.

"And here is the proof, General," he said. "This gentleman is Risa's husband. She is Sime, he is Gen—and they have two children of their own. That's why they can understand how worried you must have been—"

On cue, Joe Madison stepped out from the midst of the Tecton party—and Risa felt his father's shock, surprise, welcome, and fear. "Joey."

"Father." Then the boy snapped a salute. "General Madison, Sir! Privates Joe Madison and William Jesson request a hearing, Sir!"

Madison fought down a lump in his throat and said, "Of course. Every man has a right to a hearing in this Army. I will hear you tomorrow."

"Pardon me, General," Risa interrupted, "but what Joe and Bill have to say is vital to what we have come about. We must all talk—now. Time is growing short; the Freebanders have been reported massing northwest of here."

"We know that," Madison replied. "We're ready for them, as you can see."

"No one can ever be ready to face Freeband Raiders,

General. But you can be stronger and more ready. No Army can win its battles when operating on false information.'' She proffered her official credentials, complete with ornate seals, the General's name calligraphed in English.

That got them an invitation into Madison's tent. The whole party could not fit, so Risa, Sergi, Emstead, the young Gen soldiers, and two other channels went in to talk. Madison sent some men to clear tents for the rest of their party and took the negotiating team inside. Five guards followed, and Risa was aware of twenty more taking up positions outside the tent. Camp chairs were brought for the visitors; the guards stood at alert.

When they were finally settled, Risa began without preamble, ''You've been given false information, General Madison, by one Valry Adlay, under torture. As I'm sure you know, when prisoners have no truth to tell, to stop the torture they will spin the lies they think you want to hear. We know what Adlay told you: that the Nivet Army controls the Freeband Raiders. It was a lie, General Madison. *No one* controls them; that's why they are called *Free*banders.''

''And how am I to know *you* are not lying?''

''I bring you the truth—if you dare send out scouts to verify it. The band coming from the north is the largest ever seen on this continent. They outnumber your army ten to one. Surely you know the Nivet Army is smaller than yours. So *how* could it possibly control such a mob of people who know no law other than to take what they want and destroy the rest?''

Risa zlinned that what she said about the Nivet Army matched his information—but that he hadn't known the size of the band of Raiders and was hesitant to believe her.

''Nivet Territory wants to stop that band of Raiders just as much as you do,'' she continued. ''Perhaps you haven't heard that Norwest Sime Territory has collapsed.''

''We heard. They've been raiding *us*.''

''Yes—fleeing families trying to reach Nivet or Gulf. But have you thought what it means when a *Sime* Territory collapses? When a government can't provide Gens, the people— *all* the people—must hunt. The last-ditch efforts of the Norwest government were toppled by an invasion of Freebanders, leaving people with the choice of fleeing for their lives, as the people you call Raiders did, or . . . going Freeband themselves. What is facing you—and facing *us*, after they have overrun *your* Territory—is the *entire surviving population* of a Sime Territory, turned Freeband.''

She paused, letting that sink in. Emstead watched his friend's face, and just when Risa zlinned it was time to prompt him, asked, ''Joe, haven't you sent scouts out to estimate the size of that band?''

He nodded. ''They haven't returned. Three groups, at two-week intervals . . . and not one has returned.''

''Well,'' said Risa, ''here is the information they would have brought you if they could.''

Sergi took the master tactical map out of the dispatch case and spread it on the table, facing Madison. The positions of Madison's troops and the oncoming Freeband Raiders were clearly marked.

''Why are you showing me this?'' Madison asked.

''To convince you we mean what we say. For if we cannot cooperate, we will all die.''

He took Risa to mean from the Raider attack, and she sat back to let him study the map before offering him Klyd's letter, dripping with Zeor and Tecton seals.

Eventually, he looked up. ''This Tecton . . . is the government of the Simes?''

''No—of the Householdings,'' Risa explained. ''In Gulf Territory, where I come from, the whole Territory is moving toward being one big Householding, Simes and Gens living together in harmony. We are in the process of spreading that lifestyle to Nivet Territory.'' She didn't say how futile their efforts had proved so far.

Madison examined Risa and Sergi. ''You don't kill Gens?''

''Never. But many Simes still do; we must not mislead you. However, we have reached a point at which Simes *must* stop killing Gens, or all humanity will die.''

Madison rubbed his eyes, then looked at Risa, at the other Simes, then down at their arms on the table—his bare, hers tentacled. ''How do you expect me to believe this?''

''It's true, Father,'' the younger Madison spoke up. ''I've been there. I've donated selyn.''

"As have I," said Emstead. "Simes don't need Gen deaths to live," he explained. "All they need is the energy we produce in abundance, which they've learned how to take without killing—or pain. There's nothing to it."

Risa felt Sergi wanting to amplify that.

Bill Jesson spoke up for the first time. "And they don't ask it fer nothin'. Look!" He pulled up the short sleeve of his shirt, revealing a hairline scar below his bicep, turning the arm so Madison could see that it went almost all the way around. "We attacked this lady's home. They beat us, sure but then they healed us. General, our own medic was goin' t'cut off my arm—said he had no way t'save it. But *Risa* saved it, good as new!"

"Bill's right," said Madison's son. "When Simes and Gens work together—there's no limit to what we can do!"

"But the time is now," said Emstead. "This crisis goes far beyond that band of Raiders out there." He started to tell about Ediva's figures, and Madison dismissed the guards. Emstead continued, his plain language detailing Ardo Pass most effectively. Then Bill Jesson explained the mathematics, while Madison's field grew tighter and tighter with horror.

Finally, well after midnight, Risa finished, "And *that's* why these Freebanders are bearing down on us all!"

But Madison could absorb no more. He sat back, eyes bloodshot, and surveyed the Tecton party. "Would some of you—say you, Miss Risa, and you Harry, be willing to go to New Washington to present this to the real policy makers?"

"Yes," answered Risa. "But we don't have months for formal diplomacy."

Off in the distance she zlinned a nageric disturbance, beyond the sleeping camp and the perimeter guards.

Sergi asked, "Risa, what is it?"

"A rider—a single Gen, exhausted, frightened—"

Madison didn't ask how she knew, but went to the tent door. Now they could hear hoofbeats; the weary rider drove his horse right up to the General's tent, gave a sketchy salute, and gasped, "They're coming! They almost got me! General— there are too many to count!"

"Sime Raiders?"

"Yes, Sir! From the northwest, maybe two weeks away.

They cover the whole plain; you can see their dust cloud for half a day! Can't be less than ten thousand—"

Risa said, "Winter's early in the north. This will have to be a field command decision. General, surely you've the right to save your men from destruction while accomplishing your mission."

CHAPTER SIXTEEN

Channel Shortage

Valleroy stretched his legs to keep up with Klyd as he strode down the hall of the public changeover ward. Risa's absence had put such a strain on her volunteer staff that they had called for help, and Klyd had responded. Valleroy was gratified to see the glow of achievement on the channel's face; another life saved, another future brightened. "We should have come down here before, even when Risa was here," commented Valleroy.

"Yes, but now we're late."

Klyd's voice carried, and heads appeared in doorways. One, a patient Klyd had taken through breakout and First Transfer last night, glowed with appreciation.

He greeted the new Sime, examined the fingers the boy's parents had broken in rage at his resistance to going to the Tecton and assured him, "You'll be fine. And you won't face attrition again as long as you come to us."

"But my parents," protested the youth. "They *believed* the lorshes. The government won't pay them off in kills; why didn't you tell them that?"

"They wouldn't believe me," answered Klyd. "And—we survive at government sufferance. We don't speak against the government here."

The boy accepted that wisdom with a solemn nod. "Keep quiet, but keep helping. Put me to work. I want to help."

He had been one of the worst ever brought in, and Risa's staff had hesitated to bother Klyd with a hopeless case. But Klyd had won the boy totally.

"You can help best by attending classes," Klyd told him. "You're no use to yourself or anyone until you've learned to read, write, and figure. Then our staff can find work for you. You're right, we can use a lot of help." He smiled, capturing him with nageric reinforcement. Valleroy was sure the boy would be hatching the ambition to pledge Zeor within the week.

They left the boy staring after them and hurried to the committee meeting, arriving late.

". . . because no reasonable person makes such a total about-face in loyalties. The spy woman is lying."

"Our best channels find no evidence of duplicity!"

"Naztehrhai!" interjected Klyd, calling them all House-holders pledged.

They turned to him, shocked, and Valleroy deduced that Klyd had entered without disturbing the nager, even with Valleroy at his side. They'd had transfer less than a week before, so Klyd was high field enough to mask Valleroy's field.

"The 'woman,' " declared Klyd, "is truthful. She now understands Zelerod's Doom, and is on our side."

"She's a spy!"

"She *was* a spy." Klyd moved to his seat at the table. "Some people place loyalty above reason, and those make good spies. But we've eliminated that type of Council spy among us. Sinda is the last, and she has chosen to see reason. News of her 'death' has already been leaked to the Council."

"You're not supposed to act without committee approval," admonished an older man.

"This committee did approve the security screening," argued Klyd. "It's vital the Council *not* get word of Risa's mission; 'Collaboration with organized Gens' is treason. That means decisions must be made outside the open forum where spies hear everything." Klyd opened his file folder with a snap. "To the agenda of this meeting, then."

For an hour they discussed secreting the vast Tecton library in the vaults beneath the Tecton compound, buying horses on the black market, paying for Gulf imports, and giving sanctuary to a Gen Army officer who'd escaped from the Councilors' secret pen below the Nivet Capitol.

From there Valleroy went to a Companions' committee on training Gens to deal with juncts. The initial idealism of the non-Companion Householders had flagged when confronted with the sadistic attitudes of the average junct. So many had resigned from the program that they might not be able to meet the demand—giving the government an excuse to ransack more Householdings.

Then Klyd called Valleroy to the changeover ward, and he spent the night snoozing on a lumpy transfer lounge.

A commotion woke him at dawn as if the patient were in breakout. But the room was empty. The hem of Klyd's cape slapped the door jamb as the channel sped toward the commotion. Ramming his feet into his boots, Valleroy followed.

At the end of the hall, Ambru struggled with the receptionist and triage channel who held him in the air to keep him out of the low-field area where his excitement could easily cause a death.

When Ambru caught sight of Klyd, he stopped wiggling. "Sectuib Farris, they've taken him! You've got to help!"

Ambru, Valleroy recalled, had disappeared when Risa had left, and Klyd had assumed he'd gone along.

Klyd lifted Ambru out of the grasp of his captors. "Promise not to go in there, and I'll put you down."

"Promised!" Klyd took him into the outer lobby where there were no parents waiting anxiously for news of their children. Ambru chattered madly on about 'him' until Klyd collapsed into a chair and speared the youngster with a gaze. Valleroy moved in back of Klyd's chair and began to work on his shoulders, using his field to aid his recovery.

"*Who* is *he*?" asked Klyd.

"Bai!" He spilled out a disordered tale of Wild Gens attacking Risa's party until Klyd threatened to send him back to language class to learn to construct a report.

When they finally had the straight story, Klyd asked, "Now what's happened to Bai?"

"At the city gates! Those thieving juncts demand money to let you into town now! They stole the messenger's saddlebag with Risa's letter to you and everything!"

Valleroy went cold. Was that the Council's countermove to Klyd's demolishing their spy network?

"Where's the messenger?"

"I don't know. They took him!" Klyd didn't even swear. Ambru added insistently, "And they took Bai, too, said he was condemned for being ambrov Kiereth and government property for being Wild!"

"You told them that?" asked Klyd.

"Me?" The boy's voice cracked. "I ain't no lorsh!"

"Calm down," said Klyd, working the fields.

Ambru did, and asked with wide-eyed confidence, "When do we go get him back?"

"*I* can't help Bai," explained Klyd in the tones he reserved for announcing a terminal illness. "Any interest I showed in him would only hasten his fate and worsen it."

"Well, how *can* we get him back then?"

Klyd silently shook his head, and stared vacantly at the unadorned far wall. After a while, Ambru backed away silently, scurrying down the hall. Valleroy read his sense of betrayal in the return of his street urchin posture, hunched, wary, a quarry at bay surviving by his wits.

After a while, Valleroy let his curiosity surface. "What happened to Naivel?" The one they'd worked on all night.

"She turned out to be a channel. I've sent her for training. Sorry I didn't mention it." He found a smile for Valleroy, realizing he'd thought the girl had died. "We'd better clean up. We have breakfast with the library committee."

Well, at least I get to eat at a table. But meals during committee meetings usually gave him indigestion.

This one was no exception. Valleroy picked at his food as the disputants presented various plans for preserving the library.

Klyd, seeming unruffled, listened to each side, then ticked off the strongest points of each of five plans, "So tomorrow morning I want to see a combined version including all those points. Capital could be overrun with Freebanders settling in for the winter. They'll burn our books, even original Ancient editions, for heat!"

As the group broke up, Klyd stopped a short, elderly Sime, bent with arthritis. "Girar, you've something for me on that research project?"

"Oh, yes!" He blinked dim eyes and rummaged in a battered leather case. "Here it is! This copy is at least a hundred years old. Donated by House of Invor."

"Never heard of Invor," said Valleroy, unsurprised.

"Up north. Don't know if their Territory still exists."

Valleroy read a lot, but didn't recall the imprint. The little leather-bound book Klyd held looked old but well preserved. The Simelan typeface was archaic, the language difficult to follow. Klyd handled the pages reverently.

"Thank you," he told Girar. "I'll return it tomorrow."

"Hope it helps. All I could find on the subject." Talking to himself, Girar shuffled out of the room.

Valleroy took the book from Klyd's hands. "When, before tomorrow, can you read this?"

"Tonight," he said in the tone that indicated he'd stay up all night with it if necessary.

"You know you don't get enough rest." There were more meetings Klyd had to attend that evening.

"We're sealing the library. Can't delay the research."

"Research into what?"

"Us. As I promised. If we are in fact close to an orhuen, and if that's what's causing your problems, then this book ought to tell us. But if it's something else, well—our library didn't yield anything, and Girar would know. I think he helped invent the index system. If there's nothing here, then we're dealing with an unknown."

Valleroy turned the book over. The sick feeling he'd had before the transfer they'd tried for Ediva seemed unimportant. "They had nothing on Ediva's condition?"

"They have copies of Grandfather's study on 'delicates,' but very little has been done by other Houses. I must write up Ediva's case for the library before it's sealed."

How much can he do? "I'll get her charts copied." He understood now that Klyd was driving himself because he did care—deeply—for each individual.

"That would help." Klyd tucked the little book into a pocket of his tunic and hurried back to his office.

Days flowed past in the pressure of emergencies, meetings, and strategy sessions. Valleroy saw Ediva, mostly from a distance, and tried not to worry about how worn she seemed. *It's the continual bad news,* he told himself. *It's depressing enough, and she's so depleted by illness. . . .*

But there was occasional good news. Risa's messenger was released and brought his pouch and its well-read contents to Klyd. But as it turned out, she had written of her mission only, 'Every reason to expect success.' The rest was about the Wild Gens.

And things progressed. The library project raced along, and one border Householding tapped a source of fast horses for the express riders. Another House got the Tecton a shipment of leather via connections with junct officials. And the mortality rate at the changeover ward continued to drop.

But statistics showed the drop everywhere. Klyd called a meeting. "This is not an increase in our efficacy. This is a change in the patients. I want to know what's going on."

The answers were hair-raising. All across Nivet, the government had honored their promise of kills to parents surrendering changeover victims *the first month.* But the second month some were told to take a transfer.

Occasionally, even in Capital, Pens refused to honor channels' orders certifying a junct too ill for transfer. So the children's grapevine carried gruesome stories of adults turned away from the Pens to die of attrition. That same grapevine which passed along the ever-changing routes of the starred cross now warned children to stay clear of Pens for fear of being attacked by a turnaway.

And *that* was what was driving children to the Householdings, willing to take transfer rather than become addicted to the kill and be unable to get one.

Ediva came to the meeting to collect the statistics. She had been spending days at the Nivet Capitol, winnowing the archives. Her room was papered with charts and maps. She was working feverishly, driven by her personal doom.

When she left that meeting, she looked frightened. But Valleroy had no time to comfort her. A messenger had just come over the rear wall of the compound, filthy from having crawled through the valley behind the public stables. She was one of those messengers chosen for her knowledge of the city, to ferry pouches from the city wall into the Tecton compound to avoid the search at the gates.

"Sosectu Rior. Your messenger said this was to be delivered to you only."

It was an unusually flat packet.

Valleroy checked the seals, then read, "Diorn ambrov Rior has been killed in the performance of her duty. Her name is entered in the Memorial to the One Billion."

He let Klyd take the paper from his numb fingers. "She was so young." Klyd had said she'd never make a Companion, but that hadn't stopped her from trying. And now some junct had killed her.

But she had died trying to realize her dream—Rior's dream. Valleroy remembered how sure Klyd had been that Kitty would never make a Companion, either.

And she's dead, too.

But murdered, not killed. For every Diorn there was a Kitty—no, many Kittys who learned, as Hugh himself had done, that transfer was as much a Gen's fulfillment as a Sime's.

But Klyd and the other channels immediately began to talk of closing down the Gen transfer option, and they adjourned to a conference room. Klyd took Valleroy aside. "Why was Diorn allowed to volunteer?"

"The Zeor channels probably let her train, sure she'd never get through—but she did."

Klyd nodded, and Valleroy knew that he, too, was probably remembering Kitty. They had argued violently about letting her try Companion's training. Hugh had won . . . and so had Kitty. But now Klyd said, "We must close the program, but it's not your failure. You did more than anyone could have expected with it."

"Klyd, we *can't* close it down! Every volunteer accepts the risks, just as any channel or Companion does. You sold the plan to the government on our offering a choice. We *can't* withdraw the Gen transfer option. The juncts will turn on the Houses and destroy us all."

"They are already turning on our Companions," Klyd reminded him. "Now that there's been a kill, others will be more nervous until another gets killed. The juncts will spread news of what spooks House-trained Gens. Hugh, we have no choice but to stop it.''

Something inside Valleroy cried out that Klyd was wrong. Still, he had no argument to counter Klyd's, so he was forced to agree, "All right." *But at least he gave it a try. Next time, when we've got better safeguards, when the world is better organized and the successful volunteers convince him it was good, he'll set it up again because it has worked.*

They went into the meeting shoulder to shoulder. Ediva joined them, soaking up the data as if it had no emotional significance. But her mathematics showed, "If you cancel the Gen option, within two months you'll have channels incapacitated by exhaustion. We don't have enough channels." She left to design a new model of Nivet's selyn delivery system.

Two hours before dawn, the meeting wound down, little accomplished. But as Klyd was about to adjourn, the heavily insulated door flew open. The other guard lunged after a fast moving Sime, missed, and fetched up against a table while Ambru leaped to the front of the room, quelling augmentation as he shouted, "Sectuib Farris, I did it! And here he is, Bai ambrov Kiereth, my Companion!"

Companion!? Ambru was renSime, not even Householder.

"Where," Klyd asked, "did you come from?"

"I rescued him, from the Councilors' private stock under the Capitol building."

"Rescued," repeated Klyd, eyes widening at the implications. Everyone in the room shared his reaction.

The retaliation would be against the Householdings.

Valleroy knew only one solution.

"Klyd," he whispered, tugging Klyd's cape until he bent to listen. "These boys have given the juncts an excuse to attack us. There is only one way we can keep the government from striking when we close down the direct transfer option: strike first. The Tecton must oust the Council and take over the Territory government."

Valleroy's hand was on Klyd's wrist, making a deep field contact, so Klyd's shock ripped through him undiluted. Half the channels in the room charged to Klyd's rescue on sheer reflex, checking only when Valleroy signaled them back with his other hand.

Klyd folded into his chair and surveyed each representative in the room, weighing them individually, then collectively. Then he stood to speak. Ambru and Bai, hustled to seats in the front row, were content to remain inconspicuous.

"Sosectu Rior has seen what we have been blind to. The Tecton has become Nivet's selyn delivery system. *We* have delivered every transfer requested. *We* have turned no one away to die in the streets of attrition, or to go home and attack their own children. *We* have provided medical assistance and cared for changeover victims. We have taught the juncts to rely on us. Those who control selyn hold power. *We* already *are* the Territory government! It remains only to oust the Councilors and install ourselves in the Capitol."

Under tightest security, a full Tecton session was called that afternoon. By nightfall, they were discussing how to go about taking over the Nivet government.

Ambru, Bai, and the Gen Army refugee from the Capitol's pen knew the means—an underground escape tunnel from the building to outside the city walls. A hundred trained fighters used the tunnel to enter the Capitol just before dawn and replace every worker in the building. As the Councilors arrived, they were captured and thrown in the same Pen where they'd held their personal Gen stock.

At the start of the business day, Klyd announced that the Council had retired, leaving the government in Tecton hands.

The Army officers rebelled.

At one time, the officers had held their troops' loyalty. For the last months, however, they had been forcibly conscripting people to fight the approaching Freebanders.

To control the resentful conscriptees, career troops had been promoted and given the power to discipline offenders by public attrition. The amateur officers, unable to gain respect, had abused their power—finding excuses to punish draftees with attrition so officers could have the scarce kills. The rank and file were ready to rebel.

Klyd issued an order to release all prisoners, and embossed it with the now familiar Nivet Controller's seal, his signature, and the proper military seals.

Knowing the officers wouldn't honor the order, the Tecton mobilized Householders to infiltrate the garrisons, armed with copies of the High Command's orders to destroy the stockades and display cages, giving transfer to those in attrition.

In four days, reports came from garrisons where the Tecton takeover was greeted with cheers. Klyd wasn't fooled. The juncts planned to rebel when the current crisis was over. They didn't know it would never end.

The Tecton held a tenuous but official control of Nivet Territory. To secure that hold, Householders exploited their contacts among junct relatives of their members, disseminating the most simplified version of Ediva's proof of Zelerod's Doom, accepted more on her reputation than from understanding.

So it came as a double blow when she walked into Klyd's new office in the Capitol and dropped a heavy folder before them. She raised her eyes to Valleroy's, then searched Klyd's face as she announced in ravaged tones, "We can't do it. It's not that we don't have the selyn or the transfer *capacity*. We just don't have enough *bodies* to spread all over the Territory. There aren't enough *channels*—not by half!"

CHAPTER SEVENTEEN

Third Order

Risa rode into Capital in eager excitement. Messengers had brought news of the Tecton's takeover—just what she had hoped to persuade them to do when she promised General Madison the cooperation of the Nivet Army.

She was eager to see Klyd again, for her new sensitivity raised a thousand questions. Sergi had forced her, and she had become more sensitive. Had she made Ediva more sensitive when she forced transfer into her? How did Gens catalyze Sime sensitivity? Could channels do it?

These matters faded from her mind as the city gates swung wide to greet the returning Householders.

Emstead had stayed with the Gen Army, to train them to work with Simes. Bill Jesson was explaining Ediva's numbers to Gen Army Intelligence.

Joe Madison, however, had returned with Risa. She had been almost as shocked as General Madison, who had offered young Joe a field promotion and a command. His son had replied, "I'm going back to Capital, to fight with the House-holders. I sure hope when this is over there won't be a border anymore—because I'm going to pledge Householding Dar."

She didn't know what father and son had said in private, but Joe had been subdued all the way back.

He cheered up, though, as they found people waving to them instead of flinging abuse. At the Capitol, Klyd was in conference. Risa, Sergi, and Joe Madison went to find him—and walked into a nageric pall.

Ediva was surrounded by people offering condolences as they trailed heavy-footed out the door: "Good try." "You couldn't have done more." "It's not your fault." Ediva was trying to be brave, but Risa felt the tremors in her body and her field.

Something had gone terribly wrong.

"Klyd," Risa said, striding forward, "Didn't our message reach you? We've got an agreement with the Gen Army; their western division will join with us to fight the Freebanders!"

"Your message?" Klyd asked vaguely. "We've been in here for—almost ten hours. Did we get—?"

Hugh shuffled the papers scattered on the table, and found it, still sealed. He sighed, looking at Ediva. "There's not much use opening it now, is there?"

"What is the *matter* with you people?" Risa demanded. "You've done your part. One more step, and we've achieved everything we set out to do!"

"Risa, it's no use," said Klyd. "We have taken over the Territory, but *we can't govern it*. We don't have enough channels; Ediva has finalized the figures."

"Never mind can't," said Risa. "We've *got* to do it, like it or not. We've promised the Gens our aid."

She and Klyd looked eye to eye, fields in total agreement; the promise of Sectuibs would not be broken.

"Then we'll do it," he said, "or die trying."

Risa understood from the ambient what Ediva's new figures showed: the latter would be the case. Still, she bent over them, hoping and praying to find an error. Ediva was in need; perhaps she had missed something—

Peripherally, Risa was aware of the room emptying, of Joe Madison moving to where Ediva sat curled in on herself. *Good, the girl could use comforting.*

Valleroy stepped away from the table, gauging Joe's effect on Ediva and not liking what he saw. She was at the volatile edge of hard need. Madison wasn't safe, and neither was Ediva.

He eased over to envelop both of them with his field, and then deftly cut Madison out. "Joe! I'm glad you're back. The Dar have been asking for you, and—"

"—and you don't want me near Ediva."

"Joe," protested Ediva.

"No, it's all right," replied the youth. "I just wanted you to know, Ediva—you're one of the reasons I came back."

Valleroy had to admit to a twinge of jealousy when Ediva tried to smile for Joe. All through this whole wretched business, she had not twitched a face muscle. It was worse when Joe's expression responded as if he'd been promised everything he'd ever wanted out of life.

But Ediva said, "Joe—don't. Please. I can't—"

Valleroy focused on Ediva as he realized he'd misjudged what Joe sought with her. It was Joe's turn to feel jealous as Ediva looked gratefully up at Valleroy and pleaded, "Joe, I think you'd better leave."

The youth said, "Hugh, take care of her." Then he left.

Valleroy took her hand. The crowd was gone. Risa and Sergi, boots still covered with trail dust, bent over the desk with Klyd. Valleroy said, "Let's get out of here."

"They might still want me," said Ediva.

Klyd raked a glance across them, and resumed studying Risa's maps. Valleroy looked at the meeting room, plush chairs and thick carpeting, and visualized it all a smoking ruin. *They'll think of something.* Meanwhile, he was too comfortable to move.

"Klyd didn't say anything about you being near me," said Ediva.

"Probably knows I wouldn't listen this time. He doesn't like to fight with me."

"Never stopped him before."

"Before what?"

"Giving me up for dead."

"Has he told you that?"

"He was only keeping me alive to solve the problem."

"Nonsense! Klyd's a healer!"

"Why do you suppose he's not pulling you away, then?"

"Probably figures I can do you some good."

"Or at least no more harm."

"You didn't fail. It's not your fault the Tecton doesn't have enough channels!" He put his arms around her. Klyd was near turnover, so Valleroy had little physical desire, but his love was undiminished. He let his field permeate her systems with the feeling of life continuing, but he was careful not to engage her fields.

She snuggled close in his arms, and he drowsed with his cheek on her hair, wondering how he'd survived so long without this in his life.

"Hugh?" asked Ediva.

"Hmm?"

"I don't want to die without knowing your transfer."

He sat up. "You know that's not possible."

"What can it matter if you shen me? It would be a quick death—rather than—" Raking her tentacles through his hair to straighten it, she looked him in the eyes. "My uncle—and a cousin. They went just like me; transfer dysfunctions, sickness—nobody could help the pain, the vomiting, the paralysis. Dad said it ran in the family, but he died in a duel before it happened to him. Now my work's finished I could die willingly, except I keep thinking what it would be like if you ever gave me transfer."

"Then I never will—because I don't want you to die."

"The whole world will be dead before next summer!"

"Oh, Ediva." He gathered her close.

*   *   *

"I should have seen this coming," said Klyd, zlinning Hugh and Ediva. "In the rush of the takeover, I've scattered the team of channels and Companions I trained to get transfer into Ediva."

"Then *we've* got to do something to deal with her depression," said Risa. "She's suicidal."

"That's why I'm not calling Hugh away. He's all she has left. I doubt she knows how much he means to her."

"How could she, the way she's fixed on him?"

"I admit," said Klyd, "I'm not blameless for that part of Ediva's problem." He dropped into the chair. "Risa, what would you think of me if I could be objective about Hugh?"

"I never realized you suspected you were anything but infallible concerning Hugh."

His laugh was half grunt.

"But if you know it, why do you always act as if you have all the answers?"

"I don't intend it to seem that way." He hung his head dejectedly, and the life-luster of his fields faded.

Risa'd never zlinned such a reaction in a Farris before. It unnerved her. "I'm sorry, I didn't mean—"

"You were right, on the trail," Klyd interrupted. "Hugh and I are closer to the legendary orhuen than I thought. To live and to function vigorously—I can't do without Hugh. I don't want to, and neither does he."

Risa had nothing similarly intimate to offer. Klyd continued, "Ediva's a kind of problem you'll never have with Sergi. I can't *stand* the pain Hugh feels over her; from the start, I knew she wasn't going to live. Yet she brings him alive as he hasn't been since Aisha died. I *need* that life in him."

"Aisha?" she prompted.

He told her of his first meeting with Hugh, a Gen operative assigned to rescue Aisha, the woman he loved, from Licensed Raiders. Risa saw Hugh overcoming his fear of Simes to rescue Klyd from attrition, giving him a transfer which Hugh expected to be fatal. He had given his life to Zeor, then, and to Klyd himself. Some aspects of their relationship became clearer—how Klyd could take Korin, heartlessly leaving Hugh with Muryin "because he's the type who can do anything provided there's no alternative.'' It also explained how, because Klyd was indirectly the cause of Hugh's wife's death, he was now so anxious to save Ediva.

She noticed things in his nager she could never zlin before. *He's not cold and heartless. He can't stand hurting people, so he'd rather hurt himself.* She couldn't admire it, but she couldn't condemn it.

''Maybe,'' Klyd said, ''I've let Ediva's health divert me from Territorial affairs, and maybe that's why I didn't see the channel shortage coming before we took over the Territory. But, Risa, I *know* the solution is right before my eyes, and I can't *see* it!''

At that moment, the nager lashed wildly. Risa gasped. She'd been zlinning Klyd with all her sensitivity. Sergi stepped between her and Ediva. Risa grasped control, realized that Ediva was in convulsions, and charged after Klyd.

Hugh was bent over Ediva, Klyd circling to grip the fields. He motioned Risa to come in opposite him. ''She's voiding— third time this month. Hold her with me.''

Risa signaled Sergi and extracted Hugh from the tangle of fields. Klyd sent him for a stretcher and they moved Ediva to the infirmary. Risa zlinned with fascination as Klyd titrated drugs in Ediva's system against field pressures, to control her convulsions. It took him barely twenty minutes, and he overshot only once. Risa learned more in that half hour than in any other training session of her life.

Klyd issued careful instructions to Hugh on how to hold Ediva in this tranquil state. ''Will you stay with her while we discuss what to do next?''

Hugh answered in a whisper, ''Klyd, let her have Gen transfer.''

''That's what we must discuss.'' He took Hugh's shoulders. ''Don't do anything until I get back.''

Hugh looked from Ediva's blank face to Klyd's grim expression, and nodded, but it seemed to Risa it was less than a commitment.

Valleroy watched the door close behind them. This was Ediva's last chance.

There was nothing to be gained by fighting to the bitter

end. He recalled vividly the moment he'd decided to give transfer to Klyd, even if Klyd killed him. In that transfer, he had glimpsed for the first time what need really meant, what the world was like from the Sime point of view. He hadn't known that the only way to avoid being killed was to surrender his life.

Ediva, now that her job was done, was willing to surrender, as he had been then. An easy death with a chance at one last satisfaction—wasn't that the least one could grant one's loved ones?

He was flooded with the same open, unreserved feeling with which he'd confronted Klyd that first time, beyond fear of consequences, feeling only life itself. Ediva's eyes fluttered open, focused for a moment with a smile, then went vague as she drifted hyperconscious.

Her tentacles sought his arms, and he allowed transfer grip. He couldn't let her die, knowing his healing touch had caused the desire that tormented her.

He bent to make lip contact, letting love permeate his fields. He loved her valiant spirit, her keen mind, her discipline, her dedication, her loyalty to her House, her uncomplaining acceptance of the hardships on the trail. When she was near, everything was beautiful, as if she were a lamp washing the world in the light of beauty.

But right now, with her tentacles creeping hesitantly about his arms, she was Sime, and that, too, brought a special exhilaration. He didn't expect the perfection Klyd's draw produced. But he forgot as their lips joined and he sought the ineffable thrill of transfer, taking such firm control he didn't feel the tentative flutter in her initial draw. He knew only that he had to fill that aching need.

Klyd explained his plan. "Risa, you pick up Ediva's resonance, and hold it in your showfield while initiating a transfer flow from Sergi. That will induce Ediva's system to open to transfer. If you can slow down and hold long enough, I may be able to get a transfer into her. I just wish we had time to give you some practice."

"I can do it," she said.

"Hugh won't be in on it?" asked Sergi.

"That would put too much strain on Ediva," Klyd explained. "You go on ahead. I'll find the duty channel and have a guard set on Ediva's room. We can't risk being interrupted."

Risa returned to Ediva's room, Sergi holding back so she could insert them into the fields. Opening the door, she was overwhelmed by Hugh's nager, driving a transfer.

Risa augmented slightly, making everything seem to slow, as she yelled to Sergi, "Get Klyd!" Ediva was resisting Hugh's control. Even the Gen touch had triggered the same abort reflex Risa had overriden. Hugh subdued Ediva's reflex and his own resistance; transfer flow resumed.

Klyd flew into the room, ready to leap in any direction, zlinning the transfer deeply. Hugh succumbed to his own abort reflex at the touch of Klyd's fields, and instantly Klyd ceased zlinning, plunging himself into hypoconsciousness.

Risa didn't think, she merely acted. Gathering the resonance of Klyd's nager, she shrouded herself in it as she'd planned to hold Ediva's, then focused on Hugh, nudging him back into the transfer. Before she saw any result of her effort, her head swam and she plunged hypoconscious into Sergi's support.

Klyd shouted, "Ediva's a channel! I should have known at Muryin's changeover!" He lunged across the room, scrambled behind Ediva and seized her shoulders, seating his laterals, dangerously insecure, on her neck contact points.

As he moved, he did something with the fields that disoriented Risa, and when she'd cleared her perceptions, all trace of Ediva had disappeared.

Klyd's field now dominated the room—his primary field—his own personal system, not his showfield. He was taking transfer from Hugh. Embarrassed, she wanted to retreat, but dared not.

She gripped Sergi's wrist for a signaling contact in case she had to act. Klyd was doing the reverse of what they'd planned, *imposing* his own field on Ediva's—his showfield, not his primary field, though somehow he'd made it seem so.

And Hugh was buying it. The flow peaked somewhere beyond renSime capacity, but below that of any channel.

It went smoothly to completion, carrying Risa duoconscious.

Hugh stared dumbfounded at Klyd. Ediva's head was thrown back, eyes closed, face glowing with ecstasy. Hugh's expression cycled from dismay to outrage.

Retreating hastily, Klyd clambered off the bed. "It's all right. She's going to be fine now." He edged toward the still open door, and Risa, senses heightened, felt Klyd's embarrassment at intruding on a too private moment.

Valleroy came up out of the naggingly insufficient transfer, convinced he had gone insane. He felt Ediva's hands and tentacles, Ediva's unmistakeable mouth, Ediva's body—but he *sensed* Klyd. Then he saw Klyd's face over Ediva's shoulder.

Ediva's laterals broke contact, but her handling tentacles cocooned his arms gently. Her face seemed younger, her breathing steady. He was post enough to luxuriate in the pure sensuous feel of her, but Klyd's presence inhibited him.

The channel slid off the bed and hastened toward the door—and Risa and Sergi. *An audience!* Ediva's hands were sliding onto his chest, her eyes still closed. *Surely she can zlin that we're not alone?*

Klyd said, "She's going to be fine now." He hustled the others toward the door, adding, "You've got her post with the best transfer she's ever had. You know what to do."

When the door closed, Valleroy discovered just how much their presence had inhibited Ediva. Although he wasn't at his best, he was sufficiently inspired.

"What do you mean, she's a channel?" asked Risa as soon as the insulated door had closed.

"Didn't you zlin the stutter? I don't know why I couldn't put it all together before. It's so obvious!" Klyd bounced up and down the corridor. "There must be hundreds of them!" He stopped in front of Sergi to add, reverently, "Thousands!"

"Channels?" asked Sergi tentatively.

"Yes!" Klyd swung around and paced. "And we'd never have known if Hugh hadn't tried that crazy stunt." He palmed his forehead. "*He* tried a crazy stunt! I can't *believe* what I got away with! But we can do it now! We really can!"

"Do it?"

"The alliance with the Gens, the securing of this whole Territory, even defeating the Freeband Raiders!"

He's gone manic on us. "*How* has this changed anything?"

"The 'delicates' are channels! That's where that odd stutter comes from—their secondary systems. I *knew* there was something familiar about that shenned stutter; it's the *same* as you zlin in a channel, only so much smaller and fainter it doesn't seem so. When I zlinned it in Muryin, I should have known, but it's so much *bigger* in us!"

Suddenly, it all began to fall into place.

"It's a fight now!" he declared. "We can do it!"

Risa, having nursed a Householding through the training and incorporating of new channels, didn't see how, at this late date, discovering thousands of eager channel trainees could possibly solve their problems. If Klyd's jump to the conclusion that all 'delicates' were of this strange new channel type was accurate, then it was all the more tragic for humanity. Nature might have intended humanity to be able to survive, but they'd discovered the key too late.

CHAPTER EIGHTEEN

Cooperation

In a moment, Risa's hopes rose. "We *must* find a way for these new channels to begin distributing selyn *now*."

"Yes—if that's *all* we ask of them," said Klyd, "we can have each one in the field within a week of his first good Gen transfer. Thank goodness trained Companions far outnumber channels—though we're going to run them ragged."

"Companions won't mind," Sergi told him.

"Uzziah!" Risa exclaimed. "He's not delicate now—not since he's had Bethany! And he's already got a Companion, Klyd. His wife has been working to him for years."

"Are you sure?" Klyd asked.

"I'll certainly know once I zlin him again."

Suddenly Klyd's attention focused on Risa. "What has *happened* to you?" he demanded. "You handled that situation with such finesse, I'd swear you'd been trained at Rialite!"

Sergi grinned into the nager. "Thank you," replied Risa, "—I think." Then she admitted, "I didn't know before how what I did felt to you. I honestly couldn't zlin it, Klyd, and I apologize for my annoyance. But after what Muryin did to Sergi, our next transfer was—"

"At your age—I wouldn't expect such a change," said Klyd. "It will be a pleasure working with you—both of you."

Age and lack of adaptability was the major problem with the new channels—Third Order, Klyd called them, labeling channels like himself and Risa, with their high capacity and sensitivity, First Order. The others, the ones who never achieved high rank but were the backbone of any House, he termed Second Order. Risa disliked the terms, as it sounded as if they were second and third class citizens, but Klyd had said it, and the terms stuck.

The Householding Thirds were delighted to be channels; not only did it mean an end to their chronic deprivation, but most of them had hero-worshiped channels all their lives. To move from being a depressing annoyance to being channels themselves was as blissful as Gen transfer.

Of course, it took work to design a safe method of opening the vague secondary system of the new channel. But Ediva, healthy and learning to collect and dispense selyn, provided the incentive until Klyd, Risa, and a team of channels hit on the method that reduced fatalities to acceptable levels.

They set up the new channel for a transfer from a First Order Companion at high field, with a channel/Companion pair taking transfer in the same room. The new channel's Companion had orders to attempt what no Householder would *ever* attempt with a renSime: to force selyn into the Sime's system, inducing a spontaneous internal shunt from the primary into the secondary system at the transfer peak.

This was why the 'delicates' had remained undiscovered channels for so long. Their systems could not be perceived as separated until the secondary system was energized, but it could not be energized by accident, as often happened to the higher order channels, even at First Transfer. After several dozen 'delicates' had been opened at Capital, they sent teams to teach the process throughout the Householdings.

Becoming a functioning channel was well worth the invasion of privacy—to Householders. Juncts were another matter. Ediva, riding a wave of good health and high spirits, found that her new calculations showed that if they were going to pull this off, they would *have* to recruit Thirds from among the juncts. While juncts were lured by the prospect of Gen transfer, they balked at becoming channels.

Valleroy suggested, "Try the military. If we can convince the troops that they can raise channels from their own ranks— channels *better* than the Householder channels because they know what a kill is really all about we'll get the volunteers."

"That's brilliant!" said Risa. "The healthiest able-bodied citizens are already *in* the army! The delicates who can be opened will be given non-combat roles. Surely they'll go for that."

It worked better than trying to explain to juncts that they'd been born with a disorder which would destroy them early in life unless they became working channels. Health had never been such a strong ambition with these people that it inhibited them from enjoying themselves.

Valleroy feverishly restructured his Gen training program, no longer aiming to serve juncts in transfer, but to train Companions for the new Thirds. The world suddenly made sense again. The yearning for Sime touch which was such a deep part of him, and which so many Gens shared, was surely the mark of the born Companion. Many of his successful volunteers must be the Thirds' natural opposite numbers.

Joe Madison volunteered. The channels assured Valleroy that the young man's field truly reacted like a Companion's . . . and that he responded best to Ediva. And she to him. *After all*, Valleroy reminded himself, *she has to have a Companion she can satisfy. That will never be me—so it's good she can now turn to Joe.* He sensed, however, that the younger man wanted to be more to Ediva than just a Companion. So did Valleroy. But his Companion's training and

Madison's military upbringing allowed them to set aside rivalries and concentrate on the crisis at hand.

As they labored to hold the Territory back from civil war, the Raiders thundered closer. Messengers raced between Capital and the Gen Army Headquarters until at last the Gen Army crossed the border to the most strategic point at which to meet the oncoming horde.

The Nivet Army was massed to move up beside the Gens— but that was not an efficient deployment. So Klyd, Valleroy, Risa, and Sergi rode out to talk strategy with Madison and Emstead.

Emstead, Valleroy noted, still wore colonel's insignia. That meant the chiefs of staff had not yet made a decision, for if they had not believed Ediva's figures and Emstead's story of Sime/Gen cooperation, they'd have called Emstead back to New Washington for court martial. But if they had decided in his favor, he would be a hero worthy of promotion.

Sure enough, Madison was still operating on his own authority. "No choice," he explained. "our scouts verified your reports. No answers have come back to my reports to New Washington, nor any message from Jesson. But that's a long trip; maybe they haven't caught up with me yet."

Clearly, the man was worried—what if some messengers had been captured? That would mean both that Raider scouts had gotten past the Army, deeper into Gen Territory, and that the Raiders knew of the proposed Sime/Gen cooperation.

Grimly, they spread new maps on the table and began to plan the most advantageous deployment of troops.

"Gens up here in the hills," Klyd said, pointing to the map, "with your guns trained on the oncoming Raiders. The Sime Army below you on the eyeway, ready to meet them and to keep them from reaching your men. Even though the channels will take your troops' fields down—"

"Is that necessary?" Madison asked.

"They'll have a better chance to survive," Risa said.

Emstead said, "Make it voluntary. I'll do it as an example, Joe—and I suggest you do, too. These people use the energy they draw for healing. I guarantee, while we're fighting, the channels will be running the most incredible hospital you've ever seen."

"I guess if Joey can do it—" said the general—but Valleroy knew the channels read fear beneath his courage.

"Listen," said Emstead, "I'd rather go into battle without a gun than face those juncts high-field!"

"All right. I'll do it, and call for volunteers," Madison replied. "Now, that position on the high land looks advantageous, but the road between the hills is narrow. Once we start shooting, the Raiders can pull back—and to press our advantage, we'll have to move quickly. If both our cavalries chase the Raiders, they're sure to get intermingled."

"You're right," said Risa. "Your people don't know how to fight in Sime/Gen teams—and neither do most of ours."

"We've got to plan this well," said Madison. "Where are your generals? We'll speak the same language."

"I'm afraid you wouldn't," Sergi put in. "Harris can translate . . . but the army officers are juncts, and inexperienced at any command of this size."

"What?!" Madison exploded. "Green officers in a situation like this? Then my officers have to do all the planning— damn! Harry, you'll be my chief advisor. Let's figure out how to use the Simes."

Emstead turned to Risa, but spoke to Madison. "Begging your pardon, Sir, but Miss Risa here beat my command fair and square with mixed Simes and Gens."

All eyes turned to Risa. Valleroy knew what was in the minds of the Gen officers. A *woman?!* Risa had dressed for this meeting as always, in practical styles but with enough feminine flair that it was clear she was proud to be attractive. If it weren't for her tentacles, she could have been anyone's wife or sister.

Valleroy glanced at Klyd, then said, "General Madison, Risa has considerable tactical talent. And she has, no doubt, trained others in her methods . . ."

" . . . most of whom," Risa said, "are back in Gulf, and couldn't get here in time. I'll run your field hospital, and remain with your army as an advisor."

Obviously she knew how Madison's men would have reacted if she were *only* their tactical advisor.

Klyd said, "Communications between the two units must

be rapid and accurate. The Nivet Army must learn your bugle calls and field semaphore codes.''

Valleroy could see the red flags of security regulations popping up in their eyes. ''The codes change so often,'' he suggested, ''there's no way *this* army can use the codes against any other New Washington command. But as earnest of our intent, we'll supply your Intelligence Division with the code books used by the Nivet Army.'' Not that they'd be able to read them. The signal codes controlling the junct troops were nageric, for most soldiers in a fight would be hyper.

''That seems reasonable,'' agreed Madison. ''Now, I'll want to meet with your senior staff commanders.''

''It will be arranged,'' agreed Klyd. ''But first, we will take down the fields of any Gen who will be at that meeting. And we will post channels at all interactions between the two groups—to translate, and to control the fields.''

''It will be hard to coordinate a battle using officers I can't even talk to.''

''After the strategy is agreed on, Householding messengers will carry translated orders. I'll put a corps at your personal command, General, and we'll accommodate you in every other way. Together, we're going to win this battle and found a whole new way of life. I have a child, too. I want her to grow up in a world where she doesn't have to learn how to run an army as well as a House.''

That spoke to Madison's sense of rightness, and he responded as if at last he understood Simes. ''I want that for my granddaughters, too. No disrespect, Ma'am,'' he said to Risa, ''but a man should see his women don't have to fight.''

She eyed him. ''No one should have to fight.''

Three days later, the combined armies were actually performing a coordinated maneuver. Risa watched them from the highest rise, attuning her ear to the Gen bugle and drum signals. She had Householders spread among the juncts to translate the Gen signals into nageric codes.

So many plans had gone awry, she'd hardly dared hope this one would work. But it did.

''Enough!'' said Madison. ''We can maneuver. Whether

your troops can hold discipline under fire, I won't know until it's too late. But here's where we dig in.''

They had chosen a defensive position using their best information on the Raiders' course and had been moving toward it as they tested their drills. Now the two armies separated, the Gens with their artillery taking the high ground behind the Simes who would meet the initial charge.

Everything was working smoothly until the General's last order was echoed by the nageric corps. Suddenly, a different bugle alert rang out—from a detachment ahead of the main body, around a sharp bend in the trail.

Risa racked her brains for the interpretation, but Sergi said, ''It's a real attack—not a drill!''

''General!'' said Risa urgently, understanding that a field commander had issued the overriding order. ''Echo your commander's orders, or my people will not respond!'' *I knew it! There had to be a flaw!*

The General stared at her, then gave the command to his signal corps, and it rang out clearly over the whole army.

They rode forward to the skirmish, a place where the eyeway dove through a narrow cleft riddled with caves. Emstead's Gens mixed with about fifty Simes—Raiders. A raiding party? Or scouts? Or both?

Risa's impulse was to take command of the Sime unit that was Emstead's point. But if she did that, she'd lose all credibility with Madison. She gritted her teeth and told the General, ''We've got to take prisoners! They'll know the Raiders' plans!''

Madison raised an eyebrow. ''Can your people hope to capture one of *those* alive?''

''Certainly.'' *I hope.* Another hole in their planning. The ambient shivered with killbliss—the first time Risa had zlinned it with new sensitivity. She gripped Sergi's arm as the edges of the Raiders' force were cut down by Gen guns, but the core of the charging unit penetrated the Gen ranks and took kills. Others grabbed up Gens, slung them unconscious over their saddlebows, and attempted to escape. About ten of them made it, and Risa said, ''General, order Simes to pursue, Gens to hold back in reserve.''

Madison eyed her, clearly fighting the impulse to point out

who was in command of these armies. She knew it didn't go
down well with him that half the Sime army was female. But
escapees would tell the Raiders about the combined armies.
He issued the order, then asked, "Do you always think so
fast?"

She realized that it wasn't that Madison had reacted slowly,
but that she had been augmenting. "Only when I'm excited.
Let's get down there and see what Emstead has to say."

They rode into the canyon where the action had occurred.
Risa's medic corps was sorting the wounded from the dead.
The Raiders had done considerable damage, which augered ill
for the coming confrontation, but the tenuous alliance between Sime and Gen soldiers had held, even been reinforced
as they fought their common foe.

They found Emstead at a field table. "General!" He stood
crisply and reported. "Eighty or ninety Simes attacked us,
seven got away with prisoners. We've lost six men, all killed
by Raiders—none by our allies."

Risa had the most experienced channels in her field hospital and selyn collectorium, and all the Gens in Emstead's
command had given selyn before the engagement. She pointed
this out, and Emstead concurred. "I saw it working. Several
times one of your troops would square off with one of us, and
then collect himself and go back to fighting the Raiders."

"The ambient was disturbed by the kills that were taken,"
said Risa. "It raises the junct's—appetite for the kill. But
your men zlin like Householders, very unappetizing."

"Then why did the Raiders kill?"

"Because they're desperate," said Sergi.

The damage statistics poured in, and Emstead continued to
work efficiently under the General's scrutiny. Finally, a group
of the juncts reported in with two of the Raiders alive, and
four of the kidnapped Gens surviving as well.

Risa grinned at the General. "If you'll detail me a tent,
Harris, I'll question the prisoners."

But the information Risa extracted with her new sensitivity
destroyed all their plans. The Raiders were not heading for
the Nivet border region, but had only feinted in that direction
while the main fighting force circled west to another eyeway
that headed due south—into Capital.

The band Emstead's scouts had flushed from hiding was composed of scouts and spies detailed to track the armies and bring back Gens. By guessing numbers and zlinning her captives' reactions, Risa found the total number in this band had been seventy-four. Counting bodies, Emstead reported, "None got away, General." And they all breathed a sigh of relief.

Making camp, they sent messengers to Capital and spent the night poring over the maps. They couldn't wait for word from Capital, so Risa, Madison, Emstead and half a dozen junct and Gen officers made the decision.

"We get onto the High Eyeway here, and move west to Shen. That's a big town, not a swear word," said Risa. "We'll send people ahead to prepare the populace for your army moving through—" She stopped, aware of the sharp objections.

Emstead asked, "Are those mountains like the ones near Capital?"

"Worse," said one of the junct officers. "There's a few Householdings, but beyond Shen is the Army stables. Close to a thousand mounts there; don't know how many troops."

"I hate to say this, an alliance is an alliance," said Madison, "but we've no real reason to defend your capital, or your horses. My men aren't mountain trained. Our orders are to secure the plain east of here."

"Do that," said Sergi, "and be cut to ribbons by the Raiders when they've dispensed with us and stolen our horses to ride against you."

"And killed our Gens," added the junct officer, "leaving us nothing to do but try to take your men."

Madison just nodded, accepting that he had to move with the combined armies. Since the action of the afternoon, word had spread among the troops that, awkward and inefficient as they were in this first engagement, the Simes *had* protected their allies. The alliance was real now. The men would follow if Madison ordered them to defend Nivet's Capital.

"We wait for them in Shen," said Sergi. "There's enough flat ground there to maneuver, and the Gens will hold the high ground for us."

"We'll never get the artillery up those mountains," warned one of the Gens examining the map.

"By yourselves," Risa said, "no, you wouldn't. But with Simes to help and your selyn to use—consider it done."

Madison's eyebrow quirked skeptically, but Emstead just nodded. "They can do it, Sir."

They moved out at dawn, riders, wagons, and infantry stretching for miles along the eyeway. Risa carefully scattered the medic corps throughout the length of the column, and at every rest stop her channels worked to keep the Gens lowfield and to treat the inevitable small injuries, winning the trust of the Gens.

The juncts came to trust her medics, too, surprised that Householders would lavish such care on mere troops.

Risa rode ahead into the town of Shen, a very large town for a secluded mountain valley. Here the Tecton takeover was welcomed, for Shen had been surrounded for generations by Householdings. The town juncts had many Householder relatives.

When scouts reported the Raiders a day away, they transformed the northern entry to the valley into a trap. Concentrating on the north, they became nervous as the expected horde of Raiders didn't scream down on them. But before they could react, their eastern lookouts came pounding back into town shouting, "Raiders! This way!"

As battle was engaged, Risa realized her error might prove fatal. At the command post, she unrolled the maps and gathered the local Householders who had joined Madison's staff. "Here!" pointed Risa, when she found what she'd been looking for. "And here! From these points, with one of those spyglasses you use, they could have *seen* us from beyond zlinning range! Couldn't they?"

The locals nodded, horrified that they'd missed posting scouts to clean out those overlooks.

"Then we retreat," declared Madison, already rolling the map up. "West along the eyeway to a defensible position."

Their eastern defenses caved in under the assault. They were pushed back gradually until Madison ordered the total abandonment of the Sime town. It was a strategic necessity, Risa realized, but she hated leaving the defenseless behind.

They took as many townspeople with them as they could, but when they moved, they moved fast. The Pens were left full of Gens, and many residents refused flatly to leave their ancestral homes to the marauders. There was no time to argue. The army moved out.

The Nivet Stables were a day's hard ride beyond Shen, and they were on the only road that went there through the narrow passes. They decided to make their last stand at L'rimie.

But it was a battle they rode into.

The Raiders' fighting detachment had split—some attacking Shen from the east while others worked west along an old gypsy trail and were bearing down on L'rimie from the north.

The allied armies arrived just in time to relieve L'rimie's defenders and save the Nivet horse herd. But the Raiders fought savagely. These were not dissipated and ignorant people; these were shrewd invaders bent on taking a new homeland.

And the half-coordinated combined army was not able to stop them all. They took prisoners and managed to keep the horses, but the Raiders fought through the disintegrating ranks of the armies and rode hard east—for Shen, held by their own people, and the connecting eyeway into Capital.

This left the combined Armies strewn along the eyeway and in the small settlement around the stables.

Nothing stood now between Capital and the invaders.

And then it began to snow.

CHAPTER NINETEEN

Winter Siege

Valleroy opened the inner shutters and stuffed another rag into the leaking window. For three days it had snowed off and on, remaining cloudy between blizzards. The fancy Capitol was too drafty for Gens in winter.

He pulled his wool cape closer, scrubbed ice from the glass, and peered into the gloom. "Klyd, what's that?"

People preparing to flee the imminent invasion had been stopped by the freak early snowstorm. And as the days passed, though the weatherwatchers declared such snow meant the drought would be over in spring, tension increased. The Raiders were only delayed, not stopped, and nobody knew what had happened to the combined armies.

Klyd pulled away from the roaring fire and came to the window, zlinning. "That's Sergi!"

They raced for the front entry, plunging into the raging winds. They slipped and slid along the icy walkways, reaching the city gate as the lookout winched the gates open.

Klyd put an arm around Valleroy's shoulders and squeezed, "It's Risa *and* Sergi! And hundreds of others!"

The frostbitten, half-starved troops told a gruesome story of defeat. Risa reported, "As soon as this snow melts, the Raiders will bear down on Capital. We lost a third of our number—equally among both armies—and we're not equipped to winter in the mountains. We lost Gens to exposure, and the Simes' selyn demand increased from augmenting to keep warm."

"It's amazing you made it this far," said Klyd.

"Some gypsies showed us their secret trail, a shortcut actually, from L'rimie to Capital." Risa continued, "We had

238

to abandon the Gen artillery, but we hid the ammunition. The Raiders won't have *that* to use against us.''

Over the next few days the temperature plummeted. Stragglers came in aided by gypsies, who seemed to have spread through the mountains in a massive rescue operation. But most amazingly, the small groups who survived to rejoin the army were *both* junct and Gen, working together for survival, becoming a real team. At least one pair returned with the Sime high-field, the Gen low, their nagers defying anyone to make something of it.

Of the ones who didn't return, no one spoke save in the collective memorial service.

Soon, Capital was at full occupancy again, abandoned buildings commandeered to house the troops.

Heartened, Risa joined in planning a new offensive against the Raiders. She ascribed the defeat to several causes, not least the mountain sickness suffered by plains-bred Gens. That could not have been helped, but she took responsibility for allowing juncts in the signal translating corps. ''I should have made the junct commanders accept all Householders,'' she said. ''When the fighting started, too many juncts went hyperconscious and couldn't *hear* the bugle calls.''

''At the time we made our plans,'' said one of the junct officers, ''my people would never have taken orders from a Householder.''

Now, that was all changed. Junct, Householder, and out-Territory Gen had been welded into a unit.

They took the field again, traveling north over snow-packed eyeways on snowshoes and skis, pulling their equipment on sleighs. From the highest officer to the lowest trooper, they were determined to stop the Raiders this time.

But it wasn't that easy.

The weather did not break. There was barely a glimmer of blue sky until Year's Turning, and the temperature stayed below freezing. The combined army controlled all the exits from the valley of Shen, and there they sat, day after miserable day.

The Raiders fielded foraging parties, which the defenders attacked eagerly. If they prevented foraging, the trapped Raiders would consume all they'd brought with them and run out of the Gens they'd collected along the way.

Risa, Klyd, and everyone who'd seen Ardo had no stomach for this idea. The Gens objected because their comrades were in those Pens. But what else could they do?

At the first thaw, the Raiders would boil out of Shen and attack anything that moved. Risa sent to Gulf, telling Mor to mobilize the Territory and bring her reinforcements. The core of that troop would be militia trained in mixed fighting, but they wouldn't be mountain hardened. She warned Mor, hoping he could bring them high enough soon enough to condition them.

While Risa worked with the tacticians, Klyd drove the Third Order program to superhuman limits. Supported by perfect transfers, the result of Klyd's orhuen study, Valleroy and Klyd functioned like one person in two bodies, making independent decisions that dovetailed operations instead of clashing gears. The offices became quieter, the halls less full of augmenting Simes, and yet more work got done.

Ediva spent much of her time with Valleroy and Klyd, inventing new ways of training Third Order channels. With Joe Madison as her Companion, her transfers improved, and she chose to spend her post reactions with Valleroy—who had never enjoyed it more.

But as they rounded the dead of winter and counted the weeks until spring thaw, their situation deteriorated.

Food supplies were critically low. News of starvation came in with every messenger that fought into Capital.

Risa requisitioned supplies, and Klyd had to return the requisitions denied, for there was little left in Capital. Necessary kills depleted the Pens at an alarming rate as the usual round of winter plagues took their toll. The juncts educated enough to grasp the figures appreciated that the channels had kept more Pen Gens alive than the Keepers ever had. Talk of rebellion against the Tecton never got beyond mere talk, but it kept them worried.

One pouch, delivered by a gypsy, held a letter from Mor, promising food if it had to be carted on Sime backs over the snow. Gulf bred, Mor didn't understand mountain snow, but the spirit of the promise vitalized everyone. Klyd encouraged brainstorming, putting up suggestion boxes and offering prizes for workable ideas. Of course, it backfired.

Ambru submitted a suggestion that nonjunct Simes from the Tecton changeover program go into Shen as spies. The place must be bursting with young Simes. No one could know everyone there. Klyd assured the boy it was an excellent idea, but far too dangerous—how could they get inside the fortified city? And if they did, their good health would give them away as quickly as their Nivet accents.

The next thing they knew, Ambru, Bai, and a dozen young Simes—and Gens!—returned from Shen, hungry, frostbitten, and full of news. Risa felt her field mesh with Klyd's once again as they faced the adventurers; how could they punish, or even scold, youngsters who had risked their lives, unauthorized—but brought back exactly what they had to have?

For the information they brought had a double impact—not only what they had learned, but *how* they had learned it, renSimes and young Gens working as closely as channels and Companions to slip through Sime defenses.

Klyd and Risa met with Madison, Emstead, and Ediva to plan strategy. Klyd's desk overflowed with suggestions, most of which would be impossible to implement. They were running out of supplies; they were out of time.

As Klyd listed the attributes of the allied armies against those of the Raiders on the chalkboard, they saw one clear difference. "What we have and the Raiders don't is Sime/Gen cooperation. We are a single unit. They, Ambru tells us, are deeply divided. His outrageous scheme shows how effective Sime/Gen cooperation is against them."

As if reading his mind, Risa took up, "Their deepest cleavage is between Norwester and hard-bitten Raider. The leaders are Raiders. The Norwesters expected to use the Raiders to capture a new land, but the Raiders plan to use the Norwesters to splinter Nivet and join up with the Raider band to the south. The Norwesters have discovered the Raiders' intention. We must *use* their conflict."

She spread the map of Nivet, pointing to the Ruined Lands. "The Norwesters, we've agreed, are valuable to Nivet because Nivet has lost so many craftsmen, artisans, and Genfarmers. We can *bribe* them to settle here peacefully by *giving* them this section of Nivet. The location shows we trust them, for they could cut the Territory in half. They won't know the condition of the land until they see it, but now the drought is breaking, it can be made fertile again. By the time they've restored the land enough to farm Gens, we'll have them living semi-junct and racing each other to bring in crops to feed the increasing Gen population!''

But their immediate problem, as the weather to the east cleared, was their *own* increasing Gen population. The Gulf Army arrived, with plenty of provisions. Risa greeted her son with joy—but was astonished to find him Companioning Susi Darley. How could she be free to make such a trip unless her father—?

''Daddy's *here*!'' Susi told Risa, eyes bright with unshed tears. ''He managed . . . he managed a kill late in the summer—but oh, Risa, I know it will be his last.''

Risa did not voice her hopes to Susi—and was glad she hadn't when she had the chance to zlin Tannen Darley with her heightened senses. No, he was no ''delicate''; Susi had inherited her channeling ability from her mother.

Nevertheless, Risa decided, ''He should have Gen transfer from now on.''

''Mama . . . we tried that,'' said Mor. ''I forced two transfers into him before he finally was able to kill. My transfers did him no more good than Susi's.''

''I don't mean a Companion,'' she explained. ''I couldn't find the right Gen for Tan at home, but surely here—''

Yet it wasn't that simple. The new Third Order Companions had all been ''spoiled'' by their transfers with Third Order channels. None of them would respond to a renSime except with selyn . . . and pity. She considered asking Ambru to give up Bai for a month—but their teamwork could be crucial to the morale of the young warriors. They dared not risk putting that teamwork off-balance . . . and besides, if Bai was a good match for Ambru, chances were he wouldn't be for anyone else.

As Darley's cycle approached need once more, Risa and Sergi brought up the problem at the end of one of the strategy meetings. ''Klyd, Hugh, do you know of any likely candidate who's not already training for Third Order?''

''No—I don't,'' the other Sectuib replied, zlinning Darley carefully. ''Hugh, is there anyone you can suggest?''

"Back at Rior, two or three people." He shrugged helplessly. "I'm not at Rior."

All eyes turned in astonishment to Harris Emstead, and Risa felt Klyd go wholly hyperconscious for a moment of detailed zlinning. Emstead looked to Risa and spoke firmly. "You told me months ago that you were certain I could give transfer to a renSime. Ever since, I've been wondering what it would be like."

"Harris," said Klyd, "with a crucial battle looming, we cannot risk one of the commanders of our army."

"Zlin me," the Gen soldier responded. "I'm not risking anything—except getting healthier yet. Look at all of us in this rotten weather, on short rations—there's hardly a sniffle, let alone the flu and pneumonia I'd expect under these conditions. I *know* now that nature meant Simes and Gens to live together . . . and I believe Hugh is right that it's not just the Simes who are supposed to enjoy transfer."

Risa zlinned Sergi's amused approval and saw Klyd glance at him in annoyance. "It's too dangerous," said the Sectuib in Zeor. "Risa, we'll arrange a controlled cascade, and you or I can drive transfer into Tannen Darley while—"

"Sectuib Farris!" Emstead interrupted, drawing his white enameled chain from under his flannel shirt. "With all respect, Sir, you have no right to make this decision."

"As Tecton controller—" Klyd began.

"I am not a Householder," Emstead reminded him, "nor is Tannen Darley. Neither of us is a citizen of Nivet Territory. We are here as your allies, not your constituents."

"I concede," said Klyd. "However, I wish you would accept my *advice* not to attempt this experiment."

If that statement was meant to frighten Emstead, it didn't. But Tannen Darley was horrified at the Gen's offer. "No," he said firmly. "I will never, *never* risk killing somebody I know."

But Darley and Emstead were only acquaintances. Darley, unable to make the journey with Risa, had not witnessed the changes in Emstead.

"You can't kill me, Tan," the Gen soldier said gently.

Darley was close enough to need to be unable to keep from zlinning—and Emstead was clearly displaying selyur nager, the seductive Gen need to give. "Please don't do that," Darley said flatly.

"I'm going to go right on doing it till you agree," Emstead told him.

Risa watched the two men. They were not far apart in age, both suntanned and weatherbeaten, but Darley looked much older than Emstead. He had been a handsome man when Risa first met him. Now he was far too thin, his shoulders rounded, and the lines in his face, though actually fewer than those in Emstead's, deeper and all turned downward.

And his nager bespoke despair. Matching him with the right Gen was his only chance now. Already he was in the pattern of aborting out of attempted kills. Irrevocably junct, he would always eventually go for the kill—but his abused system would collapse under the stress of aborts.

Harris Emstead was true to his word, sticking to Darley like a cockleburr as the hours brought him deeper into hard need. There was never yet a Sime in need who could resist so persistent a Gen, and ultimately Darley and Emstead retired to a transfer room, Risa and Klyd stationed one behind each, their Companions balancing the fields.

For a Gen with no experience beyond donation, Emstead handled the situation phenomenally well. His selyur nager attracted, while his confidence overrode Darley's killphobia. There were no aborts, not even a false start. Emstead gave himself over to the pleasure of his first real transfer—and came up grinning as he lifted his head at termination.

Then he frowned. Tannen Darley lay still on the transfer lounge, eyes closed. Although his laterals had retracted, his handling tentacles clung to Emstead's forearms.

Then Darley's eyes opened, and he sat up. Seeing the puzzled look on the Gen's face, he forced a smile that didn't go beyond his lips, retracted his tentacles, and took Emstead's right hand in his, shaking hands in the Gen manner. "Thank you," he said.

"But—" Emstead began.

Darley got up off the lounge, testing his limbs as Emstead looked at Risa in bewilderment. She shook her head, and he held his protest until she and Klyd had examined Darley and sent him off to the lounge for tea.

The moment the door had closed, Emstead said, "It felt great to me! Why didn't it satisfy Tan?"

"It did," Klyd assured him. "You gave him plenty of selyn, and so smoothly he didn't abort once. That means he can heal old injuries, Harris, instead of having new traumas created by the transfer."

"But it wasn't *right*," Emstead insisted. "You think I can't tell by now when a Sime's not post?"

"Harris, that is too much to expect," Risa told him. "He's far too traumatized from aborts and bad transfers. You gave Tan something none of the channels or Companions could: a *good transfer*. Klyd is right. You've given him time to heal old wounds."

"Then—next month I should be able to give him more than just selyn," the Gen soldier said confidently.

When Emstead had gone, though, Klyd said to Risa, "They're not matchmates."

"I know that," she replied. "Still, by not adding to his problems, Harris gave Tan an additional month of life. Can a Sime ask more of a Gen than that?"

"But it won't be better next month, Risa. Your friend needs killbliss—and that's the one thing he cannot accept. Harris Emstead, for all that he can murder Simes or Gens most efficiently in a battle situation, hasn't got the slightest touch of the sadistic pleasure in pain a junct needs. Tan will accept his transfers because he knows killbliss isn't there. But his body will rebel at being denied—"

"Stop it, Klyd!" said Risa. "You can't predict the future any more than I can. Today's experiment was successful. Maybe Tan and Harris will manage a second time—and maybe by the time Tan starts aborting on Harris a Gen will turn up who's a closer matchmate. Maybe by next month we'll *all* be dead. Or maybe we'll make some new discovery to save the semi-juncts, the way we discovered Third Order channels!"

But Risa's optimism was strained to its limits in the next few days. Hard on the heels of the Gulf contingent came a Division of the Gen Army, under General Dermott, who was *most* unhappy to have been sent on this mission, and to have to deliver Bill Jesson, new orders—and a promotion—to Harris Emstead.

The Gens had been bombarded by reports of the size of the Raider band; the devastation it left as it crossed their north quadrant; verification of Ediva's figures by their best mathematicians; and new successes of Sime/Gen cooperation in the west. Finally the chiefs of staff had decided Madison's field decision had been right. Then it had taken over two months to move troops out here. Madison got another eight pointed star to decorate his helmet, and command of the combined armies, while General Emstead moved into Madison's old command.

But sending Dermott—and troops loyal to him—was a mistake. To him, Simes were ravaging beasts to be shot on sight, and this mission was a punishment. One of Madison's first orders was to override Dermott's order that his men were not to fraternize with Simes or donate selyn. Not surprisingly, few of Dermott's troops volunteered . . . and that mass of ripe Gen nager remained, dog in the manger, right within zlinning range of juncts living on transfers. The channels swore, knowing what good that selyn could do—but unable to tap it.

For Risa and Sergi, the worry over integrating new, reluctant troops into their well-practiced blended army was balanced by their joy at having their son with them. It was almost a year since they had left Gulf—and Mor had grown, both physically, giving promise of becoming as big as his father, and emotionally. He led the Gulf trade contingent with confidence, old semi-juncts accepting the young Gen's orders without question. *He's so used to running Keon,* Risa realized, *it'll be hard for him to return to being Second Companion!* But he wouldn't be going directly home. Once the Raiders were defeated, the world unified, she would send Mor to Zeor. What a Companion he would be with such training in his youth!

One day, Valleroy and Klyd were called to deal with a Gen who had offered to donate selyn, then killed the Third Order channel taking the donation.

"I'm not going back in there!" said the triage channel in the collectorium.

Valleroy met Klyd's gaze, and without discussion they marched into the room. The youth lay curled on his side on the lounge, shuddering with suppressed sobs. He had long brown hair and a gaunt look that bespoke more than the tight diet of this winter. His bare feet were calloused from going unshod. At closer range, Valleroy noted callouses on the fingers—bow and arrow callouses.

He touched Klyd's arm and whispered, "He's one of the Wild ones the junct Army cleared out of the ruins."

Klyd circled to sit on the lounge in front of the youth, asking in Simelan, "Are you one we liberated from the Pen under this building?"

The young man saw Klyd's arms, raised his eyes to recognize the face, then cringed. Klyd hugged him gently. "We won't punish you. But we've got to know what happened."

"I—I don't know," he quavered.

Valleroy moved to support the fields, and the youth looked up at him. Klyd said, "My Companion."

Valleroy smiled. "I'm responsible for training our Third Order channels. The man you killed—was my student. I've got to find out what happened."

"I'll never try to donate again!" The boy pulled away. "Everyone else is dead. Why didn't I die, too?"

"Don't say that!" responded Klyd so urgently that Valleroy knew there was real potential in this young one. "What did you do that hurt the channel?"

"I—I don't know! It just happened!"

"Then I'll find out by taking your donation."

"No!" The youth shrank away.

"Don't worry, you can't hurt me—not with Hugh here."

"How do you know!"

Klyd explained how inexperienced the Thirds still were, and how critical it was for them to perfect their training. The boy calmed down enough to say quite rationally, "I didn't mean to hurt him. He never done me no harm."

"I *know* that," assured Klyd. "Channels accept the risks before going into this duty. But we also minimize those risks. Now, may I take your donation?"

"You're *sure*? I couldn't stand it if—"

Valleroy said, "*I'm* sure." But, just to be sure, he ordered the special Farris emergency kit from the hall locker.

Meanwhile, Klyd coached the youth to relax, gaining his

confidence. When Valleroy braced the fields, Klyd completed the contact. He shuddered once during the brief transmission of selyn, but emerged with neither himself nor the youth damaged. Afterward, he stared at a blank wall with that totally abstracted look he hadn't worn since they'd discovered what was wrong with Ediva. Valleroy was left to assure the boy that all was well, and that he could leave.

Finally, Klyd roused himself. "Now I know what hit Risa's group! Put a notation on his chart that he's to be handled only by Seconds or Firsts, and if he asks for Companion's training, he's to be sent to me."

They rushed to a meeting, and Valleroy forgot the incident as they prepared to send Ambru and a squad of his loyal followers back into Shen.

Valleroy worked with Klyd for two days to prepare the group. He found two natives of Shen and three refugees from Norwest to coach them in accent and manner, and two ex-Raiders to coach the Gens to act cowed and inconspicuous.

The Simes wore blood-stained whips and daggers captured from Raiders. Makeup and artistic tailoring created a haggard look, and when they cracked the whips just shy of Gen flesh, the Gens reacted with an impressive nageric clap.

"You'll pass," declared Klyd and dispatched them.

"I hope we're doing the right thing," said Risa, watching the group ride off.

Her confidence, Valleroy knew, had been shaken by her last defeat. "They'd have gone anyway," he told her. "At least now they have a chance of getting out alive."

"If they don't," Sergi said grimly, "we'll be dead before summer."

Supplies were critical again despite the shipments from Gulf. Mor assured them that wagons were waiting just beyond the passes for a thaw, but as soon as it was possible to move on the trails, the Raiders would attack. The supplies would be of value only after they defeated the Raiders.

Mountain Bells' weatherwatcher, who had predicted every storm except the first one, declared a thaw two weeks hence. Days passed without a sign of warmer weather or word from the infiltrators, and Risa began to nibble at her tentacles.

At a conference with Klyd over the food shortage, she

said, "When the fighting erupts, our Gens won't know Ambru's squad from the Raiders!"

Valleroy saw that abstracted look flow over Klyd's face again, but this time it was interrupted by Dermott striding into the office unannounced.

Dermott waved a paper at Klyd, "What is this? We *brought* supplies to support ourselves and feed your town. We're here to defend your miserable capital, and you won't even give us basic provisions! I'm not required to stay in the field under these conditions. Either feed my men, or we're leaving!"

Valleroy captured the paper from the General's hand and gave it to Klyd. It had REQUISITION DENIED stamped across it, but without Klyd's initials and seal.

"This," Klyd observed, "was handled downstairs."

"Mister Farris, my men are hungry *today*. I will feed them *today*, with or without your cooperation. Do I make myself understood?"

Emstead waited at the door. Valleroy beckoned him in and moved to readjust the fields. "Your orders," said Emstead to Dermott, "are to stop those Raiders *here*. Move your men out now, and they'll either chase you down the mountain and pick you off in the snowdrifts, or they'll mop us up, take Capital, and then capture Nivet and join up with the Raiders on the south border."

Risa could see that Dermott knew the stakes, and had never had any intention of pulling out—only of feeding his men, even if someone else went hungry.

Klyd sat down in his chair, one tentacle idly riffling a stack of suggestion memos. He tapped the stack, then steepled his fingers and looked up at Dermott, eyebrows arched speculatively, tentacles dancing among his fingers. There was a long silence as the Gen stared at those writhing tentacles. Sergi moved closer to Risa.

Finally, Klyd's eyes searched Valleroy's, then Risa's and Sergi's, looking for agreement.

Dermott broke out sweating. Risa zlinned his terror, Klyd's determination, and the worry of Hugh and Sergi.

"You can't!" said Emstead, though no one had spoken.

"We can if it's only another week to spring thaw."

Dermott exploded. "What are you people, witches?"

Emstead edged nearer his colleague, as if to shield the Simes from him. "No! Just—after a while, sharing selyn, you get to share a point of view, a way of thinking."

It was absolutely the wrong thing to say. Hugh spoke up to distract the Gen. "General Dermott, we're thinking of *giving* your troops—all the Gen troops who've endured so much for us—the rest of our food. Simes can go long stretches without eating. It's bad for their health, but they can survive without food longer than we can and still fight. Your troops *can't* fight without eating. We must have our full combined strength when the Raiders break out of that valley."

Klyd continued, "This requisition wasn't denied capriciously, General. There is *nothing* left in stores. Our food is down on the plain waiting for the thaw."

Dermott's face hardened, and Risa took up the thought. "There's one thing, though, that Simes can't fight without."

But it was Sergi who said, "Selyn. You have it, General Dermott, in quantity. You can't use it. We need it desperately. You go into this battle with your troops high field, and the Raiders will go for you in preference to us. There'll be nothing we can do to protect you."

"We'll trade you," said Valleroy. "Food for selyn."

"And," added Klyd, "our troops will *eagerly* protect you, because you're the source of selyn."

Emstead cautioned, "You *do* want their protection, as they want yours." He circled, to put Dermott's back to the Simes. "Listen to me," he said softly. "Raiders are savages who kill wantonly for survival, power, and pleasure. The difference between them and us, is that *we* cooperate. *We* keep our word and do our duty, however unpleasant."

It sank in. In the space of two deep breaths, the man straightened, and turned to face them again, square-jawed but no longer belligerent. "I'll have to make it an order. The men won't do it willingly. And if there are any of your—accidents— they won't be forgiven."

Klyd said, "We'll send our best channels. There won't be any 'accidents,' however unwilling your troops. Each donor will be issued rations afterwards. If we can hold this operation together just one more week—"

"You feed us, we'll be there to fight. I guarantee it."

Implementing the promise took more than an order. Klyd had to explain why people were being asked to empty their private larders, keeping only enough to feed their children and Gens. In the end, the only reason it was possible was that most of the juncts in town were on transfers, saving their kill allotment for just before the battle, and they had no appetite anyway.

It wasn't just Dermott's men they fed. Madison's Gens were ashamed to eat when others fasted; he had to order his men to eat, and the channels had to turn away volunteer donors trying to give more selyn than they really could in payment for the food.

Meanwhile, they heard not a word from their infiltrators.

Finally, the weather broke. Icicles dripped; the sun shone; Valleroy shed one of his wool sweaters. Klyd said, "It's time to move out of the valley."

Valleroy had not expected Klyd to be on the battle scene. "This time," the channel explained, "there *is* no safe refuge. If we fail, there's no reason to want to survive."

So they gathered a large percentage of their channels, trekked north to Shen through slush and ice, and found Dermott, Emstead, and Madison at the command post. The maps had been pinned to a board, the tables littered with forms. Madison was pacing. "Why haven't they come out yet?"

Visions of Ardo Pass floated through Valleroy's imagination.

Klyd said, "They're still alive. Joe, they can zlin the condition of our nerves. We've got to boost morale."

"The problem is," said Madison, "we've no offensive strategy that hasn't failed before. Intelligence hasn't even discovered their fighting strength. We know nothing of their plans—and twice now they've outmaneuvered us."

Risa said, "I don't like the look on your face, Sectuib Farris."

Valleroy knew that abstracted gaze. Klyd had an idea.

So did Risa. "It won't work," she said firmly.

"Oh, yes it will," contradicted Klyd.

"Let's hear it," said Sergi.

"You mean you don't already know what he's thinking?" asked Dermott.

"Of course not," replied Risa testily. "But I already know I won't like it." She was only half teasing.

"It's a variant," said Klyd, "of the technique those Wild Gens used on you, Risa." He explained to the Gen officers, finishing, "A Sime can't take selyn without becoming— hyperconscious."

Sergi explained, "Able to zlin the fields, sense the energy he needs."

"If," said Risa thoughtfully, "we could keep the Raiders hypo, we'd have them whipped. But Klyd, it *won't* work. Even if we had enough trained Companions, it'd drive all our own Simes hypo, too! And—" she added in Simelan, "it can kill a Sime with shock."

"But Simes react proportionately to their degree of kill dissipation." Klyd answered in Simelan, and then apologized as people started trying to translate. "I don't know how to discuss this in English."

"Can't be done," supplied Emstead. "That's why I learned some Simelan, but I still can't follow the technical terms."

"But I bet you could use this method," said Klyd.

Valleroy had to ask, "Klyd, do you really want to turn something like this loose among people who hate Simes so?"

But Klyd persisted, in English. "As I see it, we must *trust* each other, and the Gen troops will learn they're not outclassed, even by a Raider berserk with need."

Risa stared meditatively at Sergi. "Yes, that would be very important to a Gen. I don't know why I hadn't thought of it before. Explain your idea."

"Juncts will be extremely sensitive to this," Klyd told them. "It's a variant of the Companion's technique which controls the level of consciousness of the working channel."

He broke off and drew a rough diagram of the valley and their fortified positions. The Sime and Gen armies were deployed separately, each with its own area of responsibility. At the borders between commands they had posted the troops who had returned to Capital with Risa, keeping them with their team mates.

Klyd stationed a channel and a group of Companions at intervals around the sides of the valley. "As the battle develops, these squads will move with the skirmish line right into the fray. Raiders in their area will be forced to fight without zlinning.''

He raised his eyes to Dermott's. ''Our main advantage is surprise. They won't understand what's happening to them.''

''No,'' said Emstead. ''The main value is morale. You're right, Klyd. *This* is what our men have to have right now. They ate the last of the food this morning.''

Risa said, ''Mor has gone to meet our shipment. They took pack mules to bring up an emergency supply.''

They set about mobilizing the combined armies, Klyd teaching the channels in the medic corps to modulate his technique and finding enough Companions and high-field donors to generate the effect. Then they scattered the channels to encircle the town.

Nobody mentioned Ambru. He and his squad were counted lost.

Just before noon, the Raiders came.

CHAPTER TWENTY

Battle of Shen

They massed their best troops at the south exit from Shen, blocking the road to Capital.

But the Raiders came out over the eastern wall of the town and drove east, to the eyeway down to the plain—where the Gulf food wagons waited—with many more Gens.

Madison ordered his reserves to move to the eastern end of the valley and support Emstead's command, but Klyd said, ''No! Wait—Risa, do you zlin?''

''They're coming out over the walls in every direction!''

But the assault on the east was the strongest. The Raiders wanted *out* of the trap.

And if they got out, the destruction would never stop.

"Come on Sergi, Emstead's got to have help!" said Risa.

Valleroy watched Risa gather her crew of high-field Gens and circle east. A runner brought a body count from the west. "Bealer's Company's been wiped out. General Dermott sent two platoons under Lieutenant Jesson to cover." He rattled off worsening statistics.

Klyd realized, "Their desperation is overriding our effort to keep them hypo. Hugh, let's go."

They rode west behind their own lines, encouraging each channel's group to increase their efforts, Klyd adjusting the fields to pull the Raiders down to hypoconsciousness while affecting their own Simes least.

Unable to zlin, the Raiders were disoriented, frightened—easy targets for the Nivet Army.

Having brought Emstead's eastern front under control, Risa zlinned about her and found Madison's command post under assault. She took half the reserve Company, in which Ediva worked with Joe Madison, Jr., and led a charge against the rear guard of the Raiders. The Gulf Militia with them used their tactic of the Gen attracting the Raider and the Sime dispatching the attacker. The juncts at the core of their flying wedge used their long whips to disarm the Raiders, who were either fixed so hard on the Gens they didn't notice the whip coming at them or had been driven hypo and couldn't zlin it.

Risa let Ediva hold the fields while she flitted from one side of their flying wedge to the other, keeping their juncts from succumbing to the kill-heated ambient. Suddenly Ediva, still more Dar fighter than channel, grabbed a Gen's rifle and used it as a staff to defend herself. She dropped the fields and the Raiders about her bounced hyperconscious.

Joe Madison, Jr., surged forward as three Raiders zeroed in on Ediva. Madison, with Dar training, threw one of them while Ediva drop-kicked the second. Madison leaped in front of Ediva and intercepted a frenzied Raider's killgrip.

Risa got a grip on Sergi's field amidst the chaos and sent a releveling pulse through the ambient. Her own juncts staggered, and she realized they had no warning of impending nageric shock. A split-second before the pulse hit, Madison had shenned the Raider anyway.

But these troops had worked together for months now; they accommodated such mistakes and pushed on. They bored a hole in the Raider line from the rear. Split, the Raiders were easily surrounded and wiped out. The Army's orders were to take no prisoners. They had no way to deal with hardened Raiders.

Joe's father grinned proudly at the boy as he emerged from the battle, bloody but with Ediva safe at his side. Madison didn't know how Joe's traumatic injuries zlinned to Ediva— but then, Ediva should have retreated to let the renSimes defend her.

Risa shrugged. Their central command post was safe.

At the western exit from the valley, Klyd and Valleroy joined Dermott's men, who had artillery dug in and sighted on the town walls, a batallion of Sime Army regulars protecting them. Dermott was instructing a runner, "The way those animals are behaving, all the Gens in town are dead. So I'm going to open fire—"

"No!" shouted Klyd, dismounting under augmentation.

Dermott repeated, "You heard me, Corporal."

"Sir!" And the man headed off.

Klyd intercepted so quickly he had hardly seemed to move. The Corporal drew his sidearm, but Klyd's hand and tentacles stayed his wrist. "Calm down. General Dermott doesn't have all the facts yet."

Around the command post, three channels were grouped with their squads of Gens. The nearest one told Klyd, "I tried to tell him, but he wouldn't listen."

Dermott gestured the Corporal to stand down. Klyd said to Dermott, "There are *many* living Simes in that town."

"I know! We have to get them before they get us. Our forces are outnumbered already."

"Dermott," said Klyd, patience fraying, "the Simes who have *stayed* in there may not *want* to fight."

"They expect their troops to bring us back for them to kill. If not, they'll come and get us. Madison knows that, even as soft as he's gone."

Valleroy moved closer, to shield Klyd from the savagery of the general as well as from the killing behind them. "Corporal,'' said Klyd, ''deliver the General's message to Madison, but add that *I* said the artillery should be targeted between the walls and the skirmish line.''

''That's a waste of ammunition!'' argued Dermott. ''The Simes will just move out of that area—''

''Which is our intent,'' said Klyd. ''We want to keep their reserves inside the town. Corporal, go!''

The man looked to Dermott for the final command. The General waved him off, then said to Klyd, ''*You* don't give orders in my command!''

''Yes, Sir!'' retorted Klyd and mounted up again. Below them, Raiders paused in their concerted charge, gazing about them bewildered, and were immediately cut down by the nonjunct Simes Mor had brought, who were unaffected by the releveling the channels were doing. Combat-trained Gens moved in to finish off the Raiders and protect the juncts who, despite practice, were bewildered by being thrown hypo.

Klyd looked back over his shoulder at Dermott. ''Note that, Sir. Cooperation works better.''

They continued around the field. Before long they heard the signal to start the bombardment—targeting the field, not the town.

The battle hung balanced. Suddenly, the gates of the town swung open and a squad of Raiders emerged, spreading out behind the lines as if to tip the balance in their favor.

Klyd stood in his stirrups, zlinning the distance over the miasma of intervening fields. ''Hugh, that's *Ambru*!''

''Ambru?!''

Running under augmentation, Ambru's squad launched their attack on the rear of the Raider lines, fighting hard and furious with every technique the Dar had taught them.

Klyd spun his horse and drove back up the hillside. Valleroy followed, whipping his horse's flanks. Klyd jumped down while his horse was still lunging upward, striding into the platoon's dugout while Dermott's men struggled to re-aim their artillery. ''Sorry, Lieutenant,'' snapped Klyd and snatched the herald's bugle. Valleroy had never suspected Klyd could blow one of the things, but he produced the loudest, clearest, ''Hold positions!'' Valleroy had ever heard.

The herald had frozen at the touch of Sime tentacles, but the lieutenant protested, "You can't do that!"

"Madison has to know those are *our* reinforcements outflanking the enemy."

Around the battlefield, other heralds echoed the command. More Raiders boiled from the town gates and over the walls. Klyd turned to Valleroy. "Those are the Norwesters—and they're on our side now! What's 'Stand by for reinforcements'?"

But Dermott had seen through his spyglass what Klyd had zlinned, half the Raiders attacking the other half's rear. He signaled his herald, and Klyd surrendered the bugle to the professional.

The message got through to Madison—or perhaps Risa or one of the other sensitive channels had joined him—and the main command post endorsed the field order.

"Come on!" shouted Klyd to Valleroy, "The Norwesters need transfers as badly as the Raiders!" They ordered channels onto the field, explaining that they had to give transfers to the Norwesters before their new allies killed.

From that point on, the battle became a one-sided slaughter of the hardened Raider leadership by those on both sides who wanted good homes and safe living for their families. Dermott's troops got their chance to wreak vengeance.

By nightfall, they had to turn Emstead's troops against Dermott's to stop them from slaughtering the allies Ambru and his friends had brought them. Dermott came at Emstead, screaming, "You've turned against your own people, traitor!"

But one of his own men grasped the bayonet he was aiming at his fellow officer, saying, "Sir! The battle is over—we've won, Sir! It's safe to stop fighting now."

"Yes, General, we've won," Emstead agreed, pretending he hadn't noticed the attempted attack.

Dermott's troops pulled to a halt, warily watching the confrontation. Emstead's men immediately infiltrated their ranks, calling cheerfully, "Hey! We've won!" "We're alive, and the Raiders are dead!" "Let's celebrate!"

At last quiet fell over the battlefield. The survivors were coated in mud and blood. The ambient throbbed with the shenned-out kill-lust of those who had lived Raider since the collapse of their Territory. They still ached for a kill despite the selyn from the channels.

General Madison released the troops to celebrate their victory. His men were still mingled with Dermott's, taking them off to make camp. Dermott watched his men defect with a grim stare, his nager throbbing with betrayal. When Madison dismissed him and Emstead, Dermott went to his own tent, and was not seen again until his division departed.

Klyd took Risa aside. "It will be better after they've eaten, but keep the Norwesters away from Dermott's men. Some of them really do *need* a kill."

Risa nodded. "I sent two hundred Simes to meet Mor and bring in our provisions. They should be back by dawn."

Risa's medic corps was spread thin, but organized with consummate efficiency. Burial details used the charges from artillery ammunition to dig mass graves in the still-frozen ground. The officers organized casualty statistics. And the bulk of the Norwesters had to be convinced that they would indeed get land and government help getting started—that they were allies here, not criminals.

By the time the first rays of the sun touched the battleground, order had been imposed. The wounded had been moved into the town, and Risa and Klyd were making a last check of the bodies to be sure they were dead before being buried. They found Emstead kneeling beside one of the bodies.

"He's dead, Harris," Klyd assured him sadly, looking down into the blood-drained face of Bill Jesson.

No tears got through the experienced soldier's control, but his nager ached with grief. "He was so young. Had such potential. It's always the young that the wars take."

"Maybe," Risa said, "there won't be any more wars."

Emstead rose and looked around—and this time a single tear did escape his control. "I pray you're right. I'm sick of fighting, Risa. Let's hope everybody else is, too."

A little further on, Risa zlinned Susi Darley. What was she doing here? She was supposed to be at the field hospital.

But Risa gave no reprimand when she saw that Susi knelt beside the body of her father, a gaping hole blown in his chest. "Friendly fire," Harris Emstead murmured, his nager ringing with bitter irony.

"What?" asked Risa.

"It happens," Emstead replied. "Tan was with the Simes who charged in to support Ambru's troops . . . before the shelling stopped." He put a hand on Susi's shoulder. "Your father died a hero."

The young woman rose and let the grizzled soldier take her in his arms as she sobbed on his shoulder for a moment. Then she pulled herself together, blinking tears from her round blue eyes, and said in a shaky voice, "He died cleanly, fighting for a better future for us all. You gave him that, Harris, and I will be ever grateful to you that Daddy was able to carry through the purpose of his last journey, instead of wasting away in Capital of shorting and aborts."

The burial detail, following the channels, reached them. Fighting back tears, Susi nodded and let them carry her father's body away. Then she turned and walked toward the campfires . . . alone, the way each member of a Householder's family did from his funeral.

All around them on the valley floor, groups of mixed Simes and Gens had built cook fires in anticipation of the promised food. They had spread the Third Order channels, untrained in medical skills, out among the Norwesters to try to control their restlessness, for the ex-Raiders would not return to the walls that had held them in all winter. Gradually, the Nivet troops accepted some of the Norwesters at their fires, and the Norwesters began to accept just how *different* this society was from home.

With the first rays of the sun, Klyd rose from studying the dead to zlin the north end of the valley, where a line of Simes emerged from the north pass, running under augmentation across the treacherous ice, carrying on their shoulders the crates of provisions Mor had promised. "Look at that!"

Two hundred laden Simes ran down the trail into the valley, where juncts, nonjuncts, Companions, channels, Norwesters, and Gens united in a rousing cheer.

In short order, crates were broken open, and sacks of rice, potatoes, beans, carrots, cheese, and dried fruit flew through the air to welcoming hands.

Trin tea was dispensed, Dermott's men daring to taste it for the first time, encouraged by Madison's men who had kept warm on it all winter.

The mule train, lightened by the Simes' augmenting a third of their cargo to the celebration, lumbered down into the valley, and Mor made sure his parents were all right and his Companion's skills were not required in the infirmary before joining the group of young people at the center of all the activity, listening to Ambru and Bai's embellishments of their adventures in Shen under siege.

Then Susi Darley brought out a shiltpron—Dinny's shiltpron, which Risa had entrusted to her to return to Dinny's sister. Susi was no musical genius, as Dinny had been, but she played well enough for singing, and soon voices raised all around her.

A Gen soldier brought out a mouth organ, and began to accompany Susi. More people joined the singing as they found a tune everyone seemed to recognize.

Risa knew Simelan words to the song, which she had learned in Gulf Territory as a child. Beside her, Harris Emstead sang in English—as did Hugh Valleroy, although the version he knew was slightly different. Even Klyd joined in, his East Nivet version different from Risa's Gulf version and from the bawdy lyrics Ediva contributed from her junct upbringing—but what did that matter?

The valley rang with song in two languages and a dozen dialects. Risa remembered Sergi telling her once that the song went back to the Ancients, who had had just as many different lyrics and meanings for it—from drinking song, to fighting song, to rousing patriotic march.

And even as they sang there in that winter valley, spontaneously a new lyric grew:

> Peace for Sime and Gen forever,
> Peace for Sime and Gen forever,
> Peace for Sime and Gen forever,
> Together one and all!

Risa came up between Hugh and Klyd and put an arm

around each of them. Klyd looked down at her, then put his other arm around Sergi, welcoming his field. Sime and Gen together, they joined once more in the chorus of hope, under the promise of the rising sun.

Characters

Valry Adlay—junct Sime who buys Gens from Genrunners. Captured by the Gen Army, she tells them Nivet authorities control the Freeband Raiders.

Aisha—Hugh's first love and his wife, she went to Klyd's bed to bear him an heir despite Hugh's objections. She died giving birth to Muryin, in the moment that Hugh and Klyd came to terms with each other.

Ambru—a young nonjunct Sime "sold" to the Tecton by his parents for kill-privileges whereupon he took a new name.

Bai (ambrov Kiereth)—As a young Gen, he watched his Householding destroyed by junct Nivet soldiers. He escaped to join the Wild Killer Gens and later discover Ambru.

Bealer—out-Territory Gen, leads a company of the Army.

Bethany ambrov Keon—Uzziah's transfer mate, she is not actually trained as a Companion, but is so valuable on Risa's staff that she goes with Risa on the journey to Nivet.

Biskor—a junct Sime wagonmaster who knows Nivet Territory roads. He advises Klyd's party to avoid Mountain City.

Bonnie—Harris Emstead's granddaughter, a child living in Gen Territory, and Harris's motivation to return home.

Susi Darley—the nonjunct channel who is Tannen Darley's daughter. Not pledged to any House, she works as an inde-

262 Jacqueline Lichtenberg and Jean Lorrah

pendent channel in Gulf Territory—often using the Pen her father owns as her main office.

Tannen Darley—a semi-junct Sime nearing final crisis, he made his second fortune investing in Risa Tigue's schemes for Keon's growth and is now a power in the Gulf legislature. At first, he's too ill to make the long trek with Risa.

Dazul ambrov Dar—one of the Dar Guards who travel with Klyd's party, he is obviously attracted to Ediva.

General Dermott—out-Territory Gen with high ambitions of becoming commander-in-chief of the whole Territory Army.

Dickart—a semi-junct renSime of Gulf who appreciates transfer from Klyd.

Dinny ambrov Keon—Verla's son, taught to play shiltpron by the musician at his mother's saloon. His death in an apparently meaningless riot supplies Klyd with a clue.

Diorn ambrov Rior—A young Gen wholly unsuited to become a Companion, she volunteers for the emergency program to serve renSimes direct transfer and becomes a martyr.

Dsif ambrov Zeor—He is the Companion being groomed for the heir to Zeor, Muryin. He gives his life to save Muryin.

Ediva ambrov Dar—a disjunct renSime, and one of Klyd's 'delicates.' The daughter of a whip maker, she pledges Dar and becomes the world's leading mathematician, Zelerod's successor, presenting both the problem and the solution during her battle to remain disjunct and not die young.

Harris Emstead—an out-Territory Gen Colonel who comes to believe Zelerod's Doom could happen.

Girar—The nonjunct renSime in charge of the Tecton library and archives. He is a superlative librarian who, in his younger years, created a new indexing system.

Grandfather—Klyd's grandfather who did research on the 'delicates.'

Jesse—He is the son of Kitty and Hugh ambrov Rior and is six years old at the time of ZELEROD'S DOOM. Later, he takes his mother's surname, Dumas, and the values championed by

Rior, and becomes a figure of some historical importance by tangling again with the Zeor Farrises.

Bill Jesson—a young out-Territory Gen of Emstead's command; a farmboy with a religious upbringing; brilliant, but uneducated.

Amos Kaneko (ambrov Noam)—He is a renSime of the type Klyd terms 'delicate.' His transfer mate is Enid Kaneko (ambrov Noam) and he left Noam when the Sectuib decreed they would not be allowed to become transfer mates. They made a place for themselves and their lifestyle among juncts of the city who likewise coveted direct Gen transfer though they, themselves, were trapped in the junct lifestyle. Ultimately unable to control the juncts who followed him, Amos gave his life in the attempt to maintain discipline among his followers when he led them among the ultimate temptation—Householding Gens.

Enid Kaneko (ambrov Noam)—The Gen who became Amos Kaneko's transfer mate and died attempting to kidnap Muryin.

Kitty ambrov Rior—She is a character who walked into this book out of the pages of the fanzine, ZEOR FORUM, to become Jesse's mother and one of Hugh's most valued Companions, a hero in her own right who gives her life on a spy mission into Gen Territory.

Klyd Farris ambrov Zeor—Sectuib in Zeor, and a leading figure in world affairs, he knows that few problems have simple solutions—and most solutions pose worse problems. He's not sure if Risa ambrov Keon is a problem or a solution, but he knows the 'delicates' and their odd transfer characteristics are the key to the survival of humanity.

Korin ambrov Keon—the Companion Risa brings to Nivet just in case Virena changes over on the trail. He would accompany her to the Tecton school. Householding bred, he is undismayed when he gets his first lesson from Klyd.

Kreg—Risa's younger brother who was murdered years ago.

Lenis ambrov Frihill—the renSime Guide who takes Klyd's party from Konawa to Ardo Pass.

Lorina ambrov Carre—a Companion who accompanies Risa on her journey through Nivet.

Joe Madison, Jr.—a young out-Territory Gen of Emstead's command, son of the famous General. He takes to the teachings of Householding Dar in a way that could embarrass his father. His interest in Ediva ambrov Dar is not what it at first seems.

Joseph Madison, Sr.—General of the Gen Army, proud of his son who is following in his footsteps. A man born of soldiering traditions, he is farsighted, strong, fair, and abhors prejudice even in himself.

Mor ambrov Keon—Son of Risa and Sergi, he is Second Companion in Keon. Although he is a Gen, Risa leaves him in charge of the House when she goes to Nivet because in Gulf Territory these days, a Gen can deal with most aspects of Sime law, though still not a citizen. At Risa's request, he martials the Gulf Army to bring reinforcements.

Morningstar ambrov Mountain Bells—Second Channel in Mountain Bells, she leads the relief mission to Ardo Pass.

Muryin Farris ambrov Zeor—Klyd's only child and his heir, she acknowledges Hugh as a second father because her mother, Aisha, was Hugh's wife. As with so many Farrises, Muryin becomes a figure of world history early in life by accepting an unusual First Transfer and going on to mend a quarrel that could have altered world history.

Nedd, Sectuib ambrov Keon—Sectuib in Keon prior to Risa, he could barely hold the House together. Sergi, as Keon's best Companion, could not desert Nedd.

Niavel—a channel who changes over in Capital attended by Klyd and Hugh.

Norris—out-Territory Gen of Emstead's command who learns a lot by tending the wounded.

Payel Farris ambrov Im'cholee—A most respected and skilled younger channel who teams well with Klyd in trying to solve Ediva's transfer problems, but even he misses the vital clue.

Risa (Tigue) ambrov Keon—Sectuib in Keon and the acknowledged leading figure in Gulf Territory, she is the architect of her territory's golden age and sees no reason why her methods won't work on a larger scale—until she sees the size of Nivet Territory, and modifies her ideas as well as her opinion of the Farrises.

Sahyiden ambrov Keon—He accompanies Risa to Nivet and gives his life protecting Muryin.

Sergi ambrov Keon—born into Keon under the prior Sectuib, Sergi is fulfilled as Risa's First Companion, though neither health care nor administration is his calling. He is artist and metallurgist, feeling a strong kinship with Hugh. However, he often wonders what his life might have been like had he pledged to Zeor to become Klyd's Companion. He doesn't realize what the Farris touch on him may do to Risa, or her relationship with Klyd Farris.

Simpsin—out-Territory Genrunner whose main Sime contact is Valry Adlay, an unlicensed Genbuyer and supplier of the pleasure market.

Sinda—a Sime woman forced by the Nivet Council to spy on the Tecton.

Tirlis ambrov Mountain Bells—one of the party sent to relieve Ardo Pass during unusual spring snows.

Trahan ambrov Zeor—a messenger who brings Klyd a report of massive troop movements and precipitates Kitty's mission.

Major Travers—Commander of the Gen "border outfit" that Madison and Jesson are sent to. He captured two Sime messengers.

Uzziah ambrov Keon—the husband and transfer mate of Bethany ambrov Keon. He is a nonjunct Sime Klyd recognizes as the 'delicate' type of renSime. Uzziah and Bethany accompany Risa to Nivet.

Hugh (Valleroy) ambrov Rior—the first Gen to be recognized as a Companion of a House, rather than in it. He is Sosectu in his own House, yet First Companion of Zeor, and still thinks of himself as Hugh Valleroy, though he bows to Nivet custom and does not use his surname. Fired by Klyd's own youthful, idealistic vision of Sime/Gen unity, Hugh cannot rest without making that vision tangible—in spite of Klyd's current practical pessimism.

Verla—Risa ambrov Keon's first friend and business partner in Laveen township where Risa set her up in the shiltpron parlor business so she'd have the means of raising her son, Dinny. Semi-junct, she dies of killcrisis three years before Klyd comes to Gulf.

Virena—Daughter of Risa and Sergi ambrov Keon, she is eager to go see Nivet, and thrilled with the idea of studying channeling in a real school for channels as soon as she goes through changeover—especially if it means she can be with her friend, Muryin. At the age of fifteen she doesn't realize that she is one of the primary motivations driving her parents to shape a new world in which the alliance she is building with Zeor figures strongly.

Zelerod—a junct renSime who discovered that it is mathematically impossible for Sime civilization to survive junct. Unable to convince the world of his time, he died trying to disjunct. Until Ediva ambrov Dar, Zelerod's treatise was taken seriously only by the Householdings and the few who sympathized with their lifestyle.

Zor ambrov Mountain Bells—the Householding's best weatherwatcher, who predicts the thaw that signals the final battle on what years later is proclaimed a holiday, Faith Day, the first holiday celebrated both in- and out-Territory.

Glossary

Ambient: (or ambient nager) The emotional "atmosphere" created by the combined life-energy (selyn) fields of human beings, either Sime or Gen. A Sime can perceive the ambient nager, and his own emotions and physiology may be affected by it.

Ancient: A human of the time before the Sime/Gen mutation split the species.

Arensti: The most famous regional Fair type of competition in Nivet Territory. A product which wins the Arensti is guaranteed commercial success.

Attrition: The state a Sime reaches when near or at death from having consumed all the selyn (life energy) in his system.

Augmentation: The increase of a Sime's selyn consumption to increase strength, speed, or heat production.

Border Patrol: The official guards of the Sime/Gen Territory borders. Both the Sime and the Gen governments mount such patrols, but with different duties. The Gens patrol to keep the Simes from raiding out of the borders and to prevent newly changed-over Simes from crossing in-Territory; the Simes patrol to welcome such newly changed-over Simes escaping the Gens, and to keep Gens from escaping from Sime Territory, or to keep Gens from raiding into Sime Territory.

Changeover: The sudden maturation of a child into a Sime adult, at puberty. The process usually takes less than a day. At the climax of changeover, the newly developed tentacles burst from their sheaths along the Sime's forearms, ready to absorb selyn from a Gen. Only children who are going to be channels know they will go through changeover. Other children do not know if they will be Sime or Gen.

Channel: A type of Sime able to take selyn from any Gen without killing and later give that selyn to a Sime to satisfy need and prevent the Sime from killing.

Choice Auction: A sale of Gens who will make the best kills.

Collectorium: The place where channels collect selyn from volunteer Gen donors who are unable to serve a Sime's need directly but who wish to support Simes so they don't have to kill to survive.

Companion: A Gen who has attained the Householding office of Companion by serving the personal need of a channel.

Controller: The definition of this office changes during this novel. At first, it refers to the Householding officer who constructs the transfer, collectorium, dispensary, and infirmary schedules of all the channels and Companions within the House. Klyd becomes the first to hold the office of Tecton Controller, responsible for interHouse scheduling as well as dealings with nonHouseholders on behalf of the Tecton.

Dar: A Householding devoted to the martial arts.

Delicate: A type of renSime doomed to die young from transfer abnormalities and resultant systemic degeneration. They exhibit a characteristic "stutter" in certain transfer situations and have an abnormal sensitivity to trained Companions.

Disjunct: A Sime who has killed a Gen at least once, usually in First Need, and then, within the First Year after changeover, has broken the addiction to the kill and come to live on channel's transfer.

Disjunction: The process of becoming disjunct.

Dispensary: The place where channels dispense selyn to renSimes in need.

Distect: The loosely knit subgroup of the Tecton composed of Householdings that have chosen Gens to lead them and who espouse the philosophy that Hugh (Valleroy) ambrov Rior is beginning to evolve: that in any transfer situation, the Gen is responsible for the outcome.

Donor: An untrained Gen who donates selyn through the channels.

Duoconscious: The state or "level" of consciousness in which a Sime can both read selyn fields and access the five ordinary senses. It is the most common state.

Entran: A malady some channels suffer when prevented from working at channeling selyn. It is characterized by painful cramps, and ultimately—in the higher order channels—by total loss of control of internal selyn circulation.

Establishment: The point in physical maturation when a child's body "establishes" production of selyn, and the child matures into the adult Gen.

Eyeway: A trail along an old roadbed laid out by the Ancients to be impossibly straight as far as the eye can see.

Farris Mutation: A secondary mutation whose origins are lost in history. The First Channel, Rimon Farris, was the son of a famous Genfarmer, Syrus Farris (see FIRST CHANNEL). In the time of the founding of the House of Zeor, it was noted that, by discarding all the data on the Farris channels, some very useful rules could be generalized from the data on channels. And so the Farrises were recognized as a separate mutation following rules of their own, required to use the surname Farris as a medicalert designation regardless of whether they were related to Rimon Farris. As the fame of the Householding Farrises spread, others not of that mutant class dropped the use of the Farris surname, those of the Householdings in self-defense against being mistakenly treated as a Farris, and those of the junct community for fear of being associated with perverts.

First Kill: the first intake of selyn a Sime experiences after changeover, when the Gen taken from dies. This sets the standard of excellence for the lifetime, and can be overridden but never wholly expunged.

First Need: The experience of lack of selyn that occurs immediately after the breakout of tentacles at the culmination of changeover. Only channels can exert any self-control at this moment, and then only if they have conserved selyn throughout changeover so that they are not in attrition.

First Transfer: The first intake of selyn a Sime experiences after changeover if that intake does not involve killing a Gen. The new Sime may receive selyn from a channel or a Companion. It sets the standard of excellence for the rest of that Sime's life, and for a channel is thus all important as it is this experience that is called upon to evoke satisfaction in the renSimes later served.

First Year: The year immediately following changeover when the Sime's learning rate and ability to adjust emotionally soar. To become truly proficient, channels must be trained in First Year. A junct cannot disjunct after the extraordinary pliability of First Year wanes. Gens also experience an increase in learning ability and emotional growth at this time, but since they have not developed a new sense, it is not so dramatic, and Simes tend to ignore it.

Fosebine: A mild medicinal preparation made from mutated plants which appeared at about the same time as the Simes themselves. It is used as a general analgesic, but is the specific for transfer shock and transfer burn.

Freeband Raider: Vagrant and migrant Simes who live a horribly dissipated lifestyle, banded together in order to conquer small Gen towns or caravans and kill the Gens—not one a month, but as often as they can evoke need in themselves. Becoming jaded on ordinary kills, they begin to seek ever more grotesque means of tormenting their victims to produce emotional highs in themselves. They rarely eat, and generally die within five years of changeover. Fortunately, a side effect of their lifestyle is low fertility.

Frihill: The House that has made archeology their business, and thus resurrected much Ancient technology.

Gen: An adult human whose body produces selyn but whose metabolism does not consume perceptible amounts of selyn.

Gendealer: A Sime who makes his living from buying and selling Gens.

Genfarmer: A breeder of Gens who uses his stock to farm enough land to feed them. A good Genfarmer will raise surplus food to sell.

Genrunner: A Gen who captures other Gens or children out-Territory (in Gen Territory), and sells them to a Sime contact at the Territory border. Or, conversely, a Sime who deals with such a Gen.

Gulf: The small southeast Territory which has only two Householdings, Carre and Keon.

Gypsies: Any of the many tribes of wanderers who refuse to acknowledge Territory borders, yet keep strictly to themselves. They do not raid in Gen Territory, nor claim government-supplied Gens in Sime Territory. Their tribal structure, social order, and culture are unknown, for outsiders are unwelcome. However, some tribes have been friendly with certain Householdings for many generations and have been known to trade with those who respect their privacy. Legends of gypsy doings border on sheerest fantasy.

Household: A sovereign living group constructed around a Sectuib, the best channel in the House, and consisting of up to several hundred Simes and Gens who pledge to a unifying virtue and work together at the Householding business.

Hyperconscious: The state or "level" of consciousness in which a Sime is aware only of information coming through the senses peculiar to Simes. In hard need, most Simes cannot achieve any level but hyperconsciousness. The junct term is "hunting mode."

Hypoconscious: The state or "level" of consciousness in which a Sime is aware only of information coming through the ordinary five senses. Simes often comment that it is like becoming a child again—or a Gen. Being forcibly releveled to hypoconsciousness can be frightening or even debilitating.

Imil: The Householding specializing in fashion design.

In-Territory: Inside the borders of a Sime Territory where the laws and customs are made by Simes.

Junct: Joined to the kill. It is the state of being addicted to killing Gens.

Keon: The Gulf Territory Householding pledged to Freedom and specializing in commerce. (See the novel, AMBROV KEON by Jean Lorrah, DAW 1986.)

Kill: The term reserved to designate the ruthless stripping away of a Gen's selyn in order to produce a penetrating sensation of pain counterpoint to the pleasure of repletion.

Killbliss: The extreme pleasure a junct Sime craves at the apex of the kill experience.

Laterals: The tentacles on the sides of each arm which have little strength because they are composed mostly of nerve tissue. These are the organs through which a Sime draws selyn from the Gen. All four laterals must be in contact with the Gen's skin in symmetric pairs—usually on the Gen's arms—and a fifth contact point must be made, usually with the lips.

Licensed Raiders: Simes licensed by the junct Sime government to raid out into Gen Territory and sell the captured Gens to the Genfarmers and dealers. A wise Sime Territory government keeps the activities of the licensed Raiders below the point at which the Gen army will respond with counter-raids. To do this, they must operate a Pen system, dealing in domestically produced Gens.

Lortuen: A condition of profound and virtually unbreakable transfer dependency reinforced by both psychological and physical sexual love between a male Sime and female Gen who are matchmates.

Low field: The condition of a Sime or a Gen when selyn supplies are depleted and the body does not generate a very strong field. In a Gen, this condition is invigorating and healthful; in a Sime, the edge of death.

Matchmates: A Sime/Gen pair in which the Gen's basal selyn-production rate matches the Sime's basal selyn-consumption rate. Matchmates may or may not be of opposite sexes. One of the classic locked-transfer dependencies (Lortuen/Orhuen/Torluen) can occur only if the pair has engaged in some selyn flow contact. Locked dependencies which cannot be broken short of death are mere romantic legend until the advent of the higher order channels who can have both their selyn systems matched and mated.

Nager: The life energy (selyn) field of a human being, perceptible to Sime senses.

nageric: Of or pertaining to a nager.

Naztehr: An intimate form of address among Householders.

Need: The urgent demand a Sime experiences when his selyn reserves are running low.

Need cycle: The natural cycle a Sime experiences between one intake of selyn and the next. To a Sime each day has its own character. The most prominent features of the cycle are Transfer (or kill), post syndrome (lasting up to 72 hours), turnover, need, hard need, and attrition. The total length of the cycle varies, with 28 days being the most common healthy length. A transfer or kill may be taken at any time after turnover, which will rephase the cycle, though that is not healthy and is resisted by all except Freeband Raiders.

New Washington: The capital city of the huge northern Gen Territory which has struggled to keep the Ancient traditions and has thereby united many sovereign Gen city-states.

Nivet: The Territory which amalgamated with many other small Territories to form a strip of Sime controlled lands across the middle of the continent and containing enough arable land to support a large number of Genfarms.

Nonjunct: A Sime who did not kill in First Need and has never killed.

Orhuen: A condition of profound and nearly unbreakable transfer dependency between a Sime and a Gen of the same sex who are matchmates but not lovers.

Pledge: The act of commiting oneself to a House.

Porstan: A beer the Simes favor.

Post Reaction: Immediately following transfer or kill, a Sime becomes hypersensitive to the ordinary senses as well as to the emotions which have been locked away by need. Any intolerable emotional pressures will be released at this time, and it can be marked by crying fits, elation, depression, or—in its healthiest form, by sexual excitement. Companions often find that their own rhythms fall into sync with the channels they serve, and they often speak of experiencing post-syndrome with the channels. However, this becomes pronounced enough to measure objectively only among the highest order channels and Companions.

Primary System: The selyn transport system within a channel which functions as a renSime's system does—to support the channel's own metabolic functions. It is also used to control the channel's Secondary System.

Psychospatial Orientation: The Sime sense through which a Sime discerns his placement in the universe. It is connected to the Sime's internal clock which measures selyn consumption and the hours of life left, and seems to have evolved to assist a Sime in hunting Gens. Orientation can be disrupted by moving an unconscious Sime without expert selyn field management.

Releveling: The process by which a Companion adjusts the sensory level, (i.e. hyperconscious, duoconscious, or hypoconscious) of the channel he's working to.

renSime: Any Sime who is not a channel.

Rior: The first House founded by and built around a Gen Head of Householding, or "Sosectu," Hugh Valleroy ambrov Rior. Its pledge is to spearhead the drive toward the unification of humanity.

Ronaplin: The substance secreted by the ronaplin glands located on the Sime's forearms beneath the laterals. It lubricates the laterals and conducts selyn.

Ruined Lands: The south-central area of Nivet Territory which has been turned into an arid zone of loose dirt blown by scouring winds because of a combination of a long drought and irresponsible farming by nonprofessional Genfarmers looking for a quick profit.

Secondary System: The additional nerve system that characterizes the channel, used for the storage of selyn which can be delivered to renSimes to satisfy need.

Sectuib: The best channel in the House; the channel who best exemplifies in his life and person the virtue to which the House is pledged, and who thus *is* the House. In the early days, the Sectuib was also the owner of record of all the Gens in the House, and all of its material assets, for purposes of dealing with junct law. The Sectuib is the one whose judgment prevails because the House members have *recognized* the Sectuib's judgment, not as infallible, but as representing their own.

Selyn: The energy that sustains life. Ancients both created and utilized that energy within their own bodies. The mutation that split the Ancients into Sime and Gen assigned the creation of selyn to Gens and the utilization to Simes.

Semi-junct: The lifestyle adopted by juncts who abjure the kill, knowing that their resolve will periodically desert them and they will kill. The experimentally established minimum kill-cycle for a junct is one in thirteen, though few ever manage such a level of discipline. The less often a junct kills, the more abhorrent the kill becomes, yet the more ardently is it craved until the conflicting psychological and physiological forces debilitate and eventually destroy the person. Semijunctedness is not a stable lifestyle.

Shen: One of the most common Sime expletives. Literally, it refers to the shock of interrupted transfer. It exists in six main degrees. In order of increasing intensity, they are: Shen, Shendi, Shenoni, Shenshay (which refers to transfer abort backlash), Shenshi, Shenshid. There is a milder degree than pure shen, Shuven, and a more intense degree than Shenshid, Shidoni, which refers literally to death by attrition (or Shedoni which in some dialects refers to execution by attrition). In some societies and at various times in history, Shidoni has been the one word never spoken aloud.

Shiltpron: A musical instrument invented by Simes to be played with fingers and tentacles. It can be modulated in either audio or nageric ranges, or both at once. A skilled channel playing the shiltpron can use an ambient Gen nager to control the level of consciousness of nearby Simes. Nageric modulation even by a moderately skilled Sime player can produce intoxication in Simes. Some Companions can learn to modulate the shiltpron in the nageric range using their own body's fields.

Showfield: The illusory nageric projection of a channel's systems to simulate a state other than his own true state. For example, to a renSime in need, a channel may appear as a Gen in order to give the renSime transfer.

Sime: An adult human whose body does not produce selyn but whose metabolism runs on selyn as a Gen's metabolism runs on calories.

Simelan: The language spoken by Simes which reflects their sensory perceptions of the world.

Sosectu: The Gen Head of Householding. A House which pledges through a Sosectu has no Sectuib. The Sosectu is not an office with as firm a tradition as that of Sectuib, yet much of the definition of Sectuib can be applied to Sosectu.

Tecton: During the course of this book, the definition of Tecton undergoes a significant change. At first, Tecton refers to the organization of Householdings in Nivet Territory—a loose union for mutual support in a politically hostile world. The early Tecton keeps two headquarters—one in the East Capital of Nivet, Konawa, and one in the West Capital, Capital itself. In these two major cities, the Tecton speaks to the junct government of the Territory on behalf of all the householdings of Nivet.

To be a unified voice for fiercely sovereign and very scattered Householdings, the Tecton imposes standards of behavior on the member Houses, and the member Houses send representatives to each of the two major centers. It also maintains communications among the Houses, disaster funds, training schools, and central archives. Funding comes from required membership contributions by the Houses, as well as voluntary contributions by the more affluent Houses such as Zeor.

Later, the Tecton becomes the *de facto* government of the entire Nivet Territory in order to make treaties with foreign powers and impose domestic order.

Torluen: A condition of profound and virtually unbreakable transfer dependency reinforced by both psychological and physical sexual love between a female Sime and male Gen.

Transfer: The process by which, without killing, the Sime absorbs selyn from a Gen or from a channel.

Transfer Shock: A condition of nerve-burn that can occur in either Sime or Gen under certain types of transfer dysfunctions. It is characterized by a burning headache that spreads down the neck and spine, often accompanied by nausea—or in extreme cases, by heart failure. Fosebine is the specific which not only alleviates the symptoms but also promotes healing.

Trin Tea: a suffusion made from the leaves and stems of the trin plant, a plant mutation which appeared at about the same time as the first Simes.

Turnie: A derogatory term used by out-Territory Gens to designate an out-Territory Gen who has made an alliance with

Simes based on self-interest or promises of personal protection. A person who has sold out his group to the enemy for personal gain.

Turnover: The point in a Sime's selyn consumption cycle at which half the selyn is used up. Each Sime experiences it as the activation of his primary phobia or his image of death. The quality of the turnover experience depends on the quality of the prior transfer and the immediate availability of a willing Gen or channel. Before turnover, need is only a memory; after turnover, need captures the waking attention with increasing urgency, gradually blocking out all other considerations.

Unlicensed Raiders: Simes who live in Sime Territory and poach on Wild Gens out-Territory, without being properly licensed. The Sime Border Patrol can sometimes be bribed to overlook such offenses, but generally such activity is frowned upon because it provokes the Wild Gens to counter-raid, choosing law-abiding citizens as their targets.

Wild Gens: Civilized Gens who live outside Sime Territory without Sime control of breeding or activities.

Wild Killer Gens: Gens who Establish too far in-Territory (in Sime Territory) to make it across the border into Gen Territory, and instead hole up in Ancient ruins and live by ambushing passers-by, becoming as much animals as the Freeband Raiders.

Zelerod's Doom: The point at which Simes run out of Gens to kill, then die in attrition.

Zeor: The first Householding, dedicated to Zeor, "excellence," and making its primary living in the textile industry. It is headed by descendants of Rimon Farris, the first channel, in unbroken succession, and they have all upheld the vision of the unification of humanity.

Zlin: To perceive by Sime senses, reading selyn fields or nageric interactions. A Sime can zlin only when duoconscious or hyperconscious. When hypoconscious, the Sime can only see, hear, taste, smell, or touch, using the senses the Sime has in common with Gens.

DAW

DAW's NEW WONDER-WORLD OF SCIENCE FICTION STARS

Ian Watson
The Black Current Trilogy
From the winner of the Prix Apollo, the Orbit Award, and The British Science Fiction Association Award comes this truly cosmic trilogy about Yaleen the Riverwoman—chosen agent of the mysterious sentient Black Current—and her dangerous mission through space and time to the stronghold of the creator—and, perhaps, the destroyer—of the universe....

☐ **THE BOOK OF THE RIVER**   (UE2105—$2.95)
☐ **THE BOOK OF THE STARS**   (UE2130—$2.95)
☐ **THE BOOK OF BEING**   (UE2153—$2.95)

Jacqueline Lichtenberg & Jean Lorrah
The Sime/Gen Novels
On a future Earth, a bizarre mutation has split humanity into two opposed groups, the Simes and the Gens. Gens produce selyn, the life force which Simes must have to survive, even though Simes kill Gens in the process of obtaining it. These novels tell the ongoing story of the war between the Simes and Gens, and the story as well of the Householders, the small group of Simes and Gens who have banded together to put an end to killing—before it's too late.

☐ **RENSIME (by Lichtenberg)**   (UE1980—$2.95)
☐ **AMBROV KEON (by Lorrah)**   (UE2109—$2.95)
☐ **ZELEROD'S DOOM (by Lichtenberg & Lorrah)**
                                        (UE2145—$3.50)

AN OPEN LETTER
TO THE AMERICAN PEOPLE

Astronauts Francis (Dick) Scobee, Michael Smith, Judy Resnik, Ellison Onizuka, Ronald McNair, Gregory Jarvis, and Christa McAuliffe understood the risk, undertook the challenge, and in so doing embodied the dreams of us all.

Unlike so many of us, they did not take for granted the safety of riding a torch of fire to the stars.

For them the risk was real from the beginning. But some are already seizing upon their deaths as proof that America is unready for the challenge of manned space flight. *This is the last thing the seven would have wanted.*

Originally five orbiters were proposed; only four were built. This tragic reduction of the fleet places an added burden on the remaining three.

But the production facilities still exist. The assembly line can be reactivated. The experiments designed for the orbiter bay are waiting. We can recover a program which is one of our nation's greatest resources and mankind's proudest achievements.

Soon Congress will determine the immediate direction the space program must take. We must place at highest priority the restoration and enhancement of the shuttle fleet and resumption of a full launch schedule.

For the seven.

In keeping with their spirit of dedication to the future of space exploration and with the deepest respect for their memory, we are asking you to join us in urging the President and the Congress to build a new shuttle orbiter to carry on the work of these seven courageous men and women.

As long as their dream lives on, the seven live on in the dream.

SUPPORT SPACE EXPLORATION!

Write to the President at
1600 Pennsylvania Avenue,
Washington, D.C. 20500.

DAW

DAW PRESENTS THESE BESTSELLERS BY MARION ZIMMER BRADLEY

DARKOVER NOVELS

☐	DARKOVER LANDFALL	UE1906—$2.50
☐	THE SPELL SWORD	UE2091—$2.50
☐	THE HERITAGE OF HASTUR	UE2079—$3.95
☐	THE SHATTERED CHAIN	UE1961—$3.50
☐	THE FORBIDDEN TOWER	UE2029—$3.95
☐	STORMQUEEN!	UE2092—$3.95
☐	TWO TO CONQUER	UE2174—$3.50
☐	SHARRA'S EXILE	UE1988—$3.95
☐	HAWKMISTRESS!	UE2064—$3.95
☐	THENDARA HOUSE	UE2119—$3.95
☐	CITY OF SORCERY	UE2122—$3.95

DARKOVER ANTHOLOGIES

☐	THE KEEPER'S PRICE	UE1931—$2.50
☐	SWORD OF CHAOS	UE1722—$2.95
☐	FREE AMAZONS OF DARKOVER	UE2096—$3.50
